My Fair Potion

A STARGLEN NOVEL

AE MCKENNA

STRIKETHROUGH PUBLICATIONS

Published by ~~Strikethrough~~ Publications

www.aemckenna.com

MY FAIR POTION (A STARGLEN NOVEL)

ISBN 13—979-8-9908870-0-8

Copyright © 2024 by AE McKenna

Line Edit by Lori Diederich

Cover Art by Miblart

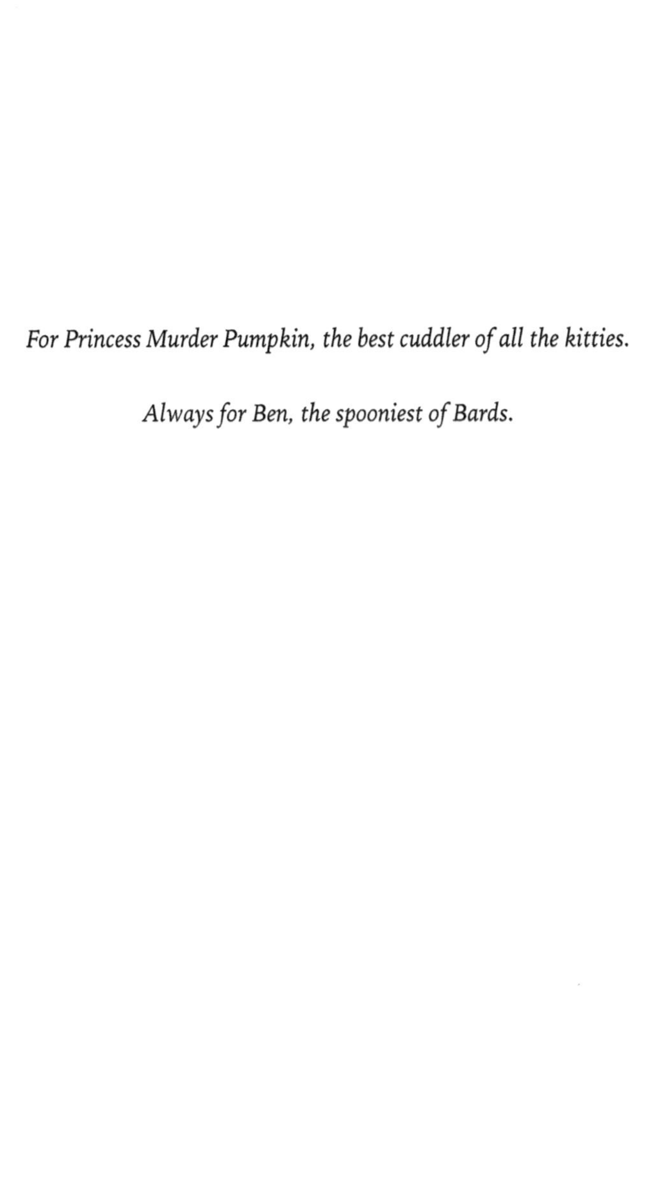

For Princess Murder Pumpkin, the best cuddler of all the kitties.

Always for Ben, the spooniest of Bards.

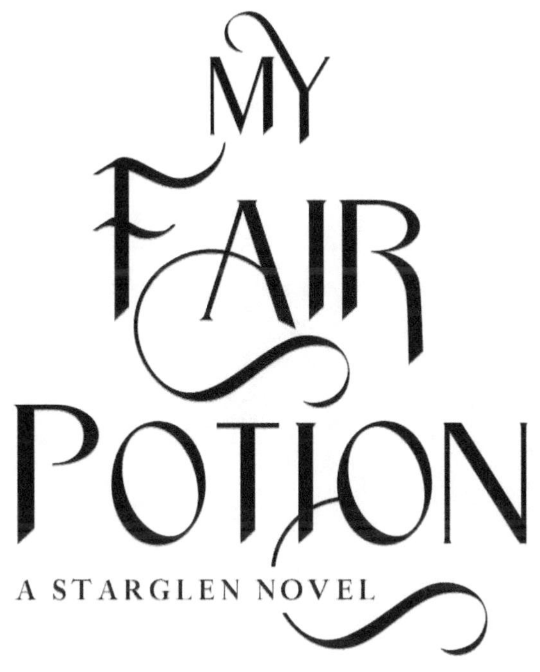

AE MCKENNA

Chapter One

"What do you mean you won't buy from me?" My fingers flexed around the corners of the heavy box full of potions in my arms. I could hear my voice rising an octave and took a deep breath through my nose and tried again. "I have a contract to sell here."

The blonde woman manning the counter flinched. I had not, in fact, managed to keep my voice from becoming shrill. I shifted the box in my arms and scanned the lighted shelving display behind her, searching for my row of potions, but I only saw bottles from Nexus—a high-end alchemy lab. Despite the mild, chilly weather, my chest grew uncomfortably warm. Swallowing, I read her name tag pinned to her blue polo and then forced a smile.

"Look, Jilly," I said, "I have a contract with Starglen Apothecary to supply your store with certain stock and you sell my potions to whoever buys them here."

A familiar sneer curled Jilly's thin upper lip. "No one will buy from *you*."

What? I glanced around the entire shop, my heart sickly

fluttering in my chest. All the lit-up display shelves on the floor had mirrors backing them, making the shelves appear fuller than they were. None of them featured my potions either. A discreet placard of a blonde woman decked out in pink and wearing bunny ears sat on one shelf. For a moment, not even the soothing scent of eucalyptus wafting through the store could calm the flash of rage that ignited in my blood.

The door to the back stock room opened and Louie, the manager, stepped out, wearing a blue polo and tan khakis. The pot lights in the ceiling gleamed on his neatly combed brassy hair. He took one look at me, winced—*oh shit*—and hurried to the counter. My fleeting moment of rage died a cold, hard death, sinking like an iceberg in my stomach.

"Lila," he whispered, placing a hand on my shoulder, "good to see you."

I frowned at Jilly and opened my mouth. "Yeah—"

"Let's go in the back." He nudged my shoulder toward the door he just walked through.

He didn't take the box from me. That iceberg in my stomach bottomed out as I stiffly walked into the back room. The door closed behind us, and I took in the racks of back stock filled with consumables and topical ointments. An industry-sized fridge for the perishables stood against the far wall.

Then I spotted a cardboard sign with "Star Trails" scrawled in black marker, and all my potions occupied three shelves. The frosted bottles bore the purple logo with a comet tail on it. All my expensive potions and a few common ones filled the space. I swallowed the bitter taste in my mouth.

"What's going on, Louie?" A bead of sweat dripped between my breasts. This wouldn't be good news. "Why aren't you stocking my potions out front? You said they were selling well."

He winced again and rubbed the back of his neck. I hated it when people made that face when speaking with me. I slid the box of potions on the shelf to give my arms a break and tugged on one of my braids. Like a switch, the rising panic reset enough that I could, I hoped, speak without sounding shrill. It did nothing for the excessive dread creeping up my back to sit on my shoulder.

He sighed, retrieving his phone and thumbing through it. "You really don't use social media."

"No." My throat constricted and I dry swallowed. "Too many bullies."

"Yeah, I get that. You've been outed as the alchemist behind your potions."

I yanked on both of my braids and shook my head. "How? I certainly never told anyone. If one of your employees—"

He gave his phone to me and a video played, showing the Star Trails logo on my popular concentration potion. It had been posted last night and had 240,000 views. The image shrank into a square in the upper corner, and a woman in impeccable makeup wearing headphones in a fancy office spoke into a tiny microphone.

"We all know Lila Townsend, the name that darkens our alchemy tables on the anniversary of her betrayal to the community. What you might not know is that this witch is practicing again—and you're buying her potions. She's disingenuously doing business under the name of Star Trails—a semi-popular potions and enchantments online store—and she sells locally in the Flower Market. I'm here to remind you *not* to give that vile woman another penny."

A picture of the same woman wearing bunny ears from the placard out front replaced my logo. This time, Georgia

Cauldron smiled brightly, holding a bunny. The host continued, "If you remember, five years ago, Lila Townsend maliciously—"

I locked the phone. "I can't watch this."

Louie tucked his phone away and glanced at the box I'd pushed onto the shelf. He lifted his hands, palms up, as if saying, "What can I do?" And there was nothing he could.

The corners of my mouth curled upwards while my brain went into overdrive. It'd happened again. No one will allow me to move past that . . . *incident* from five years ago. No one could say my name and not be reminded of what had happened to Georgia. I pursed my lips and clamped them into a firm line as I eyed the expensive bottles of potions that Louie must've pulled this morning before our appointment. He'd paid me for my last delivery, and I'd spent that money.

I swallowed, pulling my box from the shelf. "I can't buy those back from you today, but if we can come up with a payment plan, I can pay you back."

Somehow. Money was tight despite my stipend from my inheritance, and that wouldn't come into full maturity for a few more years.

"Don't worry about that for now. I can figure something out to do with these potions." Louie leaned against one of the racks and regarded me. His usual friendly face creased as he patted my arm. "What're you gonna do?"

My phone pinged, the sound alerting me I had ten minutes before my next appointment with Enchanting Crystals, but I wondered if it'd even be worth it to stop by my car to swap boxes since that video was going viral.

I cleared my throat. "Wait for the storm to pass, I guess."

"It's a shame. They're great potions."

"I know." I did everything I could to give people the cleanest ingredients in their potions. And when I listed them,

I didn't hide behind phrases like "proprietary blend" or "herbal mix."

He opened the door for me and followed me to the front. More likely, he was hiding me from view from his current customers as he showed me out. I couldn't blame him. The door closed behind me, and I took a few steps down the sidewalk before stopping outside a restaurant that only served dinner and cocktails. Placing my box on one of the outside tables, I fished out my phone. I had twenty-plus emails and a text from Winkerton, my best friend, asking if I'd seen the news.

Swallowing the sour taste in my mouth, which did nothing to the increasingly painful lump lodged in my throat, I opened my email and saw they were all from my online store with the heading "Order cancellation" and a few from previous customers. One email was a simple "You should kill yourself." I appreciated they didn't waste my time listing off my crimes and went straight to punishment. These people were why I deleted all my social media accounts.

"Oh god." I bent over and planted my hands on my thighs, sucking in a deep breath. There'd be no point in swapping out boxes before going to Enchanting Crystals. Still, I needed to grin and bear it. No one could say that Lila Townsend never faced a challenge without a smile. Because I smiled when I became upset, uncomfortable, and nervous, and *no one* enjoyed seeing it.

Making potions had been the only way I had to fit in with my family and helped me feel included. Later on, when people told me how much they liked my potions and how my brews had helped them, it had felt like I'd finally found my purpose in life. I desperately wanted to keep that feeling. Excellent-quality potions were never enough for me to be accepted.

I sucked in a breath and held it for a count of ten, tugging on my braids to shock my system into resetting, and let out the air—hoping the bad energy went with it. I snatched up my box and marched toward Enchanting Crystals.

Ahead, a brunette woman in black slacks and an emerald blouse stood near the front entrance, patting the back of her French twist. Marla had decided to wait for me. She motioned me to follow her to the back entrance of the store. Her escort was new. Part of me wondered if she was afraid I'd make a scene. She couldn't know I was too shocked by the viral sucker punch to make much fuss. I followed her inside to her shoebox-sized office and set my box of potions on the chair in front of the desk. Marla sidestepped around the desk to sit behind it.

"You've heard?" She handed an invoice to me, already prepared with an amount to buy back the charms I'd sold her.

"Yes." I scanned the items. Half of them had sold before the video broke, but it was still a pretty penny to buy back my stock. Clearly, she didn't have the same connections as Louie did in the Nettles. "Uh, can we work out a payment plan?"

Her eye twitched. "How is that even possible—"

"I have bills just like everyone else. Unlike everyone else in Starglen, the city doesn't discriminate against me and provides my utilities. They also expect me to pay, which I do. Now. This is what I can do, and I'll have this paid off in a couple of months . . . unless you want to sell them elsewhere?"

Her face pinched as if she'd sucked on a lemon while she pulled out a card reader and powered it up. "Okay, a payment plan will work. I'll hang on to the stock until they're paid off. Honestly, I don't know why I even tried to sell your baubles."

Don't react to that bauble jibe.

I unclenched my jaw. "Because they're high quality, and I

put in the effort to make them look nice so people don't know someone's hiding a wart on their nose." Tumbling crystals took anywhere upwards a month. And while it didn't improve the enchantment, I took the time to make them look like regular jewelry.

I retrieved my phone and noticed another text from Winkerton, this time asking if I was okay. I ignored her again and paid Marla.

She escorted me out the back, checking to make sure no one saw me with her. *Here we go again.* Flicking my gaze upward, I hefted the heavy box in my arms and stepped out into the main thoroughfare of the Flower Market: a foot-traffic-only marketplace taking up six city blocks in the heart of Starglen.

The air had a crispness to it despite the fog clinging to the mountains. I loved these kinds of days: overcast, a little misty here and there, with the smell of rain lingering in the air. But today—as I walked past vendors and store fronts and people brunching on the sidewalk while sellers performed demonstrations of their potions or charms—I couldn't find the calm the haze usually gave me. The potion bottles lightly clinked against one another while I forced my dragging feet on the time-worn stone pavers toward the free parking lot. My attention snagged on a billboard for a Potion Network show, *Home Brew Elixirs*. It showed Georgia wearing a fluffy pink skirt and a pair of bunny ears, standing next to her pink cauldron with a speech bubble shouting, "Hiya, Honey Bunny!" I came to an abrupt halt and stared at her enormous smile and excessively white teeth. Pressure swept across my forehead, and I clenched my jaw. One day, I'd give that bitch her just desserts and make sure she ate every last poisonous crumb.

A few bystanders noticed me and . . . I'm usually a proud person. I don't shirk from who I am and what my past was, but today, I didn't have the spoons to look anyone in the eye.

I pushed my head down and hurried through the slightly muddy parking lot before stopping at the back of an old pale-yellow Volvo and popping the trunk. As I deposited the heavy box, the thought pounding in my head finally grew loud enough that I no longer ignored it.

What would I do now that the Potion Network and Georgia Cauldron had ruined me once again?

Chapter Two

"Hey, everyone! I'm Nate." I grinned at the gathering crowd in the late morning as I lifted the leathery peony seed pod. "Today I'm going to give you some tips on the hidden gems in your alchemy reagents. A lot of you are aware of the medicinal impact of the root and leaves of a white peony plant, but did you know you're wasting?"

It was a cool day, despite the fog being burned off, but the trees covering the foothills in the distance still had clumps of the stuff clinging to the tips. I'd set up my stall close to the free parking lot. It wasn't the ideal place, but first come, first serve, and more often than I'd like, I was perpetually late. Blame it on my bike. Fortunately, this spot didn't reek of fertilizer, but I was far from the fancy shops where the real money was.

A few people leaving the gravel lot paused and tilted their heads, indulging me. A kid, maybe a scrawny teenager, wearing an oversized hoodie and beanie pushed to the front, and I just couldn't help but think I was finally getting my shot. Sure, I'd arrived late at the Flower Market and I didn't have the best spot to sell or demonstrate potions. But this was the biggest crowd I'd drawn since I'd bought the permit to sell a few weeks ago, thanks to borrowing money from Alex, my foster brother. I had a few basic potions up for sale and one glorious, beautiful healing potion. Most of these didn't require an alchemy table and the ley energy to make them. Yet most people were also too lazy to gather their reagents themselves and therefore paid for the convenience.

The fact that the permit made me mostly broke was moot. I'd used the rest of the money—well, *almost* the rest of it—to buy a vial of agua aureate. It had cost me a pretty penny since it was rainwater collected from the leaves of a lady's mantle plant. You had to spend money to make money. And I needed to make money.

I glanced at the row of bottles one more time, wishing I'd taken the extra moment to straighten them and order them from least to most expensive or effective. That had to be a sign to a formally trained alchemist that I'd never made it to Starglen Alchemy University—or any advanced training. Hell, even those classes on YouTube were behind a paywall and my money, sadly, had other more pressing priorities. But faking it until I'd made it had gotten me this far in life, and I was determined to better my situation at any risk. I had nothing left to lose.

I peeled the pod away from the peony seeds. "These seeds can block pain and act as an antioxidant, but first you need to weed out the nonviable seeds, which is easy."

I dropped them in the bowl of water waiting nearby, and after a few moments, a couple floated to the surface. I was losing the crowd, though. Some spectators had peeled away when nothing happened straight away with the seeds. I mean, it was a live demonstration; they needed to cut me some slack. If I had my own show on the Potion Network, not only would I be able to help people learn what they needed to make better potions when they lacked the formal training like me, but I'd have the magic of video editing.

I'd also have money.

"Now, as you can see, these floaters aren't viable—Hey!"

A hand slapped out of nowhere and snagged one of my potions off the table. The hoodie-wearing thief slipped away among the crowd. My healing potion was gone.

"Wait! Stop!"

Crap. This was the worst. I needed that, and yet being in the Flower Market and leaving my stand unattended was asking for more theft. But that potion he'd stolen would've fed me for three days if someone had paid for it. Healing potions were a meal ticket.

"Goddammit." I cursed more under my breath. "Stop, thief!"

How ironic that I got to say that in the market. A few passersby gaped at me, their gaze then following the fading figure. No one moved. No one offered to help. Most stores had enchantments on the doors to keep them closed if a thief triggered them, so it came as no surprise most people weren't used to what was happening right now. Catching that shoplifter—stall-lifter?—was up to me. I scanned the table and my bike parked against it. The back tire had already deflated. I really couldn't afford to lose any of this, but I *needed* that potion. It was a meal ticket and a way to rent an alchemy table so I could make more potions. That kid would sell it in the Nettles and use the money for who knew what. I didn't care; it was mine.

I snatched my messenger bag, slung it over my shoulder, and pushed through the crowds.

"Stop! Stop him." I mean, maybe someone else would help if the people near me wouldn't. Someone had to help, didn't they?

Instead, they stepped aside. I guess the Flower Market

was like that. No one cared, no one helped; they just watched and then moved on with their lives. Maybe later they'd talk about this crazy incident over dinner with their family, in their warm house with their full stomachs and a bed waiting for them.

I ran past food stalls, the smell of fried potatoes and waffle cones just as distracting as the stands of jarred reagents on clearance outside shops. The teenager shoved past shoppers and added distance between us. I was losing him.

"Stop him—"

I tripped over my feet and slammed onto the damp pavers. My teeth punched through my lip and stinging, hot pain washed over my jaw and tongue. I spat out a glob of blood.

Hands gripped my shoulders and helped me up. "Hey, buddy, you gotta watch where you're going."

I spun and looked at the man who'd assisted me. "Did you see where he was running?" I blinked, wiping at my chin. It stung like a son of a bitch. "Or she?"

"Oh, yeah." He pointed. "The long way out of the Flower Market."

I followed his finger to the dark alley, right in time to see a person-shaped shadow melt into the darkness. I didn't think; I ran after him.

I thundered down the alley, my face aching with each pound of my feet against the pavement. I didn't yell. They knew I was there. Even though they had this huge head start on me, and even though I nearly bit my lip off in a fall, I was gaining on them.

They cried out and stumbled, then their leg buckled under them. They crashed to the ground.

Yes. I put on a burst of speed and caught up to them as

they struggled to their feet. I gripped the back of their hoodie and spun them around, tearing off their skull cap.

A young girl with dirt smudging her face stared at me with large, frightened eyes that overtook her pale, drawn face. Her expression tightened and she cried out, favoring the leg that buckled beneath her earlier.

I sucked in a breath, but I couldn't find it in me to yell—couldn't find it in me to be angry. "Are you hurt?"

She glared and jerked free. She made it ten steps to the mouth of the alley before she fell, face first, on the pavement again. This time, she didn't pick herself up. *Fuck.* It'd become clear why she'd snatched my healing potion. I approached her, not as fast as before, and crouched a few feet away from her.

She bared her teeth. "Pervert."

"What?" I laughed. My lip jolted with pain, and I cradled my chin. The hole in my lip leaked blood. The pain was becoming hard to ignore.

"Chasing a teenage girl through the alleys. I'll scream."

"Okay." I inched away from her and showed her that my hands were empty. I grabbed the towel I cleaned my foraging knife with from my messenger bag and wiped my hand as best I could. "You're hurt, and you stole a healing potion from me."

"You can't prove I stole it."

When I was a junior in high school, I was caught stealing and had to serve three months in juvenile detention. It had not been the first—or any case close to being the first time I'd been caught stealing—and the judge decided to teach me a lesson. I'd seen *things.* In some ways, it'd helped me. It'd scared the shit out of me, and it'd also hurt my chances of any kind of scholarship after high school. However, I was assigned to a new foster family, and the Richardses hadn't held my past against me. I'd stayed with them until I'd aged out of the system. This girl needed a break like I had when I'd been placed with that family, and she certainly didn't need to go through everything I had to get it.

"I don't care." I shrugged, tucking the cloth in my bag again. "I know a guy who didn't take care of a cut on his hand and lost it. You're hurt. You need it. But you shouldn't take it on an empty stomach if you can avoid it."

Her gaunt features told me she couldn't avoid taking it on an empty stomach. I didn't need to rummage through my wallet to know I had enough cash for two meals. I was extremely aware of how much money I had. John wouldn't care if I crashed an extra night on his couch and bummed a meal off him. At least, I didn't think he would. He was a good friend, and that girl needed what I had more than I did.

"Come on." I straightened, then held my clean hand out to her. "I'll get you a potato spiral so you can take that potion."

She eyed me warily. "I'm jailbait."

I recoiled, wincing at the fresh jab of pain in my mouth. "What's wrong with you?"

"You can't be this dumb. You pay for my food and let me take the potion and you get the sex. I know how your kind are."

I jerked away from her and raised my hands, palms out. "No, thank you. Here, I'll just give you the money. You need to eat something and—"

"Really?" She frowned at me.

"Yeah, I don't want the trouble you're promising. Especially the trouble that comes from a misunderstanding surrounding whatever you think it is that I want."

"You chased me."

"You *stole* from me."

She scowled.

I sighed and dug out my thin wallet and opened it. I

swore a moth flew out. I winced. I only had a twenty-dollar bill—the last of my cash—and I very well couldn't ask her to bring back the change so I could eat too. I plucked it out and handed it to her as my stomach complained it was empty. "Eat well, kid. But I don't want to see you hanging around my stall again."

She snatched the bill from my hand and shot to her feet. I didn't help her; it was too much for her to accept kindness from strangers. Sometimes, that kindness was all I had to get me through to the next day. I watched her limp from the alley, hoping the healing potion would take care of that injury so it wouldn't dog her for the rest of her life. She definitely didn't need something like that on top of everything else.

Since the towel was ruined, I pulled it out again and patted my lip as I walked back to my stall. I'd figure it out. Most of my potions were gone, including the peonies, and my shoulders sagged. A week's worth of foraging disappeared in mere minutes. At least my bike was still there. No one wanted a flat tire. I scanned the crowd, hoping to see her buying food, but a sea of strangers who didn't give a shit stared back.

At least *I'd* cared.

I KNOCKED on the door to John's apartment and smiled when he opened it. We used to work at a gas station together and remained pretty good friends after he got a better job. My chin hurt. I appreciated karma, though. A caster walking by my stand had taken pity on me—I hadn't cleaned up the blood as well as I'd thought—while I hawked my herbs and reagents until late this evening. I'd barely made enough to call today a wash—especially if I didn't count the stolen potions. But at least I didn't have a hole in my lip anymore.

"Jesus, Nate." John stood aside. "What the hell happened to you?"

"I got robbed, and—"

"Holy shit!"

"Yeah." I gently rested my bike against the wall where the coats hung, careful my handlebars didn't leave marks on the wall. "I tripped and landed on my face when I was chasing her down."

"Are you okay?"

"Oh, yeah. Someone helped me out."

John nodded. "Did you get your stuff back?"

I scratched my chin—it still itched from the healing—and shook my head. "She needed the potion."

He rolled his eyes and walked into the galley kitchen. "This is why you never make any money, dude."

I sighed. "Look, man, she was starving and hurt. What else was I supposed to do?"

"Take your potion back, that's what." He rolled his eyes. "Those people aren't your responsibility."

He wasn't wrong, but he also didn't get it, either. If I hadn't been lucky with foster families, I very well could have lived the same life that the teenaged girl was living. She'd needed the break more than I did.

"So, would it be okay if I crashed on your couch one more night?" I asked, hoping he'd be fine with it, but I also knew I was overstaying my welcome.

He glanced at me, and some of the annoyance he had about him shifted. "Yeah, but only just for tonight. The girl-friend gets back from her trip tomorrow."

The tension in my muscles relaxed when I knew that once I sat down I wouldn't be asked to move along. Today had pulled a lot out of me. "Thanks, man." I quickly shucked my jacket and shoes and left them by the door. "Hey, I'll clean up for you. I know I said I'd be out of your hair today, and I really appreciate the extra night."

John glanced away and shrugged once more. "Just be more careful, man. You're fuckin' twenty-nine. Get your shit together."

His words were strange, and he seemed embarrassed to have to say something like that to me. But he wasn't wrong. I was sucking so hard at life right now. Couch surfing, trying to use my ley-given skills to make money because I definitely didn't have the college education employers thought they needed when hiring employees.

The way I saw it, this permit to sell *was* my last shot. And yes, today was a setback financially in every way imaginable, but I could recoup my losses. I'd done it before.

But just how long would it be before John stopped texting back and started ghosting me? Sometimes, people cut their losses when you don't fit into their lives anymore—especially if you inconvenience them too much. I needed to prove to everyone, including myself, that I could do this. Most of all, I needed to get back out there and forage for the rare ingredients so I could sell those and get an alchemy table. Once I had that, nearly all my problems would be solved.

I scavenged a few ice cubes from the freezer and bundled them in a wash cloth. I also refilled the ice tray. Then I stretched out on the couch and held the ice to my chin, closing my eyes at the relief the cold brought me.

Like the other bad patches, this one couldn't last forever. But it sure felt like the time between them was growing shorter and shorter.

Chapter Three

The next day, I stepped inside my greenhouse and welcomed the humidity washing over me with the bouquet of herbal-scented air, the unmistakable aroma of raw honey, and the musky perfume of flowers. Bees, butterflies, and dragonflies flitted from bloom to vibrant bloom, even to the flowering vines. Lush plants made this space a riot of rainbows. Ley bugs, their lantern on the underside of their abdomen and heavy with ley energy, lazily fluttered from plant to plant, blinking shimmery blue with every change of altitude. I had so many of them, you could call them a sparkle instead of a swarm. Every color I could imagine was here and a living thing.

And it failed to make me smile and did nothing for the pain radiating in the center of my chest. A day of hiding in my dark bedroom had done nothing to soothe me, and it was time to stop wallowing over what'd happened and move on. Again.

I'd learned that lesson the hard way after the Dead Year following the trial.

I shuffled down the main aisle carrying the two heavy

boxes filled with potions and enchanted crystals, noting a new beehive had been assembled in the rafters since the other day. There were three colonies of bees in here now, it seemed. I couldn't wait to collect the honey next year.

Shouldering into my storeroom, I quickly kicked the door closed behind me. I didn't want the pollinators to get stuck in here, since this room hosted flowers like azaleas and belladonna that would ruin a beehive should any of the pollen here mixed with the hives out there. I removed the cold charms before placing the potions back in the fridge. I'd need to recharge the charms later with a ley bug. Then I set the box of crystals on the floor and walked outside to my garden.

About a dozen raised garden beds hosting seasonal veggies stretched along the back end of the property. I was lucky to have this house on this lot. It'd been built during the height of the gold rush in the mid-1800s and sat in the middle of two lots. We were also the "last" house on the street—the sidewalk ended with us. Or it started with us. Either way, after my parents' divorce, this house went unoccupied until I graduated from Starglen Alchemy University, and my grandmother had wanted me to have it.

She'd wanted me to have many things when she'd died, and they all had caveats. Education and age. I wouldn't reach maturity on the trust until I was thirty-five. I could hold out another three years, I hoped. Thankfully, she'd died when I was a teenager, so I never had the opportunity to disappoint her like I had my ex-father.

The rainbow chard looked slightly limp, and I touched the irrigation hose. It was cold to the touch. Not unusual since I gathered all rainwater to use, but the vegetables in this box liked their water a little warmer than this. I could have the water temperature monitored with an enchantment, but I had a lot of time on my hands.

"Sir Fuzzy Pants, I need you," I softly called in a sing-song voice.

The veil parted, like someone pulled a glittery periwinkle curtain aside, and my familiar stepped into the mortal coil. Animals and even some insects could become familiars if a caster infused them with enough ley energy over the course of the familiar's lifetime. When that animal passed away, it created a spirit stone to allow it to journey across the planes.

Sir Fuzzy Pants had the build of a Pallas cat, but instead of a tan, fluffy coat, he was all ethereal blue—the color of raw magic. Centric circles, sigils, and ghostly runes covered his coat in shimmering spell workings. He brushed his spirit body against my legs, and his ley energy commingled with my magic.

Sir Fuzzy Pants was a Big Boy and had been the Townsend family's grimoire for generations, but his spirit stone was buried somewhere on our land—I didn't know where—so he stayed with the house. The more spells a familiar knew, the larger the familiar grew. I used to know a caster whose familiar was a monarch butterfly, and it'd grown as large as a road map thanks to all the spells it knew.

A couple of the spells Sir Fuzzy Pants knew were woven into his being from some of my great-great-greats that I still used to this day. However, other spells he knew, like instant communication, had become obsolete and I'd allowed him to fade out the workings. Cell phones handled a lot of the heavy work familiars had done merely twenty years ago.

I rubbed my knuckles on the top of his head, and he leaned into it. Then I dragged my fingers down to my spell working for controlling water temperature and inserted my intent. The spell working on his spiritual coat glowed electric blue and the formula appeared in the air within a tinkling blink. Then it was gone. I touched the irrigation hose one more time and it was the proper sixty-eight degrees.

"Good boy," I said. It wasn't necessary, but sometimes Fuzzy Pants stayed in this realm with me if I sweet-talked him, and I always appreciated his company.

He deserved to be doted on. Especially because he made memorized casting so fast. If I hadn't memorized that spell, I would've had to draw out the working on his coat and say each symbol aloud. It was what I'd done for a year and a day to memorize it.

A ripe tomato caught my eye and I plucked it from the vine, rubbing it on my overalls as I strolled back inside my greenhouse. This time, the fragrant air, the blooms, and the pollinators made me smile even as I contemplated renting out my greenhouse.

Was I struggling enough for that yet? My flowers were healthy, some belonged in the tropics, and I could get a good fee for them. But it'd also cut me off from that reagent and I'd have to pay *them* if I needed it. It'd rankle, especially when I was incredibly used to coming in here and taking what I needed. Fuzzy Pants hopped after a butterfly, his spirit paw going through it.

Although now that the video was currently viral, the idea of renting out my sanctuary was futile. No one liked me, and even if I offered myself up as a doormat, no one would take the time to wipe their feet on me. Not after the reminder of what'd happened five years ago on *Home Brew Elixirs*.

Not after getting outed on the internet as the alchemist and enchanter behind Star Trails.

Look where being a doormat got me, anyway. Alone in a fabulous greenhouse and alchemy workshop, unable to sell my potions and enchantments because America's potion sweetheart was a two-faced, conniving, back-stabbing liar.

Maybe I should leave Starglen and start over somewhere else, like farther north. I loved the ocean, and it'd have close to the same biomes for reagents that Starglen had. It was hard to not feel hated when I'd just lost my business. Well, most of it. I sat at my workstation and picked up my iPad where I'd left it yesterday. I needed to readjust my schedule. Fuzzy Pants jumped onto my workbench and barreled through the empty vials and corks, disturbing nothing. He leaped onto the top shelf and sat on my dried plants, tracking a dragonfly with his ghostly eyes.

"Well, at least the Vineyard hadn't canceled." I deleted all the future events with Starglen Apothecary and Enchanting Crystals. "Then again, the Vineyard's getting a great deal from me."

The Vineyard was an assisted living facility for the Muted. Nearly everyone was born with the ability to use ley energy, but sometimes that switch inside everyone never flipped and they couldn't touch the ley lines. Some people who were born with it could burn out the fuse to that switch and never touch ley energy again, also becoming Muted. *Those* people didn't handle that well. Worst case, they needed constant sedation and observation while most cases of those turning Muted needed the time to heal and accept their new normal. A lot of my calm mind potions went to the Vineyard to give them a break from the anxiety and denial of losing their magic.

My planner on my iPad—and my phone—dinged with an unscheduled scheduled brunch date with Winkerton for tomorrow. I smiled. She knew how much I hated spontaneity and had insisted that I share my planner with her so she could make these types of changes to my schedule.

I fished my phone from the front pocket of my overalls and opened our message thread.

Sorry I didn't text you back yesterday. But I'm gonna be ok

WINKERTON

I knew changing your schedule would get
you to text me back

Joke's on you. I love brunch

WINKERTON

I know. I wish I could come over today, but I
have appointments I can't break. Text or call
me if you need to talk

I smiled.

Sure thing. I'll see you tomorrow

WINKERTON

Darling, I look forward to it

I set my phone facedown. Winkerton always needed the last word. I'd tested it once a few years ago, by confirming and then reconfirming plans and giving her niceties, and Winkerton always texted back, to the point that we'd devolved into emojis and GIFs.

Yesterday had made me feel utterly alone, singled out, and reviled all over again, I was relieved to have Winkerton. If only as a friend.

THE MOON WASN'T COMPLETELY full, but it illuminated the clouds blocking it. The ley bugs' sparkling blue twinkle enchanted the area, figuratively speaking, as they signaled to each other. I stepped through the damp grass, enjoying the lush feel of the blades between my toes, clutching the bottom of my robe so it wouldn't get wet. Useless, as it always ended up that way.

I clutched my bath bomb and smelled it. Vanilla and

lavender, a calming balm on a night like tonight would be exactly what I needed to feel like myself once more. Or at least to stop feeling this sad.

The thought of relocating stayed with me. I loved the idea of Starglen and the Pacific northwest. The ocean, the rainforest, the mountains, and even the marshes were an alchemist's dream of foraging. There were beautiful plants and reagents all around me for the taking. And it really helped that the city sat on a nexus of ley lines, making my potions more potent than the southern part of California. This area would be perfect if it weren't for the people.

But because of the same reasons I loved this city, so did everyone else. They refused to let me put the past behind me, refused to let me stand on my feet. I didn't have anyone, aside from Winkerton, holding me here. And Sir Fuzzy Pants. I'd lose him too if I started over in another city. Hell, I'd probably need to switch coasts to get a good chance of starting over. I did love a good lobster roll.

But at least I'd be able to take care of myself instead of heavily relying on a stipend and then the inheritance in three years.

I glanced behind me, and the lights of the house glowed between the boughs of trees, and I took the last turn on the path to the secluded area where a large cedar tub sat. It had no water hook ups, and it was currently empty. I approached the edge, removed the acetate tab that prevented the bath bomb from activating, and tossed it in.

The ball thumped against the wood floor, then cracked opened. A rush of water nearly exploded from it in a wave, splashing my stomach and filling the tub three inches from the rim. Hot vanilla and lavender steam rolled off the surface.

"Well, it looks like I need to work on how . . . forceful the water comes out, but still." I smiled. "Good job, Lila."

I pulled my wet robe off and draped it on the corner.

Naked as I was, I wasn't worried anyone was watching. No one ever had in the past, and they certainly wouldn't now. I climbed into the cedar tub, hissing at the hot, fizzing water. I made a mental note to cool the temperature as I slowly submerged myself inch by inch.

I stared up at the overcast gray night sky, remarking that yesterday's incident hadn't made me cry. I'd almost had a panic attack, but no tears. I hadn't cried since that day Georgia almost died. Tears were useless anyway; they did nothing for me.

I scooted lower in the tub, breathing in the cedar, lavender, and vanilla vapors as ragged strips of clouds drifted across the silver half-moon shining light on the tips of the pine trees like darker triangles against the mountains. The scent of my bath was relaxing, and by the time the water cooled, I should be in a better mood and sleep easy. And if that didn't happen, I'd daydream about how Georgia Cauldron would get her comeuppance. Then one day, maybe I could let go of some of the pain she'd given me.

Chapter Four

The rain soaked through my jacket as I halted outside a two-story home some blocks away from the Flower Market. I checked the text I'd sent John this morning, thanking him and asking if there was anything I could do for him. He'd read it, but he'd never responded. My shoulders sagged; the ghosting was beginning. I recognized the signs from the other times it'd happened and knew I shouldn't have stayed the extra night. I stared at the house again, wondering if I should leave. The back tire for my bike was deflating, and even if I didn't stay here, I'd need to refill it, but I wasn't sure if I could knock on Emily's door. Yet what else was there left for me? I was broke and exhausted. After selling my remaining potions in the Flower Market—thank goodness for that, at least—I was out of reagents.

I'd ridden my bike all the way to Founders' Grove and hiked for hours, collecting ingredients, only to ride my bike all the way back into town and down to the Nettles. Then I'd spent the money I'd made today by renting an alchemy table to make new potions to sell tomorrow, and I was strapped.

My stomach growled. Broke, hungry, and tired, and Emily

was an old high school friend who'd practically begged me to stay with her until I got back on my feet. But that was before she got married and had a kid, and I didn't know if that offer still stood. Living here with her family would certainly put an end to our friendship, and I didn't want that. But I was also running out of friendly couches and I did not want to sleep in a diner again.

The curtain in the window twitched, and a small pale face peeked at me. I slid off my bike. Katie, Emily's six-year-old daughter, had spotted me. I could still go a couple blocks on that back tire before I really needed to refill it and keep moving.

"Nate!" a woman called.

Emily stood in the doorway, holding the door open and peering at me with a hand shielding her eyes. The porch light turned on, not that it could dispel the gloominess of the rain.

There was no turning back now. I waved. "Hello!"

Katie bounded out in yellow galoshes and a matching raincoat. She opened an umbrella covered in ducks over her blonde head and ran to me, splashing water as she went. "Nate, you're wrinkled like a raisin."

I glanced at my pruned fingers and laughed a little. "I am."

"Did you lose your gloves?" she asked solemnly.

If I had any, gloves would've helped only for so long. My handlebars soaked up water like a sponge. I nodded anyway, because she made a right guess.

Emily swept her arm inside. "Don't dawdle."

I couldn't tell who she was talking to, but I smiled anyway. "You better hurry, little duckling, or your mom'll get mad."

"Come along, then." Katie sounded so much like her mother. I could practically hear that phrase said to her a million times, and she was only repeating it.

"Oh, I don't know if—"

"Mom!" Katie jumped into a puddle, splashing me. "Nate's bike is broken!"

The tire was deflating yes, but—I checked it, and sure enough it'd flattened out. I sighed.

"Get in the house," Emily said. "Both of you."

I carried my bike up the porch steps and rested it against the house next to the rattan chairs. Katie shook her umbrella free, spraying both her mother and me, before sticking it in the umbrella stand.

"In you go, duckling," Emily said as her dark gaze traveled over my soaked-through clothes and wet shoes. "You look like you're freezing. Take a hot shower while I finish getting supper ready."

I paused, unable to form words to even give her my gratitude. I swallowed a lump in my throat. I didn't even have to ask. Emily simply knew, and maybe that was why we'd always got along. I knew when she needed someone to talk to, and now she knew when I needed some help. She hadn't forced me to beg for it. Which, don't get me wrong, I don't have trouble *asking* for help. Sometimes it was a little embarrassing, and today seemed to be one of those days. We stepped inside and she closed the door against the rain. It smelled like rice had been made, and my stomach growled.

I kicked my soaked shoes off and set them by the shoe rack. "Hey, I hate to intrude, but I was wondering if I could crash on your couch tonight?"

"Sure. Do you need to use the washer and dryer too?"

"That'd be awesome, Em." I smiled. All the heaviness that'd weighed me down at the end of her driveway lifted. She'd pulled her dark blonde hair into a ponytail and her sweater complemented her brown eyes. "You look nice."

She smiled. "Thanks. Go get cleaned up. We're hungry."

Two hours later, I was dry, warm, and full. Down the hall,

my clothes in the washer thumped against the barrel as it whirred into the spin cycle. Emily relaxed on my soon-to-be-bed, and I showed Katie my foraging kit while I cleaned my knife.

"Your bag's dirty," Katie said.

Emily's brows lifted, and she covered a smile by taking a sip of wine.

"That's because I use it all the time." I dragged a damp cloth along the curved edge of the blade, scratching mud free from the tiny, serrated teeth at the back end of the blade. "I was out in the redwoods a few hours ago."

"You rode your bike?" Emily asked.

"I can't have a knife yet." Katie sighed heavily, watching me clean my gear. "When I go to school, we'll have field trips to the lagoon and my teacher will have to cut things for us. I hope I'll see some otters. Did you know they can open clam shells without a knife?"

I nodded at Emily before I set my knife aside. "What school are you going to?"

"Little Stars." Katie perked. "My grandma's taking us shopping tomorrow for my first *real* apothecary set. It's gonna have a burner."

"Well," Emily murmured, setting her wine aside, "a small one that you can *only* use when me or Daddy are watching you."

"Little Stars Academy?" I gave Katie a high five. "That's so awesome!"

"I made my first real potion with Mommy at the library today!"

Emily smiled and nodded. "We did. She did really good too, Nate. You should've seen her."

"I wish I had. What did you make?"

"I made Grandma a hair tonic." Katie giggled. "It should turn her hair green. It's her favorite color."

"Nice!" Hair tonics were easy to make, but for someone new to using ley energy, they were difficult to get right. I wondered if I'd be able to hang around long enough to see her grandmother use it. I had no doubt she would; everyone indulged Katie as she was their first alchemist and enchanter in a family of solely alchemists.

Magic was a crapshoot. Sometimes a person had two abilities, like alchemy and enchanting like myself, but it was never assured you'd get the same ley abilities as your parents. Being born on a solstice was the only guarantee to get all three ley abilities.

"It took her a couple tries, but once she made the connection with the ley lines, she made the potion on her first try." Emily tucked her feet under her and reached for her wine. "The library didn't have kid-sized alchemy tables available."

I chuckled. "That's funny, because whenever I need to rent a table at the library, that's *all* they have."

Katie giggled, her brown eyes twinkling. "You're too tall for a kid's table."

"I had to kneel!"

Katie laughed. Alchemy and enchanting tables were the conduit that connected us to the ley lines to imbue potions or charms with magic. They were expensive to make or purchase, and they worked best when constructed over ley lines. Luckily, libraries rented them out for a pretty fee—the only things at the library that weren't free. They were, however, the safest place to rent one. But if you're like me, and you're short on cash, you go where it's the cheapest.

"*This* is your alchemy kit?" Katie asked.

I had it spread out, cleaning up my equipment and sorting through leftover ingredients from my last cooking session earlier in the Nettles. Nothing matched. My kit was a pieced together collection of random equipment I bought or scavenged from the garbage. If it still worked, it was good enough for me. My scales gleamed, my scissors were sharp, if almost too small for my fingers, and my mesh bags were folded neatly on top of my leather-lined gloves. Unfortunately, my twine was a knotted ball and my mask was missing.

I frowned. Something else was missing.

"Where's your mortar and pestle?" Katie asked.

"Oh no." I dropped my head in my hands. "I left them behind."

"Oh, Nate," Emily said.

"I know."

"You need to double-check your station, dude."

"I know."

"You can't keep leaving things behind."

"You *lost* them?" Katie asked in a scandalized voice.

I lifted my head and sighed. "Yes."

"Again," Emily muttered. "Hopefully, they'll still be there when you go back tomorrow. The library is really good about their lost and found."

"I wasn't at the library." My mind raced with ways to fix this. A mortar and pestle were two of the most important pieces of equipment in an alchemist's kit. Mine were basic, nothing special about them other than they got the job done. I could probably find something to work. A bowl would be easy to find, but a replacement for the pestle was a different story. If only I hadn't lost the muddler, I'd be okay.

My body grew hot, and I ground my molars. I hated this about myself. I *knew* my penchant for losing things was a bad trait of mine and I was trying to find a way to help with it, but I hadn't had any luck yet.

"Where were you cooking?" Emily asked.

"The Nettles," I answered.

"Are you nuts?" Emily hissed through her teeth.

"What's the nettles?" Katie asked.

Emily glared at me before she leaned over to make eye

contact with her daughter. "It's a dangerous place where bad people go to do bad things."

I waved a dismissive hand. "It's not that dangerous."

"Maybe for you. You're everyone's puppy, but for people like us, like women." Emily shook her head. "They sell stolen potions and charms there. That's where the mafia operates!"

I laughed. "There's no mafia there. I'll give you that there's more crime because the Nettles isn't policed like the Flower Market, but come on." I chuckled some more. "Mafia. This isn't *The Sopranos.*"

"You're right. That show's a fantasy—they don't even have magic in that world. Plus he worked out of sausage joints."

Katie stood and skipped out of the room.

Emily frowned at me. "Nate, I know you have to do what you gotta do, but the Nettles? It's dangerous there, and you just got a permit to sell in the Flower Market. Stay away from there."

I sighed. "What else am I gonna do, Em? I can't always pay to rent from the library, especially if I have other expenses I need to cover." She opened her mouth and I quickly rushed in. "I'm not your problem, and I can take care of myself."

Katie came back into the room, holding a pink plastic mortar and matching pestle. An outline of a bunny was embossed on the bowl and "My First Apothecary" was written on the side of the pestle. "You can use this."

I became motionless, staring at Katie's solution to my problem. Suddenly, all the worry I had about what I'd do tomorrow to keep my ass afloat tumbled away thanks to this little girl in duckie pajamas.

"Are you sure?" I asked, even as I took the mortar and pestle from her. I knew damn-well mine would not be waiting for me if I went back to the stacks, and really, anything worked, even Georgia Cauldron merchandise.

"Yes. Grandma's taking me shopping tomorrow for a real set." Katie beamed at me. "You can bring it back when you're done."

"You're a good egg, Katie. Thank you." I carefully placed it in my bag with the rest of my equipment. "I'll take good care of it."

A key in the lock rattled and Daren, Emily's husband, walked through the door, his dark hair and shoulders damp from the rain. "That isn't Nate's bike on the porch, is it?" His face fell when he saw me. "Oh, I guess it really is."

"Hey, Daren." I stood from the floor. Daren and I weren't as close as me and Emily were. I'm not sure why; he didn't see me as competition.

"You crashing here tonight?" He set his laptop bag down and toed off his shoes.

Emily shifted on the couch to smile at him. "Yeah, I offered him the couch. Your dinner's in the oven. Did you have a good day at work?"

He walked into the kitchen, calling over his shoulder, "There was an outage."

And then I became a third wheel. Emily, Daren, and Katie were a happy family. He was a wonderful dad, and she was a great mom. I envied Katie only a little until I realized I was jealous of a six-year-old. When I was six, I'd already been brought back to the orphanage because I had too many issues for my foster family to deal with.

LATER THAT EVENING, I sat on the couch, listening to Daren type in the kitchen. He was still working that outage or helping someone with it. I didn't know exactly what he did for work. He didn't use his alchemy skills to provide for his family, which was totally fine. He worked in tech and people liked the Internet; it wasn't like he chose poorly.

In fact, he was doing so well for himself that Emily only had to work part-time and they could afford to send Katie to Little Stars Academy for budding alchemists and enchanters. I'd never even been considered for such a school. I had to learn everything I knew from indulging foster parents when I had them, and bingeing the Potion Network. Hey, that was basically a free course of the intro to alchemy for beginners at Starglen Alchemy University.

A beer appeared in front of my face, and I grabbed it. Daren moved around the couch, sat in the adjacent chair, and leaned back.

"Thanks." I took a sip of the cold brew, enjoying the malty and slightly sweet taste.

"Look, man, I know shit's rough, but you can't keep doing this." Daren refused to look at me; the beer label was more interesting. "You need to settle down and get a job."

"I have a job." I slid farther down into the couch, pulling my shoulders up to my ears.

He flicked a glance at me before reading the beer label some more. "A job that pays you a living wage."

"I just got my permit to sell in the Flower Market, and—"

"I know, and that's great, but let me be frank with you." He lowered his beer and leaned forward, angling his body toward me. "You sleep on my couch more than us. I get it. You and Em are great friends. I'm not gonna get in the way of that. But you're a grown-ass adult man couch surfing in his *late twenties*."

I frowned at my hands. "Everything will work out. I'm getting my chance now."

"Sure, and what you're doing isn't getting you above

water, either. You can get a job and still sell in the Flower Market. There's nothing wrong with having to shlep into an office until you can do your whole potion thing."

That was rich coming from an alchemist. But Daren never had the dreams I had. I furrowed my brow. "Well, like you said, I'm couch surfing and—"

"Emily and I talked about this, and you can use our address to get you a job. Hell, you're here every other week, you may as well. And when you're on your feet, we'll help you get your own place."

I winced.

"I get it, man, I really do." Daren stood and gestured at the couch. "But if you won't help yourself, then this is the last time you can crash here."

I nodded and swallowed back my pride and anger and humiliation at being talked to like this. I sent him a strained smile. "Thanks. I'll let you know what happens."

Daren softened, and he clapped my shoulder. "Just think about it. She worries about you."

I nodded and he left, turning off the light in the kitchen and leaving me in darkness. He didn't understand. I've had plenty of typical jobs, gas station, department stores, restaurants, but something always came by and knocked me on my ass. Like at the grocery store, they announced the store closing during employee appreciation week and we'd all gotten the axe. I sipped the beer and pulled out my phone, connecting to their Wi-Fi network, and scrolled through the forums, searching for anything that'd give me a bright idea out of the hole everyone thought I was in. If I were honest, I'd been in that hole since my parents died.

Sometimes, life dealt you a shit hand, and it was taking me a long ass time to dig myself out.

I stopped scrolling when I saw the Potion Network logo—

a blue circle with TPN in bold green—wondering if they'd come up with a new recipe that I'd need to master. Instead, it was a casting call for *The Next Potion Network Star* with Georgia Cauldron and her co-host, Owen Creek.

That was an opportunity, but I knew before I even looked that they required a SAU degree because all their hosts were certified teachers. Maybe I should get an office job. I didn't know how I'd do that, since I'd only—barely—graduated high school, but if I did, then I could feed myself and sleep on my own couch.

I closed my eyes and held my breath, hating what I'd contemplate next. I'd give myself four more weeks of chasing my dream to make it in the Flower Market. If I didn't see some kind of profit, if I didn't catch *any* kind of break, I'd take Daren up on his offer. And later, I don't know, five, ten years from now, maybe I'll be able to send myself to college and get that shot at a show so someone like me wouldn't have to deal with this shit in the future.

It was a depressing ultimatum. Whatever job I found wasn't my dream and it'd suck my soul dry. It wouldn't help to make life worth living, only keep me alive. But Daren was right. I couldn't do this much longer.

I opened YouTube to catch a rerun of *Home Brew Elixirs* and dreamed big. If I ever got on *The Next Potion Network Star*, I wouldn't need to worry about money again. I'd be living the dream. Teaching people like me how to make potions and what to do if you can't get to an alchemy table for weeks, or what a decent substitute was when you couldn't get that ingredient in the tropics or the arctic. Even better, my show would be so popular, I'd get to co-host with Georgia Cauldron and no one would have to worry about little orphan Nate again because I'd finally made it.

And then everyone would want me to hang around. I might have to ghost them to get some peace and quiet.

I finished my beer and stretched out on the couch, half wondering if Georgia Cauldron was as nice as she seemed and if she really had six bunnies until I fell asleep.

Chapter Five

The soft scraping of forks against plates beneath murmured conversations and the dark, rainy, over-cast day made for a hushed feeling around our table in Brew & Chew. I speared the edge of my whole wheat toast and peered at the remnants of a smear of . . . something. Was it pimento cheese or just cream cheese mixed with tomato? Or maybe I'd confused the flavor with my bloody mary, which seemed extra spicy today, and honestly? This might be my best brunch here.

"She was coffee-housing again last night." Winkerton snatched one eclair from the plate and plucked a crumble of candied bacon from the top and popped it into her mouth.

I watched her bright red lips tilt upward and I quickly met her blue eyes. She looked lovely today with her hair in a perfect victory roll, and the stunning cranberry-red Rockabilly swing dress popped against her creamy white flesh. She was the perfect splash of bold color in this drab bistro.

"What's coffee-housing?" I made the perfect last bite by spearing the last yellow quarter of an heirloom tomato beneath the piece of toast already on my fork and topped it off with a sliver of pickled red onion. The bright tartness of the tomato paired with the sharp acidic bite of the onion sang in my mouth, and I sighed as I chewed. I was always a little sad when I finished my tomato toast.

Winkerton rolled her wrist. "She drew a card and shuffled her hand around like she didn't have the cards, but she was sitting with nine melded cards."

"How's that cheating?"

"Darling, she made me think her hand was bad and I hadn't discarded."

"I see." I didn't play rummy, so I really didn't. I picked up my bloody mary and checked around for our server, thinking another might do me good. Though now that I wasn't focused on my plate, I noticed a few people peeking over at our table.

Sure, Winkerton and I made an odd pair. She was dressed as normal, ready to go to a sock hop if asked, perfectly coiffed and manicured. And I wore my favorite clothes: overalls, a plaid shirt, and my hair in twin braids.

These people might not recognize me. During the trial, I wore my best suits, had my hair done respectfully, and wore muted makeup. I'd appeared rich, respectable, and humble. Today, I looked like I'd spent the early morning foraging, which wasn't wrong. Yet people were whispering and jerking their heads at our table.

"Darling, this is why I'm asking you to make me a charm to find out if that old battle-ax is yanking me around by my leg." She poured the remnants of the mimosa into her glass.

I quietly laughed. "I'm not going to help you cheat at rummy when you play with your elderly great-aunt."

Winkerton took a sip, studying me over the rim of her glass. "Enough about me. How are you doing?"

The remaining softness from my perfect meal slipped away, and I just knew people were watching me and gossiping. I glanced around, checking for the easiest route out of here without passing too many tables, but didn't dare meet anyone's eye. "Mostly cancelations. Though the Vineyard no longer needs me to administer the IVs."

"That's interesting." She frowned. "I thought they were always short-staffed and preferred you to help with that."

"I guess some of the patients recognized me when the video went viral, and there was an incident." I sipped the dregs of my drink, almost choking on it. I tapped my finger on the tablecloth and focused on her shoulder. "I think I'm going to leave."

"Oh." Winkerton picked up her purse. This one was shaped like an old rotary telephone. "I'll ask for the check."

"No. I meant I think I'm going to leave Starglen."

She slouched in her chair, her cherry-red lips parting as she stared at me. I squirmed. I'd never suggested moving before. After the scandal, it'd taken two years for me to not stand out like a sore thumb. Then another to build myself back up, come up with Star Trails. It was only a short time ago that I'd started to make ends meet. I was dipping less and less into my stipend for my business and really beginning to self-invest.

"You can't leave," she whispered.

"What else am I going to do?" The backs of my eyes stung and I blinked rapidly. It took me a little off guard that this wound could still bleed. "Maybe I made a mistake in staying in the same city. I should go out east where people aren't so caught up in her."

By "her" I meant Georgia Cauldron. Starglen was the epicenter for alchemist, caster, and enchanter influencers— known as ACE for short—and practitioners thanks to the node of the ley lines in this PNW city. Not only did it host the best colleges for Alchemy and Enchanting, it was the seat of power for the Potion Network. Starglen was bigger than Hollywood.

"But I thought you loved it here," Winkerton said. "And that you wouldn't let a few idiots dictate where you live."

"I've said it a million times: I came for the show, stayed for the greenhouse." I rubbed the pad of my thumb along my nails. "Maybe Starglen isn't the place where I can thrive."

Her face crumpled. I hated seeing her like this. Winkerton would be fine, and she'd thrive; she always thrived. Yes, we saw each other almost every day, and people genuinely loved her. Well, it used to be every day. Something had been *off* with her for a little while, and I'd struggled to place my finger on it. But once I'd left, she'd replace me easily enough, but that didn't mean she didn't truly feel heartbroken over me potentially leaving.

And once I'd said it out loud, the more right it felt.

"I could come back in five or ten years, depending on how things are."

"Ten years!" She clutched her purse handle and her eyes darted to the lone eclair sitting on the plate as if that were her future.

"Look, it won't be that bad, and I've only just decided." I reached across the table and laid my hand down near hers. "It'll take me a while to get everything situated, and I haven't even thought of where I'd want to land. I still have a lot to do."

She laid her hand over mine and frowned. "I hate that their ignorance is making you think you need to move away from here, darling. It's not fair."

Winkerton was right.

"It's that or I get my revenge and expose TPN for the elitist assholes they are." That was laughable; I had no revenge planned, but it at least showed Winkerton how serious I was. I stood and waited for her. We still hadn't received the check yet, but the hostess would get it for us. "Come on. Let's go shopping. I need some shimmer boxwood for a special order."

After we paid, we stepped out into the rainy, late August morning, overtaken by the smells of the damp pavement of the Flower Market. I pulled the hood of my purple raincoat up while Winkerton opened her black-laced-trimmed red umbrella. While the rain hadn't completely stopped, it'd lessened to a steady drizzle that didn't hide the smell of wet pavement mingling with fresh-cut flowers floating down the boulevard.

The Flower Market was huge, with only pedestrian traffic. It spanned six city blocks, two connecting streets, and had parking. When I came alone, I parked in the free stalls of a dirt-packed lot that was prone to become mud at some point in the day. It'd be a bog by evening if the drizzle remained consistent.

The Flower Market had everything from restaurants to clothing boutiques, flower shops, bakeries, and magic. Alchemy and enchanting reigned supreme in the market. Whether selling a finished product, like a haste potion or a charm to enhance one's appearance, to reagents, raw crystals, and wire. It also hosted two libraries that rented out alchemy and enchanting tables. Some of the fancier reagent shops allowed you to use their table for a heftier fee but more privacy.

If I left Starglen, I'd really start over from scratch. I'd have to rent those types of tables until I could afford my own, and if I had to guess, my inheritance would come through before I made enough with my potions and enchantments to buy my own.

My parents had desperately wanted a child born on the witches' new year, even if it meant my type of casting would be a common one. That not only made me an ACE, but it meant I'd been born under a water sign. When most practitioners planned for ACE children, they aimed for Samhain since it was an auspicious time of year.

We turned down the lane that'd take us on a shortcut toward the reagent shops that specialized in tropical reagents like the shimmer boxwood I needed and came across a crowd. These side streets reminded me of the county fair: fried foods and T-shirt stands off the beaten path. It smelled a little like an animal pen thanks to the fertilizer for the nearby flower shop. But people were crowding around a poorly put together makeshift stall. At least the rain had lessened to a mist now, and my hood hid most of my face.

"What's going on here?" Winkerton asked.

"Looks like a demonstration," I murmured.

Usually, these were on the main thoroughfare on the reagent street next over. We began slipping by when I glanced over. A man stood behind the rickety stand with a bike that had a flat tire leaning against it, and he smiled at his audience. His wavy blond hair was damp from the steady drizzle, and his chin was scruffy.

He lifted a stem of foxglove going to seed. "As you see, these seeds are difficult to extract from the pod, but I've got a trick."

I edged closer, curious to see this trick of his. I had a good guess how he'd pull it off, as many influencers in Starglen repeated steps from the advanced herbal prep class from SAU. A few people stepped aside to allow me to get closer. He still had dark lines of dirt under his fingernails as fresh as mine were this morning, but I'd at least washed my hands after I foraged. Truly though, I could admire that he'd gotten up early to find the foxglove in time to start a demonstration in the Flower Market.

I smiled a little. I appreciated someone sticking to a

schedule to accomplish what they needed to get done for the day, even if he was being a tad wasteful.

To my horror, he scraped the flat end of his blade—his foraging knife of all tools—along the pod, tearing that and bruising the few seeds that popped out. I clenched my fingers and bit my lip. He couldn't be serious. I moved to the front of the crowd.

He set aside the seed and pinched the end of the pod. "And if you don't get them all out, just drag your knife along it again."

He had to be joking. *Keep quiet. Keep quiet.* I chanted this in my head as he mutilated the pod. It tore.

"You're doing it wrong." Before I even knew my mouth had opened, the words popped right out.

His head jerked up, and moss-green eyes collided with mine. The skin around them wrinkled, and it took me a moment to realize he'd smiled at me.

"Oh?" He looked me over, the knife loosely gripped in his hand. "How would you do it?"

I liked that I could hear a smile in his voice instead of a challenge. His posture remained easy, and while he seemed on the skinny side, he didn't lack confidence, even now.

"You pinch them out," I answered.

His brows lifted, and his attention dipped to my hands before meeting my stare. I felt it hit low in my stomach.

"Miss, this pod is too sturdy to easily pinch them out. We wouldn't want to abuse your fine fingers by trying to pinch these seeds from the pod."

What? I tilted my head to the side and stepped closer, the edge of the table hitting my thigh. "You wrap the pod first in a warm, damp towel to soften it. Pinching the seeds out is the best way because scraping can bruise the seeds and cause oil to leak and create a less-than-potent remedy than you're trying to make."

My voice began rising in pitch. I cleared my throat. And, just to be safe, tugged on my braid. My shoulders loosened a centimeter.

Even though he pursed his lips, the smile remained in his eyes. "It doesn't make that big of a difference, and it's faster this way."

"It does!" My voice hit that pitch I recognized as "passionate" and cleared my throat again. "It does make a difference. Bruising the seeds makes them less viable, especially for replanting." I gestured at the chewed-up pod. "That's ruined. You can't use it for anything else now."

"Really?" He leaned closer, the soothing smell of the forest wafted off him. "You appreciate something that has multiple uses?"

"All plants are multi-use plants."

"What would you save the pod for?"

"I'd use it in a cream. But the pod splinters when you extract the seeds like that and it isn't recommended for salves. It'll make the salve gritty and won't rub into skin well."

His eyes traveled from the top of my head to my shoulders, to my hands—leaving behind a lick of heat—almost as if he was imagining how much skin I had. No one had looked at me like I was a snack in a long time. The sounds, the smell, the small crush of people all disappeared when I met his mossy gaze once more.

"I'd really hate for you to have to experience gritty cream. As I like to think, there's no ruined ingredient. I bet with a little work I can make you a smooth cream."

I snorted. "I'd love to see you try."

Grinning, he reached into his kit on the chair beside him and retrieved a plastic pink mortar and set it on the table. I lifted a brow. But judging him for his equipment was something a gatekeeper did, and I refused to entertain that mind-set. He dropped the pod into the mortar and retrieved a matching pink pestle. He'd certainly stayed on brand.

He twisted the pestle into the mortar and rotated it, squashing the pod again. It'd take a lot of work to get the pod into a smooth paste. He rotated the bowl one more time, mashing the rounded end of the pestle, and there, on the side, was an embossed bunny.

Ice cascaded along my veins as I studied the pestle in his hands more closely and barely made out the "My First Apothecary" embossed on the side. No wonder he was being so easygoing with me.

This man was an idiot.

Chapter Six

"You're doing it wrong."

I held in my snort. Her scandalized tone kept getting better and better. The grass stains on her knees when she walked up had grabbed my attention. She was used to doing exactly what I was demonstrating, and she had opinions. I rarely had these interactions with the crowd. People either watched and moved on, or they didn't even stop. Okay, the stealing was a new thing for me, but that hadn't happened again. Thank goodness.

But now I was getting heckled.

The hood on her raincoat fell back, no longer hiding the flush staining her cheeks or that she wore her pigtails in braids. Did I know her from somewhere? But I also knew her type, which was probably why she seemed familiar. This woman, whose voice was getting a touch shrill, had "an expensive education" and didn't like me contradicting it.

"I suppose you'd want this dried first?" I glanced at the rest of the crowd for the first time, noticing a shift in the mood and more cell phones in their hands. A flag went up in my head. What if they'd found out I wasn't qualified to demonstrate for them? I swallowed before returning my attention to the woman nagging me. "This is what you do when you don't have access to store-bought ingredients."

She blinked. A lot was conveyed in that single motion, but she simply went with, "You plan ahead."

Like I was an idiot for not thinking of that. Come to think of it, there was a shift in her attitude since I'd challenged her on the texture of my pod.

I peered into the pink mortar and quirked a brow. "You keep staring at my equipment." Then I sent her a slow, teasing grin.

Her lips moved, but no sound came out. Then her silvery eyes rounded and the soft pink tint on her cheeks turned bright red. "I was surprised to see you with plastic."

Hah! Adorable.

I half-shrugged. "Why? It's durable."

Her brows pulled together, and she shook her head. "Merely surprised. However, I suppose stone might be too heavy for some."

"I'm stronger than I look." I flexed my biceps when I ground the pod. It was lost on her because I wore a jacket, but the effort was there. The bowl nearly jumped out of my grasp from the force I'd used to show off.

"Exactly." She waved a hand at the mortar and pestle. "Stronger than a five-year-old."

She had me there. And I doubted she wanted to flirt either. Maybe I'd misread the way she'd stared at my hands and the smallest touch of approval I thought I'd seen in her expression. She certainly didn't like to be challenged.

More people in the crowd had their phones out. A few were pointing them at us, but most everyone else was reading something. A few people were chatting with their neighbor. This couldn't be typical.

"And get a tarp," she snapped in an afterthought. "The

extra moisture in the mixture can dampen the potency of the paste."

Whatever excitement I'd felt during this exchange evaporated. We were definitely *not* flirting. Usually, I could read a person well, but I honestly didn't know when the energy switched from flustered teasing to derision. She must *really* care about the consistency in hand creams.

"Seriously?" I muttered only for her ears. "Don't you think that's enough?"

The murmuring grew louder. Maybe I hadn't been as quiet as I'd hoped.

"That's Lila Townsend," someone said loud enough to reach me. "She tried to ruin Georgia Cauldron's career."

"Guess she can't stop there," someone else yelled. "She's going after yours now."

I lifted my head and stared at her. A smile, or a wince, or *something* forced her to pull her lips back in an awkward grimace. People were starting to shift closer to her, hissing accusations. I caught "poisoner" more than a few times. She practically pulled herself into the tiniest ball she possibly could, and the panic lighting in her gray eyes shocked me back into action.

"Everyone settle down," I said in my most authoritative voice, but was also grateful they were standing in the mist with me too. I was trying to find that perfect balance between not upsetting this crowd while making sure no one got hurt.

I wasn't sure what to do about that, seeing as many people adored Georgia, me included. She was so fun to watch and had some of the better techniques. Sure, she repeated them all the time, but they were classics. But the crowd before me seemed to trend more on the side of Georgia's extreme Honey Bunnies than interested alchemists as they edged closer to Lila like they were going to surround her if it weren't for my stand.

"We should teach her a lesson," someone growled.

"Hey!" I braced against the stand. I'd jump over it if I had to. They would not hurt her in front of me. "None of that."

The hipster in red swooped in and gripped Lila's arm. "It's time to go, darling."

Lila tossed one last look at me. The blush had faded, and she was pale. She was gone the next moment.

I lifted my hands in the air. "All right, all right. That's over."

Some people peeled away, already disinterested. They'd only stopped because there'd been a commotion. And no matter how hard I tried to regain their attention, I'd failed. People seemed more inclined to go over how much better Georgia Cauldron was doing since nearly losing it all when she'd been poisoned on-air.

I'd never seen much of it; I'd just heard the news, and there were always two sides. One stated the evidence, and the others clutched at that first impression.

Me? I hadn't been there, so I really didn't have an option. Clearly, the evidence pointed the jury this way, and I trusted their judgment. But that didn't make me less of a Georgia Cauldron fan; though I drew the line at calling myself a Honey Bunny.

By the time I'd finished with my potion, the crowd was finished with me too. No one bought anything. I packed up my stand, placed all my ingredients in their places, and made sure everything was tightly contained.

This was still a good day. I'd learned from the encounter —mostly that I needed to practice crowd control to prevent something like this from happening again. But I'd still taken something away from it. I'd only had my permit for a few weeks. Maybe I'd oversold the idea of how well I was at selling products, but I'd expected to be doing better by now. It felt like everything was getting worse.

Biking was prohibited in the Flower Market, so it'd be a waste of time to refill my tire now. After ensuring the straps holding my equipment to the back of my bike were secure, I wheeled it toward Main Street and the exit while I continued to reflect. It was possible I was too naïve to see that I wasn't ready for this permit, but how else was I going to get the experience?

The deadline I'd given myself to make it on my own now seemed ridiculous. Maybe I should pack it in, get that job and save for college. My dreams deflated more than my bike tire at the thought. If you didn't keep trying, nothing would happen. I clenched my jaw. Yes. Today was bad but not a waste. The road to success was never smooth.

Lila Townsend and her hipster friend stepped out of a reagent shop in front of me. They barely noticed me, as I had to pull up short so I wouldn't walk into them.

"I'm just saying, darling, the best way to get your revenge is to fool them," the hipster said. "I'm not talking anything criminal."

Lila laughed. Most of it sounded strained. "And what would that look like?"

I kept pace with them. I mean, not intentionally. They were walking in the same direction as I was heading, but they talked loud enough for me to hear them.

"You mentioned they're big on all their hosts coming with a bachelor's in alchemy."

"You've heard the SAU commercials. They have a minor in broadcasting to complement the degree," Lila said.

Those commercials she talked about were what started my dream of getting my own show on the Potion Network. But the required college education had cost too much, and I hadn't done too well the last two years in high school. Not too long after my short stint in juvie, my new foster parents were having medical issues that took a lot of my attention.

I'd helped the Richardses get to appointments, made sure they ate, and took their medicine. They shouldn't have been able to keep me. No one else wanted me because I was considered a handful, and they argued for me to stay. When Mr. Richards passed, I helped Wendy grieve. It was always one thing or another, one short end of the stick after the other, and college never happened.

Wendy was in remission in Florida now. One day, maybe I could send her money or at least visit with her. That'd be nice for both of us.

"Wouldn't it be wild—"

"Winkerton, no." Lila shrugged with her whole body.

"No, hear me out. Wouldn't it be hysterical if you could get someone on that stupid show who didn't have a degree?" Winkerton said.

"How?"

"Well, you'd teach them what they need to know."

She snorted.

I held my breath, forgetting to turn onto the street I needed.

Winkerton placed a hand on Lila's shoulder. "You could teach anyone exactly what they'd need, as if they had gone to college themselves, and you know it. They were fools for what they did, and they need to know it."

Lila sighed. "And then what?"

"And then you'd reveal what you'd done," Winkerton said. "Like in *Scooby-Doo*."

"Masks and everything?"

"Of course, darling. We're civilized people."

She laughed again, still sounding a touch strained. "But ruin someone's career?"

"Well, yes. Maybe. Even if the person never appears on television again, they'll have the skills and the knowledge. They'd still manage to get a job or a promotion. And with the exposure from the show, especially if they're a favorite, people will be lining up to buy from them no matter where they land. It'll be better than what they have now."

"Maybe you've got a point, but everyone wants to be on TV."

I stopped following. It was getting creepy. They were clearly heading toward the paid parking garage, and I didn't have any business going there—even if I desperately wanted to hear the rest while they hypothetically brainstormed about pulling the wool over a TV studio's eyes.

I stepped off to the side and pulled out a compact air pump, then attached it to my back tire. My conversation with Daren and my self-imposed deadline to live with his low-key "I know better than you" vibes played in my head again for the tenth time. I'm a grown-ass man. Get a job and do this on the side. It hit me that if something like what Lila and her friend discussed could really happen, I'd like that idea a lot. Because then I could *do* something about where I slept and still continue learning and doing something I loved.

And if getting on that show, only to be exposed as a fraud, could prove that I was good at what I did . . . hold on. That made little sense. Who would hire a fraud? Mainly, it was meant to show that I was just as good as those other people who'd received a Starglen Alchemist degree.

Maybe it *would* make my life a little easier.

Chapter Seven

I settled into the burgundy button tufted crushed velvet armchair, rested my head against the back, and stared at the coffered ceiling. Winkerton set her purse on the old travel trunk that served as a coffee table. For a moment, I could imagine an old rotary phone that looked exactly like her purse had actually sat there unironically. But it didn't distract me, not for one moment, that today had sucked.

"Martini?" Winkerton pretended she was asking, but she'd already made a beeline toward the wet bar. "Personally, I feel cocktails are in order."

My attention strayed from her as I glanced around the room. Two lamps gave this room a dim, cozy setting—so did the shelves filled with books and plants—while the heirloom couch and wing chair gave it an eclectic yet homey look. Only because nothing matched aside from the fabric. My grandmother had loved a crushed velvet anything. I hid a TV behind a closed cabinet, but I rarely watched it in here.

Winkerton cooed softly, and the glittery curtain to the veil parted to allow her familiar, a large peacock, saunter through.

He was similar in size to a black bear and covered in spell workings.

"Reginald," Winkerton whispered, "you look dashing."

She touched the spell working on his chest that would turn her hands ice cold. The sigil flashed with ley energy, and Winkerton's hands turned blue.

"Thank you."

Reginald didn't stick around like Sir Fuzzy Pants, at least not in my home. He turned around and walked back into the spirit realm, his glorious tail gliding behind him. I couldn't see anything beyond the shimmery mantle of magic he'd stepped through; the spirit realm was not meant to be looked upon with living eyes. Winkerton picked up the Boston shaker, slapped the lid on, and shook. There was no ice in that shaker, and all we heard was the liquid splashing against the insides. But by the time she'd finished, the metal shaker had frosted over. A few moments later, she handed me a chilly martini glass.

"Ooh." I took a sip and sighed. Delightfully briny and just a tad funky. "Three olives. Did I do something nice?"

Winkerton settled on the mustard yellow couch, spreading her fluffy red skirt around her. "You looked like you needed a pick me up, darling, and I know how much you love olives."

I did love olives and took another sip, planning out when I'd eat each one to how much the gin bathed them. Honestly, I should probably eat one now, so the last one on the skewer became submerged. I pulled one off and relished the salty taste.

"He was cute." She also took a drink. The cold spell was fading from her fingertips, but her cuticles remained pastel blue for now. "In a starving waif sort of way, but certainly cute."

The man's face from this afternoon flashed across my mind unbidden. Mostly, the smile lines around his mossy-green eyes. If only he wasn't one of Georgia's idiotic Honey Bunnies.

"Who are you talking about?" I took another sip—well, a hefty sip. It'd been a shit day.

"The cutie patootie in the Flower Market improperly extracting foxglove seeds. You think he's cute."

I nearly choked on my drink. I frowned at her. "I do not."

"Darling, you haven't deigned to give anyone a lesson in" —she curled two fingers—"herbal prep since you showed me how to make my hand cream thicker."

I frowned at her. Herbal prep to an alchemist was *mise en place* to a chef. Everything was gathered, prepped to the same size, and set neatly nearby so you did not dawdle when you concocted a potion. It made everything easier and you didn't mess around with it. I took a long drink, rolling the gin and olive brine over my tongue. It had been a while since I'd corrected anyone's herbal prep. I understood it was an unlikeable trait of mine.

"You liked him." Winkerton toyed with the olive skewer, her bold red nails gleaming against the dim light. Her cold spell had finally faded. "I've never seen you so alive before."

I almost choked. Swallowing and then giving in to a cough, I set my glass on the table. "You nearly made me mistreat gin, Winkerton."

"You two were flirting." She ate an olive.

I lifted a brow and checked my urge to laugh. "That man was not flirting with me."

"Darling."

I sighed and looked at her. She was lovely; she always was lovely and we both knew it. Before I knew Winkerton well, I'd thought she'd been flirting with *me*. Wasn't that why she wanted to learn herbal prep? I learned quickly, slightly awkwardly, that she'd never see me in that way. So I hid my crush from her and she pretended not to notice.

But she was right. I didn't teach or show anyone any tricks with alchemy or enchanting, because every time I had, it'd been to get closer to them—and to what end? Rejection. A flash, barely a glimpse, of blonde hair, bright blue eyes, and bubblegum lips blipped in and out of my mind, whispering, *"I don't think* anyone *can love you."*

The price was always too high. I drained my martini, savoring the crisp and funky taste while gazing longingly at the bottle of gin.

"Was it because people recognized you out in the wild today?" she asked.

I ate my last two olives and tilted my head. My expression must've given something away, and honestly, Winkerton knew the last few days had been hard for me. It was why she was babying me tonight. The past couple months, she'd spent her evenings with her great-aunt Virgie, the rummy cheater and Winkerton's namesake, instead of spending nights here with me drinking and gossiping.

I knew she had responsibilities elsewhere, especially with her great-aunt as she was set to inherit, but I knew Winkerton loved her, despite hating her name. Virgie wasn't short for anything. She'd mentioned once or twice she'd been teased because it sounded too much like virgin and insisted on going by her last name. Honestly, I couldn't blame her for not wanting to be called by it.

But . . . I don't know, those nights away from me felt different. Almost as if there was a secret hidden in those weeks. I wanted to ask, but I didn't know how or exactly what I was asking about.

A weird chime rang through the house, coming from the front door.

"Is *that* what your doorbell sounds like?" She rose from

the couch, holding her martini glass. "A half-strangled horn, too embarrassed to beep?"

I blinked, then laughed. "I guess the doorbell's starting to go."

"How long has it been like that?"

I walked to the front door. "I have no clue. No one rings my bell."

I peered through the peep hole. Since the sidewalk ended at my driveway, the nearest streetlamp was a house or two up. All I saw was a dark shape hunched in the rain.

I pulled back.

"Who is it?" Winkerton whispered.

"It's too dark to tell."

"Turn on the light."

"No!" I whispered as loud as I dared. "Then they'll know I'm home and I'll have to answer."

The doorbell croaked again, this time sounding a little more like a bell and less like a sad horn.

"Well, you won't know if you want to ghost them if you don't know who they are. We can always shut the door again." She clicked the light switch to the outside lamp and boldly swung open the door.

The man from the Flower Market stood dripping on my porch, wearing glasses. He hadn't been wearing those this afternoon.

I gaped as the martini swished uncomfortably in my stomach and uneasy fingers walked up my spine. I slammed the door shut. If he was here . . . I stepped to the window, searching the night for the mob behind him, half expecting to see pitchforks and torches. But all I saw was an empty sidewalk and my Volvo in the driveway.

He knocked on the door. I pulled Winkerton away from it. She'd opened it once before; she couldn't be trusted.

"What're you doing?" she asked, cradling her glass.

"I yelled at that man." An uncomfortable smile pulled at my face. I pursed my lips. You can't smile if you're scowling.

"Ms. Townsend?" he called through the door. "I'd like to speak with you."

Winkerton grinned, her eyes twinkling. "He wants to chat."

I smiled; I couldn't help it. I gripped the ends of my braids and tugged, but it didn't help with the expression on my face.

She tilted her head, shifting her focus from me to the door. "He makes you that nervous?"

"I embarrassed him. Or me rather." I swiped my hand over my mouth as if it'd wipe away the gruesome smile unfolding across my face. "I didn't care for it."

He knocked on the door again. "I can hear you talking in there."

"Darling, this isn't like you." She chuckled softly. "The lady protests too much."

"You said I could close the door again," I whispered.

"Please open the door." The man pounded on the door. Despite the pleading tone to his words, he had a deeper voice than I'd remembered. "I have a proposition."

"Oh, a proposition. Now I'm curious." She reached for the doorknob.

"Winkerton! Don't you dare—"

She opened the door and stepped aside while pushing me forward—all without sloshing her drink over the side.

He sheepishly smiled. "Uhm. Hi. I'm sorry to come unannounced, but—"

"How did you find me?" I asked.

Winkerton peered over my shoulder.

"Oh." He lifted his hands to show they were empty and took a step back from the threshold, making himself more nonthreatening. "I Googled you."

I blinked. His deep voice was now pitched higher, and I

realized he'd done that during his demonstration, too. But he'd *Googled* me and found my address? Oh god. Had I been doxed? Who leaked my address? What did I do about that? Maybe this was my sign that I really did need to leave Starglen.

"Oh, no. Nothing like that!" He waved his hands and took a small step forward. "I had to dig more than that. See, I get your Star Trails newsletter—"

He was a *subscriber* to my shitty newsletter for my failed business?

"—and I looked up your business—sorry about that. You should use a P.O. box."

It'd never been a problem before. Thousands and thousands of people lived in Starglen; too many businesses operated from here. I assumed it wouldn't be a problem, and it hadn't been until tonight. And it wouldn't be again since I'd delete that newsletter as soon as I closed the door.

"What do you want?" I growled.

"Oh, darling, don't be rude. It's raining." Winkerton pulled me from the door and swept a hand out, inviting him inside my house. "What's your name?"

He looked at me before making a move. Was he waiting for my consent? I knew if I didn't let him in, Winkerton would nag me about this night until the day I died.

I shrugged and gestured at the shoe rack. "No shoes in the house."

He stepped in and smiled shyly, like a person who knew they were intruding and tried to make themselves as small as possible. He toed off his shoes. He had a hole in his sock and hung his dripping wet jacket on the coat tree next to the door. I closed the door and locked it.

"Sorry, thanks," he said, keeping his voice light. "I'm Nathaniel Pittman." His brows furrowed. "But everyone calls me Nate."

Winkerton shook his hand. "Virgie Winkerton, but no one dares to call me by my first name or I'll turn them into an ice sculpture."

He shuffled his feet, his eyes darting between me and Winkerton. "Okay, that's nice."

I crossed my arms. "What do you want?"

"You're so rude." Winkerton lightly shoved me toward the sitting room and waved Nathaniel through. "Oh no. My glass is empty. Let's have a drink and chat."

Nathaniel stood beside the couch, and even though he'd been invited to sit, he didn't. I settled down in my chair, refusing to mimic him, and studied him over once more. The hems of his jeans were soaked, and so was the back of his pants. He didn't want to get my furniture wet. Some of my saltiness dissolved while Winkerton summoned Reginald once more to freeze her hands.

"Wow. He's huge," Nathaniel said.

She smiled slyly. "He knows many spells."

"Why are you here?" I asked again. I simply wanted this night over with now.

Once she made the drinks, she passed them around before settling on the couch with her own.

"Thank you." He took a sip, his mossy green eyes widened behind his black-framed glasses, and he set the martini glass carefully on the table. "So when I was leaving the Flower Market, you two were ahead of me. I couldn't help but overhear what you two were saying about faking an application to the Potion Network."

Winkerton chuckled to herself while she sipped her drink. "You only need to fake your application if you haven't been to college."

"You haven't been to college, have you?" I asked, staring at the olives—she'd merely given me two this time—and the tiny flecks of ice floating at the top.

"Well, no," he admitted.

I wasn't surprised. Foxglove seeds were a chapter in advanced herbal prep. "Then why are you here?"

"I heard what you said"—he waved at Winkerton—"about how well you can teach someone, as if they'd been to Starglen Alchemy University."

I sighed, letting the sound swirl around the room as everyone held their breath. "Nathaniel, what exactly are you asking me?"

"Nate, please. No one calls me Nathaniel."

I lifted a brow. Winkerton unsuccessfully hid her grin with her glass.

He moved to sit, then straightened and crouched near my chair. The skin around his eyes crinkled before his lips lifted. "Teach me everything you know, Ms. Townsend. Get me on that show and—"

"What show, darling?"

I sent an exasperated look to Winkerton. I knew where this was going.

The Next Potion Network Star." Nathaniel shot me something of a starstruck smile. A weird sensation wormed around in my stomach. "I watched you on season four. And I remembered how you wowed me with your tip on saving rushing catnip for when you finally got to an alchemy table. I use it all the time."

I opened my mouth to speak, but he held up a hand. I frowned.

"It's not fair that I can't get on that show because I haven't gone to their college when half the time, all their shows are about quick and easy potions this or how to forage that. I can do that and help people like me."

"What would your show be about?" Winkerton asked.

Nathaniel shifted so he wasn't solely facing me. "I want to

make alchemy accessible to people who can't buy everything. No offense."

"None taken, darling. But aren't there shows like that?" She twirled her olive skewer before biting one off.

"Not really. Sometimes people can't get to an alchemy table for weeks, and what if they come across a dawn tree right after it rains? How long is that rainwater potent, and what can I do to keep it until I get to an alchemy table? I figured this out by trial and error, and I want to share it."

I understood money was a privilege, and I'd benefitted from it by attending SAU. Even I had been blocked by a paywall on YouTube when I wanted to doublecheck a technique. He wasn't the first person to talk about this sort of thing. My classmates had brought it up, but they mostly talked about how expensive alchemy tables and other reagents could be.

Rainwater collected from dawn tree leaves was a common activating ingredient in potions, but it wasn't as easy to collect as some thought. For one, you didn't get much since the leaves were small. I stared at his profile. Blond whiskers covered his thin features. His long wavy hair was tucked behind his ears and the ends were curling. He smelled like a damp forest. Honestly, a scent that soothed me deeply and reminded me of the early mornings, fresh after a rainfall, walking off the beaten path to find a plant.

All the while, he talked passionately about making alchemy more accessible, how he'd teach people who had the innate ability but not the funds to see it through to get to a better place with their abilities. He'd thought this through, and he might even believe what he'd said. But I saw him for who he really was.

A liar and a user willing to walk all over me to get what he wanted.

"No." I stood and set my martini glass down.

"But I don't even care if I win the show." Nathaniel straightened and took a step back. He wasn't that much taller than me, but he also didn't seem to want to tower over me, either. "With the skills you teach me and the show broadcasting that I'm just as good as everyone else, I could get a job as an apprentice. I could work my way up."

Winkerton remained seated, a coy smile tilting her lips. "I like his show idea. I think it'd do a world of good to shake up the Potion Network like this."

"Yes." Nathaniel grinned and faced her. "Exactly."

"No." I headed toward the front door. "I will not help you lie and cheat to get on the show. Now you may leave."

Nathaniel's smile fell, and he followed me toward the door. "But it isn't just that. I can learn so much from you, and if you'd just give me a chance, I can—"

"I said no." I opened the door. "Get out."

He sighed and shoved his feet into his shoes and grabbed his jacket. "It wouldn't be just me you'd be helping."

"But it'd be you the most, wouldn't it?" I shook my head and made sure I wasn't blocking his exit. "I see who you are, Nathaniel."

"Yeah." He walked past me and over the threshold. He looked over his shoulder at me. "It'd help me out the most."

I shrugged. "Good luck then." I shut the door, locked it, and returned to my chair.

"Why won't you help him?" Winkerton asked.

"I'm not a liar, and doing this would be lying."

She watched me, her expression unreadable. "I know that Georgia—"

"*Please.*" I dropped my face in my hands and shook my head. "Please, can we not dissect why I refuse to help someone lie and cheat to get on that damned show?"

"Darling, you *love* alchemy, and I know you enjoy showing

people how to make their lives easier with it. I don't understand why you wouldn't help him at least do that."

I lifted my head and met her gaze. "Because it all comes down to how I won't be a doormat to further someone else's career again."

Chapter Eight

"Sorry, Nate." Sherry glanced over her shoulder into her apartment and winced when she faced me. "My little sis is in town."

I stepped back and gave her my best reassuring smile. "Oh nice. A quick break before her senior year?"

"Yeah. She's checking out the campus for the enchanters' college. She's all set to graduate early this year." She bit her lip. "Are you gonna be okay? I thought you had an apartment."

I'd talked about getting an apartment the last time I crashed on her couch, but I'd saved the extra cash for the permit to sell instead. Well, I'd meant to put it toward the permit, but shit happened. Life happened.

I waved my hand and took another step away from her door. "Yeah, no. I'm fine. Don't worry about me. Hey, tell your sister I wish her good luck this year."

I didn't wait for her to answer and jogged down the stairs and out of her apartment building. I shoved my hand through my hair and cursed. My back tire was flat again. I really need to replace the inner tube, but it was a low priority. Just like it was a low priority for any of my friends to take care of me. John still hadn't responded to my texts, and I certainly wouldn't return to Emily's place after my conversation with Daren—not until after that deadline. For fuck's sake, it wasn't their responsibility to make sure I had a place to sleep at night. Like Daren said. I'm a grown-ass man.

After refilling my tire, I hopped onto my bike and pedaled across town. Again. At least it'd stopped raining.

What a stupid idea it'd been to bike all the way to old town to beg Lila Townsend to help me. I should've known she wouldn't want to do that. No one wanted to do that, even if they weren't into that lifestyle. It was a lot of work to train someone as if they had a formal education, and I had a lot of bad habits. There was so much I didn't know, so much information I was lacking, and I'm sure it impacted my potions and my enchantments.

I hadn't even known I should've pinched those seeds out of the pod, and I'd been making that potion for years now. No wonder it was touch and go on how potent it was. I'd thought my pH strips were bad. Who was I trying to kid? My pH strips were old and probably bad anyway, but waste not, want not, you know?

My tires hummed on the wet pavement glistening under the streetlamps as I headed back toward old town, spraying up water from the pavement. God, I was such an idiot. Lila was completely out of touch; she couldn't even see what a shitshow trying to make it as an alchemist was with only a collapsible table and a hodgepodge alchemy set. She'd never appreciated what her privilege had given her: an education, a spot on *The Next Potion Network Star*, and hell, she'd even been the culinary producer for Georgia Cauldron! And she didn't want to share. She didn't want someone she didn't think worthy enough to have the same kind of life. Someone like me.

I leaned into the turn, taking the sloping road down into the Nettles. It'd been the original Flower Market back in the nineteenth century, one long street dedicated to rare ingredients, apothecaries, and crystal shops. But as Starglen grew, thanks to the massive node of ley lines the city was built upon, the bigger the market it needed.

I didn't know who swept in and reclaimed the area as the Nettles, but it'd gained the reputation as a black market for good reason. Things were cheaper, and that meant they were made cheaply too. You could find anything you wanted here, especially if you couldn't find it in the Flower Market. But you had to know what you were searching for and how to tell if it had gone bad, otherwise you were out cash *and* the reagent.

I came here when I needed to rent an alchemy or enchanting table, and every time it was sketchy. One time, the person next to me got stabbed for no reason. At least, none was given to me. The dude turned to me, pointed his bloody knife at me, and told me I hadn't seen a thing. Shit like that had given the Nettles its well-earned terrible reputation.

But while the Nettles was dirtier, more dangerous, and sold questionable items that would never grace the Flower Market, they didn't turn people away if they needed help. Maybe I should stop trying to break into the Flower Market and accept I belonged here. Would getting a job in the Nettles meet Daren's criteria? I bet they'd all love that.

I stopped at the twenty-four-hour diner, Goodies. Only the D, I, E, and S were still lit up, and I thought, not for the first time, that the Nettles was the place where dreams died. I leaned my bike against the building and grabbed everything attached to it before heading inside.

The place was mostly empty, except for a pair of men sitting in a booth talking over coffee. Sawyer looked up from an old Starglen Enchanting University textbook and waved when he saw me. He wiped his hands on his ketchup-and-mustard stained apron and grabbed an order pad.

"Sup, Nate," he said. "You hungry?"

"Yeah, but look, dude. I'm broke," I said. "Can I like, do some dishes or something?"

"Oh, sure." Sawyer set his pad down and pointed at an empty booth. "Stash your stuff there. The sink's full in the back. Whaddya want?"

I smiled and set my duffel bag down on the cracked upholstery. Years ago, someone had taped them, and it was starting to peel up. I wouldn't let my messenger bag out of my sight. "Could I get a burger and some fries?"

"Sure. Hey, I got a lemon fizzy still. You like those, right?"

"Oh man, that'd be awesome." I followed him through the kitchen, and the sink was stacked high. "You know, I could do all that and mop too, if I could sleep in the back room."

Sawyer half chuckled, half snorted. "I figured. Yeah. It's just me tonight. But you gotta be outta here by five a.m., okay?"

"No problem." I smiled. "Thanks, man."

Ninety minutes later, I had a double cheeseburger with all the fixings, a huge plate of fries, and a small bottle of lemon fizzy. I savored that fizzy. It was probably my absolute favorite drink. It wasn't sweet, not like soda, but it also wasn't so tart it made my mouth shrivel, either. It was perfect.

Someone knocked on the window next to my booth. I turned and spotted my old foster brother, Alex, and a couple of men in tracksuits. I waved. He pointed at the booth and then came inside. I wasn't too thrilled with this development, only because I owed him money. I glanced back out the window to see his buddies huddling near my bike and smoking.

He'd slicked back his dark hair and his jacket was nice, albeit he'd rolled up the sleeves past his forearms. His shoes were shiny too. He slid into the booth across from me and grinned.

"Hey, how's it going?" I took a bite of my burger.

"Not too bad, not too bad. Haven't seen you in my neck of the woods for a while." He took a fry and jammed it in his mouth. "Been working?"

"Well, yeah." I wiped my fingers on a napkin. "I have the permit, and I'm doing everything I can to make it work."

"I haven't seen you in the Flower Market, though."

I swallowed a fry, nearly choking on it. I shrugged. "I haven't seen you there either."

"Well, of course not." He took more fries, dragged them through my ketchup, then jammed them into my mayo, leaving a red smear behind. "I'm not meant to be seen there. But I was looking for you, you know? See how your business is doing."

"Okay. I got the permit. I'm selling a couple of potions here and there."

"Great. How many?"

"To be honest, it's been rough."

Alex had this "here we go again" expression that nearly everyone I knew got when I said something like that, and I was so fucking sick and tired of it.

"I don't want to hear how it's been rough, Nate." Alex eyed my drink, but thankfully, he didn't reach for it. "I want to hear how soon you're going to pay me back."

I grabbed the bottle and leaned back in my seat. "Man, I had a healing potion, and before you get excited, it was stolen from me. That hit was hard. I'm out there every morning, sometimes before the sun even rises, foraging for new reagents to keep my stock up. I try to get to the market early enough to get a good spot to sell—" I almost told him Lila Townsend heckled me, but I took a swig instead and shrugged. "I know you lent me that money a few weeks ago, but it just isn't enough time."

Alex glowered and pointed a greasy finger at me. "You said it was a sure thing."

"It *is*. I just need more time."

"You said you'd use the money I lent you, you my very best brother, and seed your business. A business I believe in. And so I gave it to you with the belief you'd pay me back."

"Come on, Alex," I mumbled. "I'll pay you back." Unpleasant heat washed over my chest and splashed my neck and face. But maybe everyone else was right and my dreams were stupid.

It'd been a mistake to ask for help for this. Once he'd given me the three grand, my phone magically broke as if it knew I had money for a replacement. It'd already been halfway out the door when it stopped alerting me to new messages or alarms. Then it stopped receiving messages, then it stopped connecting to the internet right before the screen stopped responding—it was eight years old, so it wasn't like I hadn't held on to that sucker for as long as I could. I'd had to replace that because I could couch surf fine, but no phone? I'd miss out on opportunities. I also had other debts I had to take care of—friends who were waiting on money they'd lent me first. So I paid them back, and that returned me to square one. But at least I had the permit to sell.

"I'm just not seeing you make the effort." Alex had said it lightly as he reached for a fry, but the years had layered disappointment onto it every time I heard it. Like I did it on purpose; like I *enjoyed* failing or something.

I pulled my plate away from him and forced myself to

smile. "I *am* making an effort. It takes time. I told you it'd take time and you agreed. If you couldn't afford to lend me the money, then why did you?"

He shrugged. "It wasn't my money."

"What?" My stomach clenched. "Why would you lend me money that wasn't yours?"

"You're my brother—"

"Foster brother, dude."

He waved that off. "You're my brother, and my boss thought it'd be a good idea to get into the alchemy business a little more intimately."

Intimately? I frowned, looking Alex over more closely, a bad thought forming in the back of my head. "Who's your boss?"

Alex grinned and leaned back, spreading his arms. "The Wonderboy."

"Who's that?" I didn't want to know. I so did not want to know.

Alex blinked and sat forward, pointing a finger at the table. "You don't know who Jerry 'Wonderboy' Whitemarsh is?"

"Uhh . . ."

"Are you living under a rock?"

Sawyer laughed, lifting his head from his textbook. "He's not living anywhere, dude."

I would've given Sawyer the finger if I wasn't afraid he wouldn't let me sleep in the back office.

Alex leaned in. His open expression turned stormy, and his hard eyes made me think about that man getting stabbed while cooking a potion. "The Wonderboy is a capo for the Fornaro Family."

"Oh no. What? Are you shitting me?" I set my fizzy down, no longer caring if he stole it from me.

"Keep your voice down, you clown."

"Jesus fucking christ. You gotta warn a brother when you lend him money where it's coming from."

Alex smirked. "I thought we were only foster brothers."

"Dude."

"Dude."

"Look, I didn't know that's who was lending me the money," I said, glancing around, wondering if there was a way out of this. How would I pay back someone who worked with one of the biggest families in the Nettles?

"What's done is done, Nate." Alex slipped out of the booth and paused at the table. "I just know you need to get that money back to me before too long, you hear?"

"But—"

"It won't be nothing if you pay me back." He tossed his hands palms up, then clapped me on the back. "I'll be seeing you."

"Fuck." I hunched over my half-eaten burger and the two fries remaining and stared at nothing.

A small plate of fries slid on the table, and Sawyer gave me a pitying smile. "Shit's rough, man."

"Yeah. Thanks."

I hadn't imagined things could've gotten worse than they already were. I didn't necessarily believe in karma, I couldn't with the shit hand I'd been dealt when my parents had been caught in a crossfire with a Muted and the police. I barely remembered what they looked like, what their voices sounded like now. But what the hell had I done to deserve all this?

That light at the end of the tunnel? Yeah, mine was missing.

Chapter Nine

My mind blanked as some of the gin sloshed over the rim of the glass before I dumped Nathaniel's martini down the drain and tossed the olives. What a waste. Tossing the shaker in the sink, I smacked the faucet on and . . . glared at the water rushing down the drain and sighed.

How much longer could I do this without hitting rock bottom? Honestly? Every time I thought I was at my lowest, I'd found life could always dig a little deeper.

"Do you want to talk about it?" Winkerton capped the olives as her worried gaze assessed me.

"Yes and no." I cut off the water and swiped a hand over the top of my head. "I'm peckish and olives aren't gonna do it for me."

She looped her arm through mine and guided us to the kitchen. "Then let's raid the fridge—What's with the wince?"

"I forgot to buy groceries."

"Darling, why do you never plan for groceries?" She waved her hand as we stepped into the kitchen. "You take so much care with your schedule that I had to needle you to share your planner with me so I could fit in girl time, and you can't seem to think about putting food on your sacred to-do list?"

She was trying to lighten the mood, probably knew all too well how good I was at wallowing. I appreciated it; wallowing was hard to stop once I'd settled in and memories doom-scrolled through my brain on a constant loop. I hated that loop.

I forced a small laugh and shrugged. "I have a garden, though. I'll forage. I have some popcorn in the cupboard, I'm sure."

She made a noise and shooed me out of the room. I grabbed a bowl on my way out of the greenhouse and into my garden. It smelled lovely outside, like rain and pine and clouds. I glanced at the sky, seeing the shape of the moon glowing behind the rain clouds. We were due soon for a break in the wet weather before fall really kicked in.

I stepped lightly through damp grass and picked a handful of strawberries, a couple of tomatoes, and, on a whim, a few pods of green beans before heading back inside to the kitchen that smelled like popped corn. The small TV on the counter played an ad for SAU as Winkerton pulled the silicone popcorn bowl out of the microwave, setting it on the table.

"Oh, fresh strawberries." She poured two glasses of water and sat next to me at the counter. "Darling, you're the only one I know who goes for green beans as a snack."

I grabbed a knife from the block and sliced the green tops off the strawberries, then tossed those in the countertop compost. Then I cored the tomatoes, doing the same. "Would you prefer edamame?"

"Oh, yes."

"Hmm." Northern California wasn't ideal for edamame, but the greenhouse could certainly support the plant. "I'll see what I can do."

She watched me prepare the snacks, daintily eating her popcorn. "You okay?"

I laughed sourly and shrugged. "No. I can't believe he had the nerve to come here and ask me to teach him so he could lie about his background to get on that stupid show."

"The gall."

"Who does he think I am, anyway?" I salted a wedge of tomato and shoved it into my mouth. The tartness burst on my tongue and I almost lost my bad mood.

"Clearly he believed you intelligent enough to teach him." She plucked a strawberry from the bowl and inspected it. Her nails matched the color of the fruit nearly perfectly. "I think you could too."

I froze in salting another tomato wedge. "You think it's a good idea?"

"They always choose the real polished contestants who look good in anything. It'd be a nice shake-up. Then they push the same thing over and over. Their favorite stores to get this, why they never bother with that method while they make the same potion as the next alchemist. Honestly, it's a little boring some days."

"I don't see how he'd do anything different once they give him some new clothes."

She laughed. "I *knew* you thought he was cute!"

I put my head down, my ears growing hot. Sure, Nathaniel was handsome, but that didn't mean anything. "He didn't like me giving him tips."

"You did ambush him. Sorry, darling, but I can see why he didn't appreciate your timing."

"Fair." I sighed, eating the other half of my tomato. "You really think I should train him?"

She smirked. "Absolutely, especially if helping him keeps you in Starglen. I mean, if you agree to do this and he pulls it off, it could help force some people past the whole . . ." She rolled her wrist in the air, searching for the right words. "It could get you past all of this, you know?"

"Maybe, but I don't see how." I toyed with the salt shaker, staring at a tomato seed sitting in its juice on my plate. "If you liked this idea so much, why didn't you take Nathaniel's side?"

"Because I'm always on your side, darling. However, I believe you should reconsider."

The commercial break ended and the ongoing documentary resumed. It flashed on *The Next Potion Network Star* logo, and footage of the hosts popped up. Owen Creek, who never seemed to age and remained just as handsome, and Alchemy Betty—who'd retired three years ago. The camera flashed over the contestants, and I saw myself.

"Nope." I grabbed the remote to change the channel.

"Wait, it's a new one," Winkerton said.

I hesitated. "But I know what happens. We both know."

"But we don't know what they'll say in this one." She shot me a sympathetic expression. "It's better to know now what this one will dig up than getting blindsided in public. Don't you think?"

Well, if I'd known about that viral video, I wouldn't have lugged my potions into the Flower Market or nearly have had a panic attack on the street. I sighed and set the remote down, but I'd change the channel if it got too ridiculous, or maybe . . . if I got too ridiculous.

The camera settled on Georgia. Her hair was blonde but not the platinum that she went by now. This was before she went full bunny, and there I was, with shorter hair, gazing at Georgia like the lovesick fool that I was. Ugh. I'd been so blind and stupid.

"Georgia Cauldron's knowledge potion really put her at the top slot in the semi-finals, despite having to work with Lila Townsend in the challenge," a male narrator's voice said.

He sounded British. "Georgia had the story and the know-how."

Winkerton snorted. "She had you."

I ate another salted tomato wedge.

"Before coming on the show," the narrator continued, "Georgia grew up small. Her parents had four children, which they all crammed into a small double-wide trailer on the east side of Starglen."

The camera focused on Georgia, and she smiled for the audience. "Whenever I was working on a spell, I knew one of my siblings would interrupt me or something, and I'd lose a day. I'd have to start the entire process all over again. Some-times, it'd take me two years to memorize a spell, and so I learned how to make this potion."

I ground my teeth. How had I been so stupid back then?

"Anyway," TV Georgia continued, "there's not much you can do when you don't have the support from friends or family. I had to scrimp and save to get into college, and by god, I did. And if I can do it, you can too." She twinkled.

The Lila on the TV grimaced. I reminded myself of a grinning mannequin. Well, I knew I was uncomfortable right then and there because Georgia had lied and gone off script to tell her small beginnings story all over again.

"God, I was such a fool then," I muttered.

Winkerton dug into the popcorn, shaking her head. "She never admitted you helped her, not once."

"Because we weren't supposed to allude to a relationship, especially on camera. It wasn't against the rules but strongly discouraged." I pulled open the green bean, but I didn't pick out the beans. "Probably because of this."

The documentary flashed to the final episode that announced the winner, which was Georgia. It continued to awarding the show that would become *Home Brew Elixirs* to her, which I came on as culinary producer per the deal I'd made with the network before this episode was filmed. Whoever made this documentary had received all the tape from the season because they isolated one camera that focused on me.

It felt like I was there all over again. They announced Georgia's name, and she faked her surprise and glee. I wondered then if her tears were real, and I was certain they probably were to some extent. The camera followed me, trying to smile and be happy, but it was extremely loud on set, and I was . . . I was still reeling at the news of how much the audience disliked me. All the past contestants rushed the stage, shoving me into a corner. The camera zoomed in on my smile, which had turned strained and appeared more like a skull smiling than me.

"It was never enough," the narrator said in a doomsday voice, "for Lila Townsend to share the spotlight with Georgia Cauldron. Lila became a failed TV personality, then a failed alchemist—"

I choked.

"—and a failed human being. Her jealousy led her down that dark road to a fateful, violent—"

The TV turned off and Winkerton gripped the remote so tightly, I expected her to chuck it out the window.

"Did they say I was a failed alchemist and a failed human being?" My voice sounded small, and I hated how small I felt.

I knew they'd take that kind of angle. The documentary was clearly done by the network, or a sister network, so of course they'd lift up their popular host instead of going into the details of what had actually happened. Though, to be honest, I still didn't know, and neither did the public, which was exactly why I was still being blamed for Georgia's accident.

Sometimes, I'd wished it *had* been me. At least it would've been done correctly.

"You are *not* a failure," Winkerton seethed. "You are kind. You are smart and a damned better alchemist than Georgia fucking Cauldron."

I smiled, a real one, I think, and wiped at my eyes. My fingers were dry. No surprise, but it was the confidence from Winkerton that'd made me double-check. I wasn't used to it. "Thank you, Winkerton."

She stared at the blank TV, then shifted on the stool to look at me. "I don't want you to leave Starglen, darling."

I sighed a little. "I know, but staying here isn't doing me any good."

"But you love it here."

"I love the forest, and the coast, and the swamps." I flicked my fingers at the TV. "The people can jump off a cliff, present company excluded."

"Do you really think leaving town will stop all this?"

"Maybe? I don't know. Sometimes I think that as soon as I find a new normal, some modicum of peace, someone dredges up the past and puts it on blast."

She nodded, her eyes sliding to me. "What if you gave them something else to talk about?"

"Like what?"

"Like being the only reason a non-graduate got on *The Next Potion Network Star* and won." She grabbed my hand and squeezed. "Let him take the spotlight off you."

I laughed and hugged her. "It's an awful idea."

"At least they wouldn't be able to say you're a failed alchemist anymore."

"No, what they say is when one cannot do, they teach, and—"

"Fuck that, Lila." Winkerton pinched my cheek. "Stand up for yourself, teach that cutie patootie some magic potions, and get him on that show. So that when it's time to talk about what he did, you can finally set the record straight."

"The record is straight in the courthouse."

"Yeah, but not like this." She slapped her palm on the counter. "It's time you grab Georgia Cauldron by her fake tits and tell everyone what really happened."

"And I can do this by deceiving everyone and possibly Nathaniel never getting his dream of having his own show?"

She harrumphed and tossed popcorn in the air to catch with her mouth. "If he somehow got into college and graduated and made it on the show, then, no, it wouldn't be a good idea. But he has nothing right now. He said so himself. He can only benefit from this, and you can prove you're the reason there even *is* a Georgia Cauldron."

I laughed it off. I continued to laugh when Winkerton left and I cleaned up the kitchen. I chuckled about the idea as I drank my tea that'd help me fall asleep easier. Lately, it was never enough. And I continued to laugh about the idea when my head hit the pillow.

But when Winkerton stormed into my kitchen the following morning, all dolled up with victory rolls in her hair, a red and black striped sleeveless shirt, with high-waisted black pants and kitten heels, I knew she meant business.

"Come on," she said, wiggling her fingers at me. "Let's go."

"Where are we going?" I asked, slipping off the stool.

"To the Flower Market to find Nathaniel."

"Are we even sure? I don't remember his last name."

"Yes, I'm sure, and we'll find him if it takes all week." She jabbed a strawberry-red fingernail at me. "You're taking your life back."

Chapter Ten

The sun had burned the fog off early today, but it still clogged the tops of trees on the mountains in the distance. Saturday mornings were the busiest for the Flower Market, and I . . . I was tired and anxious. I couldn't believe how idiotic I'd been to take money from Alex. I couldn't believe how unbelievably stupid I'd been to beg Lila Townsend to teach me how to be a college educated alchemist.

"Alright, so, this calm mind potion requires rainwater from a dawn tree." I gestured at the vial I was prepping. "I don't have any with me today, and that's usually how it is, isn't it?"

A few people in the crowd nodded.

"It's not too hard to get either. It just takes a lot of time and patience because the leaves are so small," I said. "So if you want to collect your own, or just don't have the cash to buy it, you can hang on to this potion as it is for two weeks. When you finally get the dawn tree water, you can activate it with the alchemy table." I flashed a knowing smile. "Thank goodness Starglen is always misty, right?"

A few people stepped away, and that was when I saw her. I nearly didn't recognize her without the braids and overalls. She almost appeared younger without them, but there was something in her stance that had me pause. In a split second, I took in her purple raglan tee and jeans with the hem stained with dirt, and sneakers. The way she hitched her shoulders to her ears and kept her eyes down when everyone else held their head high.

I don't know. It pissed me off. I didn't like seeing anyone behave like that—like she was trying to take up as little space as possible and bracing for a blow. I could only imagine what the years of being a social pariah had done to her confidence. Definitely no favors.

"Anyway, that's how you preserve a calm mind potion until you have the activating ingredient when you're ready to rent that alchemy table." I grinned. "Thanks for listening."

The crowd dispersed, aside from one attendee, and Lila and Winkerton hovered. When she met my eyes, I smiled, but she turned her head quickly. I scanned the surrounding area, looking for Alex just in case he really was watching me.

The other lingering woman approached me as I began packing up this potion and getting ready for my next demonstration. She looked about five months pregnant, and she had an infant with her.

She smiled shyly. "Is there anything else you need to do to the potion in that two weeks before you have to start over?"

"You mean the process completely?" I asked.

"Yeah. I don't always have the cash to get to a table for one potion, and . . ." She shrugged, lightly rocking the stroller to keep the baby from fussing.

"Right?" I huffed and leaned across the table. "They're so expensive to rent that it doesn't make sense to rent one for only one potion. I don't like to go in with less than four potions."

The woman smiled and nodded. "Me either. Especially if I have to buy the rainwater. You really can't wait on that from the shops."

"No, not really. So if you're wanting to hold off activating the ingredients when you have enough potions, I find the fridge is too cold, unless you can control the temperature. Sixty-two degrees seems to be the sweet spot for two weeks." I shrugged. "After that, the potion just doesn't have the kick it needs and you're wasting the rainwater."

"Oh, sure."

"But the potion would be good to an extent as it is, depending on the properties of the ingredients. Here." I passed over a sheet of paper that I'd made many copies of for instances like this. "This is a list of ingredients that are like that, and I've included some websites too."

"Oh, thank you." She took the paper and pushed the stroller off.

Lila was still there, and after last night, I didn't know what to say. No one else was around and really, maybe I should move my stand somewhere else. Winkerton nudged her.

Lila slowly approached my stand, inspecting my arrangement of semi-prepared potions and poultices. "You didn't sell her anything."

"She's more of a home alchemist than buying pre-made potions." I capped what I had and started packing up. I needed to do something with my hands. "She wanted advice on how to keep a near-finished potion stable until she had enough potions ready before she rents an alchemy table."

She nodded. "Is that something you'd talk about on your own show if you ever got on *The Next Potion Network Star?*"

I grinned; I couldn't help it. That sort of talk was my passion and she just asked about it. "Yes. Definitely. That's one of the biggest struggles for people who don't have the cash all the time to rent a table or even if they've got gaps in their education. Although enchanting is far more forgiving than alchemy, and I know all these little things through trial and error and . . ."

Winkerton grinned, watching us while Lila had kept my gaze the entire time. Her silvery eyes remained intense, and I didn't think for a moment if her mind wandered. I had her entire attention, and I wondered if she stared at everyone like only we existed. I found I didn't mind looking in her eyes at all, and it occurred to me that I'd never finished my spiel about my future show. My face grew hot.

"Well, I'm babbling, and I'm sure you have other things to do." I broke down the stand and needed to burst that weird bubble that'd enveloped me. "Like deny a poor man's biggest dream."

Lila scoffed. "Perhaps if that man so desperate for a dream hadn't been creepy . . ."

I tilted my head and caught her eye. "If I hadn't been creepy, would you have even noticed me?"

She scowled. "I noticed you ruining foxglove pods."

Winkerton laughed. "Okay. How about we get some brunch at Brew & Chew and we all have a nice, respectful chat?"

"Oh, uhm." *I'm broke as a joke.* "No, thanks. I'm not hungry."

Both women frowned at me.

Lila shook her head and faced Winkerton. "I told you this was a bad idea."

Winkerton, on the other hand, appraised me shrewdly and lifted a brow. "It's my treat. You sure you don't want a coffee at least? I promise you'll want to hear what Lila has to say."

Lila made a strangled sound. I got the feeling she was being dragged out here by Winkerton, but my stomach was complaining and a meal wouldn't hurt.

"Sure. Fine." I didn't want to sound desperate for the free meal. "Brunch'll be nice."

In a blink, we were seated in a mostly full dining area, waiting for our food to be delivered. I'd ordered blueberry pancakes with a lemon glaze and extra bacon. My mouth wouldn't stop watering. Lila grimaced the whole time. Why was she so uncomfortable? Was it me? I knew I didn't smell. My clothes were clean, and I'd showered a couple days ago. I still had a day or two left in me before things grew rank.

I glanced around and noticed a few people watching our table then leaning over to their friend and whispering. I checked for Alex again. I didn't trust him to stay in the Nettles, not after that threatening conversation over my stolen fries. Winkerton glared at the patrons, and Lila bowed her head lower. She was still getting shit from that viral video, I guessed. Which sucked. The people in this city full of influencers and TV hosts were slow to let things go. I supposed we were too close to the action. It all still felt fresh. I hoped it'd blow over soon for her. I could tell she needed a break.

All those thoughts went out of my head when a plate stacked high with blueberry pancakes dripping with a lemon glaze was placed next to me, quickly followed by a small plate piled high with bacon. Three breakfast tacos were placed before Winkerton, and a fancy-ass ham sandwich before Lila. So that was a croque monsieur. You know, I'd eat it. I swiped my finger in a puddle of my glaze and popped it quickly into my mouth. Holy moly, it was sweet, and bright like sunshine, and I would drink this stuff if I could get away with it.

Eat slow; take your time.

But my stomach knew there was food in front of me that was also intended for me and rumbled. I swiped a piece of almost crispy bacon, and—what the hell—dipped it into a puddle of glaze before shoving it in my mouth. *Yes, sir, that's how that was meant to be eaten.* If I was alone, I'd dance. I attacked my pancakes and made sure every wedge, every fluffy blueberry piece of paradise had the glaze.

"Now tell us, Nathaniel," Winkerton said, pouring a glass of mimosa from the carafe. "Why do you want to be the next Potion Network star?"

I took a sip of cider. It was made from the Starglen Brewery and a brand-new favorite of mine. I think it had guava in it. This brunch was distracting me from my mission. "Well, the show would definitely improve my living overall. Georgia has a similar story as mine, yet all she promotes are her potions, and they aren't cheap. But really, I want to help people that can't afford all the fancy equipment and reagents and share what has helped me. Maybe they're doing all right here and there, but a way to take stress off something like alchemy would be really awesome, don't you think?"

Winkerton softly laughed. "I'm not an alchemist, but I hear what you're saying."

I dragged another piece of bacon across the glaze and popped it in my mouth, quickly shoveling in another blissful bite of pancakes. I groaned in the back of my throat.

Lila watched me, her lips slightly parted. At least today she was listening to hear me instead of listening to blow me off. She suddenly winced and glared at Winkerton.

"Don't you think so too, darling?" She littered a taco with cilantro and took a huge bite.

"Yes." Lila cut a corner of her toast. "It has merit."

While she ate her fancy toast, maybe sandwich deal, I suspected Winkerton was kicking her under the table whenever she grumbled. I pushed the side of my fork down through the pancakes and shoved them in my mouth. Heaven.

"Here's what I think." I licked my lips; no lemon glaze would be wasted on my watch. "I know you said no last night, but I could really use your help to help others. Isn't that what it all boils down to now? Why make people with less struggle so much when we can help give them the tools to make at least one thing in their lives easier?" I slowly speared the last of my breakfast and reverently placed it in my mouth. I'd never forget this meal. I might even think about it in the shower.

"You're serious about this?" Lila set her fork down and stared at me. "You want to lie and cheat—Ow!"

I frowned, but how else could it be described? "Hey, this idea was your brainchild. I'm the vehicle for you to pull it off."

Winkerton glanced at her watch and then the table littered with mostly clean plates—just mine. I'd scraped the last of the glaze off the plate with my fork—and empty mimosa glasses. "So? What do you think?"

"I'm willing if she's willing," I said. And when I noticed the hesitation on Lila's face, I quickly added, "If I can get past episode four, I know that I'll have loads more opportunities than I do now. That's really important to me."

Lila tilted her head, and I was suddenly caught by gray eyes that were taking on the color of her purple shirt. There wasn't an ounce of secondhand embarrassment in them. "Why episode four?"

"That's typically the challenge when you're brought on Georgia's show, and if you do well on screen and can be charming—" I flashed my best grin. "I could get a job at one of the stores here. Maybe even apprentice with them. I'd still be helping people and giving them the tips I struggled to learn. *That's* my main goal, but if I get past episode four, I certainly hope you'd see me through them."

"And if you get eliminated at any time, even before episode four?" Lila's brows gathered over her nose. "What then?"

"Well, I guess in my exit interview I'll reveal you were my source of education and not SAU. That you taught me everything I needed to get on the show."

"That's reasonable," Winkerton said. "What do you say, darling?"

"Well . . ." Lila shifted on her chair, and her mouth hitched to one side in a grimace that didn't seem like someone had hooked their finger in the corner to tear her mouth off. For once.

Winkerton took a sip of water. "How about this: I'll sponsor Nathaniel, and you—"

"Nate," I said, tiring of hearing it and wondering why the hell I'd let it slip.

She hastily nodded at me before returning her attention to Lila. "I'll get him kitted out with a forager's kit and the herbal kit, new clothes, and whatever the application fee is to get on the show."

"I have kits and clothes," I muttered.

Winkerton waved me off. "The only thing you'll need to worry about is teaching him everything in that big, beautiful alchemist brain of yours. And hosting him, of course."

"Hosting?" I said at the same time as Lila.

"Of course, darlings." Winkerton spread her hands. "The network will want an address, and if I misunderstood you, which sorry, but you're currently without a permanent address. And a regular meal would be good for you too."

Lila took me in, and my back grew hot. I'd never been this embarrassed about my situation before. I believed eventually it'd lead to good things; everything always does. But right now, with her observant silver eyes sweeping over me, I felt like a homeless loser.

Lila nodded. "Very well. If Nathaniel agrees—"

"No one calls me Nathaniel," I said, exasperated.

She frowned. "If he agrees to this, then I shall too. But you must be open to learn the way I teach you, and you can't fight me about it."

I laughed softly. See? Things eventually blew my way and Lila—one of the better alchemists I've seen, outside of Georgia Cauldron, of course—was going to teach me everything she knew to help me. I'd be an idiot to say no. And besides, staying with her in old town would probably keep the mafia off my back long enough for me to do something about it.

"Yes, thank you," I said. "You won't regret it."

"Unlikely."

"Well." Winkerton beamed at both of us as she grabbed the check. "Then I have some shopping to do, and I'll see you dears later." She bolted for the hostess station.

I blinked after her. "That was fast."

"Winkerton doesn't dawdle when she has a mission," Lila said. "Well, I suppose we should pack up some of your things and get started today."

"Right now?" I asked, following her out of the bistro and grabbing my bike.

"Of course." Lila glanced over her shoulder at me. "The casting call for the next season is out. We don't have a lot of time."

"Wow. I can't believe this is happening."

"Me either. Your tire's flat."

I grimaced and things became awkward. She hadn't realized I carried everything I owned onboard me, and her beat-up pale-yellow Volvo could barely fit my bike. But we got it in, and the ride across town to old town was tense. Mostly quiet, and she white-knuckled it the entire way back.

I hadn't seen her house in the light of day, but I knew it was on the edge of town. Delicate white curling wood inlaid the pale blue Victorian. While it didn't have the tower like some of the other houses on the street, it sat on a large lot with lots of trees on either side, protecting the house from the neighbors.

"I'll give you a key." She unlocked the door and motioned for me to move in.

"Oh, I can always knock or—"

"Well, it's probably unnecessary, as you'll be spending every waking moment of daylight with me unlearning your bad habits, but I wouldn't want to feel trapped." She began climbing the stairs. "Let me show you your room."

She took me down a hallway with three doors, pointed out the bathroom, and then opened one to a dark room with a stripped double bed, a wardrobe, and a standing mirror.

"There are sheets and blankets in the wardrobe," she said. "Leave your things and come with me."

Alright, she was getting right to business, and it made me glad she wouldn't fool around. I set down my bags and followed her downstairs and through the kitchen. The table was scattered with notebooks and a discarded tea mug, and the sink had a popcorn bowl sitting in it.

"What's your story to get on the show?" She paused at the counter and grabbed something that looked like an ice bucket and shook it. "They like something that has meaning."

"Well . . ." I rubbed the back of my neck. I knew I had to use my story, but I hated it because people always gave me sympathy and asked a lot of basic questions I was tired of answering. But that was showbiz, right? "A Muted killed my parents when I was four, and education hadn't always been available, at least not the fancy stuff you got."

"Really, a Muted did that?" she asked.

"I understand that he'd recently lost his magic and went a little nuts."

She nodded. "That is awful, Nathaniel."

I frowned. One, she hadn't apologized, just stated the fact which I honestly preferred, but then she ruined it by calling me Nathaniel. I brushed it off. "Anyway, I aged out and missed a scholarship thanks to bad decisions, and I could never get into the university and no one would give me a loan. That's my story."

"I'd leave out the money struggles at first and focus on being alone and having no one to rely on." She pushed away from the counter, holding the container, and moved toward a window-paned door filmed with humidity. "After a challenge or two, I think you'll be fine bringing up how you managed to save to get into the university, because you need a degree for the network to consider approving your application. I can reliably say they don't check on your credentials until it's time to draw up the contract for the show."

"Yeah, you're right. I'll work on it."

I followed her into a greenhouse that took my breath away. It was the most beautiful thing I'd seen in a long while. I paused and gaped at the bees buzzing flowers before floating to a beehive—no, there were three—hanging in the rafters. Flowering vines sprawled around the walls as vibrant flowers I knew were only found in the tropics thrived. I inhaled, relishing the lush smell of plant life.

Lila turned back to me and jerked a thumb to her work-table. "Come along, Nathaniel. You've got a long day ahead of you."

I grinned, not even caring that she refused to call me Nate, and caught up to her. "You know, I kept telling myself that something would finally turn my way and I'd catch a break. I can just feel all that bullshit is getting left behind today. I've got nothing to worry about."

A strange expression slipped over her face, as if she couldn't help but poke me one last time.

"Oh, I don't know," she drawled. "You should stay worried. I was the one, after all, who gave Georgia the poison."

Chapter Eleven

"Did you have a lot of videos to link when you filled out your application?"

I slashed out an item on my temporary list and met Nathaniel's gaze across my kitchen table. He had his glasses on again and he looked . . . good in that spot. Must be the lighting. Weak sunlight slanted through the kitchen window, refracting in the suncatcher and tossing tiny rainbows across the table and onto the floor. I jiggled my knee and rubbed the corner of my notepad against my thumb.

Last night had been . . . hitch free, but still really weird. I hadn't had an overnight houseguest since about a year ago when Winkerton had been too drunk to drive home and I hadn't had a sober-me-up potion. Of course, now I kept them on hand since she'd seemed really embarrassed the next morning. But here he was sitting at my table using my laptop to fill out the application for *The Next Potion Network Star*.

I tapped the end of my pencil against my chin and nodded. "I had a few from college. I did a lot of demonstrations my senior year. I've found I don't enjoy being in front of a camera."

"Really?" The skin around his mossy eyes crinkled. "Do you still have them?"

"They're online somewhere." I returned my attention back to my notepad I used to make a schedule that'd be repeated daily. Once I got the timing perfect and every event flowing naturally, I'd update my digital planner and pen this one in my pocket planner.

I didn't want him to see me as I was then; *I* didn't want to see me then. I hadn't known I was shrill or unlikable in college. All I knew was that I had a huge crush on Owen Creek, and I'd added mint or lime to everything because he did. I'd wanted to work so badly with him at the Potion Network. In my videos from then, I spoke loudly and excitedly, and I cringed whenever I watched them.

"What are they called? I'll look them up." He popped one of the leftover strawberries in his mouth and washed it down with water.

Since he wasn't letting this go, I decided it was best to distract him. I lifted my lukewarm cup of chai. "I think I have coffee beans in the freezer. There's a pour-over cup in that cupboard."

He shook his head. "It's okay."

He'd also turned down my earlier offer for tea. I felt at odds with the morning, drinking my tea and not being able to give him something more than water. I could hear my grandmother scolding me from the grave that I wasn't being a good hostess.

"Are you one of those people who doesn't drink caffeine?"

"Oh no, I love me a cup of joe. But today, I don't know." He shrugged, peeking at me over the rims of his glasses. "I don't want to get in your way any more than I am."

"You're living here until you get eliminated from the show. Or if your application doesn't get accepted. Don't be ridiculous."

"Oh, well." He stared out the window. "In that case . . . I noticed you have a lemon tree out back. Could I slice one up to infuse water with?"

"Certainly." I frowned, the setting, the morning, suddenly feeling more intimate with a stranger than I could've ever guessed. I waved at the laptop. "Do you have videos of working on potions?"

"I have a few old ones from high school, and that's about it, I'm afraid."

"It's not only about videos on your application. It's about your story and why you would be an amazing host on your own show." I set my empty cup down and leaned on the table, drumming my fingers on my planner. "You have an intriguing story. You said a Muted killed your family?"

He winced. "I don't want to talk about that on-air every time the camera is pointed at me. It might make those who were born that way feel targeted, and it wasn't their fault some dude burned out his magic so bad he made himself Muted."

I nodded and hummed in the back of my throat. "I agree. I work with a lot of the Muted at the Vineyard too. It's a hard subject. But your upbringing into alchemy is important to your story."

Georgia would've capitalized on that tragedy if it'd happened to her, just like she did about growing up poor. I took in his threadbare clothes. I supposed that was easier to identify with than losing your family like that. Even I understood it more acutely now than I had five years ago.

"Yeah. It's been a challenge, but people—"

"Knock, knock, knock, my darlings!" Winkerton breezed into the kitchen, canvas bags lining her arms as she carried a yellow pastry box from Sugar Bliss and a tray of coffees. She set the box down and placed a cup before me that said chai on it, then pointed at the strawberries.

"Is that all you're eating, Nathaniel?" Winkerton unloaded the bags on the counter behind the table.

"It was all she had in the fridge that wasn't a salad." Nathaniel shot me a sheepish grin. "I didn't know you were a vegetarian, Lila."

I groaned and smacked my forehead. "I forgot to buy groceries."

"You know they deliver, don't you?" Winkerton threw open the box. "Never fear, I suspected Lila forgot and picked up a dozen eclairs. Oh, Nathaniel, I bought you some socks."

"Thank you." His cheeks tinted red, and his gaze flitted between the two of us. "I really prefer to be called Nate."

Winkerton sat down, smoothing her fluffy black skirt, and shrugged her slim shoulders. "As soon as she stops calling you Nathaniel, then I shall too. Your Georgia Cauldron apothecary set struck a nerve. Girl code, darling. You understand. Ah. You're scheduling. Add in groceries." Her text alert went off. "Oh." She tore off a corner from my to-do list, jotted her number down, and slid it to him. "If you need anything, please text me."

Winkerton retrieved her phone from her purse. This time it was a black and white clutch with a Dalmatian on the front. She grinned, and her fingers swiped on the screen.

I sniffed and averted my attention to my schedule. "I prefer Nathaniel over Nate." I liked the way it rolled off my tongue, like it had meaning. The other felt chilly and closed-off. Then again, I was chilly and closed-off, so maybe I should use it instead.

"I know you didn't like my mortar and pestle," Nathaniel said, catching my eye as he grabbed a couple eclairs. "My friend's little girl lent me those because I lost mine. I didn't buy it, and I totally agree it's too small for what I need, but it's all I had."

"You need to be more careful with your things."

"It's never my intention to lose things, I promise." Stress, maybe frustration, lined his words regardless of how light he tried to make his voice sound. "Trust me, it's one of my many flaws I'm working on."

My hands itched to tug on my braids. I had a few flaws I'd been working on that never seem to disappear. It was easy to guess how often he'd been chastised over that, as if he didn't know losing his possessions was careless.

Stop losing your things, Nathaniel.

Don't sound so shrill, Lila.

Well, I wouldn't nag him over that. It felt . . . disorienting to empathize so deeply with him so quickly. Standing, I opened the closest bag and retrieved the forager's and herbalist's kits and passed them over to him. There were also a couple pairs of jeans, a few checkered button-down shirts, and a pack of white T-shirts. He came around to peer through it all too.

He grabbed the package of socks and the jeans. "I'm really grateful, but how'd you know my size?"

Winkerton read another message. "Thank Lila. She's the one who wanted you to have those." She glanced up and winked at him. "I'm also a great assessor of the male body."

"You forgot galoshes." An alert that an event had been canceled dinged from my planner on my phone and I read it. "You canceled tomorrow's brunch?" It kind of ticked me off. Well, not that much, but I was looking forward to time with her. Nathaniel poked around in another bag. And *only* her.

"Yes, darling." Winkerton snagged an eclair and stood. "You need to get Nathaniel up to snuff and can't be distracted by me. I understand." She glanced at his feet before she gave him a tight-lipped smile. "Give me your shoe size and I'll pick up the footwear she demands you have."

I said goodbye to Winkerton and finished my eclair and hot chai. Nathaniel had a strange expression on his face. His neck had grown red, and his soft, mossy green eyes were . . . *pointed* at me warmly, and I didn't know what to do about it.

"Download this now." I scribbled out the link to my planner and gave him a PIN, then tore off the piece of paper and handed it to him. "The app's free as long as you use my PIN, and make sure you turn on alerts and notifications."

His eyes smiled before he chuckled. "How many planners do you have for this?"

"For your training? Just two. Schedules are important, especially if your application is approved. We won't have time to figure out what to do when filming begins. Everything must be scheduled from now."

"Even the bathroom?"

I rolled my eyes. "No, I'm not that strict."

"But there's no room for spontaneity."

"Nothing good ever comes from that." I stood and set my empty cup by the sink. "Now, if you've finished applying to *The Next Potion Network Star*, get changed. I need to see how you forage."

PINE NEEDLES lightly scuffed under my boot as I carefully picked my way through an animal trail not too far from the Avenue of the Giants and the sound of cars. The fallen redwood still stood taller than me, and saplings grew from the redwood sorrel, twisting in any direction toward the light. The air remained crisp despite the sun dappling the ground with sporadic pools of light. The greens and red-browns of the forest would've been peaceful, but Nathaniel filled the silence.

"I mean, Georgia Cauldron just made everything look so easy, and I know some of it's the magic of editing, but she makes everything look so effortless."

I snorted softly. He had no idea.

"But she came from nothing, like me. And she made it okay for a grown man like myself to use her products, even if it was meant for a child who really likes pink." He laughed. "I got one of her potions once. I saved for a month, and even the cork was dyed pink. A little much."

"Pink isn't your favorite color?" I drawled, scanning the bright green ferns for fiddleheads.

"Nah, I'm a blue guy myself. You?"

I glanced at him over my shoulder, a little surprised he'd asked about my favorite color. What'd be next? My favorite dinosaur? I scanned memories of visiting field museums and decided I liked triceratops. Weren't they renamed, though?

"No," he quickly said, "Let me guess . . . purple?"

"How did you know that?" What else was online about me?

His eyes dropped to my purple foraging bag draped across my chest and grinned. "You always have a bit of purple on something whenever I've seen you."

I blinked. Alright, fine. He was observant. That was good for foraging and using the alchemy table. I chewed on that for a second and decided it was probably good for people too. Then I realized he'd never asked me about dinosaurs after I went through the trouble to figure out which one I liked best.

"I like triceratops," I blurted.

His brows hopped into his hairline as he stared at me. "What now?"

"Well, I figured that'd be what you'd ask next when you brought up favorite colors." I was an idiot. I was not meant for socializing with people unsupervised.

"Ah." He gazed upward, a slow smile spreading across his face, and lit his eyes when he met my stare. "I'm a stegosaurus guy. I like the mohawk."

My stomach fluttered, as if a butterfly unfurled its wings. "It isn't a mohawk."

"It kinda is." He stepped closer to me. Everything around us faded, zeroing in on only the two of us. Even the air felt smaller. Just enough for him and me. "If it weren't for the show, I'd have a mohawk based on ole steggy right now."

"Ole steggy?" I chuckled despite myself. The fluttering in my stomach rose to my heart. *Oh no, not with* him.

"It's my favorite dinosaur." The skin around his eyes crinkled. "We're on a nickname basis."

His grin was contagious, and I returned it. He was cute, and not simply in the face department. Almost in a lost puppy sort of way, but not quite. I didn't want to grip his cheeks and jiggle them, that was for certain. My eyes dipped briefly to his lips. I wanted to discover what—Nothing. I didn't want anything. Nope. No way. No how.

He gripped the ends of his wavy blond hair and tugged them up on top of his head. "I bet the hosts wouldn't care about my hair now that I think about it. Georgia always has her bunny in one segment. Hey, is it true she has a whole pack of them?"

My smile slipped. He idolized Georgia and probably emulated her, whether or not he knew it. He wasn't lost; he knew what he wanted, and he was going for it in any possible way imaginable. If I wasn't careful, I could like him. Over my dead body.

I shook my head and waved at the surrounding ferns. "We're looking for fiddleheads and star moss, not chatting about how cool Georgia is."

His good-natured expression dimmed the tiniest bit. "Sure, boss."

Then he moved through the area like he was as big as an elephant.

"Use the trail!" I clutched the strap to my bag. "We leave no trace behind. Georgia didn't touch on that, did she?"

Nathaniel paused and stared at the destruction he'd left in his wake before he looked at me. "No, her shows don't have anything to do with foraging. It's not that big of a thing on most shows. Besides, store-bought is fine."

"But you want to focus on accessibility to those who can't always get reagents," I snapped.

He flinched and turned from me, shrugging his sharp shoulders. "Accessibility is important regardless of formal or a self-taught education."

"I agree with you." I'd probably been shrill there, but this was my passion, and if he wasn't teachable, then he wouldn't learn.

"Then what do you do when you need something off the trail?" he asked.

"I walk carefully, trying not to damage any of the plants. Kind of tiptoe."

He nodded and he certainly tried. I followed him as he stopped at the base of the enormous roots of a fallen giant and dug up the small thistle. I frowned as he shook the dirt out and dropped the plant into a mesh bag and straightened. He stepped away.

"Wait, you took the whole plant," I said.

He faced me. "Yeah, I'll use it all, eventually."

"I'm sure that's what they all say to make themselves feel better. Don't you see? Everyone has access to this resource. And when everyone acts purely in their own interest, they ultimately deplete the resource." I gestured at the massive forest of giants around us. "You know why the redwoods are endangered, right? Because of exactly that kind of thinking. Take only what you need and leave the rest."

"It's rushel weed, Lila. It's everywhere out here. I hear you, but I can't always get out here, and I know I'll use this."

"You hear me, but I don't think you understand. Taking the entire plant decreases the reproduction population, and then it'll be harder to forage for the plant in the future."

His brows raised. "You know, some people only have bikes, and you know how dangerous this highway can be. They can't always get out here. Sometimes taking what we'll need for a month is all we can do."

"There's always the Flower Market."

"Sure, people have jobs, but not everyone has a job that pays them a living wage. Plus, people come here and take more than what they need so they can grow their own plants." He wiped the blade of his forager's knife on his pants. "Besides, the Flower Market's expensive."

"Not all of it."

"Fine, yes. The average person can and probably goes to the Flower Market when they don't have the time to forage, but not everyone has that privilege available to them. And the other places where they can get ingredients have a different cost that's just as expensive."

Scoffing, I shook my head. "Like where?"

"The Nettles." He moved on, as if he had said nothing insane, like using the black market.

"No one goes to the Nettles without knowing what they're getting into. It's a market for criminals."

He rubbed the back of his neck and muttered something as he crouched nearby.

I scowled at the ruptured ground. "Hey! You didn't fill in the hole, either. Nathaniel, leave no trace in the forest—anywhere. Allow nature to come back and grow as it should."

He sighed. "Please call me Nate."

I squared my shoulders. "I'll call you Nathaniel until you give me a reason not to." I plopped my hand on my hip. "You're my student now, and if you don't like it—"

"Okay." He held up his hands. "I get it. Do what you say

and don't talk back. I'm sorry, Ms. Townsend. I'll fill this hole right away, Ms. Townsend."

I narrowed my eyes. "I'm not being unreasonable."

He didn't reply as he carefully picked his way back to me.

I felt . . . a little embarrassed for being such a bitch. "It's just that I love this place. I love all of Founders' Grove, and I want it to remain as beautiful as it is. And you're right. It's important that alchemy and enchanting is available to everyone who can do it. Your idea for a show is a good one."

"Thanks." He filled in the hole and met my stare. His eyes were the same color as star moss. I was sure of it. "I understand about walking carefully, and I'll do my best to take only what I need when I can. I'm sorry I didn't know better, and if you could please be patient with me, things will go easier for both of us." He smiled with his eyes first. "I really do love to learn, and I know you have a lot to teach me."

I nodded and moved past him. "That's a reasonable request."

"Hey, can I ask you something?"

"Sure." But if I didn't want to answer, I wouldn't have to.

"What was it like?"

I turned back to him, tilting my head to the side. "What was what like?"

"The trial."

I stiffened, crossed my arms over my chest, and moved away. I hated that question. I hated what that question always led to, and I hated that I ever had to answer it. I swallowed. "Exactly how you'd imagine everyone but the law behaving as if you were already found guilty. Now. I think I see some star moss. Come along, Nathaniel."

STRESS TIGHTENED the muscles around my shoulders as Nathaniel and I stored our reagents in my workshop. I'd cleared out some space for him in the cooler. While I munched on a tomato and made a mental note to order groceries, I gave him an official tour of my alchemy lab.

"Woah," he said when he took in both the alchemy and enchanting table. "You're both. Just like me."

"Oh, you're an enchanter too?" I asked.

"Yeah." He stared longingly at the tables, as if he wanted to touch them. "It's way more forgiving than alchemy. Plus, those shows always go with some weird vibe that doesn't seem real."

I didn't see a point in correcting him about all my talents, not that it'd help, but honesty ran strong in me, and I couldn't let him believe I was something other than I wasn't on his own misassumption. "Actually, I was born on the witches' new year."

"Oh-ho!" He grinned. "You and a bunch of other people. The thirty-first or the first?"

"Thirty-first." I shrugged. His sunshine smile tried its hardest to make me feel lighter. I refused. He was a Honey Bunny. "My parents wanted the best, and my mother did everything she could to ensure it'd happen."

He nodded. "Well, I'm not born on a solstice or anything cool like that, but technically, I'm only seven years old."

"What?" I took a step back and frowned at him. I couldn't have heard him correctly.

"I'm a leap year baby." He ran his hands along my alchemy table, dragging a finger through the empty channel of the five-point star, and sighed. "This is nice. I don't want to come off as pathetic, but I can't wait to cook at your table."

"I need to see what you're made of, so you'll be cooking soon."

He grinned and rubbed his hands together. "Awesome. We're gonna make an awesome team. I can feel it. And then I'll have my show. We're only going up from here."

I hung back as he walked into the kitchen to use my laptop, a sour taste coating my mouth. Of course, I'd almost forgotten he was using me to get rich, and I'd agreed to it, like an idiot. In the light of the day and the absence of dirty martinis, how had I even thought this was worth my time?

I'd vowed to never be a doormat for someone else's success again, and yet there I was.

Chapter Twelve

"The flour is here, and in the pantry there, you'll find the grater and pots," I said a few days later. I pointed toward the small pantry, which really was a glorified hall closet right off the kitchen. "I'll work on my schedule while you do this. Read the recipes completely."

I placed the recipes on the table before Nathaniel and sipped my chai, indulging in the fragrant spices and the sweet yet savory taste. The bitterness of the chicory really played well with cinnamon.

He frowned, glancing toward the hallway, then at the door leading to the greenhouse as he finished his scrambled eggs. "Why do you keep your cookware so far from your workshop?"

I set my cup down and leaned back in my chair. "I don't. What do you think's happening today?"

"You said we were going to cook."

"Yes, we are." I tapped the corner of the recipe in front of him. "Just make the spätzle."

"Spätzle?" He slipped on his glasses, and his moss-green eyes widened as he read it. "I'm sorry. When you said we were cooking, I thought you meant potions with all the reagents we've collected over the past week."

"Oh, no." Was I messing with him? Only a little. Did I enjoy it? I'd call it a perk for teaching him. "I need to see what I'm working with and how you cook. What your technique is."

"I don't cook food." He glanced at his clean plate. "I mean, just simple things like eggs. You can't screw up scrambled eggs."

"You'd be surprised. Ask Winkerton someday why she prefers pastries for breakfast."

"But I won't be cooking food on the show."

I pinched my lips together and thought over my words carefully. Mostly, I wanted to take a second. I wasn't used to being questioned like this for a while now. "You'll be cooking consumables on the show. I need to see how you do with cooking meals before we dive into potions. In case you're not at a level expected of someone who has graduated from Starglen Alchemy University." I met his gaze before nodding my head at the recipe before him. "Now, please read that and get started."

He barely concealed his scowl before he picked up the paper and scanned it. I could guess Nathaniel hadn't thought of cooking food in the same vein as cooking potions, and I was glad he'd didn't question me further. Though I supposed he simply wished to understand where I was going with the egg noodles.

He stood and moved to the fridge. His pants were baggy around his butt. Man, he needed to gain some weight. I smiled a little to myself. He'd certainly have quite a lot of food to eat if I didn't like his technique. And I'd have something other than a salad too.

He moved like he had a stutter. Nathaniel didn't know where anything was in my kitchen, which was understandable. I'd given him the basic layout like Owen Creek had for the herbarium on the first day of filming. I'd been too dazzled by his smile to really pay attention to his words. I'd learned embarrassingly quick to focus on what was happening rather than daydreaming about him being overwhelmingly impressed by my skills when I nearly didn't complete the first challenge because I was lost. Georgia had saved my ass that day.

This exercise would be good for Nathaniel. Working in an unfamiliar kitchen and still producing worthy product was an ideal quality. Claiming you didn't know your way around a kitchen might not save you on elimination day. The more adaptable he was, the better.

"Ugh, this is sticky," Nathaniel said about thirty minutes later, standing at my stove over a boiling pot of water making a mess with the egg dumplings. "It's getting everywhere."

I stood and approached him. The batter had oozed around the small cup on the spätzle maker, and it was all over his hands and the range. His shirt had streaks of flour as well as his pants. I hummed in the back of my throat and left him there, only to grab my apron. I smirked slightly. The purple canvas was worn and a little faded from many washings, but the embroidered pansies and petunias hadn't lost color.

I stepped next to him. "Here, duck your head."

When he did, I looped the tie over his head, my fingers brushing his skin. Huh. He had goosebumps. I didn't think it was that cold in here. He lifted his head and our faces were close to touching. I froze, my hands lingering at his neck, and my gaze dipped to his mouth. His lips looked soft . . . We'd only need to tilt our heads a tiny bit and—

I quickly moved behind him and tied the apron. Maybe I was a little lonely, and it'd been a while since I'd had any action. So what? But that didn't mean I should jump the first person I was attracted to that needed something from me. That was icky.

"Oh, thanks," he mumbled, setting aside the cup, and fished out the floating dumplings with a slotted spoon. "Do you make this often?"

"Yes. It's great in mac and cheese."

"Wait." He turned and looked at me, then at the fridge. "Is that what the pound of cheddar in the fridge is for? How much cheese does this need?"

I did my best to smile enigmatically and shrugged, returning to the table. I turned on the TV, careful to change it from the Potion Network. I didn't want him to be distracted, and honestly, he really idolized Georgia Cauldron and I did not want to waste any more time on her in my head today than I already had. Instead, I turned to a Lifetime movie. It probably had a ridiculous title like "Stalked by my vet because my cat had a broken tail and now the vet wants to make kittens with me." Or possibly take over the character's identity. Either way, the movie was at the point where the knife came into play, so it would be over soon.

My phone dinged with a text from Winkerton.

WINKERTON

I can't make it to brunch, darling. I'll stop by later tonight

No problem. See you then

Why was she always canceling our brunches? I sighed softly and updated my schedule to remove brunch and made a new entry for seven in the evening.

"So, are these noodles for a side dish?" Nathaniel asked.

I frowned at him. "What?"

He had a frying pan on a burner as he added butter to it.

The bowl of steaming spätzle sat on the counter next to him. "For the mac and cheese."

"What're you doing?"

"It says to pan fry the noodles in butter."

"I told you to only make the noodles."

He blinked.

"Also, do you see where it says to chill the dough for thirty minutes so it's more manageable?"

He read the recipe again and sighed. "I was just reading as I went."

"I caught on to that." I stood and whisked the bowl of noodles away and tucked them into the fridge. "First, pay attention to spoken direction. Second, always read the entire recipe before you start. Some might take as long as twenty-four hours to prep."

"That long?"

"Yes. Some potions require day-old extracts." I pushed my braids over my shoulder. "They do this sort of thing a lot on the show to see how well you follow directions."

"Oh . . ." A lightbulb practically appeared above Nathaniel's head. "You're right. Seth from season six got eliminated because the last line of the recipe said to make a hair tonic instead."

I handed him the recipe I used for mac and cheese and smiled. "Read it completely, and remember, you just made the noodles. Now. Get cooking."

I POKED at the lumpy and runny cheese sauce and pursed my lips. It smelled good. When he'd pulled the dish from the oven, it even looked like how I expected it to, but serving it revealed a lot of technical mistakes. I picked up the lump with my fork and placed it in my mouth, lightly chewing and tasting.

"Your eggs scrambled." I set my fork down. "Did you temper them?"

He shoveled it in his mouth and shook his head. "It tastes good."

"Of course it does. It's a well-developed recipe. But . . ." I shook my head and pointed into the dish. "The sauce is lumpy, and not just from unmelted cheese. The eggs scrambled."

He sighed. "Honestly? I don't see the point in this, Lila."

"Truly?" I pushed my plate back and stood, grabbing containers to box up the food. "If you can't read a recipe properly, then you won't make it far on the show."

"Alchemy is different from cooking." He scooped up some of the mac and cheese and helped clean it up. "And if it's so bad, why're you saving it?"

"This is for you to eat, Nathaniel." I snapped a lid on one. "And let me tell you, if you forget to do a step in alchemy, like improperly extracting belladonna for scopolamine, you'll get poison instead. No one wants that. Just like with cooking." I placed the leftovers in the fridge and plopped my hands on my hips. "Now, clean up and start again. This time, read the directions completely before you start."

I wondered if this was all a waste of time. Maybe he wasn't teachable; maybe I wasn't good at teaching. We'd find out soon enough whether we'd continue this ruse.

"Whisk!" I peered over his shoulder while he made the bechamel. "Whisk! Don't let it boil that much. Turn down the heat."

Nathaniel picked up the pace, making a strangled noise. "That wasn't in the recipe!"

"Of course not. You're learning. Now whisk harder."

This went on for the next week, sadly. I missed foraging in the mornings. It was a nice way to recharge, even if he was with me. But he needed to get this down before I let him in my workshop, otherwise the reagents we'd foraged would be wasted, unlike the mac and cheese leftovers. At least I had my nightly baths to myself, even if I didn't always use the bath bomb.

He'd learned his lesson on the spätzle that first day, and now he breezed through it. Last night, he'd thought ahead and made it to prepare for today, mumbling about how he does this often with potions. Another lightbulb going off for him, but I said little. Simply smiled. And he smiled back, and we'd smiled at each other for a while. Which was uncomfortable because Winkerton had been there, smiling too. To make a point, I scowled today.

When he pulled the dish out of the oven and scooped out a spoonful, the cheese slipped in to fill the void, and some of it was lumpy. I poked at it with a fork to make sure it wasn't scrambled egg again, but it wasn't.

"How is the cheese not melted?" he asked, exasperated.

"You're not getting the sauce hot enough," I answered.

"You told me to not let it boil."

"Yes, but you need to bring it to that point, right before boiling, then reduce and add heat as needed." I've eaten so much mac and cheese, I was looking forward to him getting past this point. Yeah, you can't go wrong with cheese, but my waistband was saying enough was enough. Luckily, I could go on walks and they had the same effect if he came with me. Which he did.

He groaned and rubbed his forehead. "This is stupid."

I smacked the table. "It's *not* stupid, Nathaniel. This is important." My back grew hot, and my heart gave an angry spurt of speed. "How many times do I have to explain to you that you need to be precise and careful with cooking, especially in alchemy? If you're unable to make a simple casserole, then how—"

I could hear myself. My voice was rising in pitch to possibly screeching. I tugged on one of my braids, and it yanked me out of my spiral. I tugged on it again because Nathaniel had really upset me, and suddenly I could breathe normally.

I cleared my throat. "This might feel stupid and possibly juvenile, but it's an important step."

A smile crinkled the skin around his eyes well before a slow grin spread across his face. A face that had lost a little of the sharp angles of his cheek bones. "Why did you tug on your hair? Is it because my mac and cheese is lumpy?"

"No." I crossed my arms. "You called this stupid."

"And that's why you pulled your hair?"

"Well, you're infuriating."

He chuckled. "Is that all? I've seen you pull on your hair while we foraged, while you've chatted with Winkerton . . . I don't really buy it's just because I called this redundant food exercise stupid."

"It is redundant, but it's how I learned."

His brows twitched. "Okay, I'm coming back to that, but . . ." He took a step closer; his mossy green eyes trailed over my hair. "Why do you pull on your hair?"

"Why does it matter?"

"I'm curious."

I squinted at him and then sighed. I wasn't a liar and he wouldn't let it go. "Fine. Alright. I could hear how shrill I was getting and tugging on my hair helps me check myself."

"Shrill?"

"Yes. It was feedback I'd received countless of times on the show and . . ." My ears grew hot, and I averted my face. "Pulling my hair resets me. I don't know. It's like a commercial break and lets me calm down. I don't mean to be shrill. No one does, and it's unfair that I get judged for having heightened emotions and I'm asked to control them."

I could feel his gaze on me. It was hot, and it traveled from the crown of my head to the tips of my toes before resting on my face once more. Perhaps I imagined it, but Nathaniel could read me like I was an open book half the time. I suspected he'd taken potions to read crowds when he'd first pulled something like that, but I'd spent nearly every waking moment with him this past week, and he hadn't used a single potion.

"I get it." He served himself some of the mac and cheese, not as much as he had in the past, and boxed up the rest. He'd halved the recipe with my approval a couple days ago when he realized this was all he'd eat until he got it right. "I had a foster parent tell me my grief needed to be checked at the door and that my excitement made her cringe whenever open house happened."

I suddenly felt like an idiot complaining about being told to calm down after he'd lived through something I'd never experienced. Nathaniel was definitely a brighter side of life type of person, and while I liked that side in him, I couldn't seem to force myself to look ahead like that.

"You said this was how you were taught." He picked the eggshells out of the carton and dropped them into my countertop compost bin. "What was your mother like?"

"My mother?" I snorted as I helped clean up the kitchen. "Absent. My nanny taught me."

"Nanny?" he drawled, then he looked around the kitchen and nodded. "Makes sense. You come from money."

I batted that statement out of the air. "My parents divorced when I was a toddler, and my father moved to Arizona. My mother was a busy scientist and spent most of her day at the lab. Carol was necessary. She taught me that the best alchemists were talented cooks, and I should master food first before potions. I can't say she was wrong. I can tell the difference."

He smiled bashfully as he rinsed out the small bowls I forced him to use for all the ingredients. "Is this something also taught in college?"

I laughed and placed a reassuring hand on his arm and shook my head. "No. I think it's just something picked up from other people, like my nanny."

"I bet that was nice, and before you say it wasn't, you gotta remember I taught myself everything I know from Potion Network shows, to YouTube videos, and Georgia Cauldron. She really gave me the confidence to try new things." He smiled. "You were lucky to be surrounded by family."

"My mother was too busy, and my father had moved away. Then he disowned me five years ago." I clamped my lips together; I hadn't meant to mention what my father had done. It'd slipped out. The mood soured and I stepped away, wanting to go into my greenhouse and find my calm again. "Well, I don't doubt your passion for alchemy."

"Hey." Nathaniel's soft voice stopped me. "Something's been bothering me."

I turned and tilted my head at him.

"I saw azaleas in the stock room and other poisonous plants there. Why would you even keep them after the trial?"

I blinked at him. "I have pollinators, so they need to be in a room they can't get in. I'd hate to destroy another beehive. I keep them because the leaves help banish harmful ghosts, and they're beautiful. I've sold some blooms in the Flower Market—before the trial." I frowned at my hands. "It's not so strange that I have azaleas."

"I mean, the honey though."

"Yes." I flashed him a smile that was all teeth and glared. "Honey was part of it. Now, if you're finished interrogating me yet again on something we both know is over, I want a walk."

TENSION COATED the kitchen like grease in a diner. The last few days had been tight with it after he'd asked about my flowers in the greenhouse. I supposed I couldn't blame him, I *shouldn't* blame him, but I did. That moment five years ago would haunt me forever, no matter the number of azalea leaves I burned. I may as well wear a scarlet letter for murderer even though no one had died.

His phone dinged and he opened his email. His face brightened, and I knew, without needing to be told, it was from TPN.

"I made it through to the final twelve applicants. I have a zoom call with someone called Naveen in a couple days to see if I'm a good fit." He lifted his head and grinned at me. "I'm so close!"

"That's great!" A real smile broke over my lips. "I'll get your herbal prep set up for you just in case they want you to make a potion."

"Ha! Probably a good idea."

The oven dinged, and Nathaniel pulled the dish out and set aside the towel. Our plates crowded the counter, and when it'd cooled enough, he met my eyes.

"I'm nervous," he admitted.

"Me too." I was so sick of mac and cheese, it'd be a year before I'd want to eat it again. "Go on. Dig in."

The casserole did not ooze when he scooped out a spoonful. It held its shape. He plopped it on the plate and offered me a tentative smile that almost met his eyes.

"Look, already an improvement," I said.

A lot of the tension left the room and his shoulders relaxed. The skin around his eyes crinkled even though he'd let go of his earlier smile.

We sat at the table, clinked our forks together, and dug in.

It was rich, smooth, and creamy. The cheese was amazing, just the right amount, and the nutmeg in the spätzle complemented the sauce. I took another bite.

"It's luscious." I licked my lips and smiled at him. "Good job, Nathaniel."

He pumped his fist in the air and laughed. "I had a good feeling about it. Everything was just a bit different, a bit easier."

"You did very well."

"You see? All those failed mac and cheeses were just learning experiences. They weren't a waste."

I laughed softly. "No, you're right. But I'm glad you did all the learning with cheese and noodles instead of the charged mud we collected."

His mossy eyes flashed with more mirth as he shoved a hand in his wavy blond hair. "Ha! You're right. You're always right." He struck his hand out to shake mine, and while he pumped my arm, he said, "You are amazing. When I get on that show, we're going to go far together."

Some of the joy drained from the moment, the rest following as his words sunk into my head. I pulled my hand back and wiped it on my overalls. "Well, we only have to make sure you get to episode four. You said that was the challenge that'd help you the most."

I left the table and rinsed my plate, intentionally not looking over at him. It was best to remind him why we were working together. I wanted to pull the wool over the Potion Network's eyes and make them see I was not a failed alchemist and make them seem like a not-so-credible source anymore. He just wanted to use me to get there.

Like everyone else.

Chapter Thirteen

The tapping on my bedroom door blended in well with the rain hitting my window that I thought I'd imagined it. Also, I didn't want to get out of bed; it was so much better than a couch. The mattress was perfect, and despite how light the blanket felt when I'd tossed it on the bed, it trapped my body heat well, making this moment of mostly asleep and the rain striking the window blissful.

"Nathaniel, wake up," a soft voice called through the door.

I jolted forward, everything rushing back to me at once: I was inside Lila Townsend's guest room. It was—I woke my phone—*fuck*—twenty after four in the morning. I had my zoom meeting with a TPN producer this afternoon, and if I was lucky, I'd make a potion with the alchemy table.

I scrambled out of bed and snatched up the sweatpants on the floor, tugging them on as I hopped to the door. When I swung it open, Lila stood on the other side, fully dressed in a purple plaid shirt and overalls. She'd pulled her hair back into a low ponytail, and her silvery eyes went large, skating over my bare chest.

"Something wrong?" I asked, my voice raspy from sleep.

I stared at the tip of her tongue as she licked her lips, then the movement of her throat mesmerized me as she swallowed. This attraction I had for her was distracting and becoming a nuisance. I was here to learn.

"It's finally raining," she said.

"Yes . . .?"

"We should head out to Founders' Grove and collect dawn tree water."

Sleep evaporated in a blink and I grinned. "I can be ready in five."

I was ready in four minutes, thanks to multitasking. We headed out to the Avenue of the Giants, a thirty-one-mile scenic road that paralleled Highway 101, and the sole way to access Founders' Grove. Lila snapped the radio off, suffusing the car with silence. For once, I didn't feel the need to fill it. I leaned back, listening to the squeak of the wipers clearing the rain from the window. In the dark, the redwoods stretched miles into the sky, creating a canopy of branches and needles. As if they were building a second, hallowed world with the promise of reagents uniquely available in moments like this. I'd occasionally catch glimpses of tail-lights ahead on the winding road while a few cars headed our way. Everyone had the same idea about collecting dawn tree water as we did.

I enjoyed, especially at this moment, that I didn't have to come out here on my bike. It was dark, slick, and dangerous for bike riders; we'd passed a couple, and only one of them wore reflective clothing, and I still didn't see them until we were right on them. I squirmed a little in my seat. No wonder Emily gave me a hard time whenever I mentioned I rode my bike down here.

Lila slowed, then maneuvered the Volvo into a pull off that one other vehicle had parked in earlier. She killed the engine. We were still a ways out from the parking lot for the trail.

"I thought we were going to Founders' Grove," I said, staring out the windshield. The rain had lessened some, but it was heavy enough that I was glad for my new raincoat.

"I don't know how much longer the rain's going to last." Lila reached into the backseat and grabbed her foraging bag. "This is one of the less popular trails out here. Everyone and their mother will be at the main trailhead, heading straight for where they know of some dawn trees. Here, I know a spot of dawn trees. We won't have to hang around waiting for the leaves to refill like everyone else."

She got out, and I hurriedly followed to meet her at the trunk. The light blinked on as she opened it and handed me a pair of brand-new galoshes. I slipped them on over my shoes with a grin. I hadn't had galoshes since I was a kid, and I'd quickly outgrown them. I might've been excited to wear them in my first rainfall, and I looked forward to saying goodbye to wet socks.

She pulled the hood to her purple raincoat up and brushed the embroidered embellishment on the brim. A moment later, a pale blue-tinted light poured from it, surprisingly bright, and shrouded her face in shadows. I winced and glanced away.

Lila tapped my arm and lifted her hand. A flat, oblong lunar stone rested in her palm. "I didn't have time to mount it on a chain, but your front pocket on your coat is clear."

"Oh, nice. Thanks." I unsnapped the pocket, activated the charm, and dropped it inside. Many foragers used lights like these to help when foraging in the dark, like we were now, and the clear breast pocket was designed for these moments.

"You're welcome." She stared at me. I couldn't tell what she was doing because I couldn't see her face. "Where's your foraging kit?"

I knew I'd had it in my hands as we headed out to the car, but had I rested it on the roof to free my hands or not? And had I remembered it? I stiffened and hurried back to the passenger side and opened the door. I released my held breath and snatched up my kit. "Right here." Thank god, I remembered it. I would've hated to ask to borrow from her, or worse, go back into town to get it. I should've performed my check to make sure I had everything. I guessed the soft bed was making me forgetful.

"Follow me." She didn't wait for a reply and headed out on the trail leading into the dark forest.

Our lights illuminated just enough for us to see where we were going. Ley bugs blinked aquamarine beneath the foliage here and there. Every once in a while, between trees and bushes, I'd glimpsed someone else with a light, but they weren't close enough to see clearly. An excellent reminder that even if you felt alone, you never truly were.

Lila stepped off the trail, her steps careful and gentle as she moved around the underbrush. I followed as best as I could in her path. Above, the sky was lightening, but not enough to see well by. I'd tripped over a few bulging roots even with my light, but at least I hadn't fallen. I didn't know this trailhead that well, and I was especially unfamiliar with it now that we moved off the beaten path.

Then ahead, Lila's light fell on a small patch of bushes about three feet high, covered in small golden-orange leaves upturned to form perfect little cups the size of a child's palm. Dawn trees. They typically grew in patches of three or four, and this was no exception.

We both pulled on thin gloves, since we weren't dealing with sharp plants. The first rule of foraging is to always wear gloves. It was better to be safe than sorry. Then we got to work. I pulled out a phial of the smaller size and tucked the stopper in my pocket. Then, starting from the top of the dawn tree, I placed the mouth of the container at the tapered end of the leaf and gently pressed down on the stem to encourage the rainwater to slide into my vessel. It was just a drop, as some fell on the leaves below. It was why you always started from the top.

"Good, Nathaniel." Lila nodded.

I grinned. "Thanks."

"Try to be a little gentler when pressing on the stem. You'll get more water to fall in your phial than dropping it to the leaves below."

We collected dawn tree water in silence. I, personally, didn't need to say anything, and also, talking was a distraction and I didn't want to lose any precious water. In the meantime, the rain tapered off to nothing and the loamy aroma of the redwoods fresh after a rain cocooned me. The sky lightened from twilight to a shy morning with tiny openings of the gray clouds to the blue sky ahead, and I lost track of time. I blinked tired eyes as I fished out the cap for my phial and fastened it on. I'd collected from one entire dawn tree and made it third of the way through the other one before I'd needed another phial.

Lila stepped around, tucking one full bottle and another half full in her bag. I blinked. How much water was she able to coax from those tiny leaves if she had filled another phial halfway?

"Did you finish with your trees already?" I gestured at mine. "I'm not quite done."

Lila brushed the charm on her hood and the light dimmed to nothing. I could see now that the center of a large embroidered flower there was a crystal. "You did fine. I think we have enough for the week. Let's head back."

LILA SNIFFED. She did this every time I set aside a small bowl of a reagent that I'd prepped for the speak truly potion I was set to make in just a few moments. After weighing the paste I'd made on the scale, I set it aside. Her eyes flicked to the bowl, and she sniffed again. I peered at the star moss paste. Maybe it was on the gritty side, but it wasn't for a salve, and I didn't see what the problem here was. I lifted my head and slowly turned it toward her so she knew I could be as passive aggressive as she.

"What?" She reached for a calla lily and pulled the leaves down the stem to fully expose the flower.

"I assume you have something you want to say, so I'm letting you know I'm listening."

She hummed in the back of her throat before she met my stare. "Your herbal prep is sloppy. I think—"

I sighed and tilted my face toward the ceiling.

"It is!" She placed a hand on my arm. "And that's fine. We'll work on it before you get on the show. But today, on your zoom call, I think it's best if I get it ready for you, so there isn't anything suspicious."

For a small moment, a wave of defeat washed over me, and I wondered if I would ever pull this off, if I could ever be good enough.

"Just for today." She squeezed my arm lightly. "You *are* improving, and you'll get better, Nathaniel."

I scrubbed my face. "You're right." I waved at my prep work. "What should I do with this?"

"Uh, use it?" Her brows crinkled. "You already have the calla lily pollen dissolving in vodka. How does it look?"

I lifted the small glass bottle. It had a quarter cup of vodka and an entire stamen coated in pollen sitting in it. I shook the bottle, and the liquid had turned dark yellow. "It's dissolved."

She handed me tweezers, and I pulled out the stamen and set it aside.

"Grab that jar up there."

I followed the direction where she pointed to the shelf above the work bench and saw one filled with translucent tiny petals. I grabbed it and read the label. "Ley bug wings? From the bugs in here?"

She nodded. "The benefit of having a sparkle of ley bugs is that they reproduce as often as they die. Their lantern is empty, sure, but their wings remain the same. Don't use the same tweezers. Moisture is bad for them in this state."

"I didn't know these were in a speak truly potion." I grabbed a new pair of tweezers and carefully gripped one wing.

"Yes. They make it impossible for whoever drinks the potion to lie. Drop that in the solvent."

"Really?" I'd thought the calla lily pollen merely strongly suggested to whoever ingested the potion to tell the truth. The wing dissolved right before my eyes as soon as it hit the solvent. "Is that something you learned in SAU?"

"It is. Grab an empty vessel and prep it for the alchemy table."

I smiled to myself. I've been dying to cook a potion for a while now, and I was so damned excited it would happen soon. I opened the cupboard, and a cloud of lavender wafted out as I stared at the variety of empty flasks and bottles. I grabbed a small one with a screw-on cap. Right as I was about to close the door, I noticed a few balls on the bottom shelf. They were probably the source of the lavender. I shut the door and placed my vessel on the bench. I scraped the star moss paste into the vessel with a tiny lab spatula, then added the calla lily mixture to the bottle, filling it to the neck. Using an eyedropper, I extracted some of the dawn tree water I'd collected earlier that morning. I added two drops to my vessel. After returning the unused water to the phial, I capped it.

I solemnly approached the alchemy table. It was about the size of a garden table, made from dark brown wood. While small, it was also bulky thanks to the elaborate swoops and swirls thickly cut into the legs and the sides. In the middle of the five-point star carved into the wood was a slightly raised ledge. I placed my vessel on that.

At the far top of the table, on both sides, were two indents, perfect to slide your hands in to form the connection between you and the table, which I did now. Then I dug deep, searching for the ley energy hidden within the earth, surprised to find it so quickly. The wood beneath my hands gave off an aquamarine glow. The connection between me, the table, and the ley lines was open, and the table took over.

The ley energy swept through me like an icy stream. I heard a gasp—might've been me—and my jaw locked together. My heart raced, pumping my chilly blood through my body as it distilled the raw energy. I tried to keep my focus, to watch the table, but the adrenaline and the magic took over.

It was always hard to really describe what I "saw" whenever I connected to an alchemy or an enchanting table. The best I could come up with was how the movies portrayed going into Lightspeed. The raw ley energy zipped past me and into the table in streaks of glittering periwinkle, teal, aquamarine, shot through with bolts of navy.

The colors grew brighter. My breathing stuttered and my entire body froze. It was too bright. Everything went white around me as I filtered the last of the ley energy into the table.

And as suddenly as it gripped me, it left me. My vision returned in time to see the channels of the five-point star lit up with ley blue, all racing toward the vessel, which was giving off the same glow until it dissolved into the wood to release my hands from it. Sweat sealed my shirt to my back, and I had trouble catching my breath.

"Holy shit," I panted.

"I should've warned you a ley line runs under my house," Lila murmured. She passed me a glass of water. "You'll need to make more potions to get used to it so you don't scream like that on camera."

I gulped down the water, feeling a little shaky as the adrenaline left me. "I screamed?"

"A little." She frowned. "Will you be okay? Your zoom call's soon, and I also need to drop off an order at the Vineyard."

"No, yeah. I'm fine."

Her frown deepened. "Eat a cookie or some chocolate. Sugar helps."

Lila left shortly after that, and I ate the last eclairs Winkerton had left behind the previous day. Holy shit. That'd been an *experience.* I took another moment to collect myself before I carried the laptop into the workshop and set up. Then I signed into the zoom meeting and waited for the host.

I went over in my head what to say, how to sound, and that I was good enough for the show, and by the time they started filming, I would be at my best. The screen blipped, and I didn't have any more time to prepare.

"Hi, Nate. Nice of you to join me," the man with great looking black hair said. He was in an office. Behind him were posters of *Home Brew Elixirs, The Next Potion Network Star,* and I think the other one was *Alchemy Betty's Alcove,* but I couldn't be too sure. "I'm Naveen Koti, and I'll be interviewing you today."

"Nice to meet you, Naveen," I replied. "How—"

"Let's get right into this. I've got a lot of these meetings today, and I don't have a lot of time for small talk."

Okay, this was happening. "Sure."

"You graduated from the university in . . . 2016?" he asked, scanning something off to the side.

I swallowed, but my mouth remained dry. "2017, actually." If things had gone my way.

"Right, right." Naveen nodded, his eyes flicked to me and back to whatever he was reading. "Your parents were casualties in a police confrontation with a Muted? How old were you?"

I lowered my head. "I was four when they died." For some reason, it hit differently today. Like it hadn't happened decades ago.

"You were placed into the system at a young age. What was that like?"

"Living in an orphanage?" When he nodded, I sighed. "Awful. I got moved around a lot."

"If this were on the show, you'd need to give more information without prompting, or answer questions in direct statements."

I clenched my hand and jerked my head in affirmation. "Living in an orphanage was scary. I was young and didn't fully understand what had happened or why I was there. Later on, I was placed in different foster homes, and I used alchemy to find a place in the world. You know, to connect with other people, and it was great to have something in common with them."

"With your foster families?" Naveen prompted.

I nodded. "Yes. I even had one in particular that let me read their old textbooks, and it really opened my eyes to how much I loved potions."

"If you were to have your own show, what would it be like?" he asked.

I smiled, perhaps my first genuine one since he'd started to interrogate me. "It'd be about foraging for ingredients and making potions stable before getting to an alchemy table. For people who don't have their own table, or are short on time to rent one from the library. I want to help ease some of the stress and struggle over not having your own workshop."

Naveen nodded. "And you'd make potions on set or go to one of these places?"

"It'd probably be easier to do it on set, don't you think? You wouldn't have to always request permission from rando people or find a store to allow us to film there. However, I think it'd be good to do it once in a while, like once a season, to give a business a boost and to show I'm not all talk."

He jotted something down. "That's a practical way of looking at filming."

I gestured at the alchemy table off camera. "Would you like to see me make one now?"

"I don't have the time to watch you whiteout while making a potion. We'll save all of that for the show if you're accepted. Okay, that's all our time. Someone will get in contact with you if you've made it to the show. It was nice to meet you."

"Nice to meet you too."

I wasn't sure if he'd heard me. The meeting ended in mid-sentence. Raking my hands through my hair, I closed my eyes. He'd focused more on my back story than anything else. He didn't even care that I'd gone to college, or at least he hadn't asked about it. Maybe it indicated how TNPNS would go, that my past would be all they'd ask about instead of what I was passionate about. If I won, would that be the primary focus of my show? Would I have to talk about being an orphan every episode? I didn't want to continually place the worst time of my life on display for strangers to examine and feel the need to give me their opinions.

A hand lightly touched my shoulder, jerking me from a

doze on the chair. By how sore my ass was, I must've fallen asleep a little while ago.

Lila gestured at the open laptop, the screen dark with inactivity. "How'd it go?"

"Okay, I think. The producer asked a lot of questions about my story and what I'd do with the show. He didn't want to see me make a potion, though."

She nodded. "That's good." Her gaze swept across the bowls holding reagents scattered on the workbench and gave me a tight smile. "Because we're going to double our efforts to get you top-notch. Your herbal prep leaves much to be desired."

Chapter Fourteen

I frowned at Nathaniel's herbal prep within my workshop, the small wisps of hair around my face curling from the humidity. Why had I even bothered to teach him *mise en place* if he refused to use it in alchemy? Hadn't the few weeks of mac and cheese taught him anything other than to temper eggs and melt cheese in milk? The hot air was thick and I was becoming damp beneath my flannel, so I unbuttoned it and peeled it off. Nathaniel's attention shifted to me, his mossy eyes zeroing in on me as I plucked at the trapped hot air. Except he was looking at my sides instead of my face. I peeked, making sure nothing weird was going on, but it was just bare skin. I grabbed an old pamphlet and fanned myself, lifting a brow at him. He jerked his head back to the worktable. What was his problem? It wasn't like I was indecent. Besides, my tank and overalls weren't so heavy that a little humidity would kill me—even if it was curling the wisps of hair around my face.

He nudged his glasses up his nose and stacked the thick, flat green leaves of the *aureluis herbonal* for a purpose that eluded me in a line before him. I remained quiet; I didn't want to distract him or make him second-guess himself.

But he'd hardly glanced at the recipe for calm mind. Just like he had with the spätzle. It was like the first time we'd met in the Flower Market all over again. He believed he knew what he was doing, and while I admired his confidence, I also hated being wasteful.

And he wasn't embarrassed.

"What's even the point of asking me to teach you if you refuse to learn, Nathaniel?"

"What're you talking about?" He glanced at me as he pulled his mortar closer and reached for the knife. At least he no longer used a stupid Georgia Cauldron "My First Alchemy" set.

"Stop!" I waved my hands at the leaves. "Stop. You're doing it all wrong."

He made a disgruntled noise and pulled the recipe closer. "It says to use the pulp of the leaves. I'm going to cut them fine and then mash them."

"And ruin the potion." I pointed at the rest of the plant. "This is wasteful! We need to be as careful as possible with the plants so we can reuse as much of the specimen as possible. If we went along as we did, we'd lose the leaves."

"Uh, why do you want the leaves separate from the pulp?"

As I leaned against the workbench and grabbed a pencil, his eyes followed the hem of my tank riding up my sides. A strange vibration, a secret thrill preceding a flutter, bubbled to the surface in my stomach.

Clearing my throat—as if that'd clear out his expression when he stared at me—I underlined a bullet point under the plant ingredient. "The leaves are bitter and induce vomiting. You need to scrape the pulp out with the blunt edge angled.

We can save the leaves and make a tonic to induce vomiting. The Vineyard uses this a lot."

"Oh. I didn't know that. Nothing I've read ever mentioned it." His expression turned faraway as his brow pinched. "No wonder Sawyer complained about it."

"He probably did more than complain." I folded my arms on the counter and leaned over them. Nibbling on my lip, I realized this was a suitable moment to compliment his original intention; there wasn't a point to always be so strict. I shrugged and met his stare. "Otherwise, your plan to mince and mash was a good one."

He flipped the blade over and swept it across the top of the leaves.

"No!" My voice pierced my ears and I winced. "You're doing it all wrong!"

He cringed too, then reached over and tugged on my braid. My breath huffed out of me like a startled gasp. His brows leaped on his forehead and I swore he held his breath.

I blinked at him, then at my hair he'd yanked on, and back at him. His eyes darted between mine and my hair. He reached slowly out to me as if I was an easily startled animal and pushed a curling wisp behind my ear, his fingers brushing my skin. My pulse raced and tingles spread down my arms and chest from where he'd grazed me. Then he carefully ran his fingers down my braid and made sure it rested neatly over my shoulder.

"I'm sorry," he whispered.

Was he afraid of me?

He tilted his head at the leaves. "Show me."

"Very well." My voice had returned to normal, yet that strange hot flutter had only intensified. I rolled my shoulders.

I took his knife and cut the end of the leaf off. Then I flipped it to the blunt edge. "Hold the knife at a forty-five-degree angle and drag the blade across the leaf." I demonstrated, leading with my arm, which bumped him. "It's the pressure that's important. Hard enough to push the pulp out, but gentle enough not to excrete oil from the skin." I stepped away and waved at the pulp the leaf had secreted. "See?"

"No, I didn't see any of that, actually." He frowned. "I think I caught the gist, though. Is it alright with you, Your Highness, if I try on another leaf, or would that be too wasteful?"

I scowled. I didn't like his tone, but I had to remind myself that in learning, mistakes were made. "Of course."

Yet he hadn't seen what I'd shown him, and when I corrected him again, he grew exasperated. We switched places at the workbench, but he still hadn't seen it.

"Maybe if I guide you, do you think that'll work?" I asked when we'd gone through three more leaves. At least the plant was not rare.

"Like guiding my hands?" he asked dubiously.

"Yes." I forced a smile, but I suspected I looked like I was grimacing when he didn't seem reassured. "Exactly like that."

"Okay."

He moved in front of me, and I reached around him. He was warm and he'd used my strawberry shampoo—that felt strangely more intimate than seeing him without a shirt on. I grasped his hands easily enough, but I was just too short to see everything and not grievously injure him or myself. He was only a few inches taller than me, but I supposed that was all it took to make this dangerous.

"Just a sec." I grabbed a foot stool and set it up behind him and climbed up.

Yes, this would work. I reached down and grabbed his arms, my breasts pressing against his shoulder blades. I leaned over him, my cheek brushing his ear as I slid my fingers over his hands. I could barely reach them, let alone the knife.

"This doesn't seem that safe," he rumbled, his voice going straight to my gut like a sucker punch.

I remembered now that when I was in college, the professor had an overhead camera and displayed the demonstration on a projector screen.

"How about I stand in front of you and do it this way so I can see what I'm doing and not lose a finger?" I asked.

He slid me an unreadable expression that made my chest jitter. It reminded me of going on camera for the first time. He stepped back from the bench, and I stepped forward, grabbed the knife and a new leaf.

When he didn't close the space, I peered at him from over my shoulder. "Well? Give me your hands."

He closed the distance behind me. The humidity hadn't changed, but somehow, he felt hotter with his chest barely against my back. When he didn't move farther, I reached behind me and grabbed his hands, bringing them forward and around me. He was warm, and it felt so much like an embrace that something inside me relaxed.

Oh no.

I was boxed in. He leaned closer, because I'd pulled when his fingers curled uselessly at the end of the knife. And now his chest was pressed against my back and my ass was . . . I locked my thigh muscles in hopes it'd keep me from squirming. This couldn't be happening with him.

"This okay?" His arms cinched tighter, and his breath kissed my ear.

"Yes. Perfect." My voice sounded reedy, and goosebumps scattered across my body.

I guided his hands to release the pulp from the leaf without scouring the bitterness from its skin. The greenhouse disappeared and the hot air around us thickened. Yet still, I steered him again on the leaf.

Then he shifted our hold, and his dry, rough hands closed around mine, and he guided my hands in the process. His scruffy chin moved against my temple.

"Good," I whispered, my throat a little scratchy. I cleared it. "That's very good."

I pulled my hands away, intending to get out of his space, but he kept me in the small circle of his arms, smelling like my shampoo with an underlying hint of his aftershave. It cradled me. But the more I watched his hands, the more he did well with the technique I'd shown him.

He did it again, no problems. He had it. It'd taken me longer than him to get it right, and he had it. That gentle elation at already proving those Honey Bunnies wrong suffused me, and I grinned. I could teach anyone.

"That's excellent, Nathaniel!" I half-turned, gripping his biceps to look up at him.

The skin around his eyes crinkled, and he gazed at me like he'd never seen me before. "Yeah?" His voice was low, slightly unsure.

I shifted further and tilted my head back, my smile only expanding. "Yes. You did well."

His moss-green eyes dipped to my lips. The thickened air around us charged and grew hot. That strange stage fright feeling in my chest shifted into high gear as my heart picked up the pace and somehow, butterflies had materialized in my stomach.

"Thank you, Lila," he murmured, "for showing me."

I stared at his mouth. He had pretty lips, like a cupid's bow. He was a handsome man, and he'd do well on the show if his application was accepted. These past few weeks with him, I'd seen a lot of growth, and I couldn't help but feel a certain amount of pride in my student. But it didn't explain the sudden pull I felt.

His eyes hooded, his head started to lower toward mine.

Oh no, I needed to get out of here; I couldn't get hurt like this again. Casual sex was never something I was good at. I developed feelings, and they were rarely returned. But instead of moving away, my feet only turned me around so I was fully facing him. One of his hands dropped to my hip, his fingers brushing my skin as he shuffled closer. The bench pressed against my back. I had nowhere to go, no escape I wanted to take.

His breath warmed my cheek, and if I just turned my head a little, our lips would meet. I wanted to know what that encounter would be like, and the thought shocked me out of this stupid, foolish idea of kissing Nathaniel Pittman.

I turned my head aside and pushed his hand away. "This is unprofessional."

I moved over to my apparatus and pulled down an empty bottle, handing it to him.

"I'm . . . I . . ." He took the flask. "I'm sorry. I was only excited."

I nodded. That was usually the excuse people gave me anyway, but this time, hearing the apology hurt more. The blush on his cheeks informed me he was telling the truth. He felt the same embarrassment everyone else had. A blow to my self-confidence, but we weren't here to kiss; we were here to brew. My fight-or-flight response kicked in, and suddenly this room was small, tight, and uncomfortably hot.

"Of course." I edged farther away, doing anything to distract him from my faux pas. "You should use my alchemy table for the potion."

"Oh." He brightened and looked at it. My alchemy rig was armed with clean vessels, and the channels for the ley energy to charge a potion formed a five-point star. Right now, they remained empty. "I didn't think we'd do this again today."

"Well, I think you're proving you have an aptitude for picking things up easily enough, but this is another lesson."

He quirked a brow at me. "What's the lesson?"

"It's obvious that you've rarely used a table that's sitting over ley lines."

He shook his head.

"Well, they're like this in college and on the stage for the show." I smiled and dragged my finger along the table. "And one of the reasons my potions were gaining popularity is because this house is built smack dab on top of one. When you use the table on the show, you need to behave as if you're used to the extra kick it gives."

"Oh. Right." He grinned. "I need to be used to it. Yes. This is so awesome."

"And while you're at it, why don't you make a list of easy potions to make, and we'll see if we need to forage for them tomorrow, okay?"

Was I using the alchemy table as a distraction to get away from him? Yes. I could have been called a coward then and I wouldn't have fought it. I stepped back and hovered around the edge of my workshop, the almost kiss fooling around with my thoughts while cheating on my brain with my emotions. It was best to not let anything further happen between Nathaniel and I. I reminded myself repeatedly this was exactly what Georgia had done to get me under her thumb.

"No one could truly love you." I wasn't a fool.

Later that evening after supper—we both had salads— Nathaniel checked his email. It was an old habit. Each night we'd commiserate not getting any information about his application with a dirty martini—my favorite salad of the day —for me, and a Starglen Brewery cider for him.

"Oh, my god." His voice had taken on a high pitch, and the smile he gave me made me replay the almost kiss in my head again.

I was *not* a fool.

"What happened?" I almost held my breath. "Is everything alright?"

"I got in!" He spun my laptop around and showed me the acceptance email and the first potion he'd make in the technical skill portion of the show. "The first potion we're making is a witch hazel tincture."

He jumped up and did a little dance.

I laughed and rose from my seat. "That's wonderful!"

I was in his arms again as he did a quick two-step around the kitchen before he spun me away to read the email once more. "I can't believe it! You got me in!"

I grinned. His wavy hair was still curly from the humid workshop. He appeared untouchable at this moment. I laughed and high-fived him. "Now you have to show the world what you're made of."

He tossed a smile at me. "Thank you, Lila. Really. You've already changed how I do things, and even if I hadn't gotten accepted, what I learned from you was priceless."

I pressed my fingers against my chest and took a deep, satisfying breath. And it helped to calm down my jitters. "You're welcome." I swallowed and glanced outside. It wouldn't be dark for a couple hours, but I couldn't stay in here anymore. I needed a small break from him, especially when he was this happy and kind. "Well, make a list of where we're going and the reagents we'll be foraging. I'm going to take a walk."

"Oh, do you mind if I come?"

My ears grew warm. I was going to bathe naked in the twilight. He most certainly couldn't come.

I shook my head. "We'll get started early tomorrow. In the

meantime, you have free rein in my workshop and greenhouse."

His face lit up like a kid in a sweet shop who normally wasn't allowed to have candy. "Really? Anything?"

"Of course." I headed for the stairs and glanced over my shoulder. "Alchemy rewards inquisitive minds."

Chapter Fifteen

I stared at the ceiling, my brain refusing to shut off as it went over everything Lila had showed me today. The technical potion I'd make on the first episode of *The Next Potion Network Star*, and the softness in her eyes when she'd turn in my arms. My body rock hard and ready to—

Okay, I was lying to myself. I *wanted* to think about making it past the application process, about the first episode, but all I could think about was Lila touching me. Feeling her body, her soft curves and firm breasts pressed tight to me when she'd tried to help me from behind. How she'd smelled: like a garden rioting with lush green plants and a hint of strawberries.

Not just the way her shoulders had relaxed, but her whole body when she'd been in my arms. Like stress and tension no longer existed for her. That wasn't true either—there'd been tension. Hot and electric. I had to keep my hips far from hers because then she'd know exactly how much seeing a scrap of skin and the edge of her underwear had affected me. I'd been so surprised by the surge of lust I hadn't quite seen what she'd tried to show me.

Fuck. I could rub one out right now, but I doubted it'd ease the want erupting deep from within every fiber of my body.

Instead, I rubbed my face, roughly expelling a breath.

"You're going to compete on *The Next* fucking *Potion Network Star*, Nate," I muttered into my palms. "Get your shit together."

My excitement bounced around like an overactive squirrel. I was going to meet Georgia fucking Cauldron. And Owen Creek too. He was cool, but Georgia was proof that someone coming from nothing, like me, could make something spectacular with their life.

Right now, there wasn't much to boast about. I was broke, I didn't even have a home, and I relied on friends from high school taking pity on me ten years later. Hell, this was the longest stretch I'd slept in a bed in over a month—and it was glorious.

Yet despite how much Georgia inspired me and I loved her show and modeled mine after hers, for the most part, I'd learned more from Lila in these short weeks than I had from any Potion Network show. It was a little frustrating that the Potion Network and Starglen Alchemy University were gate-keepers to knowledge. That was why it was so important that I win this competition and get my own show. People like me, with similar struggles as mine, wouldn't be left in the dark and clueless with a craft they'd had since birth.

Everything about my life would improve. No more bargaining for food, no more asking to sleep on couches or using someone else's shower. No longer feeling like a burden or a moocher to my friends. A roof over my head that I placed there from my own hard work, and the ability to open new ways of thinking to those who struggled just like me.

I had to win.

I tossed back the covers and got out of bed. The cool air

nipped my skin, and I pulled on a shirt. I had the first potion I'd make on air and complete access to Lila's alchemy workshop. Maybe I'd work on a few pitches and ask Lila what she thought in the morning. Not only did I need to work on the pitches for my show, I also needed to nail every potion I made. I went over the benefits of a witch hazel tincture in my head as I crept down the stairs—relieved skin irritations or lessened bleeding—and stepped into the dimly lit kitchen.

Lila sat at the table, a cup sitting near her hand while she nibbled her lip, poring over one of her many planners. She'd pulled her pale brown hair into a messy bun. Tendrils fell around her neck, leaving wet spots on her lilac satin robe. I halted, staring at her. Her expression when she turned to look up at me came unbidden to me. It said "kiss me" and it was a siren's call. One she hadn't heard.

She lifted her head, and her brows hopped at seeing me. "I thought you'd be asleep."

"I couldn't sleep." I approached the table. It was covered in her physical planner, her iPad had her digital planner open, and she was scribbling out a schedule on a notepad. "Do you ever have a moment that isn't planned?"

She tucked a wisp of hair behind her ear. "Well, when I sleep, there's no schedule."

I knew for a fact she blocked the time off for sleeping since she'd shared the schedule with me. I leaned on the table and studied what she'd already entered in the digital planner. "This is weeks in advance."

She squirmed in her seat before leaning back and rubbing her shoulder. Dark semicircles lined the bottoms of her gray eyes. "I can't sleep, and they obligingly sent the filming schedule for the entire show, so I planned ahead for practice and foraging. It'll be easy to fill in the biomes every week when they give you the technical. And while the producers only gave us the witch hazel tincture details for the first show, I know they give the next technical out the last day of shooting."

I stared at the planners and the notepad scattered on the table, a giddy sensation bouncing up from my core to my heart and right back down again. A new emotion unfurled inside my chest beside the lust, and it pulsed gently. No one had ever done anything like this for me before, not since I was in the system. There'd be no way I could ever repay her. I licked my lips and edged closer to her to look at what she was writing. "Really? This is all for me?"

She folded her hands around her mug and nodded. "Of course. I said I would help you."

"You also said you'd only get me to episode four."

"Well, if you make it past episode four, I don't see why I wouldn't continue to help." She shrugged. "They'd really feel foolish for not spotting the gaps in your education if you made it to the final episode—especially when you reveal it's me."

I smiled at her; I couldn't help it. While Lila's motivation to help me get on the show was to smear egg on the Potion Network's face by revealing my lack of education, she'd really pulled through for me and she didn't have to, not to this extent. She smiled shyly and dipped her eyes, lifting the mug to her lips and taking a sip. She'd enchanted me.

I tapped the table. "How long have you been working on this?"

"Well, I had a moonlit bath, certainly not intending to schedule eight weeks of filming, but I still couldn't sleep, so . . ."

I took in her lilac robe, noticing now how it gaped at her neck, and the light and shadows played together at the opening of her robe. I ate up the sight of her pale skin and the impression of her breasts beneath the slide of the fabric against her skin. My mouth watered as if a stack of pancakes were set before me and I hadn't eaten in days. Except now I was hungry for her. I wanted to peel that robe off and devour her as the rest of me worshiped—Nope. What had she said? These urges were unprofessional. One-sided. I immediately turned my thoughts to the time a friend's dog ate a crystal and I had to recover it.

"A moonlit bath?" I cleared the roughness from my throat. "I hadn't noticed a skylight in the bathroom."

"A skylight? That's an idea." Silvery eyes gazed at me with hidden thoughts. Her fingers trailed along the edge of her robe near her neck before she pulled it tighter together and shook her head. "No, I have a cedar tub at the back of the property."

"Oh really? Can I—"

"Before you ask to use my tub"—she smiled ruefully—"you should know it doesn't have a water hookup."

"Oh." I laughed nervously because that was exactly what I was going to ask next. And I imagined her naked again. "I forget you're a water caster."

"It comes in handy with plants." She took another sip of tea and rested her head on her palm, her fingers massaging her eyelids.

I studied her bowed shoulders. She seemed drained, like even sitting up was too much for her. When she dropped her hand, her eyes were heavy-lidded.

"Do you have insomnia often?" I quietly asked.

"Yes, but I just can't seem to magic my way out of this one." She set her tea down and shook her head. "I've taken melatonin, that's sleepy tea, my bath had lavender in it, and I still can't fall asleep. My body's tired. My eyes are tired, but . . ." She shrugged and shook her head. "Sleep eludes me."

My dick thought of ways to get her to sleep, and I quickly steered away from that. But I also had a moonstone elixir that helped with sleeplessness. I'd made it for emergencies, usually if I couldn't sleep in a busy environment, like the back room of a diner in the Nettles.

"Sit tight." I stood. "I have something that can help."

She made some kind of noise, probably a protest, but I was up the stairs and in my room before she could stop me. I rummaged through my duffel bag and had a stern talk with my dick about being a prick. Lila wasn't an object; she was a human being and deserved respect. I palmed the elixir and hurried back down. I set the small vial beside her cup and sat in my seat once more.

Lila held it toward the light, turning the vial back and forth. The amber liquid swirled, but it didn't spark with ley energy like most concoctions would. Her brow furrowed as she met my gaze. "What's in this?"

"I soaked a moonstone in sunlight for twelve hours. This is about three quarters of that water with a quarter cup of brandy."

I took it from her and opened it. Then I held it under her nose, steadying her shoulder. Her skin was hot and soaked through her robe. My fingers flexed. *Stop being creepy, Nate.* I don't know why I was doing this. She was perfectly capable of smelling things on her own. I guessed because she was taking care of me in a way I'd never expected and now I thought I could do something for her. Except my horny thoughts kept getting in the way. Damn, that was embarrassing.

She took the elixir. "You didn't use an enchanting table for this?"

I clutched my chest and fell into the chair beside her, feigning pain. "I can hear the skepticism in your voice."

"I don't mean to be . . . an elitist, but I've never really put much weight into elixirs that don't require ley energy."

"Don't doubt your resident pleb, Lila." I arched a brow. "It won't hurt you."

"I'm making great progress on your schedule," she murmured. Her protest was weak but still there.

"I promise your planner will still be here in the morning."

Her silvery eyes fastened on mine and a current moved between us. The dim kitchen turned cozy, and a wisp of hair fell against her cheek, begging me to move it. *Don't be creepy. Do not be a creep.* I curled my fingers into a fist and smiled at her.

She upended the elixir into her tea and then drained her cup in three swallows. "How fast does it take effect?"

I shrugged, tearing my gaze from the delicate lines of her throat. "Eh, it can vary. It works best when you're lying down and keep your eyes closed."

"Ugh." Her full lips twitched with a smile. "So I must also make an effort. Very well. I'll see you in the morning, Nathaniel."

"Good night, Lila."

I watched her leave the kitchen, and I pulled the notepad closer to me. My phone buzzed with a late reply from Winkerton. I clicked on her thread.

> How do I get Lila to be my friend? Asking for a friend who would like to not feel like a freeloader and do something for her in return

VIRGIE WINKERTON

> Darling, you're helping her reveal those odious executives at TPN for who they are. You ARE doing something for her

I shook my head. I knew Lila was using me for revenge, but in the last few weeks, the mood had changed, and not just because I found her desirable. She had a passion, and she was teaching me about it, and I was maybe her ticket to getting closure on her past.

> Not the same. I want to do something nice for her. That doesn't involve revenge

Lila had three different schedules for the same day planned out on notepads. Some with slashes through a few entries. All of them revolved around me and the Vineyard. I hadn't realized she volunteered at the assisted living center for the Muted this much. However, when she ran her errands in town, I never accompanied her. Even though one of them had made my life as difficult as possible, it wasn't all *their* fault. It was nice of her to do that, and I wanted—no, needed —to do something nice for her.

My phone hummed on the table.

VIRGIE WINKERTON

> She loves tomatoes and dirty martinis. Give her extra olives and she'll be open to be the best of friends

An idea burned in my head. I opened the digital planner on my phone for tomorrow and copied everything to my notes application. Then I cleared the day. Instead of practicing my pitch or the tincture, I worked out a special event just for her. And knowing that she would be skeptical, I included a backup plan with a backup plan.

Chapter Sixteen

I poured a cup of chai, feeling relaxed and rested. I'd slept longer than desired, but I still had time to drink my breakfast before getting on with the day. Nathaniel's elixir did well, or perhaps it was a combination of everything last night and finally forcing myself to lie in bed and close my eyes. That wasn't always something I did when I didn't feel tired yet knew I should be sleeping. Wonders never ceased.

"Sir Fuzzy Pants," I crooned as I sat. "I need your help."

The veil parted and my familiar stepped from the spirit realm and onto my table. His ethereal body shimmered with spell workings as he brushed against me. I hardly felt it, yet I couldn't help myself and rubbed his small ears before scratching his extra fuzzy cheek. He purred. Or at least, I could almost imagine it. I wished he'd been alive while I'd been a child. He would've been the best boy, I just knew it. I trailed my fingers along his coat and activated the spell working to heat my tea. The centric circles flashed sparkling periwinkle in the air, and a second later, steam wafted from my cup.

"Thank you so much," I murmured as my digital planner pinged me.

I almost ignored the banner, but the title had my name in it. "Lila's big day of planned spontaneity."

"What?" I unlocked my phone and brought up my planner.

Sir Fuzzy Pants sat, his tail merging with my tea. The good side of having a cat as a familiar? They couldn't get fur in my food.

The day I'd meticulously planned was gone. My spine snapped ramrod straight, and a high-pitched gasp escaped me. I knew I'd worked on this. I had this planned last week; I'd only tweaked it last night to reflect the change in Nathaniel's schedule since his application had been accepted. Instead, I had a day of . . . *event hidden by the host?*

Nathaniel walked into the kitchen, humming under his breath. He wore a crew neck thermal shirt that, for once, fit him. His shaggy blond hair remained damp from a shower. He grinned when he saw me.

I flashed the screen at him. "What the hell is this?" I asked, my voice harder than I'd meant. But well, when one fucked with your most sacred schedule, one must know their grave mistake.

His smile faltered. "Uhm, surprise?"

I scowled. Sir Fuzzy Pants decided it was too tense and returned to the spirit realm without so much as a nuzzle.

Nathaniel detoured to me, unlocking his phone, then handed it to me. "I wanted to do something nice for you and knew it needed to be on your schedule."

Everything came to a screeching halt, especially my brain. My schedule, my beautiful schedule that I'd slaved over, and he'd *changed* it? To do something *nice?* My brows squished together as I took his phone, and there were more details listed for the day in his than mine. I scowled, displeased he'd hidden the day from me and expected me to be fine with it. He began brewing coffee as I read it over.

There was biking in the park, but also foraging. Each time slot had a backup plan. At noon, if I hated the park, we could jet over to Arcadia and tour a massive greenhouse boasting to have some legendary plants. Then, another backup plan titled "Lila couldn't stand to have a good time and went back to her original planned programming." I snorted.

He sat at the table with a cup of coffee. "Is this okay? I saved what you'd planned in my notes."

I didn't know how to feel. No one, not even Winkerton, took it upon themselves to plan an outing *with* me for an entire day. Sure, she planned brunches or drinks here and there throughout the month, but the whole day? That hadn't happened for at least a year.

I peered at him from over the cup of chai. "Why are you doing this?"

"To say thank you." His eyes smiled at me. "There's not a lot I can do, but I know how much you enjoy foraging and I like this park on the other side of town."

"I have all the witch hazel you'll need in my greenhouse." I didn't quite get how this would be for me when we'd forage for ingredients that he needed to practice for a tincture.

He scratched at the scruff on his jaw and shook his head. "I know. You said foraging recharges you, and you've been working so hard to get me ready for filming. Will you let me do this day for you?"

"And if I don't like this plan, I can choose to go to this greenhouse or just come back here?" I asked skeptically.

"Yeah, though I hope you don't want to work."

"And it's okay if I'm not having a good time?"

"Lila"—he reached out and covered my hand with his—"you don't have to pretend at all with me."

His hand was warm on top of mine. Even with the hot

cup I cradled, his touch stole my entire focus. His kindness took me by surprise, and I found myself nodding.

"Okay, let's do this planned spontaneous day, Nathaniel."

WE WERE COASTING down Main Street toward Hoffman Park when I spotted Sweetie Pies, an artisan candy store. Since this was a day of impulses, I gave in.

"Stop!" I called to him ahead of me.

Since moving in with me, I'd insisted he replace his bike's tube so he wouldn't have to hold us up every hour to refill it when we biked out to the coast. Really, I didn't want to wait for him. I eyed the basket that he'd strapped to my bike, tempted to peek, but I'd promised I wouldn't. He'd strapped another basket to his, and I wondered once more what he could need two baskets for.

He stopped and looked back at me. "Don't tell me you're already changing your mind."

"No." I dismounted my bike and walked it to him. "I just saw something. Watch my bike?"

His eyes smiled first; they almost always did. "Sure thing."

I hurried inside the candy store, the bell jingling overhead. Someone called out a greeting, and I answered without thinking. I grabbed a bag of honeycomb chocolates and another bag of lemon hard candies that I was positive Nathaniel would love. The man went after anything lemon whenever he could. He even infused his water with lemons. Once I paid, I hurried back out to him waiting for me with my bike. And having a tense conversation with a man who'd slicked his black hair back, and wore a leather suit jacket. Two more men in tracksuits smoked near our bikes.

Nathaniel spotted me and flashed a false smile before he

muttered something to the man in the leather jacket. I approached my bike and placed a possessive hand on the seat, my attention darting between the four men.

"Just see that you do right, brother," he said, then smiled at me. "Ma'am."

I lifted a brow. The two men in tracksuits stepped away from our bikes, and the trio sauntered to an idling car parked on the curb.

"Who were they?" I asked.

Nathaniel stared at me, and I could make out the weight of his words on his tongue. This wouldn't be good.

"That was my foster brother." His lips pressed into a meaningless smile as he gestured at the bag in my hand. "What'd you get?"

"You'll see." I placed the bag next to my foraging kit in my front basket and hopped back on my bike. "Let's go."

I stared at his back as we pedaled. I didn't believe him and wondered if I should press the matter. It wasn't my business, and he certainly didn't want to talk about it, however his wagon was hitched to mine, so to speak, and this was a red flag to cut him loose. Maybe I was reading too much into it, but I hadn't thought seeing a foster brother would stress someone out this much. Maybe he'd asked how to get in contact with someone from their shared past and Nathaniel hadn't wanted to help.

When we arrived at the park, Nathaniel veered off the main walking path and coasted past the baseball field. The pedestrians thinned out drastically as the paved path plunged us into a shaded area with trees, bushes, and wildflowers scattered on the side. He took another fork in the path toward a dense woodland area. There were a few pavilions scattered along in patches of mowed grass with grills and picnic tables, but he didn't stop.

Ten minutes later, he pulled off to the side. A dirt-packed

trail led deeper into the woods, and he hitched his bike to the bike stand.

I followed suit. "Oh, I haven't been here in a while."

"I love it here."

He stared pensively at the trees beyond the path and then me, his mossy green eyes weighted with a decision that I hadn't known about.

He licked his lips and grasped my hand. "Lila, I need to tell you something."

His palm was slightly damp, and his thumb worried the top of my hand. I thought back to those men and frowned, but I nodded anyway.

"I borrowed money from Alex—my foster brother."

"Oh." Weight lifted from my shoulders, and I took a step closer to him, stilling his fidgeting fingers with my other hand. I'd thought he was going to tell me something awful, something that'd make our bargain no longer viable, and I'd been worried . . . I'd . . . grown to enjoy his company. "That was him shaking you down, huh?"

He paled. I'd meant my words to be light, but they seemed to have made it worse.

"Exactly." He swallowed and nodded. "It was seed money."

I nodded and offered him a small smile. "For your business?"

"Yes." He rubbed his mouth with his free hand and briefly closed his eyes. "He's a gangster. Said he worked for the Fornaro family and—"

"You took money from the mafia?" I jerked my hand from him and stepped backward. "Are you crazy?"

"I didn't know he worked for them!" The skin around his eyes tightened. "I thought he was being a friend. I thought it was okay."

I stared at him, half-believing him. Sometimes Nathaniel

had this innocence about him, like a puppy, and put too much faith that there was good inside people. Then a terrible thought crashed into my stomach, and I steadied myself against my bike. "Is that why you asked me for help with the show?"

"No!" He closed the distance between us and reached for me, but he stopped short of touching me. "No, I didn't know where the money'd come from until after I asked you to help with the show."

I nodded, my brow wrinkling as my mind raced over his options. "How much do you need? You can't afford for the network to find out about this."

He'd grown paler and he shook his head. "No, Lila, no." He cupped my cheeks—a thrill scattered beneath his fingers where they fluttered against my skin—then dropped his hands to clench them at his sides. "It's not your mess. I'll take care of it."

"Well, you'd pay me back."

The skin around his eyes crinkled, and a hope flashed across my mind that the crow's feet around his eyes were only from smiles.

"I'm really touched you're even considering it, but I won't take your money." He bit his lip and peeked at me from between his lashes. "Are you upset?"

"So you want nothing from me for this?" I asked slowly.

"No."

"Have you told Winkerton?"

He winced. "Do I have to?"

I blinked. "You really don't want our help with this?"

He shook his head. "The thought hadn't even occurred to me, and now that you've offered, I don't want it. This is my mess. I'll handle it. Okay?"

He'd kept this from me, and while my brain waved the

red flag like Enjolras had in a Les Misérables musical, he'd told me the truth about it. Sure, he couldn't hide it from me any longer, but I also hadn't had to pull it from him. He'd simply told me. It could cause problems for him later, especially with the show, but it wasn't my problem. And I'd offered to help but he wouldn't let me, so what else could I do?

I pushed it from my mind and nodded. "Okay. Shall we get back to our planned spontaneous outing, then?"

Nathaniel's smile struck me. It didn't just meet his eyes and light up his face. It hit me in the gut with a three-punch combo to my stupid heart. He unstrapped the wicker basket that he'd borrowed from my greenhouse and his foraging kit. His basket clinked suspiciously like bottles.

"I thought this wasn't about working." I buckled on my foraging kit and sent him what I hoped was a teasing smile before grabbing the bag of candy and the basket on my bike.

"You're not the only one who enjoys foraging for fun. Come on, I know a great spot to set up camp." He grinned.

My heart fluttered. *Damn it, don't do that with him.*

We walked in silence, and my spirits lifted. Squirrels barked from the trees, birds chirped, and I breathed in deeply, appreciating the grassy trail, damp leaves, and fresh air. This was amazing. Knots unwound around my shoulders, and while some stress remained, it felt bearable. Which shocked me. I usually couldn't recharge with other people around, including Winkerton. But with Nathaniel, it was like he respected my need for quiet.

I guess he didn't drain my batteries as much as I expected of him.

Our arms brushed. I wasn't sure if I was drifting toward him or he to me. Maybe both. Every time, a little thrill slipped through my blood, and eventually our fingers managed to tangle. I should pull back; this was only encouraging him. He'd tried to kiss me yesterday, and I'd almost kissed him first. We were merely colleagues, reluctant allies, if you will, working on allowing me to get my revenge and him to possibly get a show. And yet I continued walking, not fighting him when he readjusted our hands and loosely twined his fingers with mine. He sent me a shy smile, and I became extremely aware of him. His palm against mine, that he had a pretty mouth.

I should let go. Place some distance between us, but . . . I liked it. More than should be appropriate, but I couldn't help it. A problem, since I could get used to him hanging around, but I knew the moment he won the show or he was eliminated, he'd be gone.

I sucked in a large lungful of earthy air and banished the thought. Yes, things were temporary, and maybe after this new viral video and the documentary blew over, I could find my place in Starglen again. Or I'd move east and start over.

He squeezed my hand. "Here we are."

We'd wandered into a small clearing where the grass brushed against my ankles. There was another one of those standalone grills and a picnic table, but the table was covered in berries and bird poop. He walked past it, closer to the tree line.

"That table's always gross. I don't think people camp out here as often as the park thought." He released my hand, set the basket down, and opened it. Then he retrieved a large yellow blanket and spread it out. "You hungry?"

I wiped my hands on my overalls and took a step away. "Sure."

I needed to calm down. Why had we held hands? Why had I let him? Why did I want to do it again? He was not my type: extroverted. Despite that also being a quality of Winkerton's, I was secure in my introversion. I enjoyed self-reflection, and quiet, and spending time with my plants. There was nothing wrong with that. Why did I always seem to surround myself with extroverts?

"Want to sit down or forage?"

Nathaniel's voice pulled me out of my thoughts, and I met his smiling green eyes. I took a deep breath, a little surprised I could smell the saltiness of the ocean despite feeling secluded in a forest. From one basket, he'd spread out some plates, and mac and cheese, of all things. He removed the warming charm from the container.

I pointed at the food. "Aren't you sick of that?"

He chuckled. "You'd think so, but I really like it."

I sat down next to him and passed over the lemon candy. I almost wished I'd looked away when he saw it. His face brightened to the *n*th degree, and he clutched it to his chest.

"How did you know—"

"That you're obsessed with lemons?" I shrugged. "It was hard to figure out, but after I saw you lick the lemon frosting off your plate at brunch and infused water with them, I thought you might think lemons were okay."

He laughed, the skin around his eyes crinkling as his face lit up like a thousand-volt light. Heat crept to my cheeks, and a bubble of laughter slipped from me to join his own infectious chuckle.

"Would it be weird if I saved these for later?" he asked.

"Not at all."

He liked to savor things. I tucked that info away in my brain and opened the other basket. Inside were a jar of olives, dry vermouth, a small bottle of clear liquid, which if I had to guess was gin, and a martini glass. I was a gin girl; I bought large bottles, so I appreciated the smaller one. Next to the shaker, I saw a few Starglen Brewery ciders wrapped in a cold charm.

"I didn't pack ice." He passed me a container of tomato

wedges and the salt shaker. "I figured you could do your ACE thing."

I smiled at the tomatoes, a strange warmth blooming in my chest and taking over my body. "Oh, but if we drink all of this, we'll be too drunk to ride our bikes back to the house."

He tucked his candy in the basket and fished out two bright blue potions with the Star Trails sticker on them. "I hope you don't mind I snagged a couple of sober-me-ups from your shelf."

"No." The word tumbled off my lips like a pile of rocks. "I mean, no one's buying them, so we might as well use them." I measured out the ingredients for a dirty martini.

"You know, I never knew you were behind this brand of potions." He also began doling out food and opened a cider. "I really like how simple everything was listed. You don't hide what your ingredients are. Except that *you* were behind the brand."

"It's pretty obvious why," I mumbled.

He paused, fork halfway to his mouth. "I modeled my business after yours. Or at least, how you operate."

I almost choked. "Why? It's defunct."

"Because it was popping up everywhere. I saw people walking around with the bag or the potion and I knew there was something worth paying attention to." He swallowed and shrugged. "I really like how some of your potions and charms worked together, and that appealed to me because I'm also an enchanter."

"Oh." My ears grew hot, and I averted my face. "Thanks."

"No, thank you, Lila." He reached out and touched my shoulder. "You're amazing."

"Pfft. Eat your lunch and drink your cider." I grinned. "Sir Fuzzy Pants, I need you."

The veil parted like the stars moving aside in the sky, and

my familiar stepped into our realm. He rubbed against me and poked his nose in Nathaniel's mac and cheese.

"Wow, he's quite the cat," he said. It wasn't the first time he'd seen the familiar, but Fuzzy Pants was a handsome fellow. Who could not remark on his beauty?

I stroked his back and selected the spell working to freeze my hands, and it lit up the air in a shimmer. And I made one of the best martinis in my lifetime. Sir Fuzzy Pants moved off the blanket and crouched nearby, acting like he was munching on grass.

We ate in silence. Then, when our plates were cleared, he opened another cider and indicated I should have another martini.

So I did. "I thought you wanted to forage."

"This day is only about you." He peered at me. "Do you want to forage, or would you like to relax and drink with me?"

Swallowing, I scooted a little closer to him. The ground there wasn't as lumpy, I told myself. "I haven't relaxed like this in a minute."

"Good." He gazed at me and leaned back on one elbow. "What else do you like to do to relax?"

"Oh, moonlit baths are my favorite way to relax." I smiled and leaned back on my hands, tilting my face to the partly sunny sky. "The smell of hot cedar, and the night air with the moon and starlight shining down on me, is bliss."

I'd tried so hard to ignore him, I really did. But I couldn't help but peek at him from the corner of my eye. He watched me, a light breeze toying with his wavy blond hair, and my stomach did that dip.

"What about you?" My voice didn't sound like mine, all soft and breathy. I blamed the gin.

"Hiking mostly." His eyes crinkled. "But my new favorite is taking a picnic with a beautiful woman."

I batted his words out of the air and shook my head, but I felt a smile touch my mouth. He was a charmer.

His fingers brushed my cheek as he pushed a strand of hair behind my ear. "You're wonderful, you know that?"

I licked my lips, and his gaze followed my tongue. I should say something, anything, to break the moment. I should get up and head back home, put some distance between us. Instead, I leaned in and brushed my lips against his.

He inhaled sharply, and I pulled back. His mossy eyes danced between mine while my heart thudded in my chest. *Do not apologize, Lila. You have nothing to be sorry for.*

He slipped his hand to the back of my neck and covered my mouth with his. The butterflies in my stomach danced wildly, sending hot pleasure straight to my gut. I swallowed a squeak of surprise. I hadn't thought he would, that maybe he'd thought better of the idea when I'd told him it was unprofessional.

His lips coaxed mine apart, and suddenly I vibrated with every need I denied myself. I gripped the front of his shirt as his tongue glided along mine and I murmured something in the back of my throat. His arms slipped around me and tugged me closer as he angled his head and tasted every inch of my mouth like he couldn't get enough. Like I was lemon candy. My head swam.

I shoved my fingers into his hair, and he growled. Yes. Yes, I liked that.

He pulled me down completely to the blanket, our bodies flush against one another. I tilted my head, and he dragged his mouth along my jaw to my neck.

"You taste divine, Lila," he murmured huskily. His fingertips dipped into the gap of my overalls and caressed my hips.

Holy shit. I was turned on. I hooked my leg over his hip and pushed his head back. His green eyes cracked open, dark with desire, and I smashed my mouth against his. I hadn't been with a man since college, and if we weren't out in the open, I'd peel his clothes off and show him exactly what I wanted from him.

I broke away from him and laughed, sliding my leg back into my lane. "I think we're drunk."

He froze, an expression clouding the passion on his features. "What do you mean?"

"I mean, if I don't stop . . ." I couldn't finish my sentence. He could figure it out.

"Is that the only reason you kissed me, Lila?" he carefully asked.

I blinked and shook my head. "No, I . . . I wanted to kiss you and . . . Oh no. Did I take advantage of you? Did you not want to kiss me? Yesterday, you—"

He kissed me hard, nipping my lower lip before sucking it into his mouth. "God, yes, I wanted to kiss you. I want to do so much more than kissing if you let me." His lips slipped to my ear and his teeth grazed my lobe.

I shivered, and my eyes drifted closed. I exhaled on a sigh, turned my head, and caught his lips once more, falling into him—into the feeling of wanting and being wanted back.

Our phones dinged, and we broke apart slowly, one leisurely kiss after another. His dinged again, but the alert differed from my planner.

He perked and retrieved his phone. "It's an email from *The Next Potion Network Star*. They'll begin filming this Friday and sent the booking for the hotel." He beamed at me, stealing my breath. "It's happening!"

I grinned and high-fived him. He read over the email again, and I felt . . . I don't know. I suppose it stung just a little that he went from passionately making out with me one moment and the next barely noticing I was sitting next to him. I fished out the sober-me-ups and set one near him and upended the other. The raspberry flavor was light and made the potion go down easily.

If only remembering he and I had completely different goals regarding the Potion Network went down as effortlessly.

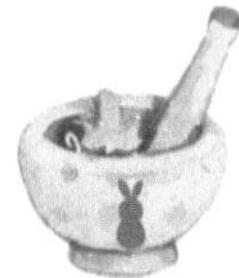

Chapter Seventeen

"Name, ID, and application number." The young man sitting at a folding table, wearing an earpiece, barely looked up at me. In neat stacks, there were badges, room keys, and something that resembled a contract.

"Sure, just a sec." I pulled off my backpack and dug inside the inner pocket for my wallet, silently berating myself for not having my ID ready. Of course they'd want my ID. "How's your day been?"

The man, who wasn't wearing a name tag, lifted his head and his expression turned beleaguered. "Fine."

Okay, he didn't want small talk. I pushed up my glasses and placed my ID on the table. "Nate Pittman. My application number is . . ." I read the document on my phone—I'd had that ready at least. "NP 229TNPNS23."

He checked my ID against my application number and glanced at me. "Oh. The orphan."

Nice. That never gets old. I shrugged.

Then he gathered up a room key, badge, and a contract. "You're in room 107. Always wear your badge when you're not on set filming, and sign this disclaimer acknowledging that the Potion Network isn't liable for accidental death or dismemberment."

"Does that happen often? The death and dismemberment?" I asked, a strange chuckle I'd never heard before escaping me.

The man gave me a million-yard stare. "I've seen some things, man."

"Yikes."

"Okay, so you're a bit . . ." He waved his hands and gave me a small map with an X marked on it. "Get to makeup and tell them you need the 'boy next door.'"

"'The boy next door?'" I glanced down the hallway he pointed me toward.

"Yes. Now move along. Georgia and Owen will want to see you at nine sharp, where you'll give them the waiver. Skedaddle. You're holding up the line."

I smiled at the Black woman waiting behind me, then nodded to the man sitting at the table. "Thanks."

The hotel was the neighboring building, and it took me a moment to navigate the skywalk to where I was going. Luckily, there were signs. I dropped my bag off in my room, which was decked out with a queen-sized bed, flat-screen TV, mini fridge, and a bathroom. I wanted to shoot Lila a text, but I didn't have time to say everything I was thinking. Then, making sure my badge was visible, I took the skywalk back to the studio and headed straight to makeup. A woman with short, spiked black hair dyed to look like an oil slick stepped in front of me.

"Oh, I can see you're not quite camera ready, are you, sweetie?" She flashed a magenta smile and tugged me toward a bank of chairs. "I'm Elsie. What did Trevor tell you to get?"

"Trevor?" I sat in the chair, blinking at the globes of light surrounding the mirror. My hair had a touch more wave to it, and the scruff on my jaw was darker than I'd thought.

"The guy you checked in with. Kind of a sourpuss." She shook out a smock cape, draped it over me, and fastened the clasp entirely too tight—it nearly choked me.

"Oh. The boy next door."

She dragged her fingers through my hair as she assessed me in the mirror. "Sure. You'll be clean-shaven, so see me bright and early every day." She removed my glasses—I hated when people did that—and set them in front of the mirror. "Do you need those to see, or do you have contacts?"

"They're reading glasses—"

"Good. Don't wear those on air." Elsie picked up some shears and opened and closed them a little too close to my ear. "Now relax and let me work my magic."

And by that, she meant cutting my hair and giving me one of the closest shaves of my life. Then she styled my hair. Including a part. I resembled the typical all-American man in the neighborhood, who was probably good at sports and had a long-term girlfriend, instead of a homeless guy with a crush on the woman who'd nearly destroyed a TV show. But that was neither here nor there.

Elsie frowned at me some more. "Is that what you plan on wearing for filming?"

I glanced down at my flannel and shrugged. "No?"

"Good. You look like a homeless waif in that. I recommend a polo or a tight monochrome tee." She gave me another appraising once-over. "Or royal purple to make your eyes pop. And get some tight jeans. This is the 21st century. You don't need to hide your figure. Wardrobe has something like that if you don't."

I left, peering down at my new shirt, dark and pale blue plaid with black buttons—which Winkerton had purchased explicitly for filming—and my jeans, which were neither tight nor baggy, and sighed. I didn't want to change; I liked what I wore. It was comfortable. I checked my watch. Ten to nine. I didn't have time for wardrobe, so I tucked my shirt in right in front of the doors leading to the set.

"A tucked-in shirt will always make an outfit look sharp," someone said from behind me.

I spun, laughing. "Yeah, there's no time for anything else if the haircut is any indication."

It was the Black woman from earlier, now decked out in makeup. The gold eyeshadow complemented her brown skin, and her curly hair brushed her shoulders. She could be anywhere between thirty and fifty. "I barely look like I have anything on my face, but it took an hour." She shook her head. "I only wear mascara when I'm home."

"Same." I grinned and stuck out my hand. "I'm Nate."

She laughed and shook my hand. "I'm Rhoda. Nice to meet you."

The doors to the set burst open, and Trevor stuck his head out. He sharply waved us in. "Have you seen Blake?"

Rhoda shook her head and walked onto the set, gasping in excitement.

"I don't know who that is." I shrugged at him and stepped inside.

I was *here* on *The Next Potion Network Star* set. I bounced on my toes as breathless anticipation nearly overcame me. I was here; I'd finally made it! It was nothing like the show when I'd watched it. I could see glimpses of it in the workbenches and the wood accents and the plants, which now in person I could tell were fake. It reminded me of a dollhouse. The back was cut off with eight stations for the eight contestants. Off to the side was the large table for judging and the occasional tasting, and the lab, where a certified chemist would test the viability of the potion.

Five people wearing badges stood in a line before the

camera crew, which consisted of a handful of stationary cameras and a couple of cameramen who'd walk with Georgia or Owen to different work stations.

And standing next to someone who might've been a director or a producer—he had a clipboard—was Georgia Cauldron with sleek blonde curls, decked out in a slim pink A-line dress, and she held a bunny wearing a diamond collar.

There she was. What should I say to her? I definitely didn't want to come off as a fanboy; I bet she got that all the time and was tired of it. Maybe I should ask what her favorite part of filming was or maybe just focus on her rabbit. Yes. I grinned. Ask about the rabbit.

Rhoda and I got in line with the other contestants. There was an older gentleman wearing a cardigan with leather patches on the elbows with an eerily similar haircut to mine. Next to him was a woman with wild, frizzy hair down to her waist and a wide ankle-length skirt and huge earrings. She reminded me of a hippie. A woman around my age with straight-as-a-stick blonde hair that faded into pale blue wore a soft blue polo and a plaid skirt. She stood next to a tall man with buzzed black hair who looked like he recently got out of work from a call center. An elderly man blew his nose. He had salt and pepper hair, wore a turtleneck sweater and slacks.

Georgia and Owen approached the stage just as there was a commotion at the door. We all turned and watched as Trevor heatedly whispered at a young man with a bun and wearing a muscle tee and leather bracelets. He tore off his leather jacket and handed it off before standing next to me.

Trevor rushed around to the fellow with the clipboard and passed off all the signed waivers. Georgia wasn't smiling; she was the anti of emotion. Someone had taken the bunny when I wasn't watching. Owen Creek came up, giving her space. His reddish-brown hair was spiked to give him a youthful appearance, and he wore a tie over a plaid dress shirt—was that why they frowned upon mine?—with a tweed jacket and slacks.

"Okay people." Georgia clapped, her loud voice ringing through the set. "Listen up. You will be on time. This is not your time. It is mine, and if you fuck with it, I'll let Melody shit down your throat. Then I'll fuck you over." She glared at the dude next to me.

Who the fuck was Melody? Owen coughed into his hand, clearly amused by something. She was nothing like her show.

"Behind you are your stations," Georgia continued. "You were assigned randomly today, and you'll keep to your stations through the duration of the filming. During your time on *The Next Potion Network Star*, you will not engage in illegal activities, you will not engage in illicit affairs, you will not get in trouble with the law in any shape or form. You. Will. Behave as you agreed when you submitted your application. If you do any of the above, I will fuck you over. This is my time, my name, my show."

What? I couldn't have possibly heard her right. Yet when I peeked at Owen, he didn't seem surprised by any of this. I glanced at Rhoda, wondering if I'd heard everything correctly, and she returned my stare with a baffled one.

Owen smiled easily and held out a calming hand. "We aren't saying you can't have fun, but be reasona—"

"Filming takes seven weeks, and one of you will be eliminated each week." Georgia stepped forward. "Just to set this straight—this is serious. Each show will be filmed over Friday, Saturday, and Sunday. *Be on your best behavior.* We don't have time to edit out your shitty personalities because we air prime time Thursday nights. Each segment is two parts, usually foraging in some area, and then you make the potion.

"While cooking, you'll have access to the herbarium for anything you'll need to make your potions pleasant to the eye and whatever you weren't able to forage on camera. A chemist will test for potency and quality, and if the potion is safe for consumption. Then it will be tasted to give feedback on taste and mouth feel."

"It's me." Owen grinned. "I'm the taster, and you know the best way to get flavor—"

"Shut up, Owen," Georgia said through clenched teeth. "If you're eliminated, you'll get an exit interview. At the end of the seven weeks, a winner will be selected for a $250,000 salary and guaranteed two seasons of your show unless you're an absolute piece of shit person who gets canceled."

Owen didn't lose his smile, but his posture had turned rigid. The clipboard man muttered something I couldn't quite make out.

"Okay, here's how it's going to go down." Georgia dropped her hands to her hips. "Today, you make your potions. Tomorrow, you pitch your show. Sunday, we test your potion and one of you won't come back next week. You'll be paid for the weekend after filming concludes. Everyone to your stations. You'll find an apron with your name on it. Be sure you put your damn badge in a fucking drawer. I swear, if I have to call you back to refilm tonight, I'll hold you down and let Melody shit down your throat."

Right. Melody was her rabbit; I remembered now. We scattered down the aisle of benches, searching for an apron with our name on it. I spotted mine in the back closest to the herbarium. Someone had embroidered my name in green thread on the blue apron. I pulled off my badge and stuck it in the only empty drawer before slinging the apron over my head and tying it at my waist.

Georgia and Owen took center stage, facing us, and introduced the potion—witch hazel tincture—and gave the audience the low-down on what good it did for skin and hemorrhoids. It was like a switch had been flipped. First, she'd been hostile, now she was approachable and knowl-edgeable. The change in her personality was so fast it made my head spin.

On our benches, we each had a sprig of witch hazel blooms still attached to the branch and a pile of star moss—the essential ingredients for the tincture. Then a gigantic sign lit up with forty-five minutes on the clock in danger-red and suddenly we were cooking.

Everyone rushed for my station. I braced for impact. And then they whizzed by as they dove into the herbarium to grab the ingredients. Two guys wearing cameras went in after them, but not before one of them took a long pause in my direction while I stared at everyone else, a little surprised. I shouldn't have been. I'd seen this show enough to know everyone always ran when challenges began.

I stepped in and grinned. I'd seen the herbarium on the show, but being inside it was like stepping into a candy store. It smelled like an expensive flower shop set up in a forest. Shelves and shelves of glass bottles of all types and sizes lined the walls directly above bins of closers: stoppers, cork-ers, droppers. Herbs, flora and fauna, clear drawers of metic-ulously labeled—thank goodness I could read them well enough without my glasses—dirt or mud stretched along another wall, and opposite to that was a wing of solvents of every imaginable kind of water and alcohol.

The camera remained focused on me.

My ears heated, but I shrugged it off with a grin. "It's gorgeous in here, don't you think?"

I grabbed a basket, dodged around the old man with the leather patches—his apron read Freddy—and headed over to the booze. There was so much to choose from, and as I reached for the vodka, I quickly changed course and grabbed the lime-infused vodka. Selecting the vessel was easy enough, a no fuss flask, and I chose an eye dropper topper, remembering that Lila had mentioned the Vineyard preferred this for something like the tincture we were making today.

I returned to my bench and saw forty-one minutes remaining, grabbed a knife, and quickly got to work on my herbal prep.

Or I'd intended to. Another cameraman showed up right before Georgia and Owen stopped in front of my bench. I sucked in a large breath and held it, but it did nothing for my racing heart.

"Hiya, Honey Bunny!" Georgia bubbled with positivity. She was great. "You seemed a little stunned walking into the herbarium."

Ha! She called me Honey Bunny. I clenched my muscles, doing everything in my power to keep myself from jumping up and down.

Owen picked up the vodka and examined the label.

"Oh, yeah." I waved my hand—*you're still holding the knife, you idiot*—at the herbarium behind me. "The greenhouse I usually work in is small compared—"

"Tell us how long you've been seriously cooking potions." Georgia's tight smile didn't meet her crystal blue eyes. Also, her dress was far more revealing than I'd thought, and her breasts looked like they were ready to fall out. Usually, not a problem for me to not stare, but she kept subtly arching her back like she was trying to draw my attention to them. "Was it before or after college?"

"Oh." I set my knife down and smiled at them both. Time to play my card. "I had a foster parent when I—"

"A foster parent?" she asked. A low ring of . . . suspicion rode underneath her words.

"Yes." I cleared my throat. "When I was a tween, he showed me what you could do with a potion when an emergency popped up, and I—"

Georgia made a sound. I couldn't really describe what it

was. A squeal, an outraged gasp, both maybe? Either way, she kept interrupting me and it'd thrown me off. I'd never seen her like this before. Then again, I'd only seen her on her shows.

"Lime-infused vodka," Owen said, setting the bottle down. "Interesting—"

"Now tell me, Nate," Georgia said. "What drew you to the Potion Network?"

"You did," I said instinctively.

She beamed and tilted her head to the side. "Me? Really?"

"Of course." I leaned against the workbench and grinned. "You're such an inspiration. We have somewhat similar backgrounds, and you made it here. I felt like if you could do it, then so can I."

She laughed. Owen had a fake smile plastered on his face.

I clasped my hands to my chest. "It's truly an honor to meet you, Georgia."

She preened.

"And you too, Owen," I quickly added on, not wanting to exclude him. "You taught me how important taste—"

"Well, it's darling that I'm a role model for you, Honey Bunny." Georgia pushed her chest forward. "I can't wait to see what you're made of."

Nearby, glass shattered and there was a *whoomph*. Someone let out a startled shriek. The camera crew and the hosts left my station. I turned to see Freddy frantically fanning the fire on his bench while cameras surrounded him.

I glanced at the clock again and put my head down. That little chat with those two had used up a lot of time. I shouldn't have stopped prepping to talk, but I knew, thanks to Lila, that I could still make this tincture before time ran out.

❧

M Y S H O U L D E R S R E M A I N E D tight from yesterday's filming, despite meeting all the contestants officially. I really got along with Rhoda. She was easy to be around and to talk to. It turned out she had one kid in college and another finishing up high school.

Abby, the girl with the blonde and blue hair and plaid skirt, was giving her pitch. I was up next, so I paid close attention to her.

"I'm Abby, and I'm a Beltane babe. I love casting and enchanting, but potions are my passion," she said into the camera.

Georgia and Owen watched from behind the camera.

"I'll give you all the know-how on which humor to use in each application and whether the mellago is a *go* or a *don't*." She laughed. "With me, you can't go wrong!"

Her set was over, and Georgia and Owen exchanged a look—kind of like "Are you thinking what I'm thinking?"

Then Owen stepped forward. "Okay, my critique for you is that you're forcing good cheer. You don't want to come off fake—"

"Too much technical jargon, Honey Bunny." Georgia slashed a hand through the air. "Sure, anyone with a college degree will know what mellago is, but that's not a term used outside the classroom."

Oh no. My shoulders grew heavy. I'd planned to use technical jargon as well to prove that I'd gone to college. I quickly revised what I'd say in my head while they finished up.

"Humor?" Owen cracked a smile. "Some people might think you'll want a joke and not liquid to—"

"She gets the point," Georgia said with forced lightness. "Otherwise, good pitch. Thanks, Abby. Next!"

I stepped onto the X and stared at the camera. I blinked the sweat out of my eyes and rubbed my palms on my jeans. Georgia explained what was needed from me, and I did what

I could to banish the nausea roiling in my stomach. I took a breath, closed my eyes, and imagined Lila and Winkerton in front of me.

"Hey guys, I'm Nate Pittman, and I learned alchemy while catching Potion Network shows and 'borrowing' my foster parent's old college textbooks. With me, anyone can learn to make potions whether you've got that potion spark or not. I'll teach you how to save ingredients until you can get to an alchemy table, because if I can learn in challenging circumstances, so can you."

Georgia and Owen stepped forward. He opened his mouth, but she was faster.

"Your pitch is good, but repetitive," she said. "Try to use more words that aren't the same."

Owen just smiled and nodded.

"Next!" Georgia bellowed.

Well, that could've gone worse. Melody hadn't needed to shit down my throat.

Chapter Eighteen

My phone buzzed in my pocket while I sat on the edge of the bed in my hotel room. Hoping it was Lila, I pulled it out and huffed.

VIRGIE WINKERTON

I'm glad to hear filming is going well, darling. What's this about Owen Creek being the only one who can wear plaid? I didn't know he had a monopoly on the textile

> I don't make the rules. I'll figure it out, don't worry

VIRGIE WINKERTON

Darling, you'll look good in about anything. Stay away from chevrons

I smirked and swapped over to my text conversation with Lila.

> Today went well. How are you?

LILA TOWNSEND

I'm glad it's going good for you. We'll still up our game for next week

I frowned when she didn't answer my question.

Sure. Are you doing okay?

LILA TOWNSEND

I'm fine. Winkerton canceled drinks again, so I'm going to take a bath outside. I'll talk with you tomorrow when I pick you up

I tucked my phone in my pocket and joined everyone at the pub later that night, thinking of Lila bathing nude beneath the moon. I might've been a bit distracted because it took the man grabbing my elbow and pulling me inside the bathroom to shake me from the daydream.

"Hey, buddy!" I jerked free and spun around. I didn't know what to expect, but I'd be ready for anything.

"Easy, Mr. Pittman." An older man with a reddened nose and big earlobes lifted his hands to show they were empty. He had on a basic gray suit with a loosened blue tie. He crouched, scanning the floor by the stalls, and when he straightened, I caught sight of a badge before his jacket closed over it.

A bolt of nauseating cold shot through my middle, and I stepped back. This policeman, judging by the badge, knew my name. That was never good. "Uh . . . What's going on? Who're you?"

He approached the sinks. "I'm Detective Burris, and I've been keeping an eye on your friend, Alex Rojas."

"He's . . ." Of course Alex was in trouble. That was synonymous with being a gangster. "Look, we're not close.

We were in the same foster family for a year. We say hi in passing."

Burris rinsed his hands and grabbed a paper towel. "Sure. I watched him shake you down the other day while your girlfriend bought candy. How much did he lend you?"

Oh, shit, it was happening. My stomach turned. This was something I couldn't avoid either. I didn't know what he wanted, but I knew my time with Lila and the show would be over if I wasn't careful.

"Woah, easy, easy." He placed a steadying hand on my shoulder. "I'm not taking you in. Sheesh, I thought you were . . . used to this."

"Used to what?" I threw my hands in the air. "I was seventeen, and it was a bunch of beer runs. I thought the judge sealed that."

He blinked, staring at me like I was an idiot. "You borrowed money from Rojas. He's looking for repayment, and from the way I saw the conversation go, you don't have it." He hitched his pants up. "So how much did you borrow?"

"Three grand." I swallowed heavily.

"That's . . . small." His bushy brows fused together. "Whitemarsh wouldn't get off his ass for three grand."

"Alex said because we're foster brothers, he'd help me invest in my business."

Burris grinned and reached into his pocket. "Looks like your friend's trying to make a side business for himself. Alright, here's what I need from you. I need you to wear this charm and—"

I backed away from his outstretched arm, not even looking at what he was trying to give me. "No way. I'm in enough trouble as it is, and I don't want to piss off the mafia."

"He's a nobody, but he's inside the family." Burris shook a

pin at me. "I need you to help me flip Rojas. He lent you money he wasn't allowed to do, and having a side gig like this cuts into Fornaro's money." He pressed the pin into my hand. It was shaped like a star inlaid with white crystal, something you could buy anywhere. "You get him talking about lending the money, you get him in the act of a crime—like extortion or an assault—and then I'll move in and take it from there."

"Are you crazy?" I handed the pin back, but he wouldn't take it. "He's never alone, and more importantly, he won't let me get away with any of that."

"First of all, once I get my hands on him, you'll be the last thing on his mind. You're in the perfect position to get me everything I need. When the charm's activated, it'll save everything it sees and hears to mine. Be sure you keep that charm charged. I know where your talents lie." Burris handed me a business card, hitched his pants again, and headed for the door, then he looked at me over his shoulder. "And if you don't help, I'll give the producers a heads up that you lied on your application."

The door swished shut behind the detective, and I sagged against the sinks, staring at the pin in my hand. It was the typical type of charm hidden in jewelry, and like the light charm Lila had given me, all I'd have to do was touch it to activate and deactivate it. I'd have to start wearing it all the time because I never knew when Alex would show up, but one thing was for certain: that pin might help the detective, but it'd probably hurt me. I affixed it to my shirt, careful not to brush against it, and left the bathroom.

It didn't look like I'd missed much from my detour, and not everyone had showed up yet. We'd split off to four tables. Rhoda had saved me a seat, and Marcia, the one dressed like a hippy, waved while Blake, the late one, jerked his chin at me.

"Oh, look, it's the charmer," Rhoda called, patting me on the back. "Good you could make it."

"The charmer?" I asked.

Marcia poured a drink from the nearly empty pitcher and passed it to me. "You charmed Georgia yesterday."

"I just—No." I took a drink of slightly chilled basic beer. "She asked a question, and I answered."

"Oh, don't be embarrassed," Rhoda said. "Getting in her good graces is smart. She barely let me finish a thought."

"She made Cole cry." Blake turned and looked at the other table. "So that makes Cole the crier."

They were talking, and Cole, the older gentleman with the salt and pepper hair, cried into his beer while Freddy consoled him. Abby bustled in, and Blake flashed her a bright smile, grabbing her arm. She'd pulled her hair back into a ponytail and changed into skinny jeans and a Starglen Alchemy University crewneck sweatshirt with "Class of '21" on the back.

"Hey, Abby," he said. "I'm 2019."

At first, she seemed taken aback that he'd stopped her physically. She stepped back and smiled at everyone at the table, then at Blake. I did not want to get roped into this discussion. While we'd looked at the list of professors and picked one for me, I had zero experience with college life. I busied myself by checking the last text with Lila, which was her nice way of saying leave me alone. I really wanted to see this cedar tub of hers.

"Who was your professor?" Abby asked.

"Oh, I had Granholm. He was a real pain in the ass sometimes," Blake answered.

Abby gasped and clapped her hands. "Me too. Oh, my god, I loved him!"

Shit. I'd picked Granholm as my professor if someone ever asked me about it.

"His lectures were so awesome." Abby leaned on the table and grinned. "I always signed up for his, even if I'd taken them already. It's always great for repetition."

Blake made some secret gesture, like a three barreled gun with his fingers, and Abby threw her head back and laughed. What the hell was that supposed to mean?

While she and Blake talked about lectures and secret societies, I guessed, I surreptitiously pulled up the SAU site. I scanned the professors that'd been available for me during my four years there, had I gone when I'd said I had.

I scrolled through the pictures of professors, quickly rejecting people who'd left the university before or during my alleged time there.

Rhoda leaned toward me, whispering, "You texting someone special?"

I jerked my head up and laughed, a little forcefully, and shrugged. "Uh, yeah. Sorry."

"Nate, you graduated from SAU, right?" Abby asked, flashing me a bright smile. "What year were you?"

"Uhh." I cleared my throat, glanced at my phone one last time, and fastened on a name. "2017."

"We were all in college together," Blake said oh so helpfully.

Marcia poured the last of the beer for herself and grinned. "I haven't been on campus since my ten-year reunion in 2020."

"My twentieth is coming up in a couple." Rhoda sighed. "Time sure does fly."

Abby smiled. "I started the year you graduated."

"Oh. Nice." No, this was not nice. Sweat gathered at my hairline, and I peeked at my phone another time. If I screwed this up, Abby would squeal to the producers and get me kicked off the show. "But you just graduated a couple years ago?"

"Yeah. I didn't realize I wanted to go into television until Owen Creek came back home for an event." She shrugged. "So that added a couple years, then last year's casting came and went when I was in Europe, so here I am!"

"You know Owen Creek?" I asked.

"Not personally." Abby giggled. "We're both from Cedar Rapids."

Everyone chorused how nice that must've been. And I breathed a sigh of relief because Abby seemed to like the spotlight on her.

"Who did you have, Nate?" Blake asked.

And he would be right next to her.

I swallowed. "Silver Reid."

They both winced. Shit, fuck, damn. What now?

"Did they seem like they were . . ." Abby waved her hands in the air and grimaced.

Blake's upper lip curled slightly, and he shook his head.

"No?" I rubbed my hand over my hair, a little surprised at how stiff and short it was, and sighed. "I had two jobs. I didn't have time for extra lectures or psychoanalyzing my professor. I needed to focus on good grades and paying tuition."

"Right. You probably couldn't afford their prices anyway," Abby said.

"Ha-ha." I coughed and busied myself with my beer. I wasn't sure what was being implied by that.

Will, the guy with the buzz cut, came over to our table and slung an arm around Abby. He nodded at us all. His posture was stiff, even if he did angle himself toward Abby the most. He gave us all a chin up, then stiffly greeted Rhoda and Marcia. Blake scowled.

"How're you liking filming, Will?" Rhoda asked.

"It's fine." He shifted away from her, pulling Abby from the table. "Hey, I got something I want your opinion on."

She went willingly with him, but she flashed a smile and waved at us as she left. Thank you and goodbye. Some of the sweat dried up, and I tucked my phone away in my pocket. I made a mental note to look up what Silver Reid had done or was like in college, so I would be prepared next time.

"I'll get the next round." Blake grabbed the empty pitcher and approached the bar.

Rhoda smiled at me and folded her hands on the table. "So who's the special someone?"

"What's this?" Marcia asked, brightening noticeably and leaning toward me. "Do you have a partner?"

"Well, it's new." I laughed nervously. "Honestly, we haven't talked about what we are."

"Like how new?" Rhoda asked.

"Like I've only kissed her once." I thought back to Lila's soft lips and the punch of lust socking me in the stomach.

"Once?" Marcia quirked a brow. "Like a peck, or are you referring to a day as once? My bestie thinks a make-out session is just once, but there are like a thousand kisses in one session, you know?"

Rhoda laughed. "Does it matter?"

My face grew hot.

Marcia clapped her hands. "He's blushing!"

"You really like her." Rhoda smiled fondly.

"Yeah." I rubbed the back of my neck. "She's smart and beautiful. Really guarded, but when she talks to me, I feel like she really sees me for me and not my story."

"Awww!" Marcia propped her elbow on the table and rested her chin in her hand. "What's her name?"

Blake returned with the beer. I poured myself another, ignoring Marcia's question.

"What're we talking about?" Blake asked.

"Nate's got a special lady friend," Marcia said.

Blake warmed considerably toward me. Considering how

he'd behaved when Will came over, I was certain he was interested in Abby.

I laughed a little. "It's really new. Nothing's . . . labeled. I don't want to jinx it."

Rhoda patted my hand and gazed at the other three tables. "I can't really believe we're here, you know? I've watched this show ever since it first aired, and you know what? I can really see the types of people from all walks of life."

I nodded. "I thought it was scripted at first, but it really isn't."

Blake chuckled. "I know, right? I coulda sworn there were paid actors for the show, but I don't think so now that we're here."

"Right? So if Nate's the charmer," Marcia said, picking up the earlier conversation from before, "then who am I?"

"The weird one," Blake said without missing a beat.

"Quirky." Rhoda smiled. "I'm the parent. Blake's the cool one."

Blake nodded, readjusting his leather bracelets.

Marcia turned in her seat and pointed. "Abby's the over-achiever and *so* fake. 'Beltane babe?' Puh-lease."

Blake stared at her but didn't disagree or agree. His eyes flicked to the other table. "Freddy's the idiot. He blew up his station yesterday. I bet y'all twenty bucks he gets eliminated first."

"And Will?" I asked, looking at the guy. He had a loud laugh.

"I don't know," Rhoda drawled out. "He has a bad vibe."

"He's rude." Marcia nodded. "His chakras are misaligned for sure."

"He's probably fresh out of the military and doesn't know how to turn off," Blake answered.

Rhoda wagged her head and shrugged. "That's certainly possible."

That was fucking true about not knowing how to turn off your brain—especially since I'd been blackmailed in the bathroom to help the cops flip a gangster, and I wasn't sure where to place my priorities.

&

GEORGIA CALDRON SMILED. "Your potion's successful, but we want to see more from you. Your herbal prep could definitely be better, but overall, it had great potency and a fresh flavor."

Owen nodded. "The eye dropper cap was an ingenious idea, Nate. It allowed—"

"I look forward to seeing what you give us next." Georgia bubbled and pushed her shoulders back.

Keeping my eyes firmly on hers, I smiled. "Thank you." Then I returned to my station.

Rhoda turned and gave me a thumbs up. I grinned and returned the gesture.

Georgia and Owen clasped their hands together and then pretended to discuss our potions and how everyone had worked. I knew that wasn't really happening. I was pretty sure they'd already decided who was being eliminated yesterday, but this was for show—quite literally.

A couple of assistants hurried out and placed down stools. They called us all to the front where they had lined up eight stools. I made sure to sit next to Rhoda, and we clasped hands.

"After careful deliberation," Owen said, "we have come to a conclusion for the outcome today."

"I have the utmost pleasure of announcing the winner."

Georgia bubbled. "Congratulations, Nate! Your potion had the best consistency and a delightful flavor, Honey Bunny!"

Air whooshed out of my lungs, and I gaped at them. I couldn't believe I'd won. I thought for sure it'd be Abby. Everyone was clapping, and Rhoda gave me a hard squeeze. I returned the hug, laughing. It was me. I'd won. I couldn't wait to share this with Lila and see her expression; all our hard work was paying off.

"And that leaves me with the terrible job of letting one of you go," Owen said, a frown creasing his near ageless face.

The air grew tense, and everyone looked at Freddy.

"Alchemy is meant to be safe," Owen said, "and with your explosion yesterday, you just aren't it. I'm sorry, Freddy, this is it for you."

Cole cried while he hugged Freddy, who didn't seem to care.

"Oh, don't worry," Freddy said. "It was my wife who made me come on this show. I think she wanted a weekend to go to the zoo without me."

There was a bell, and then the stage lights dimmed. Georgia turned and pulled her rabbit Melody from Trevor's arms and stalked off on needle-thin heels.

The stiffness melted from Owen, and suddenly a man who seemed human emerged. "Okay, you guys need to get out of the rooms and on your way to payroll. Oh, hey, there's a gift shop too, if you want to get your friends something they can't get anywhere else. Don't forget to watch the episode on Thursday at seven p.m. sharp. See you on Friday. And be on time, Blake."

When his back was turned, Blake gave him the bird. Trevor came by and handed everyone a sheet detailing the next technical. It was about foraging.

After I changed, packed up my bags, and checked out, I headed straight to payroll. It was a quick process, and I'd opted for cash. They gave me around $750 thanks to taxes, and a slip to go with it. I tucked it in my wallet, hoping I didn't lose it, and wondered if I should try to find Alex to get this pin off my shirt sooner.

Should I tell Lila about this? I told her that I'd take care of my problem, and this pin certainly was a way, but I also didn't want her to worry. I'd play it by ear for now.

I was about to go to the front entrance to wait for Lila, but the gift shop caught my eye. I knew I should save, but it didn't hurt to look. Amid shirts, mugs, magnets, and Georgia Cauldron merch—Katie's first apothecary set was here—I spotted a section filled with other merchandise the parent company of the Potion Network also owned. They had an animal sanctuary in the zoo, which streamed live births, mostly seals. But there, in the back, was a wall of dinosaurs, and a yellow triceratops with a purple daisy on its frill caught my eye. I grabbed it; I had to. There certainly had to be a law about it.

After paying, I stepped outside the studio and immediately spotted the beat-up yellow Volvo waiting in the parking lot. Rhoda waved goodbye, and a few others did as well as they walked to cars.

I barely paid them heed as I rushed to see Lila. I jumped in and she peeled out of the parking lot.

"Whoa, speedy-McSpeedy. Why the rush?" I laughed and buckled on my seatbelt.

"I don't want anyone to see you with me," she said.

I leaned over and tugged on her braid. "I'm so happy to see you again."

She bit her lip. I stared at her mouth and thought of that epic kiss at the park, just like I had every night before bed and whenever I had a spare moment to myself.

"How'd it go?" she asked.

I leaned back in the seat and rubbed my eyes. "I won."

"What? Oh, my god!" She looked at me, her face lit with joy. "That's amazing!"

"I think it was because I chose the eyedropper and lime infused vodka." I laughed. My heart still pumped adrenaline into my system.

"Owen Creek can't resist lime or mint." She high-fived me. "I'm proud of you."

Warmth suffused me at that statement, and I grinned at her. I only grew hotter when we stepped inside the house, and I gathered her in my arms and kissed her.

She softened in my arms and melted against me. When she pulled back, her cheeks had tinted with color.

"Here." I passed over the triceratops from my bag. "For you."

Her silvery eyes widened, and she clutched the dinosaur to her chest. "You got me a plushie?"

"Well, yeah. I thought of you when I saw it." I laughed a little, suddenly nervous. "It's nothing, I know, but you've done so much, and I wanted to show I appreciated it, even if it's a silly stuffed animal."

"I love it." She pressed her mouth against mine, giving me a slow kiss that reached down to my groin and made my heart pound. "Thank you."

I stared at her, wanting to ask what we were, but afraid to put a label on my desires. What if she didn't want anything more than what we had?

"Did you get the next technical?" she asked.

"Yes." I stepped back and unfolded the paper. "We're going to the forest."

"Wonderful. I do love walking in a forest."

Based on that smile on her face, it was my favorite place now too.

Chapter Nineteen

We talked into the night. I couldn't believe how much I wanted to hear Nathaniel's voice or see his eyes light up when he mentioned the people he met. He talked quite a bit about Rhoda. It was like he'd found someone that had a vibe he'd been missing.

But whenever he looked at me, his expression softened, his moss-green eyes devoured mine. I felt like the only woman in the world.

I'd never felt like that before, not really. Sometimes, I'd thought I was special, but it turned out I was more of a distraction or a means to an end. Yet I'd agreed to exactly that with Nathaniel. We both had similar-ish end goals. I knew what was ahead of us, and I wasn't barging into this blind.

He brushed his fingers against my cheek, the corners of his eyes crinkling. "I missed you, Lila." His fingers gently pinched my chin, and he kissed me. "I couldn't get you out of my mind even if I tried."

He urged me closer, his lips brushing over mine once more, then deepening his kiss. He tasted sweet, like lemons, and it made me lightheaded. All the worries and nagging voices in my head muffled to soft shushing noises while heat pooled in my stomach.

I felt bereft when he pulled back. It was difficult to keep track of what he was saying. He tasted like summer and desire.

He rested his forehead against mine. "I didn't want to try."

I blinked at him, warmth blooming in my chest and trilling through my body. The tiny voice in the back of my brain tried to remind me he only wanted me to help him win a competition, that he wasn't really interested in me personally. But I ignored it.

"Didn't try what?" I asked, my voice thin and reedy. I wanted him to kiss me more.

"I didn't try to get you out of my mind." He grasped my hands and held them in his. "Enough about my weekend. What did you do?"

Constantly thought about you. Wondered what the hell I was doing and if I really was this stupid. Complained to Winkerton about you and dreamed of what I'd do to you if we'd met under different circumstances. But there was no way in hell I'd tell him any of this. Maybe I'd listened a little too close to that voice warning me about him.

"I . . . worked on my bath bomb." I touched his cheek. It was clean-shaven. I almost hadn't recognized him with his short, gelled hair and clean jaw. He reminded me of a JC Penny catalog model. I preferred his long hair and his scruffy jaw. Maybe because he looked more attainable to me. More like someone I could find comfort in.

"Do you mean you're making one?" he asked.

"Yes." I bit my lip, thinking on the recent addition, and wondered if I would need to update the patent or not. I'd read over the paperwork later, but not now. Not when I had the person I'd missed for three days in front of me.

His eyes darted to my mouth, so I licked the offended area, just to see what would happen. The friendly expression he'd worn, even while kissing me mere moments ago, vanished and heat suffused his gaze. My breathing stuttered. When was the last time anyone had looked at me like that?

"Do you want to see?" I averted my face and stared out at the darkening twilight and the treetops crowding the purple-tinted sky. "It's the perfect time."

Fire sparked his eyes. "The moonlit baths you take?"

I nodded. "Do you have a swimsuit?"

"No, of course not. But if you're okay with boxer briefs, then so am I."

I hesitated. Maybe I was leading him by a yoke to something where I only wanted to see what would happen. Maybe this was a bad idea.

"I get it," he whispered. "You're not sure about me, even if you like kissing me. I can see what you're talking about and leave you to it."

Even if it was a bad idea, I wanted it. I shrugged and stood. "It's not perfect. I keep screwing up the delivery of water, but I want you to see it."

I led the way through my greenhouse and to the apothecary. He chuckled slightly behind me, muttering something about the herbarium missing the absolute charm of mine. My guess was the ley bugs that blinked in and out in the dusk and the soft hum of bees. I opened the locker to my stash and grabbed one of the orange swirled bath bombs waiting on a tray.

"It looks like a dreamcicle," Nathaniel said.

I hefted the ball in my palm and smiled. "It does. Come on."

I led him out back along the slightly rough stones.

Globes of light twinkled in the gathering shadows, banishing the worst of the darkness away. As we walked farther from the house, he grasped my hand and threaded our fingers together. The pine trees framed the purple-blue sky like a photograph, as the first stars twinkled into existence like a wish coming true. The moon wouldn't be far behind.

"This is really beautiful," he murmured.

The large cedar tub came into view. The fern that had been flirting with me had unfurled, and a few wildflowers had also opened; they were late bloomers just like me.

I stopped at the edge of the tub and pulled my hand from his. "It was your moonstone tincture."

"What about it?" He checked out the tub and noticed the drain. He plugged it, then took in the area with the small natural stones closed in by the trees. "This is a pretty place. Is this all yours?"

"Yeah. One of my great-greats was an opportunist." I traced the orange swirl with my finger. "When you put the moonstone tincture in my tea, I thought about essential oils, and I added amber to this one."

"That explains the orange."

"So if this works, I'll owe you."

He smiled at me, wrapping his arm around my shoulders, and pulled me to his side. "Not even in the slightest. So, are you going to cast for water?"

"Watch this."

I pulled the small acetate tab from the bath bomb and tossed it into the tub. It bounced against the corners and three spell workings flashed in twinkling aquamarine above it. The ball rolled around the tub, and a moment later, a pillar of liquid crashed into the tub, soaking us both with hot water. Steaming water lapped a good five inches from the lip of the tub with a rich aroma curling into the night.

I gasped, sucking in a lungful of air. And Nathaniel? He laughed, wiping some of the moisture from his face.

"Oh no, I screwed with the water delivery spell work." I plucked at my shirt and inhaled the rich, exotic scent of amber.

"That was . . ." He shook his head and dipped his hand in the water, then pulled it back. "Wow. That's really awesome."

"Despite getting drenched." I swiped strands of hair from my face, thinking of the work I'd have to do, etching the spell work in the Kaolin clay once it'd hardened.

"You have to look at what you did from my perspective." He flicked some water at me, making me squeak. "You created a soothing bath bomb that will cast the spell to fill the tub with hot water. You don't even need to be a caster to use it."

I beamed. "Yeah, exactly."

Warmth suffused my chest, and I felt a little drunk. He got my intention the first time he saw it. When I'd told Winkerton about this project, she didn't quite understand because she too was a water caster and could do the same.

"You getting in?" His eyes traveled from the crown of my head to my feet.

I shrugged.

He pulled off his wet shirt and dropped it. I blinked, then devoured everything he showed me. My gaze memorized the hard ridges of his back while my fingers itched to roam over the sprinkle of hair dusting his chest to his hands undoing his belt and dropping his pants.

"What're you doing?" I asked, my heart hammering my chest.

He grinned at me as he stepped out of his jeans. His boxer briefs molded to his thighs and ass as he tugged his socks off. "Getting in. I know you don't want to, but I'm not able to let this bath go to waste." He climbed in and sucked air through his teeth. "It's a little hot."

My fingers went to the buckles on my overalls and froze. I wanted to get in with him, but I also wanted to . . . I don't know. I was scared. Kissing him had already proved to be too much. What would I do in a hot tub with him? It hit me like lightning. I wanted him.

"Come on in, Lila," he whispered.

"I . . . I'm not wearing a swimsuit. I can—"

"Tell me . . ." He leaned his head back, and his hooded gaze sent a bolt of lust through me. "What's the difference between your underwear and a bikini?"

"Thicker material," I answered automatically.

He laughed and leaned his head back, his arms spread wide on the rim of the tub. "This is amazing. Shame I'm all alone."

What was the problem? I wanted him; we were both adults, and even if this didn't lead to sex, why should I hold back, embarrassed that I wasn't in the proper attire? Who would say anything? No one.

Fuck it. I unhooked my overalls and they dropped to the grass, baring my legs to the night air. Then I tugged off my shirt. He might have watched me; I couldn't really tell. I also wouldn't look at him in case he suddenly cared that I'd stripped to my underwear and hopped into the tub.

The hot water stung deliciously. But not too much that I couldn't handle it. I submerged myself to the shoulders. It smelled like romance, soft caresses, and hungry kisses.

"I might've used too much amber," I mumble.

He hummed in the back of his throat. "I can't hear you over how awesome this is."

"Yeah?"

He opened his eyes, and the heat in them consumed me. "Yeah. Come closer."

I drifted away. It was a bad idea to get close to him with hardly any clothes on. Who had I been kidding? I would've felt like this in a swimsuit. He followed me, the water hiding his fingers as he reached for me.

"Nathaniel, what are you doing?" I whispered.

He gently maneuvered me so his chest was tight against my back and his arms lightly cradled me. "Holding on to you."

"Why?" I asked, marveling over how easily our legs tangled. My pulse thrummed.

"Because if I don't, I might just die."

I scoffed and tried to pull free.

He tightened his hold. "Stay with me, Lila. I need to feel you and hold you, and damn it, I want to taste you. Because you do something deep inside me I can't explain, and all it does is make me want to hold you tighter." He dragged his nose along the curve of my neck to my ear. "Because you feel right."

Goosebumps scattered along my flesh, and everything inside me tightened. I shifted enough to peek at his profile while his fingers lightly kneaded my ribs. *Give in*, my body said. *Give in and take what he's offering*. I *wanted* him. My heart didn't object either, but that little voice answered with fear.

Fear of being hurt and rejected and discarded like every time before.

He breathed deeply and lightly cupped my shoulder and embraced me. "This is all I want for tonight."

I believed him. If I just sat, back to chest as we were, he wouldn't take it further. He'd never gone across my boundaries, not when we'd first been forced together, and never since. Even when he hijacked my planner, he'd always had the map back to my comfort zone. I dropped my head against his shoulder and stared up at the stars, a vast expanse of endless possibilities, and thought, *I'm safe with him.*

He rested his cheek against my temple. "Thank you for sharing this with me."

I kissed his smooth chin, unable to help myself. Then I kissed it again. He lowered his head slightly. Maybe to make it easier for me to assault his jaw. Probably to see what I'd do. So I angled my face to his and kissed him. Slowly, as if we had all the time in the world, and he kissed me back. I could tell he was affected by the way his fingertips pressed tighter into my skin. I caught his lower lip between my teeth, and he groaned.

"Is this okay?" I murmured.

"I don't want you to stop."

His chest rumbled against my back, and I sighed, pressing my mouth fully against his. I knew I could go as far as I wanted and that'd be enough for him. And when he gripped my sides and pulled me completely onto his lap, I didn't stop. The soft hair on his chest tickled my back, and I stared up at the stars again while his fingers lazily traced my navel. My body demanded I move against him, to find out if he was affected by our limbs sliding against each other's as much as I was. I clenched my thighs, shocked to find my own budding pressure of arousal.

"Your skin's soft," he whispered.

"Your hair is ticklish." Why did I say that?

He chuckled, the sound vibrating into my back, and he shifted. "Sorry, I'll just—"

He made to move me, and I acted without thinking.

I hooked my ankle around his calf and grabbed his hands, keeping them on my stomach. "No, it's okay."

He sucked in a breath. He was not as unaffected by me as I was beginning to think he might be, not by what was hitting my lower back.

He froze. "I don't know what to do," he whispered, his voice ragged and strained.

"Just, uhm. Scoot lower? Like you were before."

He did, and his length rubbed against my bottom, his hips lifting against mine. Molten heat shot directly into my groin, and my nipples tightened. I matched his move. His hands shifted to my hips, and he groaned.

"Bad idea, Lila." His gravelly voice made me hotter. "You're too—"

I grabbed his hands and dragged them up my stomach to cup my breasts. I sighed, dropping my head against his shoulder.

He didn't move at first, but the bulge that bumped against my ass became bigger, harder, so close to the apex of my thighs.

"I don't know if I have the control you need." His fingers lightly fondled beneath the swells of my breasts.

Maybe that'd been my problem all long, at least recently. Having too much iron control, too much willpower that I never gave in to anything that gave me pleasure or joy. Now was the time that I took things for myself when I wanted them.

"Tell me when to stop," I whispered.

I turned around and straddled him, water lapping against his chest. His eyes widened, shock and desire etched into his handsome face as I nestled against his hardness. A sizzling line of pleasure radiated from my center. I inhaled a soft gasp, my lips parting. The cool night air slipped against my skin as I reached behind me and unclasped my bra. He pulled the fabric from me and tossed it onto the pile of our wet clothes.

"You're beautiful." He leaned in and cupped my breasts before dropping kisses to them.

I arched my back, my hips rocking forward. He muttered something, my breasts muffling his words, right before he pulled that peaked tip of sensitive skin into his mouth and sucked. I moaned. His hand skated along my back down to my ass and pressed me against him, showing me what I was doing to him. I liked it. Then he jerked his hips up.

My nails bit into his shoulders, and I threw my head back, a strangled mewl escaping my throat.

He released my breast and moved on to the other, licking my nipple before grazing it with his teeth. I slid my fingers along the back of his neck before knotting them into his hair, giving in to my body.

"Nathaniel," I murmured—asking, demanding—I didn't know. My knees cinched his hips.

"Yes, Lila," he hissed, flicking his tongue against my nipple. "Say my name again."

A wild dash of intense sexual craving soaked me. I tugged on his hair until he lifted his head. Molten eyes like green fire met mine.

"Nathaniel."

He groaned. I crashed my lips against his, and his tongue plunged into my mouth, licking me. We moaned. The hair on his chest teased my nipples, and our bodies moved as if this was the small step they'd been waiting for.

I needed him.

I sucked on his tongue, nipped his lips, and then kissed along his cheek until I caught his ear lobe. His breath turned ragged as he guided my hips against his cock, and despite the thin layers between us, I could feel how rigid and unbending he was. I moaned into his ear and his hips punched into mine.

I dragged my lips along the column of his neck, gently sucking. His fingers toyed with the elastic band of my panties, lightly dipping in and out, barely getting close to my hot center, and driving me up the wall. I whimpered as he slid a finger over my slick crease through the fabric.

He tugged on my braid with his other hand, and I lifted my head. His lips parted; his chest rose with each stuttering breath. He stared into my eyes and rubbed his finger against my clit. I gasped.

It wasn't enough. I needed to feel him with no barriers. I wanted—

"More." I thrust my hips.

"Fuck." He bit his lip.

He pushed aside my panties and his finger swept across my folds. I moaned and locked my ankles behind his back. He swore, massaging my clit, and pleasure clenched exquisitely hot inside me. I let my head hang back as I arched into his hand.

He slid a finger inside me, and I moaned more. I might've encouraged him, I wasn't sure, but he worked his fingers in and out of me and his thumb tapped my clit. Pleasure knotted tauter and harsher inside me until it cracked. I cried out, my shaking body rigid over his.

"Keep riding me," he growled, pulling me closer and his hands caressing me.

Now he ground his hips up to me and despite that, there were too many layers. I rocked forward, and we gasped together. His mouth clamped on mine, and he kissed me like he'd make love to me.

Hot. Urgent.

I reached down between our bodies and slipped my hand through the opening in his boxer briefs. His kiss turned hungrier as he reacted to my touch. My fingers circled his silky hardness, pulling him free.

I broke the kiss. "Take me, Nathaniel."

He moved like a caged animal. One moment I was gripping him with my legs, the next he'd torn my panties off. His boxer briefs quickly followed. And then he had me over him once more, guiding the head of his dick to my fiery center. He rested there, staring at me, giving me one more time to walk away. Something in his gaze told me that if I didn't, if I stayed, then everything between us would change forever.

I angled my hips down and slowly worked him inside me. His jaw dropped open. His breathing came in shallow puffs until he was fully seated inside me.

I exhaled softly, relishing in the fullness, the way he stretched me and how satisfying it felt to have him so deep inside me.

He kissed me again. Water sloshed over the edge of the tub as we gently moved against each other. He groaned, pinching my nipple, and I gave up the last of my inhibitions and embraced the night, embraced him. I threw myself back, and we rocked together. Pleasure spiraled and curled with each measured thrust. He bucked up into me, shouting, holding me tight against him as he slid a hand between us and fingered my clit. If I wound up any more, I'd break apart.

I cried out. His lips smashed against mine, his tongue mimicking his cock, thrusting against mine, and he swallowed every moan of ecstasy I gave him. Pleasure curled and tightened while his dick rammed into me, twitching. He moaned as my body contracted.

Oh god, I couldn't, not again. The ecstasy was too much, too painful. If I let go, it'd break me, and then there would be no more of me left.

"Let go again." He rolled my clit between his fingers, his dick twitching inside me as I pressed him into me once more. "Come for me, starshine."

I screamed as my orgasm ripped from me, throbbing around his hard length. Shattering into piece by beautiful piece. He braced my back and rammed into me once, twice, and again before the sparkling night sky swallowed his rough cry. His arms cradled me as he slowly bucked up to me one more time, and he kissed me. Slow, sweet, mesmerizing. Branding me as his. My soul began to beat.

I'd never be the same.

<h1 style="text-align:center">Chapter Twenty</h1>

A cameraman followed me as I trudged through a part of Founders' Grove that didn't have a path. I glanced behind us and winced. Only a blind man wouldn't see the path we'd taken to here.

"Come on dude," I said easily—everything seemed a little easy this past week. "Leave no trace where we forage."

Tony, the cameraman, shrugged. "It's not that easy for me, Nate. Just keep going. We gotta get back to the parking lot so I can trade off with Marcia and follow her back out here and get yelled at for walking like I'm human instead of a fucking deer."

I faced forward, my thoughts drifting to last night, and the nights before that, with Lila—breathtaking Lila—in my arms, doing things to my heart while her body loved mine. I couldn't wait to see her again, and I'd only left her this morning. Following the sound of rushing water, I rubbed my neck, mostly covered by a turtleneck because while it was cold today, I had remnants of love bites on my skin.

We'd entered a strange dichotomy of teacher and student and friends and lovers. During the day, she'd rode my ass to perfect my herbal prep while I'd practiced making the haste potion I was foraging for right now. She'd nagged me, grew a little shrill, and sometimes we'd bicker over technique. Honestly, the first argument we really got into, I was afraid I'd already bored her.

Then that night she rode me, demanding pleasure from my body that I scrambled to give her, promising her more if she'd just let me come. And when I did, I made sure she wouldn't be able to move for hours even if she'd tried. I never wanted this to stop. I wanted more with her. More mornings at the table while she triple-checked her planners. More relaxing hours on the couch talking about alchemical theory or a new hybrid of a tomato. I didn't want our time to end when the show was over.

Obviously, I'd need to move out even if our relationship continued to grow as I wanted. No way would I let my living situation make her think I was with her for the wrong reasons. Someone in her past had done that with her, and I was already in a murky area because I'd been drawn to her from the beginning and I hadn't resisted. Who could with Lila? She never hid what she was thinking, honest in thought and in words—and her body.

Was I falling for her?

This was dangerous. We had an agreed-on expiration date, well, at least an expiration date for this ruse we were pulling on the Potion Network, but why did we have to stop there? And the pin burning a hole in my pocket. What about that? I'd decided not to wear it when I filmed, and when I was inside Lila's home. It felt wrong. But every time I wasn't on camera or inside the house, I remembered to put it on. Ironically. Maybe I hoped Burris's plan could really help me. Maybe it wouldn't, but I wouldn't risk this show because I wouldn't help the detective by wearing the charm.

"What're you doing, dude?" Tony's voice snapped me back into the present.

"Sorry." I knelt beside a creek of rushing water and opened my forager's kit.

My thoughts meandered back to Lila. Could we make it work? She behaved as if someone was always watching her. And yes, I'd seen the new true crime documentary about Georgia's poisoning, and I'd even witnessed when the public recognized her, how she reacted. But none of that mattered to me. I believed the jury when they found her not guilty. And while I never heard her side of the story—she never talked about it and I was too afraid to ask—whatever it was, we could weather it together if our nights with one another were any sign of what we could have.

I was willing to try.

"Dude, you gotta tell us what you're doing," Tony said.

I blinked. *Well, Tony, I'm thinking about my maybe girlfriend and how I'll make it through the next two nights without her.* Probably with a lot of showers.

I coughed and shrugged. "So the haste potion requires at least a cup of rushing water. You can get this from any fast-moving body of water, like this stream, or even the ocean. Sometimes, depending on your water pressure, your faucet will do in a pinch."

I dipped a plastic cup into the water and collected it. I screwed on the cap, then grabbed a pen and wrote on tape what and when I'd collected it. "Always date your samples. Rushing water has a shelf life of ten days." Then, just as I was about to stand, a rock in the water caught my eye.

I pushed up my sleeve, dunked my hand in, and wriggled it free. A rose quartz, about as big as Lila's palm and weighing barely half an ounce sat there.

I turned to the camera. "This is a great crystal, and since I found it in its natural state, it could mean unconditional love is in my near future." I winked and placed it inside my forager's kit. "Even though it was in this stream, I'll still purify it by soaking it in filtered water for a day to get rid of any negative energy."

The rest of the day went by in a slow, never-ending rotation of people trekking into the forest to get the same ingredients as I did. I texted Lila with a selfie and admitted she was right about not leaving behind a trace. She never responded, even though I knew she'd read my texts.

I sat next to Rhoda, who was reading a book, at the table next to the parking lot with a small cup of coffee and frowned at my phone.

"Staring at it won't make her text you," Rhoda said.

I rubbed my forehead and huffed. "I know. Everyone knows this. But I can't seem to help myself."

"Distraction helps." She set her book down. "I've got a question for you: I was thinking of making pills if it works with the schedule, but they take a minute to harden. Do you have a quick way around that?"

"Depends what you use," I said. "If you're making them with honey, you won't have enough time on this show. Have you thought about capsules?"

"It's my husband's fiber supplements." She shrugged. "I make them for him and thought it might be good on air, but they take days. And he prefers pectin gummies for it, anyway."

"Your show's going to be awesome, Rho."

She smiled and covered my hand with hers. "So will yours, kiddo."

She was right. All I had to do was win.

THE NEXT DAY was making the potion. The alchemy table attached to my bench was small and a little clunky to use. I got my flask set up next to the distiller and had my cap ready. This time, I chose a cork. I even grabbed some butcher's twine and printed out a label to make it cute, like Abby had last week. I had mint on my cutting board, and I'd rolled the leaves up together. I was slicing through them, creating skinny chiffonade, when suddenly, I had a camera and Georgia and Owen were standing there. I swallowed.

Georgia planted a hand on the counter and leaned over my cutting board. "That doesn't look like rushel weed, Nate."

She wore pink, as usual. She'd pulled her blonde hair off her neck and curls cascaded over her shoulder. Her large breasts were smooshed together, and I realized she was angling them at me again. It was easier today to ignore them. Owen seemed . . . Well, I'd say he was bored, but the way he'd fisted his hand in his pocket—tight jeans hide nothing—I had to think he was angry. It was no secret on set he and Georgia didn't get along.

Who did she like? Based on the way she pointed her tits at me, I was coming to the conclusion she didn't hate me. Could I use that to my advantage? I didn't see how without feeling like a slimy asshole. Still, maybe I could do this in a way that didn't give her the wrong message.

"Oh, yeah." I smiled at her. "I learned somewhere that adding mint doesn't hurt the efficacy of the potion, but it enhances the flavor."

Georgia rolled her eyes.

Owen came to life. "It really does, Nate! So does cumin and turmeric. Though I certainly like turmeric, it gives the potion a lovely yellow color that—"

"Mint is . . ." Georgia lifted her hand and wagged it back and forth. "Superfluous. We want unadorned potions. The beauty in them is that they aren't dolled up to look pretty or invent a new flavor, but to work."

She moved on to Blake's station, Tony following her with the camera.

Owen sighed and glanced at me. "Mint's a nice touch." Then he followed her.

I paused, staring at my cutting board and wondering if I should abandon the mint or keep going when raised voices caught my attention. Blake suddenly puffed up while Georgia pointed out that he'd missed the brief on the haste potion when he hadn't collected the right mud. Despite that being very much the case, Blake refused to back down.

"It'll work," he shouted.

Owen stepped between them as if trying to break the line of sight. "Oh, it just might be—"

"A haste potion needs charged mud from a redwood struck by lightning." Georgia dropped her hands to her hips. "Any mud won't do. This potion will fail, and you will too."

"Oh, so you're judging me now?"

"It isn't that hard to see you're not following the recipe."

"Fuck off, Georgia," Blake said.

The whole set went deathly silent. Owen struggled to keep his expression neutral, but he was eating this exchange up. I glanced at Rhoda, who gave me a quick smile before putting her head back down. I decided that was a good idea too. They refilmed Blake's section stiffly and then moved on.

The alchemy table nearly rocked my socks off. I'd grown used to Lila's. She'd said her workshop was over a ley line, but this . . . I think the studio had two ley lines because, all of a sudden, I thought I saw Jesus and the light to cross over to while my body distilled the ley energy from the lines. Then voilà. My potion was completed, and I was soaked through with sweat.

I WAITED at the same bar as last week, wearing the pin now that I wasn't filming. I'd come early, unable to stand being alone in my room. Today had drained me, especially the alchemy table, but . . . I liked people. I enjoyed being around them and seeing them experience the world. It recharged me in some ways that I craved. And I missed Lila. If I thought hard enough, I could imagine her scent as I kissed her with the starshine on her skin.

"Nate, it's good to finally find you."

I glanced over and saw Alex, my foster brother, settling in next to me. I jolted, then placed a hand to my chest, brushing the charm to activate it. The light shone on his slicked black hair and the gold ring on his pinky. The same two men in tracksuits sat a couple of seats down, watching me. My guts churned and twisted into knots.

"Oh, hey, Alex." I tugged my beer closer and glanced toward the door. If anyone saw us together, there'd be questions I wouldn't know how to answer. "How're you?"

"Well, I'm relieved." Alex motioned to the bartender. "I was worried because I hadn't seen you around for weeks."

"Yeah?"

"You don't answer my texts. You sent my calls to voicemail." Alex drummed his fingers on the bar as his eyes roved over me, taking in every detail. "I thought maybe you skipped town, and that pissed me off. But then, I remembered. Nate's a good guy. He wouldn't skip out on me. So he must be dead."

I winced, half wondering if this was a threat. The pin on my shirt felt like a million pounds.

"I was sad. Imagine my relief when I tuned in for *The Next Potion Network Star* and saw my beloved foster brother on the show."

I rubbed the back of my neck with freezing fingers, laughing softly. Go away. *Go. Away.* "Sorry, I've been busy."

"I see that now!" Alex smiled at me and then the bartender, who dropped off the drink. "Anyway, now that I know you're healthy and safe, I can rest easier."

"I'm sorry I caused you so much grief." I drank from my beer.

"So"—he leaned in, giving me something of a Kubrick stare—"where's my money, Nathan?"

I frowned. He didn't know my full name, and the effect was lost on me. I tilted my head, clenching my jaw. He'd suckered me into this position, and now he was trying to intimidate me. I knew who he thought he was, and I'd been foolish not to spot it sooner. But . . . I owed him that money, which I didn't have. And now I needed to figure out how to get him to incriminate himself on this charm.

A trickle of sweat itched along my scalp. "Look, I don't have anything yet."

"You're on TV now. You have to have something. I don't want to have to tell Wonderboy that my sure thing was the wrong thing, you know what I'm sayin'?"

His two pals behind him took that moment to meet my eyes. One of them lifted a brow at Alex.

"I hear you, but I don't have anything for you yet," I said, keeping my tone easy so he wouldn't guess I was panicking.

"Don't you guys get paid for this shit?" he asked.

I let out a breath, even though Rhoda and Marcia just walked in and spotted me immediately. I had an answer finally for Alex.

"Yeah, but not enough to pay you back now."

His goons cracked their knuckles.

My mouth went dry as a desert. "I'll have enough the longer I stay on the show. Maybe a few weeks or so." I shifted away from him. "I'll find you when it finally hits my account." I made a mental note to get a bank account and set it up with payroll next week as long as I didn't get eliminated tomorrow.

Alex started to say something, and I laughed, hoping not to die tonight.

"Dude, it's just the second week of the show. Who knows what'll happen? I'd just stay tuned." And I got off my stool and joined my friends at the table.

Alex glared at my back.

"Who was that?" Marcia asked.

I brushed the pin again, deactivating the charm. "A fan."

Marcia, her frizzy hair tied back in some weird loops and knots, eyed the pin. She probably assumed it was charmed but wouldn't ask unless I made a big deal about it. I hoped.

"Tell Nate what the producer was yelling at you for," Rhoda said, waving at the waitstaff to let them know we were ready.

Marcia released a disgusted breath. "I found a marijuana plant all by its lonesome today, and I rescued it."

I laughed. "What?"

"When we were in Founders' Grove, I came across some weed and I harvested on camera, and the producers said this was a family show." Marcia glowered. "Despite marijuana being great for all kinds of disorders, body aches, and a plain good time—oh *and* legal—they told me if I did that again, I'd be in breach of contract."

"Ohhh, right. No alcohol or smoking on camera clause," I said.

"Right." Marcia rolled her eyes. "Despite that, I've got the plant in stasis so I can dry it out in my apartment without their judgy vibes ruining my weed."

I laughed, and the rest of the cast joined us. Blake was

angry and talked smacked about Georgia and the Potion Network, but in generalities. Rhoda asked about my special lady friend, and I told her all about Lila and what she did to me when I thought about her.

❧

"WHILE YOUR POTION was good and had a nice flavor, I need to remind you this is the Potion Network. We aren't here for enchanting." Georgia's pencil thin eyebrows creeped into her hairline. "So don't talk about crystals."

I winced and nodded.

Owen smiled, holding the potion. "If I didn't need to stay present and in the moment, I'd drink the rest of your potion and rush off for a good time."

"You're an idiot," Georgia said under her breath. "Get back in line, Nate."

I returned to the line of stools and sat on mine. I'd been the last one judged and sure, it'd gone well for me, but not as well as last week. I didn't think I'd get eliminated, but I'd played more to Owen today than Georgia. But thanks to Blake's blow up yesterday, I knew I had a good chance of coming back next week.

"I'm so pleased with all of your progress." Georgia hoisted her bunny Melody up in her arms. "We had some amazing highs"—she smiled at Rhoda, she had gushed over the bubblegum flavor of her potion—"to some disappointing lows. But I'm thrilled to announce that Rhoda's our winner for this week. Congratulations, Honey Bunny!"

I clapped and side-hugged Rhoda. She really had done a great job.

"And that leaves me as the bad cop," Owen said, flicking a sneer at Georgia. "Today, we have to say goodbye to Blake."

As if I hadn't seen that coming.

"Your prep was muddy, but not the right kind of mud. It didn't give the potion that quickness that everyone expects when using a haste potion. Say goodbye to everyone and leave your apron."

We obligingly gave Blake the cool sendoff. Cole cried and hugged him tightly.

An hour later, I was outside the studio with cash in my pocket and searching for Lila's car when Georgia stopped beside me. Melody was wearing a harness, and Georgia had her on a leash.

She bubbled at me. "I see you're into crystals."

"Ah, yeah. I'm also an enchanter." I scanned the parking lot one more time before giving her my attention.

She flicked her hair off her shoulder and shoved her chest forward. "That's so cool. I thought I remembered seeing something like that on your application."

"You saw it?"

"Oh yes." She smiled and trailed her fingers along my biceps. "Who do you think gives the final say?"

I squirmed. "Ah, well, I guess I never thought about that."

Ugh, what a conundrum. Georgia was talking to me, and I could pick her brain. Find out how she won the show, which I knew she'd say with talent and know-how, but maybe that was a canned response and she'd give me the low-down on what to do. But I didn't want to flirt with her. I saw Georgia as a teacher, someone who would nurture me with knowledge.

"I was wondering . . ." She leaned against me, her breath washing over the side of my face. It held the sour tang of alcohol. "Is it true that fire agate enhances sexuality, and could you put a pleasure enchantment on mine?"

What the fuck? I jerked my head back. What do I do? If I

pulled away and rejected her, I might get eliminated next week. Why would she do this? It pissed me off that she made me think about my actions like this. It was uncool and not the way I imagined someone like her would ever behave professionally. Second, no. No, no, no.

I laughed a little and rubbed my chin. "I don't know if that's something I have in my repertoire."

She slid her hand from my arm and over my chest. I stiffened, checking the parking lot again, looking for an adult, hoping Lila wasn't here but that someone would please save me from this.

"Georgia!" Owen Creek, my savior. He sneered at her and shook his head. "Naveen needs you in his office about next week."

Georgia smirked and pulled away. Then she lifted Melody, propped her chin on the rabbit's furry head, and wagged her paw at me. "See you next week, Honey Bunny."

I huffed and wiped my palms on my jeans. That was gross. I checked the parking lot again and, behind a tree, I spotted a pale-yellow Volvo. I hurried over and climbed in. Lila gave me a strained smile. I returned it, wondering if she'd been here the whole time. I glanced at the entrance and my heart sank. I could see it clearly.

She pulled out of the parking lot. "How'd filming go?"

"I talked about crystals because I found one, and Georgia and Owen gave me a hard time about it."

Her lips thinned and she exhaled loudly. "I have to agree with whatever they said. This is a potion show."

I frowned and leaned my head against the headrest. "It was just there, and I saw an opportunity."

"I get it." She reached out and patted my thigh, giving me a quick smile before she returned her attention to the road. "Now isn't the best time for that, but once you have your own show, you'll have more freedom. It'll be expected because it'll be part of your brand. For now, just potions."

"Sure." I grasped her hand and brought her knuckles to my lips. "Good thinking."

For the first time in a long time, I finally had a face to the something more I wanted from life, and it looked a lot like Lila's.

<h1 style="text-align:center">Chapter Twenty-One</h1>

Rain tapped against the window as I dropped freshly sliced lemons in the water carafe before putting it back in the fridge. I checked my phone, wondering why Winkerton wasn't responding.

Shaking the countertop compost bin, I stared out the rain-smeared window. I'd sent that message at dawn, but it was almost afternoon, and she still hadn't replied. Gnawing on my lip, I stepped back inside the apothecary to find Nathaniel, his glasses pushed on top of his head, mangling the gingko leaves for the potion he'd create in the third challenge.

He was already on the third challenge. I took a deep, satisfied breath. It shouldn't have surprised me; then again, it'd been me giving him the knowledge he'd needed to fool everyone. I hadn't seen last week's episode yet, but he had told me about the foraging and what had been said. I enjoyed watching his competition and letting him know who I thought was great at alchemy. I'd pegged Abby as someone he needed to look out for. I was certain she had noted that Nathaniel, despite his somewhat clumsy herbal prep, was someone who knew what he was doing.

The image of Georgia touching him in front of the studio entrance flashed inside my head, and my heart squeezed. There was no way in hell I'd ask about it; I'd sound jealous and possessive and that what we were doing meant far more to me than I'd let on.

I huffed and jabbed a finger at the recipe he should've been paying attention to. "You're pulverizing the leaves. They need to be crushed."

"It's fine," he murmured, continuing to destroy the ingredient.

"No, it isn't. The knowledge boost requires crushed leaves. Do you know what the difference is between crushed and pulverized, Nathaniel? I can show you again."

He lifted his gaze to the shelf I hung some apothecary tools from, and the triceratops's new home, exhaled, and then he tugged on my braid.

I sucked in a breath and held it, counting out the seconds by tapping my big toe. I understood I could get a little shrill. Honestly, the feedback I'd received when I competed on *The Next Potion Network Star* always included that I could get a little shrill. I'd hated it; I hated the winces I got from people afterward, as if they knew it was a sore spot and kept picking at it. Maybe I was being juvenile right now, but Nathaniel using my little reset to quiet me hurt more than just a little. It pissed me off.

"Stop that." I flipped my braid over my shoulder.

"Look, it's going to be fine with the leaves—"

"That's not what I meant entirely." I clenched my fingers into a fist and took a deep breath. "Stop tugging on my hair just to shut me up when you don't want to hear what I'm saying. And *no,* that potion won't be fine, but go ahead. Waste the ingredients and we'll test it for potency when you're done."

I turned to leave, but he caught my arm. "Lila, no," he said, his voice soft and slightly alarmed. "I'm sorry, I didn't want you to stop talking, I just wanted . . ."

I pulled from his grasp and faced him. When he didn't continue, I lifted a brow. "What did you want, Nathaniel?"

His eyes darted from mine and he rubbed the back of his neck, grimacing. "I wanted you to stop nagging me."

"'*Nagging?*'" I jerked back, placing a hand on my chest. "I don't *nag* you."

His brows smooshed together, and his lips shifted in different ways, as if he was testing out words before speaking them and not finding the taste pleasing. "Would micro-managing be a better word for what's going on?"

I had no words. I glanced at the workbench behind him and then met his gaze. "I just wanted your potion to be a success. I apologize. Now, if you'll excuse me, I need to get some air."

"Lila, wait. It's raining."

"I certainly won't melt." I lifted a hand in farewell and walked toward the entryway leading into the greenhouse. "I'll be back before dinner."

I grabbed my galoshes and shoved my feet into them, then my purple raincoat, tossing it on before I stepped outside into the steady rain. When I sat behind the wheel, I started the engine to the Volvo and sent another message to Winkerton.

Are you ok?

Then I pulled out and headed toward the coast. I jabbed the radio, hoping to find a song I could scream to.

It wasn't fair. My emotions and how they presented were valid. I hated that he'd made me feel like I had to hide them or tone them down just to make him feel better about what I was saying. The rain hitting the hard roof drowned out most of the song, but I enjoyed that. It felt like I had a blanket of static around me and nothing could get in, and my head, my emotions, could take a damned breather.

The twenty-minute drive to the Never Peak cliffs calmed me down enough that I wasn't grinding my molars when I got there, but my jaw remained tight. I sat in the parking lot with the wipers off. The water slid down the windshield and smeared the rocky cliffs jutting out into the ocean. My digital planner dinged from my phone sitting on the passenger seat, and I checked it.

Winkerton had canceled our Friday brunch. I sighed, a heavy hollowness opening in my chest, feeling worthless. I really wanted to talk to her, and I was beginning to believe she was brushing me off for something. This was the third date she'd canceled. Then a text message came in.

WINKERTON

Sorry, darling. Auntie V has a procedure on fri that I don't want to miss

WINKERTON

We'll chat more soon

I frowned.

What about RN?

The dots appeared and disappeared. I leaned my head back and let the drumming of the rain soothe me. A few minutes later, another text came in.

WINKERTON

Now isn't a good time

She wasn't normally this vague. I wondered what was really happening, if there was something that I'd done that upset her or if she made new friends she liked better than me. I scrolled through our previous messages for any sign there was something wrong and I'd missed it. I bit my lip as I sent her another message.

Don't you even want to see how your sponsee is doing? You've been canceling everything with us

I pocketed my phone, strapped on my forager's kit, and pulled my hood up before climbing out of my car. The rain pelted my head, and it reminded me of a shower with great water pressure. I trudged out onto the puddle-strewn path, not bothering to step around the wet patches taking me far from the parking lot.

A text went off, and I bit the inside of my cheek. I wouldn't read it until I made it to the lookout. I didn't care who it was. I wanted to calm down; I wanted to stop feeling as if I was always going to be alone and good for one thing, and one thing only. It really sucked.

The ocean was angry. White swells slammed against the cliffs, breaking into sea-foam and charging the rocky shore before inevitably sliding back out as if it couldn't gain purchase. I felt a bit of the connection with the sea. I scrabbled with polite society to find my place, and the moment I made purchase, the tide changed. I noticed some henbane not too far from me, its yellow leaves with the dark purple veins patterning it popped like a bright beacon on this gray and darker gray day.

"You're gorgeous," I murmured, but didn't move to it.

Henbane was a poison, and while it wasn't as common as, say, black bryony, I wouldn't pick it up. Me collecting poison? If anyone ever found out, they'd burn me at the stake.

Despite the small pang of resentment, my anger was slipping from me as if the rain had diluted it. I breathed in the wet, salty air and retrieved my phone.

WINKERTON

There's not much I can do with him now that he's on the show. I sent him a good job on winning the first episode, but I neglected you. I'm sorry, darling. You're doing an amazing job teaching him. I miss you. We'll get together soon. Promise

I miss you too

Should I tell her I had sex with Nathaniel over text or was that more of an in-person thing? That I'd seen Georgia and Nathaniel cozying up in front of the building when I'd picked him up? What good would it do? I bit my lip and slipped my phone in my pocket and returned to the trail. Sex with him was amazing. He was a gentle lover when I needed it and powerful when I demanded it. And, please help me, being held was wonderful. I hadn't realized how lonely and bitter I'd become until Nathaniel began whispering sweet nothings into my ear while he made love to me. Calling me starshine when he was lost inside me.

It had to be that. What else was it? He was tender, sweet, considerate, and demanding, but he never made me feel used the way that Georgia had. His hands on my body, just gliding down my sides, turned me on. Probably because I knew he'd pleasure me until I begged him to let me sleep. I shouldn't let him sleep with me, but . . . I had feelings for him that were more than sex and friendship. I'd realized it when I kept reading his messages and became paranoid about texting him back when he was filming. He needed to keep his head in the game instead of me whining over how much I needed him home with me. What if I ruined his chance at his dream? I cared about what he wanted, and I wanted him to care about me.

It was the last thing I needed, if anyone had bothered to ask me.

I groaned and buried my face in my hands, shaking my head. "This is bad. You've got it bad."

Between the cracks of my fingers, I spotted a thorny, red flowered bush and dropped my hands. I jogged toward it. There was no reason to hurry. I was alone on the cliffs in the rain, but spotting the ocotillo was exciting. A common plant, yes, but usually it grew closer to the ocean, or in the scrubland, and me not having to climb to a cliff was a great incentive to run to this plant. It'd make the most excellent healing potion.

Later that evening, Nathaniel knocked on my bedroom door. I'd avoided him when I came home and hadn't eaten dinner with him.

I poked my tongue at my cheek and shrugged. "Come in."

He stepped in, worry creasing his features, but he didn't come farther in my room than over the threshold. "I'm sorry."

"It's fine."

"No, it's not." He heaved out a giant sigh, his mossy eyes meeting mine. "It's not my place to regulate your emotions, especially with a way that you use. It was wrong of me, and I'm sorry that I made you feel you weren't in a safe place with me."

The remaining ache that'd held on from my outing vanished. "Thank you."

"It might take a little time for me to find the right way to let you know I need a little space from your . . ."

I tilted my head. "Nagging?"

He winced. "See, I knew it was bad when I'd said it. And even now I can't think of a better term, and I'm sure as hell never going to say when you're being passionate, because I like it when you're passionate."

"Oh?" I lifted my brows. "You like it when I'm passionate about herbal prep?"

His eyes smiled, and the air in the room changed from stale to electric. My heart picked up speed, and I straightened on the bed.

He stepped closer. "About everything. The way you let your emotions live inside you is . . ." He gazed at me, hunger burning in his eyes. "Beautiful."

I warmed. From his expression, to the feeling of his words filling my chest, to the desire that seemed to grow the more we loved each other's bodies. I recognized the intent behind his stare, and my body reacted.

I propped my hands on the bed behind me and leaned back. "Show me."

That night, he demonstrated what movie sex was. All tangled limbs and slow, measured movements. Shared breaths and our hearts pounding in sync. I'd even bunched the sheets in my fists as he edged me closer and closer to the cliff.

We fell over the side together.

THE NEXT DAY, Nathaniel was more receptive to crushing gingko leaves than mashing the ever-living crap out of them, thanks to a failed potion. I'd plucked the flowers from my foraging yesterday and had them out to dry on their own. We worked in companionable silence, and for once I didn't feel the urge to correct him on his herbal prep.

"You're doing good there," I said.

He grinned at me, and my stomach somersaulted. Not good. I doubted I was strong enough for him to break my heart. I needed to place some distance between us because whatever we had wouldn't last, especially if he went far in the competition.

"Hey, listen," he said, working the King's seed into finely ground powder with a mortar and pestle.

I turned to him, memorizing the lines of his forearms and biceps as he worked.

"I'll need to give Trevor the name of who's going to join me for challenge six—if I make it that far." He met my stare and smiled sheepishly. "I wanted to give him your name."

I did a double-take. "Is that a good idea?"

He snorted, giving me a look that said, "why wouldn't I pick you" and that made me feel . . . I don't know. I cared for Nathaniel far more than I should, I enjoyed being around him, and I didn't feel like he was a drain on my energy. But I also knew I was a means to an end.

"The email said the challenge is to invite the person who shaped you most in alchemy," he explained. "A lot of people are inviting their professors or a relative. They want the name by the end of challenge five. You know, if I'm still in the running." He shrugged. "For me, that person's you."

"Not Georgia?" I asked, without even thinking, and I could hear the resentment in my voice. Just like I'd felt when I'd seen her come on to him.

"Well, no. I mean, don't get me wrong, she certainly inspired me because her story's like mine." He faced me completely, gathering my tingling hands in his. "But you've done the most for me in alchemy, and I'd really love it if you'd come on air with me."

The thought of seeing Georgia on the stage of *The Next*

Potion Network Star did not thrill me. She'd also have a say in it. "I doubt they'd approve."

"There isn't anyone else I can think of to ask." He stared at me, his mossy green eyes large and hopeful. "It feels right that it should be you."

"What if your connection to me hurts your chances of winning?"

He blinked, his brows bunching together. "Why would it?"

"Because of Georgia's poisoning."

"But you're innocent. You were acquitted."

I laughed soft and abruptly, averting my face. He couldn't be this naïve, could he? There was no way he didn't know that Georgia never said I was innocent and always implied I'd gotten away with attempted murder. "I don't know . . . It seems risky."

"I don't care what other people think. I only care what you think." He nudged my chin up with a finger. "I know you're nervous about all the extra attention being on air will bring," he whispered, tugging me closer. "I would be very honored if you joined me, Lila. I can't think of anyone else to even ask. And you'd get to meet Rho. Will you consider it?"

Maybe I was reading too much into everything Georgia did and I should remember this was Nathaniel asking me.

And he asked so nicely I didn't think I could say no. I grasped his hand and wanted to remember this . . . warm, tingly feeling that seemed too big and layered for something small like this.

"Sure, I'll . . . I'll join you."

A smile broke out on his face and lit up his moss-green eyes. He clasped my face between his palms and kissed me, his thumbs stroking my cheeks. "Thank you. It means everything."

I smiled, waving it off while I tried to regain my balance

by leaning against the bench. Why were my knees a little weak? Weird.

"Besides, it'll be that extra poke at the network you wanted, right? Let them know you're still awesome," he said.

I glanced at him. "Pardon?"

"Oh, your revenge, right?"

I nodded.

"This'd be the perfect time to let it all out, wouldn't it?"

"Do you mean revealing you never attended Starglen Alchemy University?"

He laughed. "Oh god, no. If I get to challenge six, I definitely don't want to admit that."

I nodded, returning my attention to my drying flowers. That'd been the point of taking him on though, hadn't it? That I'd reveal he was uneducated per their specifications. I swallowed, but the sour taste remained in my mouth.

"Besides, at that point, I could win this whole thing and have my own show." He turned toward me and grinned. "We could work together."

Ice formed in my chest and expanded.

"You could come on as a culinary producer or something. I mean, you don't like all the attention, right? I'd be on camera doing all of that and also promoting your potions. It's a win-win."

My mouth dried up and I leaned against the bench, ears ringing. I wasn't sure if I responded to him. I must have because he kept talking like he hadn't just behaved like Georgia had the day before we filmed the last challenge together.

Stupid, stupid, stupid. That should be stamped on my forehead because I was definitely a doormat and I'd *promised* myself I'd never let that happen again.

What sucked even more? I'd believed it.

Chapter Twenty-Two

Early that morning in the hotel room and before I needed to show up on the TNPNS stage, I'd debated whether to wear the pin Detective Burris had given me because while we were filming, it wasn't on set. And Alex proved determined to menace me whenever he could. But it needed to be charged, and I knew the studio had enchanting tables. With the pin in my pocket, I headed down and found Trevor.

"Hey, is there an enchanting table I can use?" I asked once he gave me his attention.

Trevor frowned. "What for?"

I frowned and tugged out the pin. "For confidence."

His brows pulled together as he examined the pin and then sighed. "I suppose that isn't against the rules. Head over to stage six. It's not set to be used today."

Stage six was a small set for *Crystal's Crystal*, an alchemy and enchantment show that was about enhancing natural properties of stones for elixirs. I wandered over and opened a cupboard. It was filled with raw and tumbled crystals, a stockpile of mason jars filled with a variety of reagents, such as water labeled with the time of day it was collected, another jar of ley bugs, still alive from their glowing lanterns, and essential oils. I took the mason jar filled with ley bugs and headed over to the table.

Red and purple fabrics draped along the alcove, and the enchanting table was decorated in gold fringe. It was like an alchemy table, however there were two thin slots in the indentation where we rested our hands. Two depressions sat in the middle of the five-point star. I dropped the pin into one of the depressions and carefully opened the jar. None of the ley bugs attempted to flee, and I wondered how they managed that. I carefully plucked one out and set it in the other depression before screwing the lid back on.

Then I slotted my hands into the indentations and called upon my ley energy. Ley needles spiked out of the table and into my palms. The feeling wasn't like anything I'd ever felt outside of using an enchanting table. As if a spirit needle was piercing my own magic, a more physically taxing use of ley energy. Which made sense, since to enchant, you suffused the item with your own ley energy and the ley lines replenished you instead of being distilled through your magic like alchemy.

It didn't hurt, but I was frozen. I couldn't move, and the draining sensation ran up from my legs and my chest to my arms and down into my hands. The channels filled with dully glowing blue energy, and it rushed through them toward the depression my pin sat on. The ley bug's lantern died out.

Then the ley lines replenished me, filling me with refreshing energy that snapped the sleep out of my head and limbs like an adrenaline rush. I jerked my hands from the table and peeked at my palms. The red marks were the only indication that I'd recently enchanted, and they were already fading.

I cleaned up after myself. The pin felt like a two-ton weight near my collar. Today would be challenging enough without having to worry about Alex and getting Burris what he needed from me. I hoped I didn't run into anyone I knew.

❧

WITHIN THE FLOWER MARKET, the fog had burned off into a gauzy haze with a dewy scent hanging in the air. I peered at the sky, but the underbelly of the overcast clouds wasn't bruised. The production crew hurriedly set up and gathered filming releases to show people's faces who would be on camera, mostly the vendors. I turned toward the crowd gathering to watch and spotted Winkerton. It wasn't hard; she'd yelled at me.

I headed over and nodded to the tall man standing next to her. "Morning, Winkerton."

"You're looking superb, darling." Then she placed a hand on the man's arm. "This is Drew."

Drew looked up from his phone and nodded at me. His phone rang, and he stepped away. She bit a bright red lip, but I wasn't sure what her pensive expression could mean. I could only guess there was something about Drew that Winkerton wasn't telling me or Lila about. If I had to guess, a new relationship.

Her gaze zipped up and down my outfit. "You really do clean up well, but . . ."

I snorted. "But?"

"I think scruffy suits you better."

Rhoda paused next to me and smiled at Winkerton. I made introductions.

"You're giving our Nathaniel a run for his money, I understand." Winkerton clasped her hands around her clutch, which was shaped and decorated like an eclair.

"Nathaniel?" Rhoda tilted her head to catch my attention.

"Winkerton's one of the two special people I must allow to call me that," I quickly said.

Rhoda's dark eyes lit up, and she faced Winkerton. "You must be his special lady friend."

I nearly choked on air. Okay, I did choke. I coughed and shook my head. Rhoda clapped me on the back.

Winkerton gave me a sly smile. "You have a special lady friend?"

Heat creeped up the back of my neck. I didn't know how much Lila and Winkerton talked. When I'd first come to stay with Lila, it was constant texting. But now I didn't see it so much, and I wasn't sure what Lila would want me to reveal, and I . . . It made me nervous. Whenever I got too attached to someone, they always ended up leaving in the end.

In fact, Lila had already started to pull away. She didn't visit my room anymore, and certainly wasn't coming on to me. I wanted to be close, but her body language had told me to back off. Maybe she was already bored with me and simply biding her time until I got kicked off the show.

"Such a frown, darling." Winkerton lifted a hand and waved, then flashed a bright smile at me. "We'll chat more later. I need to go. Nice meeting you, Rhoda. Good luck today, Nathaniel."

I turned away from the crowd and shrugged at Rhoda. "Winkerton paid my application fee."

"That fee's a little ridiculous." Rhoda nodded. "So. Challenge three today. What're you getting here?"

We headed back toward the waiting area, and Cole spotted me. He waved and hurried toward us. For challenge three, they'd paired us up with partners to shop the Flower Market for tropical reagents for the potions we'd make tomorrow. This pressure test was meant to show how well we worked with others and managed our time in the market.

Obviously, if we did poorly, one or both of us wouldn't get the ingredient we needed for the potion. I was paired with Cole.

"I need to get some king's seed and some elephant hair," I said.

"Elephant hair?" Cole gasped, his eyes welling up with tears. "Really? What do you need that for?"

"Easy, buddy." I patted his arm. "I'm going to Tymond's Oddities. I know for a fact his line of animal reagents is humanely sourced."

"Ooo," Rhoda murmured. "He's pricey."

She wasn't wrong. I'd spend most of my reagent budget there, then I'd need to go to chain reagents store to get the other ingredients.

Cole sniffed, and he seemed to have collected himself. "Why do you even need elephant hair?"

I tilted my head and studied him. His salt and peppered hair was neatly parted and his eyes looked a little bloodshot, but if I could cheer him up, things would probably go easier for me. It was worth a shot.

"Because an elephant has a long memory." I lifted my brows and smiled.

Rhoda clapped her hands. "A knowledge potion?"

"Yeah." I grinned, pleased she got it in one. "The hair will reduce the timeframe to memorize a spell working."

"Oh." Cole's expression brightened. "Wow, that's a great idea." Then his face crumpled, and he bit his lip. "I decided to go with an accuracy potion, and now I'm second-guessing myself. I should've picked something practical like yours."

Rhoda clucked her tongue and smiled sympathetically at Cole. "It doesn't matter what you pick, hon."

"All that matters is that it works," I said.

Cole nodded as he pulled a tissue from his pocket and wiped his eyes. "You're right. And if I can get really good arrow catnip, I could get the potion to last for as long as seven minutes."

"Wow." I studied him. He was clever to cry all the time and hide his thoughts. A potion that worked for seven minutes was a big deal. "That's going to be impressive."

"Oh, Trevor's signaling us." Rhoda broke away and headed for the crowd of the other contestants.

Cole and I followed. We halted at the back of the group.

"Each pair will have their own cameraman," Trevor said in a no-nonsense tone. "If you do anything inappropriate or destroy public property, Georgia will let Melody shit down your throat."

Cole sighed. "Why does he have to be so vulgar?"

Georgia, wearing a white jacket with bunny ears on the hood, rose from a chair and snapped her fingers at Owen to follow her. He was in a suit and tie.

She stood on an X made of tape and smiled at the camera. "Okay, Honey Bunnies! You have thirty minutes to shop. Once we return to the herbarium, you'll have an additional thirty minutes to cook. Alright, on your mark, get ready, and hop your tails off!"

I snagged Cole's jacket and hurried off to Tymond's. His shop was on the upside of the market, three blocks over from our starting point. We'd agreed to hit his store first since it was the farthest away from the starting point. I jogged past a flower shop that had its doors opened, their sweet floral scent bringing a smile to my face. Maybe I should get Lila some flowers. But I quickly dismissed the idea; it wasn't something she'd like, and I wouldn't use gifts as a bribe to forgive me.

We got in and, thankfully, it was mostly empty. None of the reagents were out on display, however. There were posters of some potions made with them and store merchandise. You either ordered ahead and the package was bagged and waiting for you, or you picked it out at the kiosk by the register and they went into the back to collect it. The store owner, Tymond, was already waiting for me at the register.

And for once, I felt like a baller as I strode through the roped-off lane to the polished wood counters. "I need two pinches of elephant hair, please."

Tymond made a show of checking stock before gliding to the back room and returning with a small tray holding strands of wiry black hair on a white cloth. With tweezers, he lifted them to me, one hand cupped under them. "Do they meet your specifications?"

"Yes, thank you."

He dropped them in a glass jar, wrapped it in tissue, and placed it in the purple bag with "Tymond's Oddities" embossed in gold foil. I'd keep that bag for the rest of my life. Then I paid for it without making any deals or begging for a discount. We were burning up time, so I hurried for the door.

"Sir!" Tymond yelled, waving something at me. He sniffed. "Your phone."

My ears burned. "Thanks, man."

Bag and phone in hand, I stepped out and glanced at the time. "Okay, we have nineteen minutes to run to the emporium and—Whoa, why are you crying?"

Tony, our cameraman, stepped closer and aimed the lens at Cole. "Will you explain in direct statements why you're upset?"

Cole wiped his eyes but continued to cry. "I just hate zoos, and I know they help provide humanely collected ingredients, but . . ."

It took a lot to keep my face neutral when he started explaining. I stepped out of the shot and frowned at my watch when I heard someone trying to get my attention. It was Alex, backed up with his friends in tracksuits. I tightly clutched the braided handles of my bag. How did he even know I'd be here today? I tried to pretend I didn't see him even though I knew there'd be a chance. But with Tony and Cole so close by, it felt too risky to talk with him. I checked to see if I had my wallet because I'd almost left it behind at the set earlier today. Then I patted for my phone. That was there; I knew it was there. I'd take any excuse not to talk to Alex while filming a show. If the Potion Network found out I owed the Fornaro family money, I doubt they'd give me a show any time soon.

"Nate, my brother!" Alex whispered-yelled and waved.

Damn it. Cole was still interviewing, and I didn't see Winkerton anywhere. I pretended to scratch my neck as I approached him and brushed the pin to activate the recording enchantment.

Alex eyed the bag in my hands and flicked a toothpick to the decorative pavers. "Looks like things are still going pretty well for you on the show. I caught your last episode. Too bad on that potion. Wonderboy wants you to keep your head in the game."

One of his friends looked askance at Alex, his brows lowered.

I swallowed heavily. They were watching the shows? Icy beads of sweat dripped down my spine, and I swallowed again. "I mean to."

"Because if you don't"—Alex smiled as if he wasn't purposefully scaring the shit out of me—"we'll have to demand full payment now instead of letting you play host on the TV and bring in more money."

Wait, what? I never agreed to that. The fact that I didn't even have a bank account, let alone a positive balance, shone vividly in my brain. I didn't have enough to pay him back today or after I got paid on Sunday. I forced a smile. "Then you're jeopardizing that right now."

Alex waved a hand, stepping back. "Just wanted you to know my whole family's rooting for you, Nate."

Cole stopped beside me, wanly smiling at Alex. "Who's this?"

Tony was pointing the camera at us. Oh, shit. I should give Cole the finger so the footage wouldn't be usable, but that'd only make the man cry more.

"We don't have time!" I spun Cole around and slapped his back. "We gotta hurry to the emporium!"

WE'D BARELY HIT our mark. No thanks to needing to console Cole at every turn, but that hadn't stressed me out, not today. As I sat at the pub and had a trio of carne asada tacos with Rhoda and Marcia, I wondered if anyone saw me with Alex and what I'd do if anyone asked about him.

Had I moved far enough away from the interview to not be filmed while Alex had shaken me down for money and then gave me that threat? Had Tony or anyone else on the crew asked him to sign the filming waivers? Would Alex *want* to be seen on TV? If his boss, Jerry Wonderboy something or another, was rooting for me, how much did everyone in that "family" know about me and what I was doing? Was this pin only going to get me in more trouble with the Fornaros than owing them money? Why were they so tough about the three grand? It felt like such a small number to me that a crime family like them probably didn't even notice that much. Or they snorted that much in a night. I didn't know any of them —I'd hardly kept in touch with Alex after high school.

That'd been what got me into this mess, because I'd thought it'd been safe when he'd offered to help.

"Hey, how're those tacos?" Marcia asked. "It only looks like a bunch of cilantro and a couple pieces of meat."

"They're really good." I wiped my fingers on a napkin. "The hot sauce is tasty."

"So, that woman this morning?" Rhoda lifted her cocktail glass and brought the tiny straws close to her mouth. "She wasn't your special lady friend?"

"Ooo." Marcia grinned. "You met Nate's special lady friend?"

I'd barely spoken about Lila and definitely not by name after the rose quartz incident. I shoved half the taco in my mouth, shaking my head.

Rhoda wagged her brows. "She called him Nathaniel and paid his application fee."

"Wait." Marcia set her fork down in her mac and cheese, and by my discerning eye, the sauce was too runny. "You're screwing your sponsor? Is that wise?"

"What?" I almost choked on a piece of cilantro. "No, no. I never said we were screwing."

"But your sponsor?" Marcia pressed.

"No! Li—She's not my sponsor, she's . . . my special friend, and she isn't sponsoring me. She's . . . She's more than that, okay?"

"What's her name?" Rhoda asked.

"Look, it's new between us, and I really admire her, but I don't want to put any pressure on her to commit to whatever we're doing. I just want to keep it close to the chest, alright?" I lifted my head and watched them, desperately hoping they'd drop it.

Rhoda reached across the table and patted my hand. "I think that's sweet. You must really like her."

I did. I thought about her constantly, and I missed her. Damn, did I miss her, especially when she'd started to withdraw sometime a few days ago. Tugging on her hair had been a mistake, and she'd accepted my apology. I'd never done it again afterward. But something else had happened, and I wished I knew what I'd said or done to push her away because I wanted . . . I don't know.

"I think you need to sit in nature and commune with your spirit to find out where your heart lies," Marcia said.

The thing is, I didn't think I needed to search farther than Lila.

Chapter Twenty-Three

I pulled open the door to Brew & Chew and glanced around for Winkerton. Usually, she waited for me in the lobby, but today she wasn't here. Odd, but no biggie. Maybe I was earlier than normal. I stepped closer to the dining room and scanned the diners. I could spot those victory curls from ten yards away.

"I'm here with her," I said to the hostess before she could ask me what the heck I was doing.

As I cut through the tables toward hers, I frowned. There was a man sitting with Winkerton. A leather jacket draped on the back of his chair, and he'd swept his hair back in a way that made me think of Elvis Presley, but low-key. As If he wasn't trying to draw attention to himself. Classically handsome.

He glanced up, his brows lifting as if he was about to ask if he could help me when Winkerton gasped.

"Lila!" Her baby blues darted between me and him as the color drained from her porcelain face. "What're you doing here, darling?"

"It's brunch?" I stared at her, my fingers curling around

the back of the chair, but I couldn't pull it out to sit. I peeked at the man, then back at my best friend.

She pursed her apple-red lips. "I thought I canceled . . ."

My shoulders tightened and hitched to my ears. Had he been who Winkerton had been canceling our dates for all along? She'd met someone and hadn't yet told me. Well, that was fine. I hadn't told her about Nathaniel yet, though I'd planned to talk about it today. But this was strange. She was shooting looks at him as if he knew what she meant, and if this was new then, why would . . .?

He smiled, dabbed his mouth with a napkin, and stood. "Well, since Vee isn't going to introduce me, then I suppose I can."

"Vee?" I shifted my focus to her.

Winkerton wouldn't meet my gaze; it remained glued to the eclair-shaped clutch I'd given to her for her birthday.

"I'm Drew Duke. Vee's fiancé." He thrust his hand out. "Honestly, I thought you hated me because you kept canceling, but I'm real pleased to finally meet you. She talks about you constantly."

Fiancé? I shook his hand numbly, a dreadful smile pulling my lips back to my ears. He said something else. I heard forest and liaison, but I stared at Winkerton until she looked up at me with guilty eyes. Then I dropped my gaze to her left hand and the huge rock that sat snug on her ring finger. A ruby-studded band hoisted a setting of diamonds surrounding a ruby. It suited Winkerton perfectly, considering red was her favorite color. It must've cost a small fortune. My heart dislodged from my chest and slowly sank into my stomach. The rest of me threatened to fall to the floor, but I'd managed to keep myself upright.

"This isn't what it looks like," Winkerton whispered.

Drew sat, cocking his head curiously between us. "What doesn't this look like?"

"Lila, if you'd sit, I can explain everything." Winkerton half-rose from her chair, her napkin falling from her polka dotted skirt as she gestured to the chair I'd gripped.

I swallowed a painful lump in my throat, my sinuses and the tip of my nose burning, and stepped backward. "You know, uhm." My lower lip trembled, and I quickly pinched it with my teeth. "I'm an idiot." I laughed—loud and shrill. People were watching me. "I totally forgot I have to administer some medicine this afternoon at the Vineyard. I gotta hurry before I'm late."

I spun and speed-walked as fast as I could out of the bistro. Winkerton might've called after me, but I wouldn't turn back. Once outside, I darted around the building into a side alley and covered my mouth.

Winkerton was engaged, and I hadn't even known she was dating anyone seriously. Tears spilled down my cheeks, and I clenched my eyes closed, trying to be quiet, hoping no one would see me. Why hadn't she felt she could tell me she was in love with someone? Or at least that she was seriously seeing someone? Why hadn't she felt it safe to confide in me? What was it about me that always put people off? Was Drew why I hadn't been able to talk to my best friend ever since this nonsense with the Potion Network started?

I sobbed. Oh god, I couldn't stop crying. It was getting worse. I bowed my head and shuffled farther down the side path between buildings and tripped over empty flower pots. My knees barked against the damp concrete, and sharp heat radiated into my bones. It was too much; this was too much. I was a camel, and that was the last straw that broke my back.

Covering my face with my hands, I did everything I could to bawl and remain quiet. My feelings were too big for the space I was allowed, and I knew—I just knew—this would hurt me further if I took up more room.

A noise that'd been drifting toward me grew clear. A soft shutter. I lifted my head to see a few people at the end of the path, pointing their phones at me. It was too much. If I'd been any other person, they would've ignored me. Maybe, maybe if someone was feeling charitable, they would've asked if I was okay. But I was the reviled Lila Townsend who'd always refused to cry in front of these vultures, and they captured the moment to share with the entirety of Starglen.

The ache in my knees faded, and I clenched my fists. Fire licked through my veins and flared inside my brain. Honestly, if I wasn't so aware that fire was outside my casting talent, I would've believed I'd channeled ley energy to roast these assholes.

I snatched up an empty planter and threw it at them. "Go away! Leave me alone!"

One person skipped backward, then left. The other remained, taking more photos. Probably a video. I wasn't a lucky person.

I threw another planter at them. "Is this what you've been waiting for?" I shrieked. *Shush, don't raise your voice.* I ignored my own advice. "Is this making you feel better about your-selves, you damned vultures? Well, here I am! I hope you're satisfied."

The person lowered their phone and, for a horrifying moment, I thought they were going to come to me. They took off instead, probably heading to the nearest tabloid to make their quick buck off my distress.

The energy it took to maintain my emotions sagged out of me like the air from a sad balloon. I'd only made it worse, and the timing for this had been perfect. I felt as fragile as cracked glass, and I feared that I'd lost most of my strength today.

I wiped my face and took a few calming breaths. The best

I could do now was pick myself up and go home. I needed to reexamine my options, really consider what was important, and carry that as close to my chest as possible.

I also needed to call my mother about withdrawing funds from my trust to move to the east coast.

"You idiot," I whispered.

That spanned a lot of things: believing I was worth something to the public, throwing flower pots at those people filming me—it'd only make things worse and I'd see those clips for years now. But mostly, it was stark clarity of how much value people closest to me had placed in me. Why would Winkerton have told me anything when I hadn't even hinted that something more was brewing between me and Nathaniel? Of course, she didn't feel as if she could confide in me. Had we lost something between us and I had been too caught up in my drama to notice?

I cleared my throat, but the painful tightness remained. No. None of this was my fault. Why didn't she think she could tell me, to include me in this special moment of hers? Did I no longer fit into her life? I pushed to my feet, my knees throbbing and radiating pain up my thighs and down to my shins.

I squared my shoulders and took a few deep breaths. I'd tried to talk with her every day. She canceled brunch and wouldn't engage me in conversations when I told her I wanted to talk with her. Winkerton hid this from me on purpose, and her expression told me she knew exactly what she was doing.

My phone was going off. What alarm was that?

I pulled it out and found that it was my ringtone and Winkerton was calling me. I almost declined it, but I knew this was serious. Winkerton—and I suspected everyone of a certain age—hated talking on the phone. She was reaching out and, fool that I was, couldn't deny her. Instead, I placed it to my ear and . . . said nothing.

"Lila? Are you there?" Winkerton said after a few beats of silence between us. A toilet flushed in the background. "Lila, I'm sorry. Will you let me explain?"

I pulled in a deep breath, willing my emotions to calm down.

"Oh, darling. Are you okay? Did something else happen? Why didn't you answer sooner?"

Did something else *happen?* I scoffed, eyeing the cracked planters on the pavement. And what did she mean by answering sooner? I frowned, wiping at my face, and sniffled. I dropped my forehead into my palm and huffed. Pathetic.

"I'm so sorry." Her fervent voice cracked. "I'm so sorry I hurt you. Please. Let me explain. I'll tell you everything."

"Sure." I cleared my throat; it was a little looser now. "But not today. I . . . I don't think I can listen today."

"I understand," she whispered. "Shall I come by tomorrow for drinks?"

"Will you actually keep the appointment if I schedule it?" I knew I sounded like a brat, but I didn't apologize for it.

"I deserved that, and I'll give you extra olives when I make you that extra dirty martini tomorrow."

I snorted. "Let me text you later when a good time is, especially if Nathaniel made it through this round of elimination."

"I understand." There was a pause, a shaky inhalation of explanations promising to come. "Listen, Lila, this is—"

"I'm sorry, Winkerton. I just can't listen right now. I'm— I'm too upset, but we'll definitely talk later this week, okay?"

I hung up before she could respond and took in deep, calming breaths and slowly released each one. There were two missed calls and a voicemail from Winkerton. Those must've happened while I had my . . . special moment.

I trudged back to my car, my knees protesting with each step. I wasn't surprised to find my overalls were stained with blood; it'd been quite the fall. But this time, I wished I'd splurged on the parking garage so I could get out of the Flower Market as soon as possible. Then again, with filming going on here today, I doubted I would've found a spot.

I unlocked my door and slid into the driver's seat and sighed. I leaned over the steering wheel and closed my eyes. I wondered how today could get worse and decided my brain was doing me no favors. Once I got home, I'd have an edible and take a day off from being me.

At least the mystery over why Winkerton always canceled brunch was finally solved.

Chapter Twenty-Four

The next day, I came back to the studio to find that the crew had rearranged our work stations overnight so we could cook with our partner. My head ached slightly from too much cider last night and never getting a response from Lila. She hadn't even read my messages.

Something uneasy opened in my stomach over that. I could almost always count on a text from her in the morning wishing me luck. And to remind me of what herbal prep was supposed to look like. It was kind of cute, because first it'd been pictures of small bowls filled with reagents. Then the last two times had been selfies of her holding a bowl, a shy smile on her luscious lips.

But now she hadn't opened her texts from me at all. Maybe she'd turned off sending read receipts, wanting time to think of what to say or reply. But for what reason? I'd pored over the planner, noting that she'd had a brunch date with Winkerton yesterday. Those two could drink and chat for hours without even thinking of the outside world.

It made me a little jealous, considering the only person

who had recently texted me was Emily. She'd sent a picture of Katie and her grandma, who was proudly sporting green hair from the tonic Katie had made. Funny how I replaced my lost phone so I could still keep in touch with everyone and no one would contact me.

Rhoda grinned at me. "You're hung over. I told you to drink water."

"Elsie gave me a hard time too." I swiped a hand over my impossibly smooth jaw, a little cakey from makeup. "I have to wear concealer because, according to her, I've got travel trunks under my eyes. This stuff is heavy."

She pursed her lips and nodded. "It can be. Especially this stuff."

Cole sauntered up to me, fresh-eyed, but the way he dry washed his hands made my head throb. He was nervous, maybe panicking about today's potion, maybe just being Cole. I didn't know. Today, he wouldn't cry, not if I could help it.

"Hey buddy." I smiled and gently patted his shoulder. "Sleep okay?"

"Oh yeah. The beds at the hotel are nice." He took in the changes to the set and the dry washing intensified. "They moved us."

Perhaps change terrified Cole and that was why he was so sensitive. If that was true, he was immensely brave coming on *The Next Potion Network Star* because he'd have to deal with change on a constant daily basis.

He would eventually get used to this overwhelming pace, especially if he won. I mentally shook my head, a little upset that I'd diminished Cole's abilities because he was sensitive. Just because he could cry at the drop of a hat didn't mean he was incompetent.

I retrieved my glasses from the front pocket of my button-down shirt and slipped them on. "I need to read this thing before we really start." Then I pulled out my recipe for the knowledge boost potion I'd make today. Obviously, I'd need to get my herbal prep down as soon as possible so I wouldn't lose time from keeping Cole on the level he needed to make his potion.

"You look real smart with glasses," he said.

I snorted. "I had to fail a test to get these."

A smile broke over Cole's face and he chuckled. "I never thought of it like that."

Rhoda laughed and he blinked. More of the contestants milled onto the stage. Will glared at us as he tugged Abby toward the work benches. Marcia wandered over, an easy smile on her face and her hooded eyes a touch bloodshot. I wasn't the only one with a hangover, but she, at least, was dealing with it.

Trevor blew a whistle and strode out onto the set, tightly clutching a clipboard. "Okay, people!" He blew his whistle again when no one stood to attention. "People! As some of you might have noticed, things have changed temporarily on stage. We moved stations together and placed your and your partner's aprons on the benches. Get to them now."

Cole startled, and I slung an arm around his shoulders and we buddy-walked to our stations. At least I was still staying near the herbarium. I spotted ours easily enough thanks to the fancy purple bag from Tymond's Oddities. I was glad I hadn't lost it. Yet. That was in our favor. Seconds literally meant the difference in a failed potion today. I tied my apron on.

Georgia and Owen stepped onto the stage. Owen wore a shirt similar to mine, and my neck heated. I should've listened to Elsie when she'd warned me away from plaid.

"Listen up, Honey Bunnies," Georgia snapped. "You've got thirty minutes to cook, and we strongly advise you take some of that time for presentation. Some of your potions look like a five-year-old cooked them, and if I have to pretend to like the look of one of your ugly potions one more time, I'm going to make Melody shit down your throat."

Cole's mouth puckered.

I leaned over and whispered, "How many times do you think Melody's pooped in someone's mouth?"

He gagged—not the reaction I'd hoped for.

Owen rolled his eyes and angled away from her. "Presentation is something you all need to consider in challenges going forward."

I went through what was available in the herbarium in my head while Georgia and Owen repeated a TV-friendly version of what they'd said for the cameras. I needed to get my herbal prep done as soon as possible, help Cole stay on track while brewing my own potion, and make it pretty. In thirty minutes. No sweat.

Thirteen minutes later, I had crushed two handfuls of gingko leaves and deposited that into a bowl. I mashed the pestle into the King's seeds, the tropical ingredient I'd picked up in the emporium with Cole, glowering at the elephant hair and the vial of rainwater collected from dawn trees. Pretty soon, I'd need to distill my dry ingredients in the brandy, then activate them all on the alchemy table with the dawn tree water. Not to mention I needed to make a label.

I glanced over at the cricut machine, frowning. How long was Abby going to monopolize that? I peered at the pink gradient bottle I chose, coming up with a backup plan if Abby never gave up the machine. There was just one of those cutting machines, yet a ton of mini label makers, but those only did two shapes. Maybe I was thinking about this the whole wrong way.

Cole hummed softly over the distiller, his eyes red-rimmed and a little puffy. How was he already distilling? I was so far behind. He'd already had a mini crisis over what stopper to use, and I had to use precious moments to get him to stop crying and to think clearly. My neck had yet to release all the knots, and I was sure I wouldn't unwind until Sunday evening.

Cole leaned over the distiller, and steam puffed in his face. He jerked back with a high gasp. I didn't think; I acted.

I grabbed his shoulders and spun him to me. His face was damp, but it wasn't reddening. His eyes were glassy. My brain scrambled. If he cried and I ignored him, I'd be an asshole. I was his partner for this challenge. I had to make sure he was okay and not leave him twisting in the wind.

"Don't cry, it's okay," I chanted. I grabbed a clean towel from his station and patted his cheeks. "Don't cry, you're not hurt."

He jerked from me and snatched the towel from my hands, his lips flattening. "You don't need to talk to me like I'm a child, Nate."

Oh shit. I had been acting like he was a foster brother, and I was afraid he'd tattle on me for something I had no control over. I lifted my hands and stepped back. "I'm sorry."

"Mind your own business." Cole blinked rapidly, tears catching on his lashes.

I sucked in a breath, but he just walked away.

I shook my head forcibly to get that out of my brain and my mind back on my potion. I wasn't here explicitly to make sure everyone else was okay. I had to win this show. I reminded myself of that while I distilled my reagents in brandy, filling a dark pink bottle up to the shoulders of the neck. I shifted over to the alchemy table, placed the vial on the ledge, and activated it with the dawn tree water. I fitted my hands into the slots and reached for the ley lines. The table lit up with ley energy, pulsing through my body, snapping my jaw shut, and the brightness of magic blinded me.

When the world came back to me, I had three minutes

remaining. I stopped the vial and hurried over to the mini label maker. At least I could still have a gold sticker. I chose one with an image of a brain inside a head, smoothed it on a wooden medallion, and looped some twine through it to tie it on. With ninety seconds remaining, I melted some wax and pressed the medallion into it to make sure it stuck.

"Time!" Owen Creek yelled gleefully.

I set my bottle on the counter and lifted my hands in the air. Sweat dripped down my temple, and my heart raced. I hadn't made it back to my station, but I'd finished my potion. I hoped my only mistake today was how I handled Cole.

THE STUDIO LIGHTS were hot as I stood in a row with the other contestants that Sunday morning. Cole was beside me, surprisingly dry-eyed and cheerful. Figured.

As I thought back on yesterday, I wondered if I'd lost my touch with being compassionate or at least having the tact that came along with being able to guess how people were usually feeling. In any case, he'd only cried one more time yesterday—at the bar we all ate at—and today it wasn't my responsibility to keep him focused.

Georgia bubbled in front of the camera and snuggled Melody. I could imagine the rage the hare felt and the need it had to shit down someone's throat. "It's my absolute pleasure to announce this week's winner. As a caster, it's important to practice a spell every day to memorize it, and an elephant never forgets. Nate, your knowledge potion was off the charts and shaved days off a year. It was a risk to gather that extra ingredient of elephant hair, and it paid off. Congratulations, Honey Bunny!"

I laughed, surprised. I thought for sure Abby had it in the bag this week with her calm mind potion and the really awesome label she'd made with the cricut machine. She'd decorated the entire bottle in calm colors and chakras. Cole clapped me on the back, and Rhoda gave me a hug.

"And that means it's my job to be the bad guy." Owen pouted. "It gets harder and harder each show to say goodbye to any of you. Unfortunately, one of your potions failed, and it belonged to Marcia."

"Aww, no." Rhoda swooped her into a hug.

Marcia shrugged. "It would've happened eventually. I was surprised I made it past the last episode."

I wrapped her in a hug and passed her down the line so everyone else could say goodbye. Then I found myself in the herbarium, stubbornly holding on to my Tymond's Oddities bag, with Tony and a producer for my interview. They'd asked me to explain in direct words what made me go for elephant hair.

I rubbed the back of my neck and shrugged. "I'd actually chatted with a caster friend of mine, who mentioned the year it took for her to memorize a spell. I couldn't imagine waiting that long for a potion to cure. It sounded awful." Then I grinned sheepishly and lifted the bag. "And going to Tymond's was an *experience.*"

When I got inside the Volvo, the drained, haggard expression on Lila's pale face was like a shock to my heart. I needed to make her smile, to take care of her and soothe her sore emotions. It was nothing compared to how I'd felt with Cole. If Lila wasn't happy, I wouldn't rest until I helped her.

She whistled and wiggled fingers at the purple bag in my hands. "Ooo, fancy."

"It's a nice bag." I dropped it to the car floor and nudged it aside with my foot. "I missed you." I leaned across the seat and caught her lips with mine.

She squeezed my fingers and tried to give me a smile, but it didn't reach her eyes.

I didn't need to commune with nature, like Marcia suggested. There'd be nothing else I needed to find outside of Lila that called to my spirit.

Whatever was bothering her about us, I'd make damned sure it didn't last.

Chapter Twenty-Five

T he weekend sped by despite not chatting with Winkerton and Nathaniel being gone. However, he texted all the time. By the lack of notifications, I could tell when he was filming, eating, or sleeping. It was nice, but it was also . . .

When would the other shoe drop? I tapped the steering wheel, waiting for him to emerge from the studio, wondering if Georgia would escort him out again or not. Pain shifted beneath my breastbone, and my insides heaved. I'd debated whether to tell him what really happened with Georgia. It was a difficult decision. She was his hero, for some reason that made little sense to me, and he wouldn't want to hear it from me that she was an awful person.

Not many aside from Winkerton and my mother believed me when I spoke about what happened. After the incident Saturday, it was clear they still didn't. If I'd been minding my own business and came across someone in emotional distress, I would've tried to help them instead of filming them. I was so humiliated; I'd let my phone die overnight instead of recharging it. I'd only powered it back on when I got in the car.

Yet Nathaniel came out alone and slid into the passenger seat. I think I said something inane about the bag he held because he tossed it down, said he missed me, and kissed me. Some of the gloom dissipated.

He'd missed me? I thought about this as I drove from the studio. I'd missed him too, but I couldn't bring myself to tell him. The weekend weighed too heavily on my heart, and I feared even mentioning my vulnerabilities that someone could exploit. It barely registered that he said he'd won again.

I blinked away the rain cloud taking shape in my head and forced a smile. "That's fantastic."

Happy energies just flowed from him, cramming my Volvo up with good vibes and sunshine, and I didn't have it in me to reciprocate. I felt awful when the smile faded slightly from his mossy green eyes; he deserved to celebrate his happiness. So when I pulled to a stop at the traffic light, I patted his hand.

"That's truly amazing, Nathaniel." I grinned at him, meaning every word. "I'm proud of you."

He leaned in and caught my lips in a slow, tantalizing kiss that sent shivers up my spine and butterflies to my stomach. That bad feeling, the moroseness that'd clung to me after finding out that Winkerton had been hiding a relationship from me for however long, drifted away as my mouth moved with his.

Someone honked. The light had turned green. We chuckled together as I drove off and listened to him talk about what he'd done and mostly how he had to console Cole.

"There's always a crier in these competitions," he said. "I hope I don't get paired up with him again anytime soon. It took time away from buying things."

I pulled into my driveway and parked the car. "But you managed. I'm sure you were amazing with him. Do you have what you need to work with on the next challenge?"

He stopped me at the doorway and dropped his duffel on the bottom stair. "Is there something bothering you?" He cupped my shoulders, his earnest gaze searching my face. "You can talk to me about anything, you know that, right?"

The memory of Winkerton and Drew Duke sitting at a table in Brew & Chew assaulted me, and my vision grew blurry. "Winkerton has a secret fiancé."

His jaw dropped as his brows smooshed together. I wondered if I'd looked like that when I'd realized what was happening. Stunned. Dumbfounded. But he didn't seem hurt by the announcement.

"What?"

My chin trembled, and for a split second, it horrified me that I might crack. But Nathaniel wouldn't just watch me cry and take pictures. Still, he'd had to put up with a lot of tears this weekend already. He didn't need mine.

I turned to the parlor and cleared my throat. "Yeah. He's why she's been canceling brunch, I guess."

He spun me around and crushed me to his chest. "Are you okay?"

His arms were strong. He smelled like eucalyptus and the ocean, and my body relaxed against his. *Home*, it said.

I tilted my head back. "Why did she have to keep it a secret from me? I thought we were best friends. And she hid me from him like I was some kind of ugly sweater she's ashamed of."

A hot tear leaked from my eye. His lips parted, and he ushered us down onto the button-tufted crushed velvet couch.

"Does this mean she doesn't want to be my friend

anymore?" I hiccupped. "That she doesn't have time for my drama?"

He swiveled both of my legs across his lap and cradled me, his broad hands rubbing up and down my back. "Oh, baby." He kissed the top of my head and hugged me tight to him. "Have you talked with her about it?"

"I'm not in the right headspace to really listen to her." I clenched his shirt in my fist. "I don't want to cry—not in front of her when we talk."

He made a soft noise in the back of his throat. "It's okay to let it out now. You're safe."

So for the second time this weekend, I cried. Nathaniel held me for as long as I wanted, never asking me to be quiet or to stop. He simply listened and comforted me.

THE NEXT MORNING, I zested a lemon into the glaze I'd made for pancakes. Nathaniel had taken care of me last night, and I wanted to show him how much I'd appreciated it. Bacon sizzled in the oven behind me, making the kitchen smell divine. I brewed him a cup of coffee, which sat on a warmer, and all I needed now was for him to come downstairs.

His feet announced him before he stepped into the kitchen. "Oh, my god, it smells amazing in here—*are you making me pancakes?*" His smile transformed his sleepy face into joy.

I grinned. "Yeah. Sorry, no blueberries, but this glaze is really good."

He swept me up in his arms and spun me around the kitchen before planting a wet and passionate kiss on my mouth. "If you're not careful, I'll never leave."

I chuckled and pointed to the batter. "In that case, make your own pancakes."

We sat at the table with plates before us. He had a stack of five pancakes, but I'd only grabbed one with a side of toast and half a tomato—salted, of course.

I set my chai down. "You never got to tell me about the next challenge. I'm sorry."

"I'm not sorry." He squeezed my fingers before he passed me the paper. "Challenge four! I need to make something that plays off some of my earlier potions, and I think a concentration elixir would be really nice, but can you make that in the seven minutes I'll have on her show?"

It dawned on me that the challenge he was most excited about was the one where he appeared on Georgia's show. Only the winner of the competition's segment would air, so he'd need to be really on top of this. I nodded, my fingers turning to ice. If he made it past this challenge, he'd be a real contender for being a TV host for the Potion Network. Or an influencer. He might even get his own cookbook or something if he made it to the last challenge.

". . . brought it to the conventions." Nathaniel dragged a triangle through the glaze. "The vendors would love it."

"What?" I set my fork aside. "I didn't hear the beginning of that."

"Oh." He smiled. "I was just saying that you should bring the bath bomb for challenge six. Of course, if I make it that far, but I feel really good."

"Why would I do that?"

"Because we'd go so far with it. You'd have a chance to show it to the vendors while we're filming." The skin around his sparkling mossy eyes crinkled. "It really fits in with the accessibility theme I have. A bath bomb that non-casters and Mutes can use that magically conjures hot tub water. We'd be the talk of the Potion Network and—"

"No." My ribs crowded my heart and it hurt to breathe. I no longer wanted to eat my tomato.

His smile fell. "You're not coming to the studio for challenge six?"

"I will if you make it that far, but I won't bring my bath bomb."

"Why not?"

"Because it's not for you to use, Nathaniel." I nudged my plate away. "It's mine. I put in all the work on it." A headache began taking shape behind my eyes.

He grimaced and shook his head. "I know it's yours, but if you bring it to the convention, I can show it to Georgia or Owen, and they'll help—"

"No!" I threw my hands in the air. "I will never show this to Georgia or any of the executives at the Potion Network."

He blinked at me. "Why not?"

"Because the last time I had something like this bath bomb—teeth whitening—Georgia wanted it for her show, and she kept it. Then I'm suddenly number one suspect for her attempted murder." My face was on fire, and it pissed me off I could still *feel* like it was fresh and happened yesterday. Five years should've been enough time to get over it and move on. "I lost my career."

Nathaniel stared at me as if I'd sprouted a third eye in the middle of my forehead—right there at the breakfast table. "I don't understand."

"You want to know what really happened? Fine. I'll tell you." I snatched up one of the posters he had for the show. "Georgia couldn't hack half of the potions on the show. I had to help her stay on *The Next Potion Network Star,* otherwise you'd"—I jabbed a finger at him—"be idolizing me"—I jerked my thumb to my chest—"instead of her."

"I think you're quite wonderful, starshine," he whispered.

I shook my head. "That's not the point. I'm telling you

that I helped her win, but the day before they announced who'd won, the producers came to me to let me know how unlikeable I am. That I'm shrill, and that while my potions are sound and of excellent quality, *I* wasn't." My hands balled into fists, and my nails dug into my palms. "And oh, by the way, would I like to back up Georgia for her own show and be on that with her?"

He stared at me as if I'd just revealed Santa Claus wasn't real.

"Except it wasn't like that." I yanked on my braids, but the ugly emotions only intensified with the pitch of my voice. Damn it, this was exactly what I didn't want to happen. I couldn't stop now that I was on a roll. "Georgia didn't feel having two hosts for *her* show would work well, so I was demoted to culinary producer and then she dumped me. She broke up with me because it wasn't professional and she wasn't sure if she liked women, anyway."

His eyes widened, and he reached for me.

I scooted my chair back from the table before he could touch me. "I watched her use everyone, and when my potion line started to really take off, I had to sign an NDA about being behind it. Then . . . Then she managed to get me to hand her poison on-air and destroyed *everything* I've ever dreamed of. So *no*, Nathaniel, I will not allow the Potion Network to find out about my bath bomb, and I will not let you use it to win."

He stared blankly at the floor, as if it had all the answers. It didn't. "I don't understand," he murmured. "How did she do all of that?"

I shrugged and shook my head, crossing my arms, trying to hug myself. "I was stupid, and thought I loved her, and afterward . . . I don't know. I was still doing most of what I wanted, and really, you said it yourself. I don't like being on camera, and people don't like listening to a shrew."

"But how did she trick you?"

"Into poisoning her?"

He nodded.

I shook my head and stood, pacing behind my chair. "I don't know. I made her potion, the tooth whitening one—which was a stroke of brilliance when I invented it." I swallowed painfully, thinking back to that day. "She didn't like how bitter it could taste, especially if it came down to room temperature, so we sweetened it. I dosed it with honey. The assistant who hands things to her was gone, and someone needed to do it because this was live." I rolled my lips into a line and shrugged. "So I did."

I fell quiet, staring back into my memory of Georgia convulsing on the floor. "I thought it was your basic clover honey, but it was really azalea honey. Do you know what it's like to watch someone succumb to 'mad honey' poisoning? Apparently, Georgia's sensitive to it." I lowered my eyes, unable to meet his gaze. "Her legs were too numb to hold her, so she dropped like a ton of bricks. Her speech was extremely slurred, but she was too busy vomiting anyway. And when she wasn't . . ." I coughed, the memory of the smell coming back to me. "I tried to get her to take the antidote I had on me—because safety. But I couldn't get it down her throat. She was screaming, and someone shoved me aside, and then she was being charged to keep her heart going."

He stopped by my side, his fingers curling and uncurling, like he didn't know what to do with his hands.

"They tore my bee hives down," I whispered. "That was the only way I was acquitted."

Nathaniel grabbed my hand and pressed it to his chest.

"A botanist and beekeeper confirmed that my bees never pollinated from azaleas, and I was acquitted." I met his eyes. "But I'd already been judged guilty by the court of public opinion, and I was asked to leave the show. They bought me out of the potions, and now you know everything."

"Did they ever find who poisoned her?" he asked quietly.

"It's Starglen's biggest mystery, and I'm still the number one suspect." I pulled away and wandered through my greenhouse. He followed me to the door leading to the little poison garden that was mostly belladonna and stared into it. "After that last documentary, I don't know how much longer I can stay here."

"What?" Alarm coated his words.

I turned and looked at him, realizing too late he mattered to me on the same level as Winkerton did, except . . . the warmth in my chest when we kissed. When he tried to comfort me, it felt soothing. And he wanted to use me like everyone else. I truly was unlovable.

"Don't worry about it, just thinking out loud." I forced a smile and could tell it hadn't worked. "Anyway, you said concentration elixir? I think that's a really great idea."

But I never really felt happy helping him make it. He never brought up Georgia, but I could see the wheels in his head turning, and all his questions were around her. I needed to back off if I were to survive this experience with him.

One thing was clear: I still wasn't safe.

Chapter Twenty-Six

Georgia Cauldron grabbed my ass.

Even the next day, after the endless shooting and reshooting, I still couldn't get over the fact that she'd grabbed my ass while we were filming the short seven-minute segment over the concentration elixir I'd made. While in makeup or eating lunch in the studio cafe, I'd heard bits and pieces that Georgia could be a little demeaning, especially if someone didn't treat Melody as well as she believed the bunny should be treated. But I chalked a lot of that up to her being a diva.

Because she most certainly was. I'd learned on the first episode that if I didn't constantly fawn over her, she'd interrupt me. There were also some whisperings that Georgia didn't like anyone prettier than her, and based on the enormous crowds of women waiting for Owen Creek at the end of a day, I understood his and Georgia's dynamic better.

Yet sitting on this hard stool, waiting to learn who had won and who had been eliminated under the hot lights of the studio, it felt more like another kind of spotlight was on me.

Because I had one of my speak truly potions in my bag *and* Georgia Cauldron had grabbed my ass and who saw it?

Please don't let me win.

I didn't want to be that person who won because they were screwing the host, even though I wasn't. And now, considering what Lila had said about Georgia's poisoning, I had doubts.

I'd almost taken her bath bomb with me on Friday. When I'd grabbed the speak truly potion, the bath bomb was sitting on the next shelf, practically begging me to show off how fucking awesome it was to the producers, and I'd grabbed it to go along with a half-cocked idea to prove to Lila that her invention would remain hers. That I only had her best interests in my heart. That she was wrong about the Potion Network, and when they saw what she could do, they'd beg for her to come back. This time, she'd know better and demand credit for her inventions. And she'd know there were people out there looking out for her best interests.

That I'd fallen so hard for her that I couldn't get her out of my head even when I was literally living my dream. I'd had it in my bag; I was running late. She'd been waiting for me in the car, and all I had to do was zip up my bag, but I couldn't do it. She'd never forgive me if I'd taken it, so I'd removed the bath bomb and left it there. I yanked on my shirt collar, the fabric far itchier than yesterday even though I'd washed it.

Georgia glittered under the spotlight as she broke out into an enormous smile that was all teeth. "It's my utmost pleasure to announce this week's winner is Abby! Your serenity potion granted me the peace of mind to do the things I needed to do. Congratulations, Honey Bunny!"

We all cheered, and Abby covered her face.

"And that gives me the . . ." Owen frowned at one of us lined up. "*The Next Potion Network Star* is to promote wellness and accessibility into our homes and maybe even as a life-style. What we don't promote is hate. It gives me much satisfaction to spot a problem and root it out. Will, your comments yesterday regarding your fellow competitors and the Muted are unacceptable and we refuse to tolerate your intolerance."

Will stiffened, and the mulish set of his expression turned mottled. He jerked both hands up and gave the double, single finger salute, said a few choice words that would become a long series of beeps on the airing next Thursday. Cole burst into tears, and Rhoda growled. Will stormed off stage. Apparently, he was a white supremacist and a ley energy purist. I doubted he'd get an exit interview after that.

They detained Rhoda and Abby for an interview.

I hung around, wanting to talk to Rhoda about the revelation Lila had given me, about the speak truly potion in my bag and revealing the nature of the bath bomb and see if she agreed with me about talking to the producers about everything.

Instead, I went to the producer, knocking on Naveen's door. I'd get him to take the potion so when they talked about the bath bomb, I'd know the truth. That they wanted the bomb purely for Lila's invention and wouldn't take it from her like the teeth whitening potion.

"Who is it?" he barked, not even opening it.

I cleared my throat. "Uh, it's Nate Pittman. I'm a contestant on the show?" I cringed. Why had I made that sound like a question?

There was a bang. "I'm busy editing. Don't fucking bother me unless you're bleeding out of your eyes and your asshole."

I winced, fished in my bag, and palmed the speak truly potion so I'd be ready to dose his drink. "No, see, my girl-friend has a really awesome prototype for a—"

Something crashed against the door. "You're fucking banned from knocking on my door until you have six figures in your bank account. Fuck off, Nate Pittman."

I let out a gusty breath of air, honestly glad Naveen never answered the door. I shouldn't talk about the bath bomb to anyone. Why had I thought I could help her with her potions and concoctions when she knew so much more about alchemy and show business? I guess it came from the desire to help her because she was helping me try to get my dreams. I tucked the potion gently back into my bag and returned to the set, hoping to catch Rhoda.

Georgia loitered by the snack table, and the terrible idea that'd taken shape in my head a few nights ago saw another, better opportunity to help Lila clear her name. The speak truly potion shifted in my pocket. I could get the truth straight from the horse's mouth. Swallowing the sour taste in my mouth, I approached the table right as Georgia turned around with a plate full of strawberries and mango.

"Well, well, Honey Bunny." She bubbled at me. "You did well yesterday." She licked her lower lip, then stuck it out in a pout. "Sorry your segment won't be aired on my show."

I smiled and nodded, a little surprised being called Honey Bunny by her wasn't thrilling at all. "It's okay. It was interesting to watch you film your show. I could learn so much from you."

It was like a switch had flipped. One moment she was glancing over my shoulder, the next her blue eyes turned sly along with the curve of her mouth. "You think so?"

"Oh yes." My stomach cramped. "I'd do anything to learn from you."

She lifted a shoulder and turned slightly from me. Was she being coy? "Well, I see a lot of . . ." She lowered her gaze to my feet and slowly dragged it up my body. When she got to my chest, she bit her lower lip and lifted her eyes to mine. "Potential in you."

I swallowed the excessive, bitter spit in my mouth and locked my knees to keep from walking away. "Oh wow. Really?"

She placed her free hand on my biceps and leaned up, deliberately pressing her chest against my arm. "If you come by my trailer," she whispered in my ear, "we could talk about the business, and I can give you tips."

I rubbed the back of my neck to dislodge her. "Really?" I'd already said this and knew exactly what she was suggesting—it wasn't business—but I couldn't, for the life of me, think of a better response than that.

She chuckled, deep and throaty, and stepped back. "Oh, you bet, Honey Bunny. I'll see you in an hour. Shave off that scruff."

She walked off, and I couldn't bear to watch her. I glanced around and caught Trevor frowning in my direction, and when he noticed me noticing him, he quickly left. I raked my fingers through my gelled hair, wrecking it. I needed to get a hold of myself. This was a stupid idea. Abby walked away from the interview, and Rhoda stepped in to take her place.

I waved at Rhoda, but she didn't respond. Hopefully she saw me and knew I wanted to talk to her before she left, but I sent her a text just in case she didn't read into my wave. Then I went upstairs to shave, check out, and get paid. Hopefully, I'd have time to talk with Rhoda.

RHODA

Oh no, I didn't see this until I got into the car.
Everything ok?

I need to talk. You got a minute?

Rhoda has notifications silenced. Alert anyway?

WAS my crisis that important to bug Rhoda while she was driving home? No. Despite being frazzled and having locked my key in my room and then my wallet, I needed to do this on my own. I retrieved my phone and sent a quick text to Lila and fucking lied.

Hey, there's an afterparty for surviving the challenge. I won't be home tonight if that's ok

STARSHINE

Have fun and congratulations for surviving!!

I knocked on Georgia's trailer door, feeling like a shriveled piece of shit, but this needed to be done.

Georgia answered the door holding her rabbit and wearing a sheer pink bathrobe layered with pink feathers framed in faux pink fur that didn't hide her enormous boobs. Her hair was done and her makeup pristine. "You're late."

I peered into the rabbit's shiny eyes, wondering how many throats she'd been able to shit down. Was it two? Ten? Hundreds? Melody chewed on the fringe and stared back, giving nothing away.

I laughed nervously. "Would you believe me if I told you I left my keycard and then my wallet in my room?"

She lifted a brow and moved out of the doorway. "Yeah. You're rather absent minded. Come on in. I've got something to help with that."

I hitched my bag higher on my shoulder and climbed into her trailer. Georgia quickly locked the door. She'd drawn all the blinds and turned on some fake candles. The inside of her trailer had a long pink leather couch draped in shaggy pink blankets, with white and pink bunny pillows. The smell inside her trailer reminded me of a pet store. An opened upper cabinet revealed multiple bottles of alcohol and glasses, and a full ice bucket sat on the counter.

Georgia set Melody down and attacked me.

Okay, she draped her arms around my neck and rubbed her tits on my chest. "Come closer, Nathaniel. I have something for you."

I stiffened. "I only let extra special people call me Nathaniel."

She pouted prettily. "Aren't I special for that? You idolize me."

I pulled her arms down only for her to rake her fingers along my arms. "Well, you're close, but—Hey!"

She had my ass in both her palms, and I could feel her nails digging into my cheeks through my jeans. She laughed and launched at my face. You know that scene in that parody movie about seeking the holy grail with the killer bunny? She looked a little like that just before her lips latched onto mine. I gripped her shoulders and pushed her back.

She chuckled and licked her lips. "You've got to loosen up, Nathan—"

"Nate. Please." I lifted my hands and swallowed the alcohol taste Georgia had planted in my mouth. She was drunk already, and based on the flute of champagne that was mostly empty, I knew I was playing with fire. "Hey, let me make you a drink. Let's get comfy and cozy, yeah?"

Her face brightened. "Good idea. I've had a bottle already, and you need to play catch up, Stud Muffin." She sat on the couch and crossed her legs, dragging her fingers down her thighs and smirking at me.

I grabbed the bottle of whiskey and mixed up a Manhattan. Melody easily distracted Georgia, and when she was kissing the rabbit, I set my phone up on the counter between the ice bucket and the empty bottle of champagne to record whatever happened on the couch.

With the drinks mostly mixed, I slipped my hand into my pocket and grabbed the speak truly potion, and right as I was pouring it in, she caught me.

"What's that?" She sat taller, snuggling Melody closer to her face, and peered at me.

"It's, uhm . . ." My brain raced through what it could be, and I thought of Lila sitting in the dark over a cup of sleepy time tea. "It's a fire agate elixir. You'd asked if it enhances, uhm, you know. And I thought—"

"Oh, Nate," she purred. "I love that you came prepared. You better give yourself some too."

"Sure." However, I'd already emptied it in hers. I capped the vial and pocketed it, then I grabbed both glasses and gave Georgia the one I'd spiked with the speak truly.

I was an asshole. I stared at the phone, wondering if it was worth it, and imagined Lila staring back. She'd hate how I went about it, but after everything she'd said about Georgia, I knew this was the best way to clear Lila in the eyes of the public and the Potion Network. Maybe it'd give her back some joy. But mostly, I wanted her to know I loved her, and if this destroyed everything I'd worked for and cleared her, then it was worth it.

It was like I'd been sucker punched. I loved Lila. I'd do anything for her, and the first thing I did in the name of love was sit on a couch with her scantily clad nemesis.

"Mmm . . ." Georgia wiggled on the couch, getting closer. "I can taste the animal magnetism. Hey, go on and drink. I want you horny."

I sipped my drink and peered at her. She laughed and tipped hers back, draining it.

"Holy shit, be careful." I took the glass from her, but it was already empty.

She clapped her hands. "You're gonna fuck me so hard tonight, I can already tell."

"Jesus Christ." I should leave. I looked at the door longingly. It wasn't too late, was it?

Georgia clambered on top of me, and I held my drink out to keep her from knocking it from my hands. She straddled me and started biting my lips.

I jerked away. "Stop that."

"You want it. It's why you keep telling me how much you love my show." She gripped my shirt and tugged. "Take this off."

"Georgia, stop." I set my glass on the counter, hopefully not blocking the camera, and picked her up off me.

She whined. "What's wrong? Oh! You haven't touched your drink. Drink that and you'll be good for it."

"Okay, but can I ask you some questions while I drink?" I grabbed it again.

She rolled her eyes. "I don't really want to talk about anything with you. I just want an orgasm."

I blinked. The speak truly must've kicked in, and I may as well take advantage before she became too out of control. "Okay, fine. What happened the day Lila Townsend poisoned you?"

"Lila?" She laughed. "Lila never poisoned me. I doubt the thought even crossed her stupid little mind. Drink! Drink, Nate."

I took a sip. "If she didn't poison you, then what happened?"

"Oh, a lot of things happened that day. I almost went into a coma, and I finally got fucking Lila off my show and kept my potion line."

"Why?"

"Drink!"

I drank. "Why did you want her off your show?"

"Because *Home Brew Elixirs* is mine!" Georgia scowled. "I had to be 'on.' I have to be Georgia Cauldron all the fucking time. Be who the fans expect me to be, and Lila didn't. She didn't work a quarter as hard as I did. She didn't deserve what I had then, and she deserves what she has now. Nothing."

I clenched my jaw. "Did she let you win *The Next Potion Network Star?*"

At her sharp look, I took a gulp of the drink.

Georgia waved a hand. "She makes better potions, I'll give that nutjob that much credit. She was so shrill all the time. The audience *hated* her. So of *course* TPN wouldn't crown her. I *saved* her. I offered the idea of me winning and hosting *Home Brew Elixirs*, and she'd work on my potion line. She took it."

"Why would she do that?"

"Cuz she was in love with me."

This fucking bitch. I jerked away, washing my palm over my face so I wouldn't have to see her smug expression. "You used her."

"Hell yeah, just like I'm gonna use your body. Hey, you want to do a reverse—"

"Lila never poisoned you. Do you know who did?"

"Yes." She bit her lip and then sighed. "Make me another drink."

I opened the fridge and saw a few bottles of the champagne she'd drank earlier and grabbed it. My hands shook as I popped the cork and refilled her flute. Then she demanded I join her drink for drink, and I did. Once I got her talking about how smart she was, she didn't need any more prompting.

Georgia boasted about how she and the producer were in a casual relationship, and she'd convinced him that Lila was trouble for the show. After filing complaints to get her fired, the network declined. People complained Lila was too hard to work with, and still the network wouldn't fire her. She was shrill and militant, but she was a cash cow in the potion line.

Then the tooth whitening potion came out, and it was a hit. There was no way they were going to get rid of Lila now that she had come up with an easy way to whiten one's teeth. For a year, everyone kissed Lila's ass, and Georgia had had enough. She was the queen, she was the face of the business, and she was the one selling it.

Lila had to go in more ways than one.

"So I went to the Nettles," Georgia said, half laying against me, her voice slurring. "I got some azalea honey."

I stared at my phone, the red bar at the screen telling me it was still recording. "What did you do with the azalea honey, Georgia?"

"Well, the whitening potion's a little bitter, everyone agreed. So I had Lila's assistant swap out the honey we'd sweetened it with, then I told her to take the day off."

"Why did you do that?" I asked.

"Because I wanted Lila gone."

"No, why did you have the assistant take the rest of the day off?"

"Oh." She laughed and clapped her hands. "Because I'm a genius, and if Lila handed me the potion on live TV, there'd be nothing the network could do but fire her."

"She almost went to prison," I said.

"Worth it."

"She's suffered, Georgia," I said, my voice hard. "People don't even take her acquittal into account because you keep approving documentaries about your mysterious poisoning, and it was you. You did it to yourself and framed Lila for it."

"Meh. Lila doesn't matter."

"She matters to me," I said.

"What?" Georgia leaned back, but her eyes were glazed, and she barely had control of herself.

"You destroyed something special we all could have experienced for what reason?" I stood and raked my hands through my hair.

"I deserved it." Georgia stood, swayed, and fell back onto the couch with a huff. "I deserved the money and the parties and the adoring fans because I put the work in. I sold the potions, and they should be mine."

"What did you ever come up with in your life?" I asked.

"Well, I'm definitely good at framing people." She cackled and sighed, sliding over to lie on the couch. "I'm drunk."

"Yes." I pulled the shaggy blanket over her and set Melody on her stomach. "Sleep it off."

Georgia let out a rip-roaring snore. I grabbed my phone and turned off the camera. Then I grabbed my bag and left the trailer. It'd grown dark, but the light nearby allowed me to see where I was going. I readjusted my clothes and then headed out.

I needed a drink, needed to get my head on straight, and figure out the best way to approach this. Georgia was a predator, and Lila had been set up, judged, found guilty by her peers, and left to hang.

As I walked around town, I wondered what the hell I was doing. Was the show worth it if this was the cost? Especially if it was someone I admired who had done such a heinous thing? My idol had pulled back the curtain and showed me she was a monster.

Chapter Twenty-Seven

The waitperson set tomato toast before me and shepherd's pie croquets drenched in brown gravy before Winkerton. We smiled shyly at one another, the air thick and awkward between us. Last night, she'd sent an invitation to brunch through a separate planner instead of inserting it into my own. It'd felt more like a formal request and, well, Winkerton was special to me, and I didn't want to lose her. Plus, I had a week to come to terms with my feelings and understand why her secret had hurt so much.

"Thanks again for joining me, darling," she said, dipping the tips of her fork into the gravy and sampling it.

I cut a corner of the toast. "The invitation was very fancy. I couldn't refuse."

She took a drink of her mimosa and then dropped her hands to her lap, staring at them. "Lila, I want to apologize. I kept much from you over the past year."

"Is that how long you've been engaged for?" My heart sank, and a little voice that had been quiet for so long whispered in my ear, reminding me that I wasn't that lovable.

"No, Drew proposed six weeks ago."

Right around when she convinced me to help Nathaniel get on *The Next Potion Network Star*. I set my fork and knife down and picked up my iced chai, glancing around at those nearby. I'd noticed over the past couple weeks that people didn't stare too hard at me. Like they were no longer trying to figure out a way to get me to confess to a crime I never committed. Unless I was hysterical in the Flower Market.

The wind always changes, doesn't it?

"Is . . . that why you asked me to teach Nathaniel?" I whispered.

Winkerton's blue eyes widened and fastened on mine. "No. I thought you two had chemistry, and I wanted you to . . . stay here. I don't know. You seemed so sad and there wasn't anything I could do to help, and I thought this might take your mind off it."

"You thought me helping someone with *that show* would take my mind off what happened?"

"Well, I realized too late that wasn't the case, but you had a spark back, darling." A red lacquered nail tapped the side of her plate. "And he needed help."

"Alright." I wanted to talk about him more, but first, I needed to know why she'd hidden her relationship from me. "Then why didn't you tell me about your boyfriend?"

Her cheeks flushed pink. "Now that I'm going to say it out loud, I hear how self-centered it sounds."

I stared at her, waiting. I wanted to patch things up with her, but she needed to come clean with me.

"I thought you still had that crush on me." She sighed, straight from her heart as if she knew she'd made a mistake and regretted it. "And I didn't want to hurt you."

I frowned at my plate, my chest aching dully. "But why? You set me straight early." I blinked. "We've been best friends for years after that."

"I've caught some of your glances, darling. You aren't as smooth as you think."

I groaned and rested an elbow on the table, dropping my head in my palm. "You're a lovely woman, and I'm not dead inside."

She chuckled slightly. "Thank you? But it was hard to not give you the impression that I was interested. I didn't want you to think I was teasing you."

"No, of course not." I pinched my lips together. "I never thought you were trying to tease me. But I also thought I respected what you'd said. I didn't know that small admission had placed so much weight on you."

"And that's why I didn't tell you when I met Drew. I didn't want to lose you as a friend, and it felt like it might be a breakup I couldn't face."

"Okay, I hear what you're saying, but I'm having a hard time." I paused in the middle of sawing through my toast and set my knife down. "It was unfair of you to keep this from me because I had a crush on you when we first met. I'm an adult with mature feelings, and I can rationalize you don't swing in my direction and get over it."

She nodded, her expression downcast. "It just went on for too long, and I didn't know how to tell you, so I kept putting it off and off. I'm sorry, Lila. Can you forgive me?"

There was a slight buzz floating around the room. Whispered conversations, which had barely any substance, grew louder. I quickly scanned the dining room, but no one paid attention to us. I sipped my iced chai, watching Winkerton over the rim of my cup. I knew she was telling the truth, and I also knew Winkerton always had my back and would continue to. She was closer to a sister than a friend.

"I can, yes." I reached across the table and touched the back of her hand. "I do forgive you. Thank you for telling me why you kept the secret, and I'm sorry you felt you had to take care of my feelings."

She smiled and flipped her hand, grasping mine. "Your feelings are important, and I'll always wish to protect them, darling."

"How did you meet Drew?"

She grew animated, her eyes lighting up as she described the sock hop she'd met him at and the dance off they competed in. After she'd thoroughly embarrassed him, he'd asked her out. Then it was a simple fast track to love. I smiled. It felt good to see her so lively, not that Winkerton had been the opposite, but the beginning of our brunch had felt somber and funeral-like. And both our appetites returned. My tomato toast was exceptional.

"And your Auntie Virgie?" I popped a triangle of an heirloom tomato in my mouth. "Did her surgery go well?"

She grimaced. "There was a slight complication with her anesthesia when they were attaching the fourth lead to her pacemaker. She's confessed to cheating at rummy, but she's on the mend." She smiled. "And back to cheating."

I chuckled. "I'm glad she's feeling better."

"So, tell me." She leaned in, lowering her voice. "What has training him been like?"

"He's eager to learn, and while it can take him a couple of tries to get something right, once he does, he only improves." I bit my lip, thinking of other ways he'd improved. "We had sex."

"What?" Winkerton squealed.

Nearby tables glanced at us, then returned to watching their phones. Which I thought was more odd than usual. My ears grew hot and I ducked my head, peeking around. It wouldn't be odd if my hysterics last week finally made it to everyone's phone. I wished these people would find someone new to fixate on. Mostly everyone had their attention riveted on whatever was on their screen instead of me.

"Keep your voice down," I said, half-laughing.

"Tell me everything."

I told her about the way I had to show him how to scrape the pulp from leaves and that he'd almost kissed me, then the planned spontaneous outing and the kissing.

"It was so sweet. You should've seen him." I grinned, the warmth in my chest spreading like a healing balm. "He'd even kept a copy of my plans for that day if I didn't want any of it."

She grinned, sipping her mimosa. "Smart man."

"Then there was the moonlit bath." I didn't give her much detail, only that I'd taken things further with him . . . and how he'd made me feel more each and every time. "I've never been with anyone like that before. It was . . . exhilarating to let go like that."

Winkerton fanned herself. "Darling, I'm impressed." Then she clapped her hands. "Oh, I'm so happy for you. I thought he had an extra spring to his step when I saw him at the Flower Market last week." She lowered her voice further. "How did he do on challenge four? I know that was his big goal to get to."

"I don't know." I bit my lip. "He had an after-filming party he wanted to go to and hasn't come home yet. I'm sure he had the best time doing it." I couldn't help the sour tone in my voice. "You know how much he idolizes her."

"Everyone must have a fault, darling." A chime came from Winkerton's purse, which was shaped like a cardinal. She brightened. "That's his Google alert."

I swallowed the last bite of my toast, which had the perfect amount of cheesy eggs, avocado, tomato, and pickled red onion. "You have a Google alert on Nathaniel?"

"Of course I do, darling. I'm his sponsor, after all." She retrieved her phone. "I need to keep tabs—Oh fuck."

The fragile buoyancy of the beginning of a good day burst. "What's wrong?"

Her brows gathered together, and she moistened her lips. "Maybe we should go someplace else."

"What?" My shoulders instinctively curled inward. "Why?"

"Let me order you a martini at least."

"Winkerton," I said a touch sharply. I didn't like that she was hesitating. It was about Nathaniel; it was her Google alert. What happened? He'd never came home, and he hadn't texted good morning or anything yet like he normally did. He didn't have his bike; he was walking, and if he was heading home by foot, had some drunk driver hit him? "What's wrong?"

She scooted her chair next to mine and showed me her phone. A gossip site had gotten their hands on leaked security video from the lot where the TPN hosts park their trailers, and it was replaying the footage with captions. "*The Next Potion Network Star* contestant Nate Pittman seen entering Georgia Cauldron's trailer, where he stayed most of the night." The video was grainy, but I recognized the shape of his shoulders as he climbed inside the trailer. I knew his silhouette in the window from staring at it so many times from the kitchen. And then the security footage sped up and a new timestamp showed up for three in the morning of Nathaniel stepping out, fixing his clothes, and walking off.

A fissure appeared in my heart, and I pushed the phone away from me, yet I couldn't tear my gaze from the broadcast. Scandal, affair, contestant. Clips from challenge three where he was fawning over her, and every time he did, she bubbled. When they showed them all together like that, instead of separated by weeks, it was obvious there was something more going on between them.

"Let me get you a martini," Winkerton said, locking her phone.

"No, I'm fine." That was a lie.

This wasn't happening. Everything had gone numb, and I felt as if I was floating; I wasn't really here. I checked if I had a text from him yet, but there was nothing. Did that mean he knew the cat was out of the bag, or was he sleeping it off? He didn't have a bike. I clapped a hand over my mouth, images of ambulances and life support slotting through my brain. Was he hurt?

"Darling, it's utterly indecent you aren't having a martini right now." Winkerton waved her hand to get the waitperson's attention.

A terrible feeling bubbled up from the dark pit inside my stomach. What if this was another ploy to get me? No, that was ridiculous. Georgia had already destroyed me; what more could she want done? What more could I suffer to make her feel good about when she already had everything of mine? The image of him leaving her trailer and fixing his clothes burned into my brain, and it was all I saw when I closed my eyes.

Apparently, she had found one more thing, an idea, a feeling, to take from me.

"I need to go," I whispered.

When the waitperson came, she paid the check instead. I was already on my feet, blindly walking out into the foggy day. The images smeared before my vision, and I squinted, doing everything to keep it together. My throat ached.

"Lila, wait!" Winkerton hurried after me. "Let me come with you."

"What?" I blinked at her. The more the seconds ticked by, the more my chest caved in, puncturing my heart. "Why?"

She cupped my cheeks. "Because I love you and I don't want you to be alone. Let me drive you."

I nodded. The ride home was a blur, yet I could hear every lyric of *Stray Cat Strut* as it played on her speakers, and it made sense. Nathaniel had used me to get what he wanted all along. He'd used me for alchemy, he'd used me to get into Georgia's good graces, and when that wasn't enough, he'd used me at night. My fingers clawed my overalls as I dragged my hands up and down my thighs, unable to sit still. Unable to wrap my head around what he'd done.

Winkerton followed me into my greenhouse. "Lila? Lila, talk to me, please."

"I'm not thinking clearly." I made a beeline straight for my defunct potion stock and grabbed a calm mind elixir. And that was when I noticed it. Ice opened in my stomach and spread beneath my sternum. "What the fuck?"

"What?" Winkerton pushed close against me. "What's wrong?"

I opened the cupboard completely, my hands shaking so hard I couldn't grasp the knob. My bath bomb was missing. Random potions were missing, especially some from the practices we'd done for his later challenges that we'd guessed on due to prior seasons of the show. The speak truly, but what kept drawing my stinging eyes was the missing bath bomb.

"He asked me to let him show it to the producers, and I wouldn't let him," I whispered in a shaky breath.

My heart hammered in my chest, breaking apart as the reality came crashing around me. My knees threatened to give out; my throat closed up.

"Show what, darling?" Winkerton asked.

"My bath bomb," I whispered. "It's gone."

She sucked in a sharp breath and stepped back. "The one you've been working on?"

I went to every cupboard. Maybe I'd moved them to make space for Nathaniel's potions and forgotten about it. But every time I did not find my bath bomb, the more I knew he'd stolen it from me. My blood froze.

"How could he? Why?" I was in a cycle. My breaths came in strangled, high-pitched wheezes. I opened cupboards I'd already checked and rechecked and then triple-checked, slamming them closed harder and harder each time. "He took it. He took it from me. I'm such a fucking idiot. I knew he wanted something, but I hadn't thought it was so he could run straight to Georgia *fucking* Cauldron and stab me in the back."

I stormed through the door to my kitchen, slamming the door so hard the window rattled in its frame. Tears streamed down my cheeks, and I clenched my teeth, wanting to scream but refusing to give him that.

Winkerton dashed after me. "Where are you going?"

I stomped up the stairs and barged into Nathaniel's room. "I'm not going anywhere, but *he* certainly is." I heaved his tattered duffel bag from the bottom of the wardrobe and yanked it opened. Then I began packing. "This is the last time I'm a doormat."

"Then stop folding his clothes nicely. Here, let me help." Winkerton pulled the clothes from my hands and wadded them up.

I laughed and nearly sobbed, so I snatched more of his shirts and crumpled them into balls. They smelled like him— similar to walking in an airy forest near a stream. I swallowed, the painful lump in my throat choking me. I turned to the bed and spotted my bath bomb sitting on the nightstand.

"What?" I picked it up and turned it over in my hands. The acetate tab was still in place and it didn't appear to be tampered with—though I would've known the moment he had. The room would've been flooded. "It's here. My bath bomb."

Winkerton stopped beside me and took it in her hands. "It's orange."

"I added amber." I lifted my face to the ceiling. "I don't understand why he took it. For what purpose?"

"Maybe he was organizing another planned spontaneous outing with it."

The leaked security video of him leaving Georgia's trailer replayed, and it broke my heart again.

"It doesn't matter. I believed him." I sobbed; the tears felt like splinters pushing from my heart. "I believed him when he said he wanted me and that he had feelings for me. I never believed he'd do something like this to me. I thought he really liked me." I threw his old shoes on the floor and kicked them. "I thought we could have something." I covered my face, ashamed I'd let myself become so stupid, so vulnerable. "Why am I not worthy? Why am I only good enough to use? *Why?*"

She hugged me, and I clutched her, foolishly weeping over a boy who had lied to me.

Chapter Twenty-Eight

My body felt as heavy as a fallen tree, and every yawn grew longer and louder. My head pounded as I shuffled my way up the driveway and into the house. Well, I tried to get into the house, but she'd locked the door. I juggled my bag forward, my head pounding as I blearily searched the pockets for my keys. I couldn't find them.

"Sonuvabitch." I pulled my bag off and set it on the doorstep next to my bike. My stomach stirred strangely; I hadn't left my bike on the front porch because Lila preferred it in the garage. Crouching, I checked every pocket of my bag again. I hardly ever needed the keys to the house, and when I finally forgot to bring them, the door was locked.

The door jerked open, and I lifted my head to find Winkerton glaring at me. I frowned, unable to shake the sudden trapped feeling that gripped me on the porch.

"Is it him?" Lila called from somewhere inside the house.

"It is," she called back, her hard eyes never leaving me.

I swallowed and straightened on my feet, my pounding

head briefly subsiding to dizziness. I cleared my throat. "Hey, Winkerton." I moved to step by her, but she blocked me. "What's up?"

"You have a lot of nerve," she muttered heatedly to me, keeping her voice low. "You texted me about her and what you could do to become friends, and I helped you. And then you . . . you seduce her while you're fucking Georgia? How dare you?"

The short hairs on my neck lifted as ice shattered all around me. I drew back. "What do you mean?"

Lila came up behind Winkerton, her gray eyes red-rimmed and puffy, her light brown hair pulled back in a messy bun. When she saw me, her vulnerability switched off, like a wall of iron had been erected between me and her. I felt it in the very fiber of my being.

"What's wrong, Lila?" I stepped forward, but Winkerton moved to block me. I frowned at her before looking back at Lila. The pain in her expression broke my heart. "Lila?"

She whispered something to Winkerton, who scowled at me once more before stepping away.

"He only needs one testicle to live," she muttered. "And that's stretching my kindness."

My brow furrowed as I returned my attention back to Lila. "What—"

Lila heaved my duffel bag from the floor and shoved it into my arms, forcing me back, my heel tipping over the edge of the step. Then she came outside, curling her bare toes and crossing her arms over her chest to grip her elbows. "I know everything, Nathaniel." Her voice was raw. "You're not welcome here any longer."

Winkerton pulled the curtain aside and watched us from the window.

"Will you please explain to me what's going on?" I asked.

Spots floated across my blurred vision as vertigo threatened to wipe away my hangover. I wasn't sure I understood what was happening.

Her jaw worked and she shook her head as if feeling out words and unable to utter them. I ached to hold her, to bring her close and breathe her in. But when I reached for her, her expression turned flinty.

"I was a fool, and I've learned my lesson." Her face flushed and her eyes turned bloodshot. She blinked rapidly. "I'd thank you, but I don't even have that left inside me."

"I don't understand," I whispered.

"Everyone saw you leave Georgia's trailer, Nathaniel." She clucked her tongue, making a disgusted noise in the back of her throat. "I can only be glad you never spoke of me to anyone, but it's over."

"No." My breath hitched painfully. "No, it's not. We still—"

"We?" She shrugged. "What we?"

My heart thudded painfully at that nonchalant gesture and the tears welling in her eyes. "I need you."

She scoffed, her fingers trembled when she rubbed her mouth, then shook her head once more. "For what? You made it to challenge four. We agreed you wouldn't need my coaching after that."

"No—"

She lifted a brow.

"Well, yes, but that's not what I meant." I pulled my phone out. "Lila, I need to show you something."

"Oh god, no." She backed away. "I don't want to see whatever you have to show me."

"I have something you need to see." I unlocked my phone, bringing up the video I'd watched a hundred times while getting too fucking drunk to walk or even sleep.

"I know everything I need to know about you, Nathaniel."

She pushed a wild chunk of hair behind her ear. "I know you're fucking Georgia—"

"No!"

"I know you were planning to steal from me." A tear skated down her cheek and she growled at me. "I know you took my bath bomb—I found it in your room. I'm not sure who put you up to it, but I can guess you and Georgia had some cute pillow talk about me and how you were pulling the wool over my eyes, but I'm done. They're wide open, and I do *not* like what I see when I look at you."

My heart broke and stopped beating. Somehow it restarted, sluggishly spreading sharp, needle-prick tingles across my chest. "No, you have it all wrong. I didn't tell anyone about the bath bomb. I'm not fucking Georgia."

"Everyone saw you, Nathaniel!" She laughed and wiped her hands clean. "I saw it, and it serves me right. I just can't believe how foolish I've become to be swindled twice by people like you. Or were you going to steal my bath bomb so you could pay back the money you owe to the mafia?"

"No way, I swear. I didn't tell anyone about it or use it to pay off my debt."

"Then why did you take it?"

"I was going to show one of the producers who—"

"Who works for Georgia. Don't shake your head, Nathaniel, and don't be so stupid. If a producer works on any show with her, they're hers. They're loyal to her first because without her, they don't have a paycheck. I hope it was worth it, because I registered the bath bomb with the patent company when I was close to being finished. You'd do best to believe if any kind of bath bomb like mine comes out before I release it, I'll see you in court." She gripped the doorknob.

"No, wait, you have to believe me that I didn't take it to steal from you."

She chuckled harshly and glared at me over her shoulder.

"How can I believe a word that comes from someone like *you?* Look at you." A ragged laugh spilled from her. "You cheated and lied to compete on a show you could never qualify for on your own. You're a swindler. A conman." Her expression turned flinty. "And you thought you could get the upper hand on me." Her hard gaze swept over me and found me wanting. "Maybe you did. But I learned one thing when it comes to potions: if they don't blow up in your face, someone will try to take them. I never want to see you again."

She opened the door and slammed it behind her, the deadbolt clacking into place. Winkerton left the window. Numbly, I heaved my bag. It was packed lumpily and off balance. But I still strapped it to my bike, then clipped my backpack on.

I called Rhoda. I didn't know who else to call and ask for help. I left a voicemail with Rho and walked my bike toward . . . Where? Maybe Emily would be up for a visit, but then what? I had no place where I belonged because, as always, people end up leaving my life. I went to the only place I knew that was as desperate as I was. The Nettles.

IN GOODIES, I stared blankly at the table. My phone and the star pin sat side-by-side with my empty plate. In my head, I replayed the moment I'd taken the bath bomb from the cabinet and cursed. If I hadn't given in to that impulse, at least she wouldn't think I'd tried to steal from her on top of screwing Georgia. Not that my situation would be any better, but I wouldn't have attempted theft on her list of grievances against me. Maybe she'd have believed me when I explained what'd happened last night. But once I'd seen the video? Fuck. I winced and covered my face with my hands.

This was bad. I couldn't even bring myself to read the comments, and there were thousands of them. This couldn't be happening.

I should show the producers my video, but something told me they would hide it until the shooting for the show was over. Or maybe for forever.

I should release my video to the same gossip site that showed the leaked security footage of me at her trailer. Who had seen me go there? Trevor had watched us talk in front of the buffet table, but I'd assumed he'd protect Georgia's image for fear of Melody and her partiality for shitting down throats.

I opened the email for an editor at the gossip site and uploaded the video, but hesitated. What was I supposed to say? Here's why I went into Georgia's trailer: to clear the name of the woman I love, but it backfired horribly on me and now I've lost everything? Please help me get my girl back? I frowned. My gut told me that wasn't the right way to go about this, and even though I didn't understand why, I deleted the email.

"You made quite the splash, Nate," someone said with a laugh.

I jerked up and sighed. Alex hovered at my table. I heaved out a long, exasperated breath, vibrating my lips. I grabbed the pin from the table and activated it in the process of clipping it on. Everything else was going down the drain. Maybe this was one thing I could get done right.

"I'm not the best company right now," I said, hoping to push him off. A long shot, but you miss every shot you don't take, from what I've heard.

"Good thing I only want my money." He sat across from me and frowned at my lone cup of joe and the empty plate with dregs of syrup and bacon grease. That's when I noticed he had a split lip and a bruise on his cheek. Then I saw other bruises and slowly healing scratches on his hands.

"Look, I told you it'd take a minute before I could get you the money." At payroll yesterday, I'd opted for a check because I didn't want to miss an opportunity to speak with Naveen about the bath bomb. I didn't know his schedule. For all I knew, he bounced as soon as possible. But now that I think about it, if I'd told him what it could do, he'd probably have it figured out within months and overpower anyone else who came out with something like it.

The thought alone killed me. I tried to swallow the painful ball in my throat. She deserved this bath bomb; it'd never been an option to take it from her. But I just thought I knew better. I was on the show; I saw the executives whenever I was there. They would want it. She'd worked so hard on this. It'd taken her years to come up with the right spell working and then to have Sir Fuzzy Pants memorize it whenever she came up with a better calculation. I'd thought I could do at least one thing for her, like I was some big shot now. But I knew the truth. I was a wannabe.

Alex slapped the table, startling the shit out of me. "And I told you that I want my money. You promised me you were good for it."

"Hey!" Sawyer's sharp voice cut through the tension. "It's time for you to go."

I bared my teeth at Alex, grabbed my backpack and duffel bag, then left the diner. One of his buddies in a tracksuit stood by my bike, smoking. I pulled up short and searched for the other guy that was always around but didn't see him. This was ridiculous.

I clenched my teeth and strapped my duffel to my bike. "Hey, where's your other friend?"

"You don't need to worry about him, Nathan," Alex growled behind me.

A wild thought went through my head that maybe Burris was right and Alex hadn't had the approval he'd needed when he'd lent me the three grand. I mean, that had to be chump change. Beneath their notice, and Alex had said it wasn't something he usually did but was willing to because we were family.

"Did I really borrow money from your 'family' or was it just you?" I asked.

The goon flicked his cigarette across the street and faced me, arms apart from his sides as he crowded closer. The acrid stench of cigarettes and body odor saturated what little breathing room I had remaining.

A dangerous vibe radiated from Alex. "I told you not to be asking about my business."

The tracksuit guy punched me. *One-two-three!*

The blows came out of nowhere. The air barked out of me. I groaned and doubled over, falling to my knees. He reared his leg back and slammed a kick into my side. I coughed, rolling on the sidewalk. I couldn't breathe. Alex loomed over me, crouched, and slammed two more blows into my face.

"Next time I see you, you better have my money, bitch." He and his friend left.

I wheezed, trying to breathe through the pain in my stomach, side, and face. Staring up at the dark sky. The S in Goodies had gone out since the last time I was there, and the flickering neon bulbs only illuminated the D, I, and E.

RHODA OPENED THE DOOR, and her delighted smile slipped off her face when she saw me.

"What in the world?" She pulled me inside. "What happened to you?"

I wondered if I could tell her the truth about everything—that I'd never gone to Starglen Alchemy University, that I owed the Fornaro family money and they were done waiting, that somehow I was supposed to get Alex to admit his crimes while I wore Burris's enchanted pin, that I fucked things up with Lila . . . Glancing at the TV, I saw the video of me readjusting my clothes before walking off. Guessed Rhoda already knew what happened there.

"I screwed up," I said.

"It looks like it." She shook her head and guided me to the table covered in homework, a couple beat-up alchemy textbooks, and a notebook resting beside them. The room smelled like garlic, onions, and the sea, and I was sorry I'd already eaten. "Dandre, get me the first aid kit from the bathroom, would you please?"

Dandre dashed from the couch. He couldn't be much older than fifteen, and his short haircut only accentuated that he'd yet to grow into his ears. He ran back into the kitchen with a small bag and sat at the table. His wide, dark eyes took me in, and I knew this had to be more exciting than anything else that'd happened that day for him.

Then she pushed me into a chair and pulled out some salves and swabs. "Tell me everything, kiddo."

So I did. This felt oddly similar to a time when I'd gotten suspended from high school, probably the same age as Dandre was now, and my foster parent listened while they cleaned me up. I was so glad I'd found Rhoda; she gave me that warm feeling I'd missed since then. I started off from the day Lila crashed my demonstration, to finding out where my permit money came from, and the ruse Lila and I had agreed to. Rhoda found that part especially delightful. So did Dandre.

"Well, you can stay here as long as you need." Rhoda stood and walked down the hallway. "Gracine doesn't use her room anyway, so you can have it." She faced me and gripped both my shoulders. "But you need to tell Lila what really happened."

"I tried," I said. "She won't listen."

"Life's too short for you to stop trying now, and you of all people should know that." Rhoda frowned, then patted my cheek. "You hungry? I've got fish chowder on the stove."

Chapter Twenty-Nine

Delete all future events?

The words became blurry as I stared at my planner in my quiet kitchen on this dark morning. A storm had gone through in the night, washing away the sins of those who'd trespassed into the dark, but left behind truculent clouds as a reminder. As if saying, "I know what you did."

That was how crying myself to sleep felt. I still knew what he'd done in the morning.

I jabbed the confirmation button on my digital planner. It removed all of Nathaniel's sessions for training, foraging, and cooking potions from my calendar. I slid my aching gaze to my cooling cup of chai, then to the thick planner sitting on the table, and sighed.

"Maybe it's time to go strictly digital."

Not that I needed two planners. I hadn't for years, but the habit soothed me. Enter it on one, enter it on the second, and it'd burned into my mind. Instead, now Nathaniel's face—wounded and pleading only to become closed off and as hard as steel—had become branded into my memory.

Why did he have to make me fall in love with him? He *knew* he'd turn around and destroy everything that I'd built. Couldn't that have been enough? What was it about me that pushed people to spit on me like this? Maybe Georgia was right. No one could love me.

My eyes grew unbearably hot and itchy, and I rubbed them while releasing a frustrated growl. "It's too damn quiet in here!"

I turned on the TV to give me noise, to distract me from these thoughts endlessly doom scrolling through my head. Nathaniel used me to further his career exactly as Georgia had. My heart never should have been involved.

I'm such a fool.

"It could mean I'll find unconditional love."

I'd recognize his warm voice anywhere. To my dismay, my heart hammered faster and a flutter of hope rippled across the sour surface of my stomach. I glanced to the hallway before I realized I was hearing a rerun of this season's *The Next Potion Network Star*. I gaped at the screen, staring at his handsome face as he dropped a crystal in his pouch. Then it cut to commercial break, which was a pre-filmed advertisement for the show. And Nathaniel stood with seven other people, decked out in his embroidered apron in front of the herbarium, grinning.

"Nope." I snatched the remote and turned off the TV. "Nope, nope, nope."

I abandoned my chai at the table and pushed into my greenhouse. The scent of grass and soil assaulted me as I approached the workbench. It felt as if the plant-covered walls were closing in. I used to find this room so full of life and joy. While I stared at my ferns, flowers, herbs, and beehives, everything felt empty, leaving only room for memories of him. My eyes wandered to the shelf and the triceratops sitting there, and I sighed, wandering over to the bench to torture myself more.

His written recipes for potions lay wrinkled on the counter. I brushed my fingers over his handwriting, noticing the scales he'd forgotten to return to his foraging kit. He'd need those. What would he do if he came upon something he needed the exact—No. It wasn't my problem anymore. It never should've been.

And now, what was once my most sacred sanctuary no longer belonged to me. I used to joke with Winkerton that I'd made this greenhouse for the show, and now I only stuck around Starglen for my greenhouse. And he'd taken this bit of peace from me.

Feeling heartsick, head aching and eyes threatening to leak again, I headed for the outside door, grabbing my purple raincoat on my way out. Sitting in my Volvo, I refused to acknowledge the empty seat but instead stared through the water-dotted windshield at my house. It stood odd, distorted, like the very foundation was coming undone board by board. Like every essential part of my soul had shattered apart and only bones remained inside me, and even those were threatening to break. I flicked the wipers on to clear the left behind rain, and my house still didn't look like my house. I didn't feel like myself, either.

I tore out of my driveway and drove to my favorite place on earth. I gripped the steering wheel, wondering if I should email the network and tip them off to check Nathaniel's college credentials, or if a call would get it started faster. But would they even listen to me?

I parked and jogged across the road into the woods and followed a deer trail. Yet once I was deep in the piney and dew-scented forest of Founders' Grove, it reminded me of walks with Nathaniel and criticizing him for the way he foraged.

"For fuck's sake, Lila," I muttered. "You were such a nag to him. It's no wonder . . ."

I pushed off deeper, staring at my shoes and finally realizing, after they'd become covered in mud and pine needles, that I'd forgotten to put galoshes on over them. He had me so screwed up that I couldn't do anything right.

I couldn't come here and enjoy the solace, because it was silence that I was trying to escape. There was no joy here for me, no recharge. No reset to my emotions.

Balling my hands into fists, I did the only thing left to relieve the twisting tension inside my body. I screamed.

I screamed because I was hurting and frustrated. I screamed because I still loved Nathaniel—even after knowing what he'd done. I screamed until my throat grew sore and my heart lost some of the aching weight strangling it.

"Hey there? Are you hurt?" someone yelled between me taking breaths.

I startled, winded, and glanced around, searching for whoever was calling out to me. My chest ached and my head hurt, but I no longer felt the urge to cry. And I no longer felt the peace from the redwoods.

He'd stolen everything that'd mattered.

"Ooh, she's dirty," I murmured appreciatively and took another sip of the martini a couple of evenings later. I pondered the tops of the bookshelves and the overgrown ivy plants trailing leafy legs down to tickle the book spines.

"I thought you might like that." Winkerton grinned and sat next to me, kicking her socked feet up on my travel trunk coffee table. This evening, she wore black skinny jeans and a pomegranate red blouse.

"It's delightful." I took another drink, this time draining half the glass. "Thanks for coming over again."

Winkerton kept me company at night, sometimes walking me up to bed. Other times I'd wake up on the couch with a blanket on me. I hadn't had to ask. She was just there, and I loved her for it. If I really could go through with leaving Starglen, I'd miss her terribly. I'd scheduled a call with my mother next week to discuss a withdrawal from my trust to help me start over in the northeast.

Winkerton petted my hair, smiling slightly, but she shifted away, swiveling to face me like she was ready to catch me if I needed to fall. She tipped her head toward me. "Of course, darling. Even if I didn't feel responsible for what you're going through right now, wild horses couldn't tear me away. We'll get this figured out."

I shook my head and emptied my glass. Then I stood, holding my hand out. "Another?"

"No, no." She got to her feet and took my glass. "You're pouring too heavily on the gin, darling. I don't want to pass out and have a hangover tomorrow. I have that brunch with Drew's mother and mine."

"I could make you a potion," I said, falling back onto the mustard yellow couch, rubbing my hand against the grain on the velvet cushion. "I'd have to go into my apothecary, but I'd do it for you."

"And they say chivalry isn't dead."

I closed my eyes against the idea of going into my greenhouse or apothecary, listening to her cast and shake the Boston shaker. I had done nothing regarding alchemy or enchanting since that first day. Hell, I hadn't even casted. I just sat on my couch and played one of those murder mystery hidden object games on my phone.

"Do you like his family?" I asked. "Drew's, I mean."

"They're nice people."

I opened my eyes. Winkerton's peacock had stuck around, and he strutted through the burgundy wingback chair, dragging his glorious tail behind him. I could only imagine what he'd looked like when he was still alive, all turquoise, blues, greens, and purples, and now he was spirit blue and covered in spell workings.

She placed the drink in my hand. Four olives this time, with one just rolling around the bottom of the glass. She settled next to me on the couch. "I actually wanted to ask you something, once I had all these gifts ordered, but I can't wait."

"You can ask me anything." I sipped the martini. It was a little icy on top, which was phenomenal considering Winkerton hadn't used ice.

She smiled and cleared her throat. "Darling, would you be my maid of honor?"

"Really?" I sat upright and faced her. "You want me to be your maid of honor?"

"Yes. Who else would I ask?" She clasped my free hand. "I know you don't like being around a lot of people, and this wedding will be a lot, but will you consider it?"

"You're my best friend." I gave her my first honest smile all week. "I'm honored and delighted to be your maid of honor."

"Good, but you must know you'll be wearing red."

I laughed. "I bet your family will love that."

"Drew's mother isn't thrilled. She's trying to convince me to go pink." She rolled her eyes and patted her victory curls. Her phone dinged, and she reluctantly retrieved it from her purse—this one resembled a vinyl record. Her brows pinched together.

"Is everything okay?" I whispered.

"It's my Nathaniel Google alert," she whispered back.

Time froze as what-ifs—more rumors of him and her;

more lies coming to light; he was hurt and needed me—scrolled through my brain so fast I grew dizzy. I bit the inside of my cheek and stared at my olives. "You still have that?"

"I wanted to keep tabs on him in case he pulled another bastard move, but this isn't what I expected at all." Her phone bathed her porcelain face in a blue glow. She gasped and gripped my arm. "You gotta read this."

I leaned away. "I can't. I need space from him."

"No, this is different." She held her phone out to me. "Ainsley from season six accused Georgia of sexual harassment in light of *his* video."

"What?" I sat forward and read her phone.

It was a still from the leaked security footage of Nathaniel and Georgia, her wearing a ruinously stupid pink nightie and standing in the door, and he . . . I couldn't see his face. Next to it was a headshot of Ainsley and the headline "Georgia Cauldron had me eliminated from TNPNS because I complained about her inappropriate behavior."

"Whaaat?" I took the phone from her and set my martini down on the side table. "It goes on to say that a couple of other contestants talked about her advances but were too afraid to come forward."

"Georgia is disgusting," Winkerton said.

"It speculates that Nathaniel was also being threatened by her and they have it from a source that the next day Georgia was in a terrible mood and hungover." I frowned, scrolling through the article. "What's that supposed to mean?"

"I don't know, darling," Winkerton said. "You know her better than me. What do you think it means?"

I sighed and pinched the bridge of my nose. "I knew her five years ago. People change."

"Does Georgia have the capacity to change?"

"No." I handed back the phone. "I don't think so. I don't know. Back when we were together, she—" I bit my lip, thinking back on our relationship and then our working relationship. "I always knew when she had a quickie at the studio because she was so smug and cheerful."

Winkerton made a noise in the back of her throat and lifted her glass. "Maybe . . . Maybe he felt he had to visit her but got her drunk instead of sleeping with her?"

"It doesn't make sense. He's a user." I popped an olive in my mouth and furiously chewed it. "They're the same, you know. Small beginnings, willing to do anything to get ahead. She accused me of poisoning her, and he stole my bath bomb."

"They have similar backgrounds, yes, and he tried to steal your bath bomb, which, if I know you, it was really mine, so I should be the wounded party here."

I scoffed out a laugh and nodded. "You're not wrong that it was supposed to be for you."

"I knew it." She pursed her lips, and her expression softened. "What I'm trying to say is that Nathaniel isn't Georgia. That man doesn't have a mean bone in his body, and he'd rather give his last dollar to someone who needs it more than hurt someone."

"How do you know that?" I looked away. I couldn't meet her eyes, not when my vision became hazy. "You barely visited when he was here."

"We chatted a lot in texts. Someone stole his healing potion the same week we met him. When he caught the thief, not only did he insist they keep it, he gave them money so they could take it on a full stomach. Would Georgia do something like that?"

No, she wouldn't, and Winkerton knew it. I swallowed, but the hard lump remained painfully lodged in my throat. "Even if none of this had happened, it'd never work out between us."

"Why's that, darling?"

"Because we're too different, and I'm me." I flashed her a sad smile. "There are die-hard Honey Bunnies out there who'll always spurn me, and they'll turn that hatred on him. And then what? It'd be easier for him to stay far, far away."

"Hmph." She tilted her head, lifting her chin. "Do you know that's never happened to me?"

"No one could hate you, Winkerton."

She *tsked*. "My father wanted me to stop being friends with you, and I told him it was a bunch of bullshit to do that when you're perfectly innocent and my dearest friend."

"Really?" I blinked. I'd never known.

"Auntie Virgie set him straight when I couldn't."

I loved her great-aunt even more. "Remind me to make her some hand cream."

"I did all of that because you're my best friend and you're like family to me. He's stupid in love with you."

"No, he isn't."

"You're blind, Lila. You're always so logical that you overlook other people's emotions because you believe you know better."

I fell quiet. She wasn't wrong. I couldn't read people, and I really did dismiss emotions in favor of logic because logic got me through everything. When I was on trial, when I was left alone to deal with the fallout with Georgia, I relied on rationality to get me through to the next day when the previous night threatened to take everything.

Even in the brightest of times with him—and I'd forgotten that I was unlovable—fact still trumped emotion. It'd always be difficult to face the truth, but the truth was always there; it'd never leave me no matter how cold or shrill I became. And there was still one thing I couldn't dismiss.

"He still made me his doormat to get what he wanted in the end."

Chapter Thirty

Chaos surrounded me. I just wanted to drink my coffee in peace, but Rhoda's family was loud. First, Rhoda continued to scream up the stairs for Dandre to get moving. And when he missed the bus, she had to drive him to school. But when she asked if I wanted to go to the Flower Market, I jumped at the chance. Even if I hadn't been able to write out a list of what I needed, or even check which reagents I had in my herbalist kit. I also made sure to wear the enchanted pin; Alex was angry and possibly desperate, and there wasn't anything I wouldn't put past him.

I missed the structure of my day, of knowing what was to come and being ready for it. And heaven help me, I missed the quiet mornings and evenings with Lila. Sure, I fed off this energy; it was great. I loved Rhoda's family, and I loved that they accepted me, but damn. I didn't need all this energy. When I'd been with Lila and it'd only been us, I wasn't starving for people; I wasn't lonely. Why had I tried to do something she hadn't wanted? I'd known I was taking a risk, but I thought . . . I thought I knew better.

Desperately wanting to know what she was up to, I opened the planner on my phone and saw nothing scheduled. The window I had into her life was gone, the blinds drawn. It was as if it'd never existed. I rubbed my sore eyes, unable to believe it. She'd deleted me. I shouldn't be surprised, not after that stupid video of me leaving Georgia's trailer. I rubbed my chest, but there was no way to soothe the ache there.

"He's doing it again," Dandre said.

I locked my phone and glanced at him over my shoulder. "I was looking at my calendar."

"Ugh." His eyes rolled to the ceiling of the car. "You're too sad."

Rhoda glanced in the rearview mirror, then at me. "You do look like someone kicked your puppy, Nate."

I sighed and waved my phone. "She deleted our practice sessions from the calendar."

"Then delete her from your life," Dandre said in a sing-song voice. Well, more like a death metal voice, since he did it in a whisper roar and drummed his thighs to the beat drifting from his ear buds.

Rhoda smirked and pulled to the curb and Dandre got out. Once he was safely on his way into the building with his friends, she pulled off and headed toward the Flower Market.

"Maybe you should remove that calendar app from your phone. All you do is stare at it and look heartbroken."

I dug in my pocket for the printout of the next challenge and what we needed to buy in the Flower Market, but I couldn't find it. "Crap. I forgot the list from Sunday. Do you have yours?"

"You really do practice," Rhoda said.

"Yeah, it's how I get everything down and improve my herbal prep." I sighed. "You can never practice too much."

She laughed. "Well, the prices at the Flower Market and my bank say that I can."

Rhoda didn't have an alchemy table, or even a small one. She rented from the library outside the Flower Market. I'd grown extremely used to Lila's greenhouse and apothecary.

I thought of the checks sitting in my wallet. I'd planned to use them to open an account, and they wouldn't do me any favors of eventually getting my own place sitting there. "Hey, can we also go to the bank? I need an account."

"Sure. I'll take you to mine. I need a couple of checks, anyway." She pursed her lips. "I don't know why I have to send a damn check for renewing Gracine's passport when everyone else in this century takes cards."

"It's like fax machines—no one else uses them except insurance companies."

Rhoda groaned and shook her head.

But the bank wouldn't open an account for me since I didn't have a permanent address. However, they agreed to cash my checks. The Potion Network was good for it, and I had my new ID. For a moment, I wished I'd left it behind. I'd use any excuse to see Lila right now.

I stared at the slip as I walked toward the Fine Cupboard, a shop that had some of the cheaper prices on reagents in the Flower Market. The wad of cash in my pockets felt heavy. I'd never had this much, and I wondered if it'd get me an apartment. Probably a one room kind of deal, and despite this prospect, I couldn't help but think nothing was going my way. At least I didn't feel like I could show my happiness.

Lila's tear-stained face kept flashing in my head. She was right. I'd used her to get what I wanted. And in the beginning, it'd been mutual: she'd wanted to prove she wasn't a failed alchemist, and I wanted a chance on *The Next Potion Network Star*.

I guessed we'd both got what we wanted, but I felt so empty. The success I was having on the show up till now and the cash in my pocket couldn't lift my heart. It didn't soothe my worry about what would happen in the future, either. If Lila was taking care of herself or if Winkerton was comforting her. At least I knew those two had made up. Broken friendships hurt, and I was relieved Lila hadn't lost her. But I'd failed her, and I'd paid the price by breaking both of our hearts.

None of it was worth it without her, and I didn't know how to show her that she was my everything.

I could release the video I took in Georgia's trailer, yet that still felt wrong. Maybe it was because Georgia approved all those documentaries about the attempted murder to make Lila look like she'd gotten away with it. No one had ever considered what that was doing to her, and I wouldn't be a part of that. She deserved to be the one who decided how that video would be released and to whom. I'd send it to her as soon as I had access to free Wi-Fi.

I stepped inside the Fine Cupboard and browsed through the ingredients. They had decent verbena, which I grabbed. I passed the calla lily pollen needed for the speak truly potion. I already had that down, and I didn't want to buy something I didn't need right away. As I headed toward the counter to pay, I wondered if I could convince Rhoda to take a trip to Founders' Grove for the rest of the ingredients. Because I didn't want to spend twenty bucks on ten ounces of redwood bark.

"Oh, hey! You're the guy from *The Next Potion Network Star*," the clerk said. His nametag read Peter.

I forced a smile, not sure what to do in a situation like this. No one had recognized me before. "Yeah. How're you?"

"Great, man. Just want to say I like your approach to

potions. It's real simple. My sister is Muted, and she really appreciates your tips for reagents that have similar benefits that don't require an alchemy table."

"Oh, that's great."

He paused and leaned toward me and whispered conspiratorially, "Is it true about Georgia? Two more people have stepped forward about her."

Ever since someone had leaked the security video of me going to her trailer, it was all that people talked about. And four people had complained that Georgia had made unwanted advances on them.

"I can't speak for anyone else but me," I said in my most final voice. I didn't want to talk about this. I had a feeling Naveen would read me the riot act the moment he saw me.

Peter nodded knowingly. "You know, if you don't win, you could have your own special corner in the market." He rang up my items. "My ma—this is her store—thought about having something like that here. But she's too sick to do it herself, and I don't have the extra time, what with this shop and taking online courses."

"That's a great idea," I said, not really feeling the excitement I should have considering I'd already reached someone with my ideas.

He passed me my change, and I quickly divided it up among my pockets. I'd learned long ago to not keep all my cash in my wallet because pickpockets went for that.

"Hey." He laughed and bagged my items. "If the Potion Network doesn't work out, stop by. I could use the help."

"Sure thing," I said.

I left the shop, leaving Rhoda to check out alone. What had just happened in there? This was exactly what I was hoping for, wasn't it? A chance to prove myself on air and get a job based on that instead of my work history, which was null because no one hired anyone who didn't have any kind of alchemy degree to work in their alchemy shop.

The victory felt hollow and tasted bitter.

Then I spotted Alex walking in my direction with the same big dude in a tracksuit. I sighed, already knowing I'd lose the weight of the money in my pocket within the next five minutes, and activated the enchanted pin. His buddy cracked his knuckles when he saw me, and my face throbbed in pain from a memory not too long ago.

I stuffed my sack in my messenger bag. Alex picked up his pace, his expression turning angry as he stormed up to me. "Bitch better have my money," he growled.

I jerked my hands up and took a step back. "Yes, of course. It's here." I grabbed the wad in my front pocket and started counting out the three grand that I owed him.

Alex snatched all of it from me. "This'll do."

"Woah, that's more than—" His expression had me changing my tune. "Uh, please give my thanks and apologize to your, er, boss, for the delay."

His buddy spat at my feet, and they walked off.

At least I had one monkey off my back. For the first time, I was glad to see a friendship go.

NAVEEN SLAMMED the door behind me and jabbed a finger in my face. "Are you fucking stupid?"

"Uhh." I blinked at his angry dark eyes. "Yes."

He shook his head and backed out of my personal space. "I can't believe you thought it was a good idea to have a relationship with her."

For a split second, I thought he was talking about Lila and I saw red. My hands balled into fists, and I took a step forward.

"Georgia and Owen are off-limits," Naveen said before I decked him. "How does no one realize this?"

I stepped backward, the crimson fading fast from my vision, draining the tension from my limbs. This wasn't about Lila but the colossal shitstorm I'd found myself in.

"I . . . She . . ." I shrugged, throwing my hands in the air. "How do you say no to Georgia Cauldron?"

He stared at me, aghast. "This fucking bitch." He wagged his finger at me. "You signed a contract. That means you do not comment on anything regarding this studio until this show has finished airing. Don't talk to her. Don't look at her. Even on camera—nothing. You make no comment to the media, you do not hint to this or any chance you might still have after this is over. Do you hear me, Pittman?"

I nodded.

"I'll make sure she also understands." Naveen pinched the bridge of his nose.

"Who leaked the security video? Do you know?"

"No, and as soon as I find out who, their ass is fired. Un-fucking-believable." He exhaled an angry breath. "Alright. Get back to your hotel room."

When I left Naveen's office, Trevor was waiting for me, clutching his clipboard.

"I need the name for the guest you'll have for challenge six," he said.

I glanced at the door, then back to him. "Let's just see how this weekend goes, alright?"

His brows lifted. "You think they'd risk more talk about this scandal by eliminating you? Don't be naïve, Nate, it doesn't suit you."

"They should eliminate me if I have the worst potion this challenge."

"Sure." Trevor sounded like he didn't believe that'd

happen. He tapped his clipboard. "I want the name by the end of the day on Sunday."

I made it to my room incident free and sat at the desk. Everything was in shambles, but at least I could give Lila some closure over the poisoning and Georgia's motivations behind it. The video was too long to send in a text, so I sent it in an email.

I never heard anything back from her.

THE WATER-LOGGED ground soaked into my shoes, and I wished I still had my galoshes that following Saturday. I was pretty sure I'd forgotten them in Lila's car—an excuse I was afraid to use to see her. To me, it sounded like I was only coming back for the things I'd gained by our partnership and anything else I'd say would ring hollow.

Rhoda remained a couple steps ahead of me, and the cameraman filming us stayed a few feet behind. I really liked her. She kind of felt like a surrogate mother, better than a foster parent who cared, but definitely a friend as well. I knew she'd always be a figure in my life as long as I didn't overextend my welcome with her.

I'd learned yet again that everyone would eventually kick me out of their life.

"Oh look, there's some lion's mane." Rhoda picked up the pace.

I followed her, stepping in the same place as her. She crouched and reached out. She'd never put on her foraging gloves, but if she'd really found lion's mane mushrooms over here in the swamp, she didn't need them. I came up behind her.

Lion's mane mushrooms grew in clumps, the white caps long and stringy, resembling a mane of hair. Rhoda reached for the cap of a single mushroom, the color perhaps more buttery than white, and there was only one.

"That isn't lion's mane!" I tried to grab her arm, but she was too quick.

She frowned up at me, and then at the mushroom she was attempting to grab by the stem. The mane writhed, spreading its hair over the back of her hand.

"Oh shit." She dropped the plant and staggered back from it.

I helped her to her feet. "Are you okay?"

She examined her hand and gave me a tight-lipped smile. "I'm fine, kiddo."

I studied the plant and grew more worried. It wasn't a mushroom, but a manticore's tail. A carnivorous plant that absorbed smaller insects like snails, praying mantis, and even some smaller amphibians. The tails had barbs to scratch the skin and left behind a toxin that'd paralyze and putrefy its meal. In a human, it'd induce dizziness, vomiting, and it could even cause organ failure if they got enough of the toxin in their bloodstream.

"Rhoda, that's a manticore's tail."

"It barely touched me. I'll be fine. Now, let's move on." Rhoda stepped around the manticore's tail, and Tony pointed the camera at me.

I frowned and went after her, keeping my attention more on her than where I stepped. We walked a few more yards when Rhoda stumbled.

I rushed to her side, and her lips were turning blue at the edges and the side of her palm had a long, thin slit that was growing puffy before my eyes. I flipped her hand over and gaped at the angry, wet welts covering her skin. "Rhoda!"

"I . . . feel strange, Nate." She gripped her jacket. "I can't breathe."

"Sit down." I eased her to the ground and dug in my kit for the antidote I always kept in there.

I uncorked the potion and held it to her mouth. Tony circled us, filming.

"Don't just stand there!" I growled. "Call a fucking ambulance, man!"

Rhoda's hand dropped; she hadn't finished taking the potion.

"No, Rho, finish that." I held it to her mouth and tipped it back.

She coughed and sagged onto her back, her eyes blinking rapidly at the sky. "Nate . . ."

I grabbed her hand and, after verifying Tony was calling for help, gave her my full attention. "I'm here."

"You gotta tell that girl you love her," Rhoda whispered. "Life's short."

GEORGIA HELD her bunny as she stood beneath the studio lights beside Owen Creek the next day. She'd been in a foul mood the entire time filming and barely spoke. I'd guessed the allegations over her misconduct were getting to her. And I probably pissed her off. I wondered if Naveen saved me from Melody shitting down my throat since I doubted Georgia would let the rabbit do her business by herself.

Yet I already knew the outcome of today's elimination before they would announce it—we all did. Rhoda's accident saved my ass. If she hadn't gotten so sick, I'd probably be the one going home today.

"It's finally my pleasure to announce a winner." Owen grinned. "And it's no slow poke to be sure. Abby, our Beltane babe, got us with your delicious potion. It's true mint makes everything better."

Georgia scowled. Abby covered her mouth, and we all congratulated her.

"As for the elimination today . . ." Owen cleared his throat. "Due to Rhoda's accident with a manticore's tail, she's being held for observation at the hospital to ensure a full recovery and she's unable to continue. That means all of you get to come back next week!"

Cole cried, and honestly, I almost did too.

Chapter Thirty-One

"You gotta tell that girl you love her," Rhoda slurred, the captions stark white at the bottom of the TV screen in my kitchen. "Life's short."

Nathaniel clasped her hands, his brows smooshed together and the fear and sorrow in his mossy green eyes hit me right in the chest. I almost choked on my martini. I had to glance away. Seeing his pain and worry made my chest cramp. Reginald, Winkerton's familiar, perched on my kitchen counter next to the bottle of gin and vermouth. We'd grabbed the essentials from the wet bar and brought them into the kitchen to watch the show.

"You're going to be fine," Nathaniel whispered with emotion on the TV. "You're going to be fine."

"Jeeze," Winkerton said, reaching for a mini eclair. "They really played that up."

I shook my head. "That's Rhoda. He really took to her. I bet he's scared shitless she might be seriously hurt. Look."

I pointed at the disclaimer that talked up safety first when handling mushrooms and unknown plants, the silent killers of the woods. Never forage without gloves, always keep your foraging kit stocked with an antidote, and make sure you are handling the fungi properly—even though it'd been a manticore's tail that'd stung her. Rhoda had broken a cardinal rule of foraging.

"None of that was staged." I toyed with the olive skewer, wondering if she'd give me the stink eye if I got more olives to snack on.

Nathaniel appeared on screen, watching the flashing lights of the ambulance as they drove off. He bit his lip, a faraway expression on his face. Someone spoke to him off camera, and again there were captions asking how he felt about the whole thing.

"Her family's going to be worried about her, and I feel like I let them all down." He nodded slightly. "But always, *always* make sure you have an antidote potion in your kit before you forage each time."

The show broke for a commercial for one of the gossip shows on a sister station, discussing more people stepping forward about Georgia Cauldron, ranging back from the beginning of her time as a host on *The Next Potion Network Star*. Most of these people coming forward now were employees of the station.

Winkerton muted the TV and grabbed a pastry from the plate, the ruby on her left ring finger glinting in the light. It still smarted she'd hid her relationship from me, but I couldn't hold it against her, and time would take the sting away.

She faced me. "Have you talked to him in the past week about the next challenge? You said you'd go on the show for him."

Tomorrow, they'd start filming for challenge six. I unlocked my phone and showed her the message thread between us. He'd texted me every day with an apology, saying he missed me or pleading to meet up so we could talk again now that some time had passed. There had even been an email with an attached file, but I deleted that and never responded. "And do what? Expose him as a fraud on national TV like we'd planned?"

Her baby blue eyes widened as if the thought hadn't entered her mind.

"I don't want to. What's the point anymore? It won't help anyone." I shook my head. "No, and I don't think I'll be going on. I hate being on camera, and there's that new documentary . . ."

"Don't you want to talk to him?" she asked before biting into one of the mini pastries and softly humming in the back of her throat.

"All the damn time." I sighed. "I miss seeing him every morning, miss talking to him." I shrugged and sipped my martini. "Even if it is true he didn't sleep with her, it all comes down to him using me as a stepping stone to get where he is today. I just can't be that for anyone but me."

"Are you in love with him?"

My heart hitched painfully, and I bowed my head. Of course I was, but what good would it do me now to admit that? He was gone; we were done. I'd thrown him out of my life as quickly as everyone else had kicked me to the curb as soon as he'd done something wrong, never giving him the chance to defend himself. I wasn't avoiding him or my feelings because I was embarrassed; I was *hurt*. My chest ached as if a physical blow had been dealt to it and there was no recovery from this in sight. The back of my eyes grew hot and my head throbbed. I didn't want to cry, not again. If I started, I didn't think I'd be able to stop.

"It doesn't matter. Even if I'm willing to overlook the lying it took to get on this show because the heart wants what the heart wants." I rolled my eyes and sneered. "He used me from the beginning. He told me he was going to use me, and then I was surprised when he used me and tried to steal from me." I rubbed my mouth as if I could wipe away the trembling deep inside me. "I can't really blame him, either. There's not much about me that's lovable."

Winkerton scoffed. "I've heard you say that you're unlikable off and on throughout our entire friendship. What does it say about me if I like you?"

"You're very kind and—"

"Nathaniel *really* likes you." She stacked her hands on the table and lifted a sculpted brow at me. "So does my great-aunt. Drew desperately wants you to like him."

I swatted that last statement out of the air. "That's because I'm your best friend and he thought I hated him."

"True. But he still wants you to like him." She picked up her drink and poked me. "Where did you get this idea that no one could ever like you?"

"Well . . ." I thought back over the years. I was always an introvert, comfortable with silence, but I managed to make a few friends here and there. But the real tipping point came from this show. I'd always been nervous in front of a camera, so that awful smile came out. And then when I spoke passionately about something, my voice would rise in octave. And then there was my ex-father, but politicians were born snakes. "A lot of the producers told me my expressions made people uncomfortable, and no one enjoyed hearing me talk."

"Lila, darling, I've never thought you enjoyed being on TV. You don't talk of it fondly, and when you did, it was about the potions you'd created for that show. You're very much a behind-the-scenes type of person, and there's nothing wrong with not wanting the limelight."

"Georgia told me all the complaints on the set were about me when we worked on *Home Brew Elixirs* together. She said the reason why I went through so many assistants was because I was awful and it was hard to like me, and—" I looked down at my hands. "She said I was unlovable when we went our separate ways."

"Assholes." Winkerton stood, and the spell to chill the booze flashing in the air over Reginald's head in glittering swirls and lines. She poured another round of martinis. "You're believing assholes because they needed to tear you down to lift themselves up."

"I know they're assholes," I whispered. "It's . . ."

"What, darling?" She covered my hand with hers and crouched beside me. "You can tell me anything."

"Well, you know my dad disowned me because—"

"He's an asshole and decided you were guilty before the verdict was in. Couldn't walk that back, could he?"

"Oh, we were always distant. My father was running for congress in Arizona then and couldn't be linked to me. I haven't talked to him since. But how could he do that so easily?"

"I can't guess. It's so wild to me."

"And my mother isn't much better. We chat every few months, but she sends me gadgets on birthdays to make up for my childhood."

"Okay, so you got the rotten end of the stick with parents and your first love." She stood and gripped my shoulders. "And it's time you stop believing those lies about yourself because Nathaniel is in love with you and you can have that with him if you can forgive what he did."

"But he used me."

She sat down and drummed her fingers on the table. "I know in the beginning, it was mutual, but everything you've told me about him feels like you two are really great together. And I've never seen you with these feelings for anyone."

I shrugged.

"I don't want you to lose something special because

you're too far in your own head, listening to farting assholes."

I laughed a little. Mostly because Winkerton was trying to make me smile and she deserved something for her efforts.

"You know, it's just really easy to see what they say about me." I swiped at my cheek. "*I* don't even like myself sometimes."

"Darling." She smiled gently at me. "Everyone's brain is an asshole."

"Even if he hadn't done this, and taken from me like he had, we're still too different. And being with me is social suicide, especially if he wants his own TV show."

"My social life is entirely unaffected by what other people think of you." Her red lips thinned, and then she jerked her head at the TV. "Georgia's the only one who cares where everyone stands on the social ladder, and she has done everything she could do to be on top. I don't think Nathaniel cares as much as you think he should."

"I'm just so afraid of being hurt even more by him than he already has," I whispered.

"I get it, darling. It sucks. But if he hurts you again, it's because he doesn't deserve you, not the other way around. You're an absolute treasure. I love you. Nathaniel loves you. And the world would love you if you gave it a chance. It's time you love yourself too."

I ROLLED OVER IN BED, staring at the silvery beams of moonlight slanting across my room. The rain had finally stopped for the time being, and I missed the sound of it hitting my window. I grabbed my phone and unlocked it.

I had an unread text, which had my phone not been set to do not disturb, I would've known. I couldn't sleep, not with the conversation I'd had with Winkerton and everything that'd happened these past weeks.

She was right. I was letting the mass public opinion of my trial guide how I thought, behaved, and even worked with vendors. I let them undercut me because I believed no one wanted to work with me. That I was a difficult person to like, and if I kept myself bland and didn't fight back, then I'd still be able to ghost on by, barely disturbing people.

Sure, many people were Team Georgia, and they were the loudest because she still had that damn mystery about her poisoning and I had azaleas, no matter that none of my bees had pollinated them. I was still guilty because Georgia didn't like me.

I'd lost so much, and most of it was who I was before I let people talk me into believing I was a terrible person, but mostly okay in small doses. These people couldn't handle me in my worst moment, and they didn't deserve any consideration from me.

I opened the text and my stomach flipped.

NATHANIEL

I'm still going to list you as my partner for tomorrow, but if you don't want to see me, then I understand

Dots appeared. I dropped my phone like it was a hot potato. How did he know I was reading his message?

NATHANIEL

I'm sorry for taking the bath bomb and giving you a reason to distrust me. I promise I didn't tell anyone about what it could do. I'm so sorry, Lila

I was sorry too, because he was someone I never felt awful around. Sighing, I clasped my phone to my chest and stared at the ceiling. I felt alive and beautiful and smart around him, and that was why his betrayal hurt so much. He'd seen me, the real me, and not some act I'd put on for people who I did business with, and he still went into Georgia's trailer and did what he did with her.

For the first time in years, I deep dived into social media for scandal rumors. Tons of results came up, but I just picked the first one and gasped when I read the first paragraph. Six men and three women had come forward about sexual misconduct and verbal abuse from Georgia while filming *Home Brew Elixirs* and *The Next Potion Network Star*. Nathaniel wasn't one of them, but I knew he wasn't commenting. I doubted Naveen would let him until the show was over.

There was a TikTok video of Georgia. She wore all black and her makeup was subdued, and her bunny wasn't in sight. "There's a lot of talk about me and my past relationships, which should stay in the past. They've all been mature relationships, and I'm sorry if some people are uncomfortable with my lifestyle. It's crazy to judge people for who they choose to have in their life and how they choose to break ties with a person. I respect each and every person I work with and have been in relationships with, and these accusations that I don't are wildly inaccurate."

I frowned, letting it play again and focusing on the captions more than her voice and her face. "That's not an apology. That's barely an acknowledgement of what's happening."

I watched it again because I was a masochist. "She's gaslighting!"

I closed the video and sat up in bed, rubbing my face. It never surprised me that Georgia gaslighted. I'd been aware of this trait of hers for years. What surprised me was that she believed every word she said. She didn't see that she'd done anything wrong, and she never had.

Nathaniel, on the other hand . . . I read over the apology he sent. I'd never given him the chance to apologize, and this was the only way he had, and it was . . . I believed he was sorry. I'd been wrong about him because I'd believed he was just like her.

What else had I been wrong about?

I swallowed and placed my phone back on my bedside table and pulled the covers back up to my chin, blinking at the ceiling. If someone like Nathaniel could see the truth about Georgia and me, then maybe I was holding on to something that I had no business clutching so closely. I'd protected the idea that I was unlovable because it'd resonated perfectly with everything I thought. But, fuck.

It'd taken a long while, and I don't know . . . Seeing her behave toward everyone who complained about her to the entire world like she'd behaved to me freed something from my heart. I wasn't the villain, and I was done acting like an outsider.

For the first time in many years, I fell asleep with a kind thought for myself.

Chapter Thirty-Two

Trevor glared at me and swiped the ear bud and microphone off his head, bundling the cords in his hand. "Are you out of your fucking mind?" He shook the electronics at me. "You want *Lila Townsend* as your guest? On *this* show?"

I glanced around, checking to see if anyone had heard. They had. Abby and an older gentleman exchanged a look that clearly said someone would have rabbit turds in their mouth soon, and that someone would be me.

"Yeah." I pushed his hand from my face. "She's really smart—"

"I don't care if she's the Queen of Sheba! Georgia will shit kittens if that woman sets foot on this stage."

Naveen lifted his head and frowned at us. He gestured us to come to his chair, and we did. "What's the problem now?"

"Nate's telling me just now his guest is Lila Townsend," Trevor said like a tattling toddler. "It's why he waited until today to spring it on me."

Naveen's eyes shifted to mine, and he stared at me.

"She's innocent, and she's really shaped me in alchemy," I said. "Look, you can say no, and I'll go alone." I let the unspoken part of my statement hang thick between us. They were too scared to let Lila on.

"Trevor, put her name on the list and let Georgia know she needs to be on her best behavior." Naveen returned his attention to the show notes.

Trevor turned sheet white, curled his lip at me, and stalked off.

But it hadn't mattered. Lila wasn't here.

I stood on the set, the herbarium behind me as we all took our places at our workbenches. It was only the three of us, and I could see Abby's and Cole's partners waiting off in the wings. I wiped my hands on my apron, then drummed my fingers on my workbench.

I couldn't blame Lila for not coming. Not after what I'd done and what everyone else thought I'd done with Georgia. I licked my lips; she was talking in the camera, but I could tell by the set of her jaw and the rigidness of her shoulders she was pissed. Owen Creek, on the other hand, was in the best mood since filming started. I suppose he was feeling some schadenfreude and couldn't fault him for it.

I glanced to the wings one more time as they introduced everyone's guests as if it would change what I'd already known. Lila hadn't showed up. It reminded me of those days in school, especially elementary, when I'd stood alone while my classmates showed their parents their desks. Bowing my head and staring at the workbench before me, I wasn't sure what I'd expected from her. I wished she'd responded to my texts. Maybe I should've gone to her house instead of visiting Rhoda in the hospital, but I also hadn't wanted to force her to listen to me. She didn't owe it to me to hear my apology; I didn't deserve to be listened to. But I'd hoped one day, when the wound wasn't so raw, I could let her know what had really happened.

I stared ahead and smiled when I saw other people smiling. Cole hugged someone and cried as he did it. He was emotional, and he was free to feel that way, but I was certain that was his wife and she'd driven with him to the studio. Abby and Granholm, her professor, were chatting. I could tell right away they had a genuine friendship and respect for one another. I was also worried about that night weeks ago when we'd talked about our time in college. I hoped they wouldn't want to chat about the glory days with me.

"And what a surprise tonight! One of our own from five years ago, who almost stole the show from our Georgia." Owen cheesed it up so hard when his cohost's scowl replaced her strained smile for a flash. "Please give a warm welcome back to Lila Townsend!"

I spun, my jaw hitting my chest when she stepped out into the light. She'd pinned her pale brown hair back with a purple flower while the tail dangled over one shoulder, curling at the end. Our eyes met. For a moment, I couldn't breathe as her strained smile relaxed into a semi-nervous one. I erased the distance between us, opening my arms, and she stiffened. I dropped them, half reached for her hands and then stopped.

"Lila," I murmured, smiling at her. "You're . . . lovely."

She wore a blue plaid shirt, unbuttoned enough to tease at her cleavage, and her gray slacks hugged her shapely hips. Her cheeks flushed.

Georgia laughed. "I see you're still just as awkward on camera."

My fists clenched tight enough for my nails to leave marks on my palms. I turned slowly, but Lila placed a hand on my arm, her fingers flexing on my biceps.

"I see you remain the same, Georgia," Lila said.

A pin dropped. Silence sucked all sounds from the studio as Georgia fumed. Owen cackled, then coughed and shoved his hands in his pockets. Lila and I settled behind my workbench.

Owen clasped his hands together and faced the camera. "You have sixty minutes to prepare these potions. That includes making them in the appropriate flask, labeling them, and of course, making them part of your brand. On your mark, get ready . . . *Cook!*"

As soon as he finished speaking, I turned to Lila, but she was already dashing into the herbarium. I ran after her, snagging a basket and following her inside.

"Lila, I—"

"You're still making the six you decided on?" she asked, pulling some reagents down and tossing them into the basket.

"I'd never stray from the plan."

"Good. We need six vials of dawn tree water and two eyedroppers," she said in a stern voice. "Go get it."

I hopped to it. Lila raced around me as if she'd always known this place. And I guess she had. After collecting all the ingredients, we hurried back to the bench. I set out the reagents, and she went along prepping the vials and toppers for what was going to be what. As I was prepping the star moss, she peered around my shoulder, the smell of lemon candy catching me off guard. This reminded me of her greenhouse, and I desperately wanted to take her in my arms and beg for forgiveness.

"Not so fine, Nathaniel." Lila poked my pile of moss. "You want to catch most of this when you strain."

Georgia chuckled. "Nate doesn't like being called Nathaniel."

I jerked my head up. I hadn't noticed the hosts

approaching our bench, but I supposed having Lila on set with me would demand immediate attention. Oh, if only I could've been a fly on the wall when they'd both found out.

"Naw." I shrugged and smiled at Lila. "Only the special ones can call me that."

Her silvery eyes lit up with the genuine smile curving her mouth. Georgia bristled and Owen laughed. Lila cleared her throat and resumed printing sticker labels, that cute flush staining her cheeks again.

Owen leaned against the table. "Lila, how does it feel to be—?"

"How did you two meet?" Georgia asked, but it sounded more like a demand for an answer. "Nate's a little younger than you, isn't he?"

"What were you going to say, Owen?" Lila continued affixing the labels to the medallions she'd chosen without looking up.

I grinned and continued prepping. I was so thrilled she was here, and I couldn't believe my luck. I knew she put much on her word and loyalty, and if she'd said she'd do something, then she always did. She was amazing. I'd do whatever I could to win her back. Spend every dime I ever made to give her the best planner book available; take her to every forest imaginable for the rarest of ingredients; extra olives in her martinis—whatever it took, everything would never be too much for her.

"How does it feel to be back in Potion Network Studios?" Owen asked, grinning from ear to ear when Georgia glared daggers at them. "Is it like riding a bike?"

"I'm nervous, of course." Lila glanced at me, a shy smile on her face before moving on to the next potion. "But nothing seems to have changed."

"Plenty has changed," Georgia said with forced cheerfulness. "I'm the head executive producer and a host here. And you're . . .?"

"Oh, but you're still the same Georgia," Lila said with a sharp smile. "Isn't that right?"

She opened her mouth.

"You two need to move along. We have work to do and little time to do it, don't we, Nathaniel?"

"Absolutely!"

Owen chuckled and walked off with the camera crew. Georgia hovered, glaring at us, then stalked off. I let out a breath I hadn't realized I'd been holding and grinned at Lila. Then we put our heads down and finished making the potions.

Afterward, when the chemist deemed all potions safe and viable, Lila wandered off. She hadn't said anything about us or the video I'd sent her; I still hadn't had the chance to make amends.

I chased after her, my apron strings trailing behind me. "Lila, wait!"

Her hands clenched into fists, and she spun around. That strained smile stretching her soft lips into a nervous baring of teeth appeared on her face. I hated it was for me.

I grasped her hand. "Will you get a drink with me and talk?"

She gently extracted her hand and clasped her fingers together, taking a step back. "No."

My heart crashed into my stomach and drowned. My ears buzzed.

"I want you to concentrate on the show," she said, "and when you're done filming, I'll have that drink with you."

"I . . ." At most, it wouldn't be for another week. It wasn't a no. I clutched the promise like a lifebuoy ring, the tightness in my chest easing. I nodded. "Sure. I'm really glad you came."

"I gave you my word I would." She fiddled with her hair and then shrugged. "Winkerton's waiting for me."

"I'll see you tomorrow?"

"Yes." Her lips tipped upward at the corners of her mouth.

I watched her leave as if my heart were walking away with her. Rhoda was right. Life was too short to not put her first every moment I had.

THE VENDOR HALL stretched for half a football field with fresh maroon marbled carpet, and it smelled as if the cream walls had recently been painted. A sliding beveled partition blocked off most of the room. Black cloth draped over plastic tables all arranged to force people to mill in weird circles. I chugged my water at my table, examining the perfectly packaged potions Lila and I had made yesterday. I scanned the hall.

Abby and Granholm were arranging their potions on the table. They had healing varieties that would fetch really high prices for whoever sold them. She'd flown under the radar earlier on in the show. She'd won the last two competitions and between her, me, and Cole, she was the one I was really worried about.

Cole and his wife—I forgot her name—had filled their table with utility potions like accuracy, speed, calm mind, and steady hands. It surprised me, as I hadn't pegged him for that. Then again, the accuracy potion he'd made when partnered with me had lasted nearly seven minutes; his arrangement shouldn't have shocked me.

Lila walked into the hall, a vision wearing a wraparound navy-blue dress. My breath stalled and our gazes met as she walked toward our table. People turned to watch her, and I couldn't blame them.

I smiled when she stopped beside me. "You look amazing."

"Thank you. It has pockets." She did a little spin; I loved her in blue. "I declined the petticoats from Winkerton, much to her dismay."

Trevor appeared like a ghost and sighed. "You're supposed to wear the same thing you had on yesterday to promote continuity."

Lila tucked her hands in the pockets and shrugged, smiling serenely. "I didn't want to."

"Georgia says that if you can't, then you won't be able to participate in filming today." Trevor flicked nervous eyes at the woman in question glaring at us.

"Wouldn't that also disrupt continuity?" I asked.

"Georgia can tell me so herself," Lila said. "I'm not going to change."

Trevor whipped out a bottle of Pepto-Bismol and groaned. "I don't get paid enough to relay that message." He walked off without another word.

"I hope this doesn't mess things up for you," Lila whispered.

"I don't care."

She jerked her eyes to me, studying me. "But if this messes things up, you won't get your show."

"My show isn't as important as I thought it was."

Her lips parted. I could tell this was the moment to let it all out, that she'd let me explain. I stepped closer, brushing my fingers down her arm to—

Trevor clapped his hands. Lila took a step back.

"Places, everyone!" Trevor pushed an earpiece into his ear. "The vendors will be let loose, and you need to sell your potions. If you cause a scene and embarrass the studio,

Melody will shit down your throat!"

Then it was happening. People came by and examined my potions, checked their viability, but a lot of them seemed nervous. Like they didn't know what to do with Lila or me and the situation with Georgia. I knew before that it'd been a mistake to visit her trailer. Now I saw exactly how big it was. Not just because Lila kicked me out, but people knew where the wind was blowing, and thanks to my colossal mistake, it didn't seem to be in my direction.

But Lila was poise and graciousness. Her smile was strained at some point, but I brushed her arm and lightly gripped her fingers, showing support as best as I could.

"You've got a lot of balls tying your talent to someone who can't have a viable business," a woman said.

"Marla." Lila threaded her fingers together. "I didn't know you'd be here, since you specialize in shiny baubles over at Enchanting Crystals."

"I'm a vendor. Why wouldn't I?" Marla smirked. "I'm a silent partner with Jeffrey in a lot of things."

Her partner, Jeffrey, sniffed dismissively. "No one wants to do business with her." He shook his head at me. "Career suicide before you even get started."

"Nathaniel and I aren't in business together," Lila said.

At least she hadn't said we weren't together. There was that, right?

Jeffrey lifted his hands palms up and shrugged. "Immortalized forever as soon as this is aired." He jabbed a finger at me. "You'd do well to stay away from her before she really ruins everything for you. The jury might've cleared her of poisoning Georgia, but I'm positive she worked some magic to force someone to do her evil deeds."

"No," I said, half-shouting.

Lila blinked while Marla and Jeffrey stiffened. Owen

smelled drama. He and Tony wandered over to join the crew. Georgia hurried after them.

"What's going on?" Owen asked through clenched teeth.

"We were just warning young Nate here to be careful of who he does business with," Jeffrey said.

"That's true." Georgia's brows lifted on her forehead, and her cold blue eyes speared Lila. "This is pathetic, even for someone like you."

Lila sucked in a breath, and her spine grew ramrod stiff. "Pathetic? D'you mean as pathetic as you not being able to cook a potion and begging me to help you not get eliminated or that you're not able to invent your own potions?"

First blood went to Lila, and like sharks, everyone in the auditorium turned to watch.

"Ha!" Georgia let loose a shrill laugh. "You couldn't hack it in front of a camera, not with your terrible personality. No one liked you then, and no one will now. What do you think you're trying to pull here, huh? At least *I* didn't try to murder anyone on camera! The public has spoken about you long ago, and you're nothing."

Lila winced, her wounded gray eyes darting to me, and she took a step back. "I never tried to poison you, Georgia."

"Liar!" Georgia pointed at her. "It's all on video of you handing me poison!"

"Enough!" I tugged out my phone. "Why don't I let the cat out of the bag, hmm?"

"What're you doing?" Lila had that uncomfortable smile on her face.

"I'm sorry. I wanted you to decide what to do about this, but I can't stand here and let her lie about you. I can't let you allow her to walk all over you again." I lifted my phone up. "I found out exactly what happened regarding Georgia's poisoning five years ago." I opened the video and fast forward through the beginning. Tony pressed tight to my back, angling the camera over my shoulder as I played the video.

It showed me pushing Georgia off me multiple times and growing louder the drunker she became. My neck heated. Then it came to the sweet spot.

Georgia's voice cut from my phone, describing why and how she set Lila up. Georgia heard herself and froze, turning as white as a ghost. Then she lunged for me, but Owen caught her around the waist.

"People don't even take her acquittal into account because you keep approving documentaries about your mysterious poisoning, and it was you. You did it to yourself and framed Lila for it."

"Meh. Lila doesn't matter."

"She matters to me," I said.

"What?"

"You destroyed something special we all could have experienced for what reason?" I stood and raked my hands through my hair.

"I deserved it." Georgia stood, swayed, and fell back onto the couch with a huff. "I deserved the money and the parties and the adoring fans because I put the work in. I sold the potions, and they should be mine."

"What did you ever come up with in your life?" I asked.

"Well, I'm definitely good at framing people." She cackled and sighed, sliding over to lie on the couch. "I'm drunk."

"Yes." I pulled the shaggy blanket over her and set Melody on her stomach. "Sleep it off."

Lila covered her mouth, tears swimming in her eyes as she stared at me. The room was silent, and I took another chance. I turned and faced everyone staring at us.

"You've called her a bad alchemist, a failed practitioner of the magic acts, and that you wouldn't let her train your dog to sit." I cleared my throat and laughed, my palms sweating as my stomach turned a touch queasy. *Here goes everything.* "News flash. I owe her everything."

"Nathaniel, don't," she whispered.

"Lila taught me everything I know. I've never stepped foot inside Starglen Alchemy University. I never took any courses. Everything that you've liked about my alchemy, she taught me while I waited for you to approve my application for this show."

They closed the set after that. The big wigs whisked Georgia off. Owen was . . . I didn't want to say he was as happy as a pig in shit, but I also couldn't say that wasn't the case thanks to his suppressed smirk. Cole blinked dry eyes at me as I sat beside him in the hallway while we waited for filming to resume. Abby got up from the other side of him and strode across the hall to the empty bench.

Cole turned to me, tilting his head. "That was . . . enlightening."

"Yeah, I bet." I looked around for Lila, but I couldn't find her.

Two hours went by with no news.

Eventually, Naveen and Detective Burris strode down the hall, and when spotting me, the detective abruptly stopped and held out a hand. "You still got that pin on you? I need to return that back to Enchantments."

"Oh, uhm. Not on me." I grimaced, wondering who he was here for and hoping it wasn't for me. "Is . . . is it over? Did you get what you wanted from it?"

"Oh yes, everything I wanted. He'll flip like a pancake." Burris hitched his pants up. "Good work. Make sure you turn that in soon."

I shook his hand. "Sure."

Naveen threw a confused look at me while he ushered the detective into one of the nearby offices.

I didn't know how I felt about Alex and what was happening with him and the mafia. If they weren't careful, they'd probably get him killed. I sighed. Then we were called onstage.

Owen was alone, professional, and he gave me a resigned expression. "In light of recent events, we must call a stop to today's challenge. Nate, you have admitted you falsified your application about your formal education. While you've . . . brought light to the disparity and depravity of what goes on behind scenes, regretfully, the president of the Potion Network has given a vote of no confidence in your continuing forward. I'm sorry, but you won't be the next Potion Network star this year."

Chapter Thirty-Three

The police had been called immediately after they stopped filming and sent the vendors away. Of course, they'd questioned me. Again. Five years ago, I'd sat in a gray-on-gray room in the police station with a botanist next to me and two detectives across a table. I'd been shaking in my shoes with fear and worry and so stunned I didn't know what to do. The memory of the cold cuffs lashing my skin tingled across my wrists.

Today, I sat in a small office with a cup of room temperature water on the desk. Framed stock photos of popular TPN shows lined the wall. One of them was of *Home Brew Elixirs*. I stared at it, remembering when we'd decided on the title and that I'd given little thought to it because the idea of a teeth whitening potion was taking shape to me then.

Detective Burris sat on the other side of the desk. He was older, going bald, and his nose had a red tint to it from excessive drinking. The room was growing warm, or perhaps it was just me, but that old terror of not knowing what was happening didn't grip me by the throat.

"Thank you, Miss Townsend," Burris said, jotting something down on his notebook. "I'll be in touch if I have further questions." He lifted his tired eyes to mine and tapped the end of his pen on the desk. "You might want to consider contacting a lawyer about a civil suit against Miss Daugherty."

Daugherty was Georgia's legal name. She'd adopted an alias after she'd been selected to compete on the show. I nodded and stepped out of the room. I didn't know how things would change, if at all. But it felt good to finally know what had happened those five years ago. *I* knew I was innocent, and I'd been acquitted rightfully, but now the public knew, or would soon find out. If the producers didn't strike on this drama first—talk about exciting TV!—something told me Nathaniel wouldn't wait to share the video. I didn't know what would happen next.

But mostly, I knew Nathaniel had sacrificed his dream to clear my name.

My thoughts swirled too fast in my head for me to latch on, but one kept hammering home. When he'd taken the potions and made that video, it'd always been for me. Yeah, he'd gone about it the wrong way, but it'd been for me. I smothered a laugh. My body couldn't decide how to react. Possibly to drop dead from my stalling heart. I shook out my tingling hands. Or maybe I wanted to jump for joy. I walked as fast as my heels would carry me toward the set. I had to get to Nathaniel. I had to find him and ask him why he'd done all this when Georgia stepped into my path.

"Well, well." She sneered. "You're like a bad penny."

"Georgia." I looked over her shoulder, eyeing the doors to the stage. I didn't want this confrontation with her anymore. I had my answers. I needed to find him, make sure he was handling the elimination okay. To see him.

"So, how long have you been planning this?" She crossed her arms. "It was brilliant. I didn't even see it coming."

"What're you talking about?" I asked.

"You found Nate and made him seduce me. You catfished me."

I blinked, a startled laugh bursting from me. That was an idea. However, I'd waited years for this confrontation to unleash all my negative feelings about what she'd done to my life. I'd lost a wealth of belief because of her. Trust in people, trust in myself. Friends. And now that the moment was here to dump all my feelings on her over what had happened, all I wanted to do was find Nathaniel.

I dug deep inside me, intending to grab the anger, sorrow, and betrayal and give them back to Georgia. I was tired of carrying that emotional weight for her. But I came up empty. Somewhere between last night and now, I'd let it go. There was room to breathe fully. I closed my eyes and took the first real breath I had in a long while. It tasted sweet.

"You can think whatever you want about me, Georgia." I lifted my hands, showing they were empty, and laughed. "You're just not important enough for me to care what you think." I bumped my shoulder against her as I brushed by.

She screeched. "You'll regret this, you harpy! You haven't heard the last of me yet. I'll see you in court again!"

She would see me in court again, but it wouldn't be from the same table as last time. With every step I took away from Georgia, it was like closing a door on that chapter of my life. Now that the world knew, or would soon know, I couldn't even give her the prestigious pedestal of being the villain in my story any longer. I let go.

When I stepped onto the stage, I expected to feel regret and loss for a time that no longer existed. Except I only felt . . . indifference. Nathaniel wasn't here. Trevor hurried around with the crew, cleaning up papers. The lights were off, save for a couple. I stepped into the herbarium and smiled. It was beautiful in here, and it smelled like a fresh garden. I hadn't lost this; I still cherished alchemy, and I doubted there was anything that could take it from me. I left the stage. I still needed to find him.

A teary-eyed older man stepped in front of me. "I just want to apologize for all my mean thoughts about you." He sobbed. "I believed her and—"

"Cole, right?" I said. It was a silly question. He still had his apron on, and I watched the show.

He nodded.

"Yeah, I don't care what you've thought about me in the past."

He gasped. I'd shocked the tears right out of his eyes.

"That's where it is, and I'm okay with it. Have you seen Nathaniel?"

He cried even harder and blubbered something about the locker room. I don't think I ever saw that man without a wet face. His wife must be a saint. I ran down the hallways until I made it to the locker room. I placed a hand on my racing chest and opened the door.

Owen Creek was in his underwear, high-fiving Nathaniel. He didn't look like he wanted to be high-fived, but when he saw me, he tossed a towel at Owen.

Owen frowned and turned. Then he yelped and tied the towel around his waist. His nipples were pierced. Wonders never ceased. "This is the men's locker room!"

"I really need to talk to you, Nathaniel." I walked farther in and then grimaced at Owen. "In private, please."

"Well, I suppose that's fine." He grabbed his pants and smiled at me. "I hope you're happy."

That was the first time someone had said that to me without malice. I blinked and nodded. "Thanks."

Then we were alone. I licked my lips. Nathaniel was so handsome, and the more I'd grown to know him, the more attracted to him I became. It hadn't faded. If anything, it felt like too much. But . . . I'd kicked him out of my house. Told him we were over and then ghosted him, never giving him a chance to defend himself. I shoved my hands in my pockets and balled my fists. What if I'd damaged things more between us? What if he didn't feel the same way about me?

"I'm sorry. For not letting you explain what happened." I swallowed and met his concerned gaze. My heart skipped a beat. "But what were you thinking back there in the convention?"

My voice sounded strangled and shrill. Oh god, I was nervous. Calm down. I could talk to him about anything, I knew that. But . . . he'd thrown everything away on a whim.

His face fell, and he raked his hands through his hair. "I just couldn't listen to them talk shit about you when I knew the truth."

I forced myself closer to him. The distance between us was too much. "But you got eliminated."

"Yeah, well, maybe I don't want to work for this network if they're going to let people like Georgia rule the roost." He wiped his mouth, his mossy green eyes locking on mine.I took another tentative step forward. "You could've had every-thing, and you ruined it. I don't understand."

"The show isn't important, Lila." He shrugged, then matched my step.

"But it is!" I shook my head and swallowed, trying to get some moisture in my mouth. "It's a wonderful idea, and I'd love to watch it."

"It's not important." A sheepish expression slipped across his features. "It's the people in my life, and if getting that show meant losing you, then I'd have nothing. I'd rather do right by you now and lose the competition than win and still have nothing important."

"What're you saying?" I could barely catch a breath and

my heart raced so fast I was sure it'd fly out of my chest at any moment. "This is your dream."

"I'm saying I love you, starshine." He smiled and the clouds inside me parted, allowing the sun to shine again. "I'm deeply, madly, ferociously in love with you, Lila."

Emotion tightened my throat. My body vibrated with the desire to launch myself into his arms, heat blossomed in my chest, and I didn't hold back my laugh. "Well, then fuck the show, because I love you and if you'll have me back, then I'll have everything I've ever needed."

He gathered me up in his arms, and his mouth captured mine. And oh! My body sang. I tilted my head, stretched against the solid planes of his chest, and threw my arms around him. Our mouths moved together, as if they were made solely for kissing. I could feel his heart hammer inside his chest. I'd forgotten to breathe, but any millisecond of time parted from him was too much.

Slowly, he broke the kiss, our ragged breathing comingling between our lips. My blood was on fire, and I was sorely tempted to undo his jeans and hitch my dress.

He rested his forehead against me, whispering hoarsely, "You're wrong." His hand stroked down my back and his lips brushed mine as he spoke. "I totally won today."

Epilogue

One year later . . .

Winkerton stood in my shop while her brand-new husband placed a potion on the counter. They'd been married for four months, and she absolutely glowed. Although now that she was officially a Duke, I couldn't seem to stop thinking of her like that. At the wedding, Drew had pulled me aside and said I should start calling her Vee.

Since Nathaniel exposed Georgia and TPNS hadn't censored it, everything had changed. I'd received a loan to open my potion and enchantment shop six months ago on the main thoroughfare of the Flower Market. Outside, a hanging sign shaped and painted like a comet with the name "Star Trails" displayed hung over my door.

My shop was small, pale gray wooden floors with racks and tables filled with enchantments, raw and polished crystals, and salves or poultices. Behind the counter, I had a glass-fronted refrigerator filled with potions and one staff person to help fill online orders. Unfortunately, I'd had to stop volunteering at the Vineyard; there wasn't enough time in the day, but I gave them the potions they needed at cost.

I could pay my bills without worrying. It helped I had a roommate.

"Did you see the TPN exposé last night?" Winkerton asked. "They trashed her so hard."

I bagged the potion. "I assume there are a lot of legal issues happening with Georgia and her show behind the scenes."

A few months ago, the state had heavily fined Georgia for falsifying a crime, and the Potion Network had an ongoing libel suit against her. My lawyer had decided that it was in my best interest to wait for that to be all settled. New things may come to light, and I deserved everything I could get with my civil suit. It was like watching an extremely famous couple divorce. Nathaniel and Winkerton ate it up. In fact, the four of us usually played rummy while they had it on, so Drew and I could have something else to do. Between this scandal and the recent upheaval in the Nettles regarding the Fornaro family—high ranking members of the mafia had been arrested—we had our hands full with drama. Alex fell off the face of the earth a few months back, and we assumed he was in witness protection.

The backroom door opened, and Nathaniel stepped in. His hair had grown back out and regained some of its wave. He was a little scruffy, and when he saw me, his smile lit up my heart. He only had eyes for me as he came over and kissed me.

"I'm sorry, I need to pay and get back to the site." Drew tapped the bag. "You guys can finish this up after rummy tonight, right?"

Winkerton laughed and said something under her breath, which made Drew blush.

Nathaniel lifted his head and grinned. "Oh, hey guys. I didn't see you there."

"You don't say, darling," she said.

"What're you doing here?" I wrapped my arm around his waist. "Not that I'm upset to see you, but don't you have shooting to do today?"

It was true that he hadn't won *The Next Potion Network Star* that day. It'd gone to Abby, and they'd awarded her a show. Filming hadn't started, as they wanted her to compete on other potion making shows to really get a fan base going for her. However, PBS offered Nathaniel a show that focused on foraging and cooking potions. It was called *Gone Foragin'*. Last week, Katie, his friend's daughter, had joined him. She was adorable in her duck-themed foraging outfit.

"Hey, they give me a lunch and you're right here. I couldn't resist." He leaned in and nuzzled my neck. "I missed you."

Drew cleared his throat. "I need to pay, really."

I waved him off. "Best friend husband discount, get outta here."

Winkerton laughed and dragged her husband out the door. "See you later, darlings!"

Nathaniel pushed me against the counter and dipped his hands into my overalls, gripping my hips. "I was wondering if you wanted to appear on my show."

My heart raced as heat shot through me and pooled between my thighs. "Again? Aren't you worried it's too much?"

"I'm the star, sure, but you're my star, Lila."

"Oh." I sighed and kissed him. "I'd love to."

"But?"

"No buts." I nibbled on his lip. "Well, except you'll have to draw me a bath."

"On set?" He pulled back, amusement dancing in his eyes. "Lila Townsend, it's a family show."

I laughed, glancing at the bath bombs on display before grinning. "You know I only like them at night."

Acknowledgments

I'd like to give a huge shout out to Matt Dewar and Lori Diederich! Your comments and insights to this story has been so helpful and supportive. Your encouragement to kick things up a notch are always well thought out and welcomed. I can only go further with your words.

Thanks so much to Auren, my secret sister who made me hug her when we first met. I was okay with waving, but she's a hugger. Your thoughts were excellent.

A special thanks to Kimberly and allowing me to pull her back in to my stories and talk about them with me. Thank you for all your help!

Thank you to Kayle Crosby for taking a chance on me. Your comments were really helpful.

An extra special thanks to my husbandface for letting me talk his ear off. Also, for taking my new interest for poison mostly in stride. But to be honest, you had to have seen it coming when we visited that poison garden.

Last but not least, to Funshine Butt forcing me to get up every so often to follow her to the kibble bowl and pet her while she ate. Those breaks are always important.

About the Author

AE McKenna is an Urban Fantasy and Paranormal Romance author who enjoys writing books with healthy relationships and interesting magic systems. She's not too shabby with fight scenes, either.
She lives in the Midwest where she drinks beer, eats cheese, and pets cats. All at the same time.

www.ingramcontent.com/pod-product-compliance
Lightning Source LLC
Chambersburg PA
CBHW022004310726

48972CB00006B/1509